THE LIES OF PRIDE

(THE SEVEN SINS, #3)

LILY ZANTE

AUTHOR'S NOTE

The Lies of Pride is the third book in **The Seven Sins,** a contemporary romance series of steamy, angsty and emotional stories featuring characters who are loosely connected.

All books in this series are STANDALONE but loosely connected.

Underdog (prequel)
The Wrath of Eli
The Problem with Lust
The Lies of Pride
The Price of Inertia
The Other Side of Greed

Sign up for my newsletter and get a FREE book:
https://www.lilyzante.com/news

CHAPTER ONE

NINA

I hide in the kitchen, even though I'm aware that it is a silly thing to do, hiding in the diner at the height of the lunchtime session, but I try, anyway. I'm good at making myself invisible; it's a skill I've learned and honed over the years, out of necessity. Call it a survival skill.

I hover around at the back, pretending to look for something.

Except that I'm starting to sweat.

I thought I was over this.

Palpitations pitter-patter in my chest. I remember this from before, needing to run for my life. It was flight or fight, and I couldn't fight, not as an eight year old. It happened a lot back then in that children's home. But I never managed to escape.

I used to be scared back then, except I'm not scared now, just anxious; I get like that when someone pays me too much attention, too much of the *wrong* type of attention.

I'm supposed to be used to this; getting hit on by customers. It should be part of the job description of a waitress. A twenty-five-year-old shouldn't react like this just because a guy is hitting on her; and he's a nice guy, Office Guy, we call him. Frankie and Joni tease me about him because he comes in here regularly, and he always seeks me out.

I'm just not interested. I used to be able to handle this better, but ever since Elias's news surfaced, ever since I discovered what happened to him, I've started to fall apart again.

I pull down the cuffs of my long sleeve turtle-neck top. It's not part of the uniform. We have a maroon waitress dress with white edging on the collar and at the ends of the short sleeves, but I told Frankie that I feel cold. She's let me wear this long-sleeved top which is good because it covers my arms right up to the wrist.

Joni thinks I'm doing it to get attention. I remind her that I'm not like her. She's the queen of attention. She's already pissed that a lot of the customers often ask who Elias Cardoza's sister is. Ever since Elias won the boxing heavyweight title, Frankie's Kitchen has become a famous landmark in Chicago. My brother used to be a regular and he still hangs out here most weeks. People come here hoping that they might get a glimpse of him. It's the same story at the gym where he still trains. People hang out outside hoping they'll catch him going in.

It amazes me that people are that fickle.

Still, I get good tips at the diner on account of being Elias's sister. It makes Joni jealous. She doesn't even try to hide it. She hates that I get more customers asking for me, and that I get bigger tips. But if people think I'm going to give up any juicy nugget of information about my brother, they're wrong. I'm good at keeping things secret. I even hate the way people, celebrities especially, post boring facets of their lives on social media. As if anyone cares.

"What are you doing in here?" Frankie asks. "We've got four tables that need waiting on. Food's not going to come out of thin air!"

Most of the other waitresses would be scared of her, but I'm not. She's always got my back, and I've always done over and above what's needed. I turn around. "I just need a moment," I say, fanning my face.

"You take a moment, then." Frankie's voice is soft, just like her expression which has suddenly changed. She's never that angry with me, though, I've never given her any cause to be. But I've sensed that she's been watching me carefully lately. It's like she can sense that something is up even if she doesn't know what it is.

"Do you need to take a break?"

I shake my head. "

"Who are you hiding from this time? Joni's friends again?" She puts her hands on her wide hips and looks as if she's about to go back out there and do something about it. She's protective of me and her staff, in the same way that I am protective of my brother. The customer is always wrong, as far as Frankie's concerned, though she might smile sweetly to them and then curse them behind their backs once they've left.

"No, they're not even here." Joni's boyfriend Rhys sometimes hangs around here and sometimes he'll come in with his friend, Scott. Apparently, the guy likes me, and Joni keeps trying to get me to go out with him. She says it would be fun for us to be a foursome. Scott's not so bad, I don't mind him, but I'm just not interested in him the way Joni says he's interested in me. It's Joni's boyfriend I can't stand. There something sick about him; something dark and menacing that takes me back to my childhood.

Frankie peers closer. "You've not been in a good way ever since Elias won the fight."

I laugh off her concern, but I know what she's getting at, even if she doesn't. What happened to Elias shattered my heart. I don't like talking about it and there are nights when I can't sleep. I can't handle facing the past. All that time, growing up together, I thought I had protected him. I believed I was saving Elias by doing what the janitor asked and finding out that this hadn't been the case crushed me.

I thought I had finally put this behind me, thought I had fixed myself. Not *completely,* but enough to be normal. Now my broken past lingers in the periphery of my mind and I can't shift it. I don't think I ever will be completely okay.

I'm back to my old tricks again. Things I hadn't done for a long time.

"What's going on in that head of yours?" Frankie looks at me as if she's trying to X-ray into my brain. "Do you want to talk about it?"

I shake my head, to try to indicate that I'm okay. I am. I really am. I get nervous when people want to get too close to me.

"It's Office Guy," I say, in an attempt to derail her interest. I'd pulled out my pen and was about to take his order, and then he suggested we could go for a drink sometime. He's never been that forward before. Up until he made the drink suggestion, I was handling the easy-going banter just fine, and then he went and said that, and I clammed up.

"He's not so bad looking," Frankie says, a hint of a smile

curving up on her lips. "He's smartly dressed, handsome and polite too. What else are you waiting for?"

It's a going joke around here that I push all the interested guys away. I get asked for my number, more so since Elias won the fight, but I always say no, tell them that I'm too busy, or not looking for a relationship. The guys are easy to push away, but convincing Joni and Frankie isn't.

"You think you're too good for anyone 'cause your brother is the heavyweight champion?" Joni often comments. "What are you holding out for? A superstar?"

I'm not holding out for anyone. I can't handle getting close. Intimacy gives me the shakes.

But I hate being this way. I hate falling to pieces. It's a problem, especially with the job I have—facing customers all day long. Maybe with my latest course in interior design I might actually do something with it. I should move on from waitressing. Elias is always telling me off. He wants me to work for him. I don't think so. I like it here. The diner might not be a great place for career advancement, but the familiarity of it all makes me feel secure. I take a long deep breath. "I'm going back out. I can handle him."

"It's not him I'm worried about," I hear Frankie say as I move towards the door and force myself to go back out into the diner serving area. With a smile plastered to my face, I sail up to the table where Office Guy is sitting and ask him what he wants to order today.

"I didn't mean to cross the line," he says when I return. He seems sweet enough, the overreaction was on my part. Now that I'm back, I widen my smile—make it sweeter, make it count—the way I learned to do from way back; when I needed my little brother to know that I was fine, and that the world was a good place, and that we would be okay.

I shrug. "What can I get you today?"

"A cup of coffee, eggs, sausage and bacon. Maybe you sitting opposite me and keeping me company," he adds, with a wry grin that's enough to make me sprint back into the kitchen. But I stand my ground.

"I'm afraid I can't do that. I have to work. Frankie would sack me."

"You can always come and work for me."

"You don't let up, do you?" I say, with some of my old feistiness coming back.

"I'm a persistent guy."

"And I'm not interested," I tell him with a smile he buys. I rush back into the kitchen and pin the order along with the others.

When I come back out, I see another table that needs waiting on. The customers crane their necks in my direction and look eager to order.

Elias's win has almost doubled Frankie's footfall to the extent that she's had to take on a couple of extra waitresses for when the place gets super packed.

I heave in a breath, and go and deal with the other customers, while keeping an eye on the food orders I've already placed. When his order is ready, I give Office Guy his food, thankful that I can rush off because things are so hectic. I am rushed off my feet for the next hour.

"He seems like a nice guy," Frankie tells me, as I pin another order to the board.

I almost roll my eyes but manage not to. "So do psychopaths."

CHAPTER TWO

CALLUM

"If you play things right, and don't mess up in your private life, this could be it—the role that catapults you to A-list glory," Rudy's voice comes through on my cell phone which I've sent to loudspeaker mode. I don't see him often. He's based in LA, but as my publicist he touches base with me daily.

I stop flexing my muscles in front of the mirror and I briefly consider firing my publicist. "I *am* an A-lister."

"I mean, A-list *Oscar* glory," Rudy clarifies. "This could be the role to do it."

I smile at myself in the mirror and imagine myself holding that coveted Oscar in my hand. I even have the first few sentences of the speech floating around in my head. I'm trying to move away from my usual action roles, and try something that's a little darker, a little different.

I've poured my heart and soul into this role. I want to be known as more than just a hunk. I want the Oscar, and accolades, and I want to be talked about for decades. I want to do what De Niro did with 'Raging Bull' even though 'Death of a Legend' isn't as gritty and as hard-hitting as that classic, it's a step in the right direction and away from the formulaic action-packed movies I've been making so far.

I'm no De Niro yet, but that's what I'm working towards. I've been studying hard for this role, and I've gone through rigorous physical training, and even taken part in a couple of real boxing matches. I even won one of them. It was good publicity for the film, with critics talking about how I've been getting into character with this role. I've even read up about all the boxing greats, and I feel like I kind of understand them a bit more. Most of them were guys who need to prove themselves. Needed to get a one up in life and fighting was the only way to glory.

Most of the filming has been done, there's a romance element to the film, and all those scenes with my co-star, Alyssa Watts, have been shot. The studio wants us to be the next romance in Tinsel Town. We have a few sexy scenes. I wish we didn't. That shit takes away from the grittiness of the film, but the people financing this film say they need romance in it.

Now we're in Chicago in order to shoot some of the big boxing scenes as well shooting those scenes that women like, the ones where I'm training hard. There are plenty of shirtless scenes, and I have to say, I'm pretty pumped by my physique. I've never looked better.

I puff out my chest again, posing once more like a bodybuilder so that the ridges and dips of my muscles are well defined. "I look the part." I nod approvingly at my reflection, and an image flashes through my mind again of me in a tux, raising my Oscar as I make my speech.

The door to my suite opens, and Dottie walks in. "Your

dry-cleaned shirts," she mouths, seeing that I'm on the phone. She sets my green and healthy smoothie down on the table near me. I would be lost without my personal assistant. She goes over to the table and sits down and starts typing away on her laptop. She's staying at a cheaper place a few blocks from here, and we go through a few things once a day. She lets me know what interviews and meetings I've got, though now that I'm filming, this is where my focus is.

"Any luck with Cardoza's camp?" I ask Rudy.

"I'm working on it." That seems to be Rudy's stock response.

"How hard can it be?"

"I'll see what I can do."

I don't understand it. Rudy doesn't have much to do, it's not like he's the one getting into the ring and fighting. He's not the one who's had to get up at 4 AM most mornings and workout for six hours every day. "Did you speak to his manager?" All he has to do is set up one meeting with Elias Cardoza.

Just one. I've been trying to get Rudy to set up a meeting with the guy, but Rudy says Cardoza is hard to get a hold of. Even his manager doesn't seem keen. I get that the guy has a huge fight in a few months' time, but our coming together, even for a one-off meeting, would help us both.

"I'm having a hard time reaching him."

I wonder if I should put Dottie on the case. She's clever, and quick-witted, and thinks outside the box.

Though this last part of filming is going to be intense, I feel prepared, but I want to have the edge. I've read about the boxing greats, legends like, Calzaghe, Hagler, Chavez, Ali and Tyson, and now there's Cardoza. I want to meet with him and get inside his head. Maybe talking to him for a few hours will help get me even more into character.

There's nothing like having a real life boxing champion to talk to. This guy burst onto the scene back in the summer, dethroning Trent "The Tank" Garrison with his raw power and nimble moves. The world took notice. I read up everything I could on him. I watched the fight over at some big producer's house. We weren't expecting to see the fight of the century, with this unknown underdog coming out on top. From that time on, I've been wanting to meet the guy.

It's weird how we've ended up filming these final scenes in Chicago because Cardoza comes from these streets. This is *his* city. This is where he trains. It's where he's lived all his life. I've also been reading another biography on him, and I've found out about his terrible past. I see now why he was never going to lose, even to an opponent as formidable as Garrison. Cardoza's past is a bonus for me. All I need to do is to get some glimpses of his life which will help me with my role. I swear to God I can almost feel that Oscar within my grasp.

My film, 'Death of a Legend', might seem as if it's based on Cardoza's life. It's not, but it so freakishly mirrors his story that critics might think we had hopped on the back of Cardoza's story. The truth is, this script came into my hands two years ago. They didn't want me for the role. The producer and director had someone else in mind, but my agent campaigned hard for me, and luckily, the guy they wanted was already signed to do another film. They couldn't wait for him, so I got the part.

That part is similar to what happened with Cardoza. From what I've read, he wasn't supposed to fight Garrison, there were others in front, but for one reason or another, through injury or failing a drug test, they couldn't fight, and Cardoza got the opportunity.

We're not so different, me and Cardoza, in that respect.

His story, the fighting underdog pitted against the world heavyweight champion, who then goes on to win the title against all the odds—that's real. I admire the guy. Cardoza ignited people's hopes and dreams and went on to do the impossible. In a much smaller way, and less important, I want to prove to people that I can do parts that require depth. I am so much more than my action roles.

"What if *I* ask him?" I suggest. If Rudy isn't having much luck, maybe I should turn up at the gym? Surely Cardoza wouldn't dare throw me out.

"I told you. Leave it with me."

I snort. "This is an important role for me. I only need one visit. You can make that happen, can't you?"

"I'll see what I can do."

I breathe out in irritation. I'm a famous actor, and this kid is new to his fame. I don't understand what damage a quick visit will do. This is my chance to prove to everyone that I'm more than just a handsome face, that I don't only have the body of a Greek god—thanks to my training—but I'm a serious actor as well.

"Try harder." I hang up.

Dottie looks up. "Do you want me to book you a flight back to LA at the weekend?"

"For what?"

"Rudy says there's a party you both need to be seen at."

I pull a T-shirt over my head. "I'm not going to LA until we're done filming." Screw Rudy, screw the studio and screw the fake romance. It's lucky I'm not dating at the moment, because something like this would piss me right off.

"You have to go back next month. Alyssa has a film premiere and you're her date."

"Remind me nearer the time."

Alyssa's been working hard and done two films back to back. Our sexy scenes in 'Legend' worked well and now the studio wants us to pretend we're getting together. Rudy said it would be a good idea for me to attend the premiere of the film she shot before Legend. I agreed only because I have no real life girlfriend who might get pissed off about something like this, and I'll do what the studio wants me to do. "Anything else?"

She nods her head. "Do you need anything else?"

"My disguises." A faux beard, moustache and wig come in handy.

"In your suitcase."

Because we're shooting, I'm mostly going to be on set and in my hotel suite, but even I can get bored of being cooped up all day. I only have bodyguards when I'm attending an event where there are big crowds, but I hate losing my anonymity. Using disguises is my way of going out without fear of being recognized. Dottie picks up her laptop and moves towards the door. "You're not supposed to go out alone, Callum."

"I'll be fine."

"Don't do anything stupid."

"As if I would."

"You're meant to be on set at four."

"Make sure you have my smoothie ready."

CHAPTER THREE

NINA

It's cold and I hunch my shoulders as I bury my mouth and chin deeper into my scarf. I brace myself for the long walk to the bus stop.

Elias would be mad at me for getting the bus home at this time of night, especially now that he's flush with money. He's always trying to give me some. He's always telling me I don't need to work at the diner, and has tried to give me some admin jobs to do for him. I know it's a ruse for him to make sure I don't work all the hours I do, but I love my job at the diner. It's flexible, and Frankie looks out for me, Joni is okay and the other waitresses are nice. I can't complain. Plus, I get to do my assignments there, and Frankie won't bat an eye.

They often joke about my night school classes—Harper and Elias, and my work colleagues, but I like learning. I want to better myself. I want to prove to myself that I can be more. Still, my waitressing work fits in nicely around my studying, and I still get to keep a roof over my head.

I don't want him to spend his money on me. He had a chance to change his life, and he grabbed it with both fists. He did what many thought was impossible, and he turned the boxing world upside down, but who knows how long this might last? I want him to save and invest his money, and not feel like he owes me, because he doesn't.

Besides, I'm not so broke that I can't afford to get a bus home. As I walk along the street, I hear a commotion coming from an alleyway further down. There's hardly anyone else around and I can feel my heart rate starting to skyrocket. I speed up my footsteps as the shouting gets louder. It's not the rational thing to do, but I can hear a man shouting. It sounds as if he's in trouble, and I can't walk away. As I approach nearer, I hear the clattering rattle of iron bins being knocked about.

"Get the fuck off of me!" someone shouts.

I race down the alleyway and see a group of men wrestling. I crane my neck further, and can make out a man on the ground being attacked by two others. One's on the ground, pummelling him, and the other one is standing and kicking the guy on the ground.

"Hey!" I shout, without thinking. "Leave him alone!" It's an insane request, and only someone as delusional as me would make it. I don't like those odds, two to one, and I've always fought for the underdog because I can relate. "Hey!" I yell out, because they didn't hear me the first time around.

The moment freeze-frames, as the two guys turn to look at me. I whip out my phone and hold it in front of me, as if it's a handgun. I'm not thinking straight, and I accidentally take a picture by mistake.

I didn't mean to do that. I meant to show them I meant business and that I was going to call the cops.

"What the fuck?" The guy who's standing looks at me. My insides hollow out. I'm tiny and this man looks pissed. The light from the street lamp is enough to illuminate his features. Terror paralyzes my muscles, and I stumble backwards, just as the guy starts walking towards me.

The other guy stops fighting with the guy on the ground, and yells, "C'mon! I got it." He holds something up.

But the guy coming for me doesn't listen. My heart crawls up my throat. "You little bitch. Give me your fucking—"

The piercing sound of police sirens cut into the air, loud and sharp. They're near, and it scares the guys. They dart off, and I rush to the man lying on the floor. My eyes widen in shock. His beard is hanging off him. My first thought is that he must be in so much pain. I wince as I kneel down, over him. "Your beard," I exclaim, and wonder at the same time why it's come off so cleanly.

Blood pours out of his nose. "You're hurt," I cry, shocked, and scared, yet concerned. I examine his face; it's bloody, but I've seen worse. His beard hangs off even more, and I miss a heartbeat, until I see the loop hanging off his other ear. It doesn't make sense at first.

I must be in shock, too, and then I see that it's a false beard. I remove the loop from the other ear and take the beard off entirely.

He groans as he clutches his sides, and mumbles something which I can't make out.

"What?" I say, lowering my ear to his face.

"They've got my fucking wallet."

"It's okay. They've gone. They're not going to hurt you."

"I had them. I almost had the fuckers."

I stare at him in disbelief. Two against one? I think not. "At least you're alive," I say. He groans again, then wipes his hand over his face, so that his hand is now covered in blood. "Owww," he moans, as he touches his nose.

I can't tell if it's broken, but I've taken some tissues out of my bag and I attempt to wipe his face clean, as gently as I can. This doesn't look too bad. It's not an Elias-level injury. I won't ever forget those days when my brother used to stagger through the door with his face mashed to almost unrecognizable when he'd come home from those underground fight clubs.

The police siren gets deafeningly louder. I glance over my shoulder and stare into a flood of lights as the car's headlights shoot straight at us. I hold up my hand to block out the light because I can't see into the bright lights. The car stops at the mouth of the alleyway, because it's too narrow for the car.

An officer gets out and runs over. She takes one look at the injured man on the ground, then says something into her radio.

"Backup is on the way," she tells me as she drops to the ground to survey the injured man. "What happened?"

"Some guys were beating him up," I reply.

"They stole my wallet," the guy says, slowly trying to sit up. He looks slightly familiar, but again, I can't be sure.

The police officer is about to say something when her eyes widen. "You're...you're... you're *Callum Sandersby*," she gasps, and her mouth falls open. I stare from her to the guy, and back to the police officer again. Her mouth is still hanging open.

"Yeah," the guy says, and manages to smile.

Is he for real?

The officer seems to be caught in a web of

enchantment. "Callum Sandersby," she gasps, as her professional demeanour slips away.

Callum who?

I don't know who they're talking about. I take another look, and now that he's sitting up and the headlights are on him, he does look familiar, yet I still can't place him yet.

"Sir, sir, are you okay? Are you hurting anywhere else?" The police woman's sudden concern intensifies.

"I gave back as good as I got," the guy replies. I peer at him, but giving back as good as he got isn't how I'd describe it. He did well to put up a fight against the two of them, but his sudden bravado surprises me.

"The ambulance is on its way."

"Thanks," he says, and as the blood pours out of his nose he attempts to wipe it with the already soggy tissue.

I pull out another tissue and hand it to him. He dabs his nose again and winces in pain. "Thanks," he says to me.

"Don't mention it."

"I suppose you'll want an autograph."

I almost choke in response.

CHAPTER FOUR

CALLUM

I wouldn't say she saved me, the woman from the alleyway who is now sitting in my hospital room while the doctors and nurses tend to me.

She was in the right place at the right time, and I was in the wrong place. I'm going to be in big trouble with the director tomorrow.

Shit.

Dottie got here before I did. I called her on the way here and told her not to tell anyone else. She took one look at me and her face turned pale. I'll have to see what the doctors say. Rudy's on his way here because Dottie, against her better judgment, panicked and called him. She's on the phone to him again. He keeps calling, and I keep refusing to speak to him.

I have no idea why that woman is in here though. I'll happily give her the autograph or selfie, both those things if she really wants them, but she doesn't need to be in here.

She hopped into the ambulance when it arrived, and now she's sitting in my hospital room looking bewildered. Maybe it's because the police officer wanted to take a statement from her.

"Rudy is *really* pissed." Dottie hands my phone back to me.

"No shit," I reply.

"Bruised ribs, no broken nose, and a black eye which should go down in a few days time," the doctor informs us.

That's lucky.

"Thanks, Doc." I try to grin at him. You'd think I'd suffered a major trauma given the number of medical staff in here.

"You need to rest up."

"Can I go home?" I try to sit up but it hurts.

"It might be better if you stay here tonight, and we can do final checks in a few hours' time. You were knocked to the ground, so we'll need to keep an eye on that."

"You shoulda seen the other guys," I tell him. He nods but is too busy scribbling on his notepad.

I am lucky that I don't have a broken nose, or broken ribs. I'm lucky to walk away with these superficial injuries. I'm certain that my recently acquired boxing skills, and my recent fitness regime, helped. But, it looks like filming is going to have to be delayed, maybe by a week or so.

I've messed up bigtime. Delaying a film costs money. It's a big no-no. Worse, Rudy and the director are going to have my balls for being out by myself at that time of night.

All at once the room empties. And it's just me, Dottie and the woman who saved me.

"You've delayed the film," she says.

"Maybe only by a few days." I'm being hopeful.

"Or weeks."

"It won't be that long. I'm in good shape." I try to sit up, then wince when it hurts.

"Take it easy. You heard the doctor. How much will it cost the studio, to delay filming?"

That's something I don't even want to think about. "Can we talk about something else?" I say, growing irritated. Personal assistants don't usually have so much power, Dottie is good at keeping me in check. She met me here, so that by the time the ambulance arrived at the hospital, she had already secured me a private room, and the best doctors.

"I told you not to go out."

"I was checking out the area," I reply, suddenly feeling defensive. Before I get a chance to explain myself, the door bursts open and Rudy charges in. "What the hell were you thinking?" he cries, looking at me in shock.

"It's not as bad as it looks," I tell him, marvelling at the speed with which he got here.

"I don't know why I'm still here." The woman from the alleyway speaks up. "Can I go now?"

Rudy glances at her suspiciously. "Who are you?" he growls.

I cough in exasperation and wish Rudy hadn't turned up right at this instant. There's an implication behind Rudy's tone, and I shake my head, letting him know that there was nothing going on. I glance at the woman again, this time looking at her properly for the first time. She is small, and slim, with a cute face. Like, a *normal* face. No botox, no beestung lips, no plumped up cheeks or surgically sculpted cheekbones.

"She's a friend," I reply, without thinking.

"Are you *together?*" Rudy asks me.

"No, we're not *together*," the woman replies. She looks slightly disgusted.

"Then who is this?" Rudy demands, his face twisting as if he's in pain. Inside that calculating head of his he's probably worked out how much my little detour has cost the studio. It shouldn't be such a big concern to him. He's not going to have to take the brunt of the director's wrath, but Rudy's job is to make me look good, and I guess right now, I'm not looking so good. The media are going to have a field day with this.

I should have been more careful. "She's just a passerby," I explain. "She was with me with the cops arrived."

"I heard shouting coming from the alleyway," the woman says. "So I took a look."

"You were in the *alleyway*?" Rudy cries, glaring at me.

"I wasn't walking *down* the alleyway, those losers dragged me in." I just happened to be unlucky.

"I stepped in and tried to help him," the woman tells Rudy before I can get a word in.

"That's either very stupid, or very brave," says Dottie.

"For both of you," Rudy cries, looking from the woman to me.

"Look, those guys jumped me," I reply. "I wasn't expecting it."

"That's how muggers usually operate," remarks Dottie. Rudy's face turns red. "What were you doing wandering around the streets of Chicago so late at night?" He stabs a finger in my direction.

"I warned him not to," says Dottie.

I try to shift in the bed but it hurts to move. These two ganging up on me is the last thing I need. "I was getting a feel for the streets. Soaking up at atmosphere," I protest, though with hindsight, what I did was foolish and reckless.

"Soaking up the atmosphere?" Rudy echoes in disbelief. He rests his palm across his forehead as if he's got a sudden headache. "Miss, why are you still here?" he barks, talking to the alleyway woman whose name I don't even know.

"Don't worry, I'm going," she replies stiffly.

"I expect you want an autograph," I say, reminding her.

"No, I don't."

"A selfie?" I ask, sounding desperate.

"What for?"

What for? I start to chortle, but my ribs hurt, and I wince instead. What for? I look at her scrawny little face, and wish she would scuttle away.

"I wasn't staying here for the entertainment." She walks over to the door. "They bundled me into the ambulance before I had a chance to leave. I had to make a statement to the police."

"Oh, god, no." Rudy looks worried. "We can't have this," he says to me. "How would it look? We don't need that kind of publicity. The studio won't want it."

"You went to his aid?" Rudy asks, slowly, walking towards her.

"She didn't save me," I protest. I didn't need saving. I can take good care of myself.

Rudy takes some cash out of his wallet. "This should take care of things." He holds out the bills for her to take. The woman looks confused. "Why are you giving me money?"

Rudy coughs lightly. "So you won't sell your story."

"To who?"

"To the tabloids."

She makes a noise in the base of the throat, as if she's trying to stop herself from laughing.

"Don't you ...don't you know who he is?" Rudy asks, slowly.

She looks at me again. I'm actually surprised she wasn't any warmer to me in the ambulance, and now I realize that it's because she has no clue about me.

"He looks familiar, but I don't care who he is. I certainly don't want your money."

"Take it," Rudy insists.

"I don't need your money," she throws back, looking disgusted.

"Leave her alone," Dottie says, and I'm inclined to think the same. But this is something new to me, having someone, a woman no less, turn down the chance to take a picture with me.

She leaves, and I don't even know her name. Doesn't matter, because I sure hope I'll never run into her again.

Dottie gets ready to leave and asks me if she needs to wake me up at 4 AM tomorrow, and buy me a smoothie. 4 AM isn't that far away, and yes, I tell her, "Do both." Because it might ease things if I explain to the director in person, even though the sight of me looking like this will send him into cardiac arrest.

"I was joking," she cries. "You're not going anywhere for a week at least, right?" she asks Rudy.

"It's a good thing I'm here and not in LA," says Rudy. "I'll have to explain this mess you're in to everyone. We'll have to work out a story to explain this."

"Call me and let me know what you decide," says Dottie. She waves as she leaves.

Damn it. Now it's just me and Rudy. It looks like I'll be staying in the hospital for tonight, routine precautions and all that. It's not a bad thing because it means anytime soon, Rudy will be heading off.

But, he starts to lecture me first. "You need to get a grip, Callum." He points his finger at me.

"I didn't ask to get attacked."

"Some of these streets aren't safe. How could you be so stupid?"

"It's not too bad." My attackers could have had a knife, or a gun. This thought only comes to me now, and I realize how lucky I have been.

"Not too bad?" he yells, raising his voice, "Not too bad? The studio is going to have to delay filming until your ribs heal. The makeup can take care of your black eye, but miracles can't reduce the swollen face."

I raise a hand to my face. It does feel puffy. I remember the punches to my face and chest, and then that woman yelling at them. Maybe she did come at exactly the right time.

"You were lucky," he says.

"I'm aware of that. Let's leave it at that."

"Why did you put up a fight? They only wanted your wallet. Why didn't you throw it at them? It's not like you need the money."

I have my reasons, but to him I say, "What's my lead role, huh? I wasn't going to give in to those two losers that easily."

"You might be one of Hollywood's favorite sons right now but things can change very quickly in this business. You could have gotten yourself killed."

"I'm okay. I'm not dead."

"You were damned lucky. At least I don't have to be in your shoes when the director sees you."

He's right. I wish I wasn't in my shoes either.

CHAPTER FIVE

NINA

The strong smell of freshly made coffee fills the air. It's relatively quiet at the diner first thing in the morning. I sit in a corner trying to get a little of my assignment done. I'm not due to start my shift for another hour, but I prefer being in the diner and surrounded by people. It beats being in my apartment where sometimes I can't trust myself.

This is safer.

Elias and Harper walk in about half an hour later, but go and sit on another table when they see me with my school stuff spread out. A few of the regulars nod their heads in acknowledgement, but otherwise no one bothers them at this time of the morning either. It's mostly only the tourists who come up to him asking for selfies and autographs.

I pack my work away and go over to them. I still have a little time before I start my shift.

"I don't play golf," I hear my brother say.

"Then tell him you don't."

"I did. He thinks he can convince me. I should ask him if he'd like to step inside the ring with me." Elias grins as Harper swats him gently.

"Be nice. He just wants to get to know you better," says Harper. Her dad was mad at her when she and Elias first got together. He saw some intimate photos which a douchebag journalist work colleague of hers sent to him. It's taken a while for the rift to heal.

"Hey," I slide into the booth opposite them.

"Hey yourself," says Elias.

"What you got there?" I ask. Harper has the newspaper spread across the table.

"Callum Sandersby," she says.

"Who?" I ask, even though I know, because I looked him up online after I got back from the hospital. He's some big actor from Hollywood, and I realized he was in that film I watched once, with one of my favorite actresses, Leanne Rose. It wasn't such a bad film. Actionpacked. She was better than he was. Trust this idiot to be walking around Chicago that late at night, given who he is.

I peer at a photo of the actor leaving the hospital, and then I almost cough in shock as I read the headline.

Taking his role too far

"What do you mean, *who*? Callum Sandersby," repeats Harper. "He was in that big action movie last summer." She clicks her fingers as if she's trying to remember the name.

Elias leans forward, places his hefty hand on the paper and sniffs. "He looks like a pretty boy to me." He turns to Harper. "I thought you liked your men rough around the edges."

She leans in and stares up at him adoringly. "No one for me but you, honey." Then she kisses him and thankfully it's only a short peck on the lips.

"Less of the PDA, please," I beg, and turn the paper around to me so that I can read it.

Reports say that the actor injured himself during filming in the city of Chicago. The last part of filming for his upcoming film, Death of a Legend, was due to begin this week, but has now been delayed.

"He's making a boxing film," I state.

"Yeah?" Elias turns the paper around so that it's the right side up for him.

I swat his hand gently. "Hey, I was reading that."

"This must be the guy Lou was talking about."

"You know him?" asks Harper.

Elias taps his finger over Callum's face. "I don't know him, but someone from his camp has been on Lou's back. Says the guy wants a few hours of my time."

"For what?" I ask.

"Says he wants to make sure he's properly in character or something. He's playing the part of a boxer."

I recall what the actor had said on that night, about giving as good as he got, and his constant boast of 'you should have seen the other guys' to the doctors and nurses. So that was why he'd stood up to his attackers, or tried to?

It's on the tip of my tongue to tell Elias and Harper the truth, that he wasn't injured on set. He got mugged, and then beaten up.

"Why don't you meet with him?" Harper suggests.

My brother raises his eyebrow at her. "I have a rematch with Garrison coming up. I don't have time to waste on this guy."

"Not even an hour?"

"Do you have the hots for this guy or something?" Elias asks, sliding his arm around her shoulders, all territorial like. She snuggles up close to him. "I have a hot guy all to myself, and I don't need anyone else."

"Are you sure?" Elias asks before turning to me. "Should I be worried about this fangirl?"

I shake my head and grin. "Don't be silly. Harper adores you. She's like a puppy dog following you around."

This comment elicits a stern look from Harper. "I'm not like that!"

She likes to think she's a strong, independent career woman, and I know the kinds of hassles she's had at her last work place, but Harper is all soft and squishy around my brother. She's madly in love with him.

They're madly in love. I've never seen my brother look so happy, and it fills my heart with happiness to see him like this. It isn't because he's riding high on the waves of success, or the fact that he's proven himself as a boxer, but the other things—finding a soul mate, feeling complete, and content— things I can never hope to have, my brother now has them. He deserves them.

"He's eye candy," says Harper, then turns the paper the right side up for me. "What do you think?" As well as the main photo of him leaving the hospital, there is another, smaller more classic close up of his face further down the page. This guy has an intense look about him, as if he's staring right at me.

I shrink back in disgust. "He's an actor."

"Hollywood A-list," Harper states.

"I'm sure he's full of himself," I throw back.

"Yeah, full of bullshit, I'll bet," says Eli, coughing into his closed fist. He's saying this because a teeny-weeny part of him is jealous, but he's not far from wrong. I've had a taste of Callum Sandersby, and I didn't like him one bit. This guy assumed I'd want a picture taken with him. I want nothing of the kind. I can see why telling the truth would sabotage his carefully honed image, especially given the fact that he's got the lead role in a boxing movie. I'm not so callous that I'd sell his story, despite what his slimy friend thought, when he tried to pay me off with money.

I also respect the fact that people want to keep their stories and secrets to themselves.

Besides, if I tell Elias and Harper the truth of what really happened, Harper will ask me a million questions, and she'll hassle me into getting in touch with him. For a confident, self-assured woman, I'm surprised by her excitement over this guy.

But I steal another glance at the newspaper and I see the actor's face again. He cleans up quite well. The lighting wasn't so great that night in the alleyway and his face was covered in blood, but he's not so bad looking. Dark hair, dark eyes, green I think. A strong jaw. I don't normally take much notice of guys, but this guy has something. Hollywood appeal.

Thank goodness I walked away.

CHAPTER SIX

CALLUM

I found out the freakiest shit. The woman who found me in the alleyway happens to be the sister of Elias Cardoza. One of the nurses at the hospital told me.

Un-freaking-believable.

Talk about hitting the jackpot.

This has to be fate, because, what are the chances of that happening?

The guy won't let me meet with him, but now I have a way in. Sure, I'm grateful that his sister happened to come by the alleyway, she thinks she saved me, but I had those guys. There was no way I was going to give up my precious wallet, and then she waded into the rescue. I had no choice. I had to give it up otherwise one of those losers was going to go for her.

After getting a huge telling off and a warning from the director, and being blamed for the delay in filming, I've been told to take a week off.

I'm in a baseball cap and shades, and I haven't shaved in days. It's not a full disguise, but nobody bats an eye. I take a cab to the boxer's gym now that I have the perfect excuse to come here and get acquainted with Cardoza. I have no idea how to get hold of his sister—she's hardly my type—but it gives me a way in to seeking out Cardoza. At least I can approach him and, in the process, introduce myself.

As I arrive at the gym there is a group of people outside taking pictures of themselves. Some of them turn to me, then turn away. A teenage girl looks at me and smiles. I smile back. Clearly, she's recognized me. I pull on the handle of the gym door, and wait for a fleeting second, expecting her to come up behind me and ask me for an autograph or something. But instead, she flips her hair over her shoulder and takes a selfie of herself with the gym in the background.

She didn't recognize me either.

I take off my shades and baseball cap as I walk into the gym. It's more rundown than I expected. It's filthy, actually, and nothing like the place where I trained. Paint peels off the dirty walls. It doesn't smell too great here either. I hate to think what the locker room must be like. I'm shocked that a place like this turned out a champion like Cardoza.

An old guy walks around with a tool kit. As I look around, everyone is doing their own stuff. No one looks up; they're working out, fighting, punching, flexing some serious muscles. I hate to look at them because my hard-earned ones seem so much smaller in comparison. I used to think I had a great physique until I walked into this place.

But then a pretty woman walks up to me.

"Hi, I'm Harper." She holds out her hand.

I shake her hand. "Hi. I'm Callum."

"I know. We read about you in the paper."

I swipe my hand across the back of my neck. "That story got out, did it?" I wince.

She nods. "That must have been one heck of a fighting scene. How are you feeling?"

I laugh, and then cough, because it still hurts, though I feel better now than I did a few days ago. I heeded the doctors' advice and stayed in my suite for the past few days, taking it easy. But I'm keen to meet with Cardoza and make the most of my time away from filming.

"I'm better now thanks."

She glances over her shoulder and waves. Cardoza is sitting on the stool, and some guy is talking to him. He's taken his helmet off and sweat drips down the sides of his face, then he looks at the woman next to me, then at me, and scowls.

"Don't worry about him," Harper tells me.

"Does he ever smile?"

She grins. "That's his fighting face. He wears it with pride."

"I don't think he likes me."

"He doesn't trust many people."

"Does he always look so mad?"

"When he's fighting, yes."

I'm relieved that someone, his trainer maybe, is talking to him, otherwise I have a feeling the guy would march up to me and demand to know what I'm doing here. I'm pretty sure he knows who I am.

The woman motions for him to come over, and I stand up taller and flex my muscles at the prospect of being face to face with Elias Cardoza. I didn't expect to see him this quickly.

"Why did you want to see Elias?" she asks, as the guy still doesn't make a move towards us.

"I wanted to know how to get a hold of his sister. I need to thank her."

"Nina?" Harper suddenly perks up.

"You know her?"

"I'm Elias's girlfriend, and yes, I know Nina. How do *you* know her?"

Cardoza comes over just then. "What's going on?" The boxer walks up to us and adopts the kind of fuck-off pose that I've sometimes practiced in front of the mirror—hands on hips, a scowl, muscles bulging. He doesn't look so happy to see me, and while there is no need for him to look ecstatic, I didn't expect him to look this sullen.

"This is Elias," Harper says.

"I know. Pleased to meet you." I start to hold out my hand, but something about the way the guy's face is set, makes me hesitate. The guy nods at me instead.

I nod back.

"I know who this guy is," I joke, to his girlfriend. "I mean, who wouldn't?"

"What are you doing here?" He's direct, I'll give him that. When a man with a physique like Cardoza says anything to you, even if it's not funny, it helps to smile. So I smile. A part of me wonders if he thought I was hitting on his girlfriend, her being so super friendly and all.

"I just came in to introduce myself."

"What for?" he growls.

I step back first, because that's the logical and safe thing to do. Then I shake my head and hold my hands up. "I was passing by and I was just taking my chances."

"That's what I don't like the sound of."

"Eli!" His girlfriend places her hand across his chest. He's dripping with sweat, but the way her hand lingers over his sleek muscles, as if she's almost caressing them, makes me feel like the third wheel between these two. He stares at her, and I feel it in my blood.

Talk about sizzling chemistry.

These two are putting images in my head I have no right to be seeing. I shake my head as if to clear it.

"He's looking for Nina," his girlfriend tells him.

"What do you want with my sister?"

Holy shit. I almost take a step back. That's got to be the sharpest warning to stay away from her. It suits me because it's not her I'm after, it's *him*.

I try to win him over. "I need to thank your sister," I say, lowering my voice.

"For what?" Cardoza growls, staring at me as if he'd like to gouge my eyes out with his fingers. His manner is so abrasive, that I can't think of a good excuse on the spot. So, I'm going to tell them the truth.

"Despite what the papers are saying, I didn't injure myself on the set," I announce. I'm aware that the studio's PR machine tried to put a spin on things, but these two will obviously know what really happened.

"What?" Harper asks. Cardoza angles his head as if he's suddenly taken an interest in the story. I stare at them and my jaw goes slack. I'm not so sure that they know they truth now. I tell them that I got mugged that night, and that I was set upon by two guys.

"What does my sister have to do with it?" the boxer asks. Sweat lines his face, and his muscles, and I steal a glance at them, and inwardly flinch.

What have I let myself in for? I can't even begin to think of a way to talk myself out of this. "She didn't tell you?" I say, as calmly as I can. Why would the boxer's sister keep this a secret. It wasn't going to reflect badly on her.

Cardoza gives me a look that could split my head in two.

I cough lightly. "She ... she came to my rescue."

"Say what?" Harper exclaims.

"*She* came to *your* rescue? Nina?" Cardoza's voice is protective and rough.

"I was out a few nights ago and some guys jumped me. We got into a fight and your sister heard the noise and..."

"Jesus Christ," the boxer wipes the sweat off his face with the back of his hand. "She was in the alleyway, *walking into a fight?* What time was this?"

"About eleven o'clock."

Cardoza winces as if he's in pain. "Why's she fucking walking around the streets at that time of night?" he asks his girlfriend.

"She might have been walking to the bus stop."

"She doesn't need to get a bus that late. Why didn't she jump in a cab? Why's she still doing those late shifts?" Sounds to me as if Cardoza's angry with himself. "Did she get hurt?"

"Did she look hurt to you?" I can't help but retort, then I remember that I'm supposed to be appealing to her brother's better nature. "I threw my wallet at the guys and they ran off."

"Oh, Jesus." Cardoza looks as if he could punch a hole through a wall. "Why didn't you give them your wallet in the first place?" he asks quietly.

I press my lips together because I don't want to get into the details of that night. This boxer dude looks so mad that even if I told him the truth, I don't think he would care.

Cardoza shakes his head and points his finger at me. "Never *ever, ever* get into a fight if you're being mugged. Give in. Give them what they want. Who the hell did you think you were?"

My silence hangs in the air as uncomfortable as if Cardoza had grabbed me by the balls.

"Eli! That's not fair." Harper seems to be my fangirl and I feel lucky that she's on my side.

"The police came, and the guys ran off, and your sister came with me to the hospital."

"She did what?" Harper cries. "She hasn't said a word of this to us." She looks at Elias. "Why didn't she tell us?"

I wonder the same thing.

Cardoza shrugs. "I'll be damned if I know. Wait until I see her. You were lucky the police came," he points to me. "Because if she'd been hurt..."

"Eli, it's not his fault."

I'm about to echo the same thing. Yeah, dude, it's not my fault, but I decide to stay silent.

But I'm curious about his sister and why she didn't tell Elias and his girlfriend of all people. It shocks me to the core, and I don't understand it at all. I've been around people who try to take, take, take and this woman whom I hardly know not only comes to my aid, she then keeps quiet about it.

It's bizarre.

"I gotta get back," says Cardoza suddenly.

"Already?" his girlfriend asks. I detect a slight annoyance on the boxer's face. Looks to me as if the girlfriend, this Harper, is the only ally I have.

"I have a fight to train for," he mumbles, and I'm so transfixed staring at his frame, at the muscles rippling all over his body, that it's only when he walks away that I realize I forgot to ask him for his time.

"I was hoping to ask him if we could meet for an hour or so sometime. I know he's a busy guy, training for a rematch, and it's the last thing he wants, some actor guy stalking him."

This gets a laugh from her. "I stalked him before. I was sent to the gym to do a story on him, and I had to shadow him for a few weeks, maybe a month or something. He didn't like it. Don't take it personally."

"Thanks for the advice."

"You just want to talk to him?"

"I want to find out what's in his head."

She winces. "I'm not sure you'd want to know."

Emboldened, I say, "I want to know what he's thinking when he sees Garrison walking towards him, at the weigh-in, and then again when they meet for the first time in the ring. I want to know what goes through his hand when he hits the guy. I've trained and all, but I'm no fighter. I actually hate the idea of violence."

"How odd for you to go for this role."

"It's a change from my usual."

She nods in understanding. "I'm sure we can work something out."

This makes my insides sing. I might have time to spend with Elias Cardoza, the heavyweight champion of the world. "I'd appreciate it."

"Are those injuries really from that night?"

The way she says it makes it sound as if I got a good beating. "It's not so bad," I tell her, raising a hand to my face. The director is still so mad at me he can barely bring himself to talk to me.

"She's a feisty one, Nina, getting involved and coming to your help," Harper says. "Lucky girl."

I smile. I think I just caught Elias's girlfriend say something without meaning to.

"I mean, I expect she asked for your autograph or something," she ventures.

"She didn't want a thing."

"Right," she says, nodding to herself. "That's more like her."

It reminds me, I still have no idea how to get in touch with her. I should at least thank her, I suppose, though if Cardoza had been friendlier, I wouldn't have need to make the extra effort. "Where can I find her?"

"She works at Frankie's Kitchen. It's a diner not far from here." She proceeds to give me the directions. "She'll be there now, if you go."

Looks like I have no choice. "Thanks."

"Nice meeting you."

I'm so lucky that his girlfriend likes me. If Cardoza gives me some of his time, I'll make sure they get tickets to the film premiere and get VIP access to the after party.

CHAPTER SEVEN

NINA

I'm waiting on tables when I hear the commotion. When I turn my head, I see that actor guy sitting at one of the tables. He's surrounded by a group of giggling young girls, having their photos taken with him. He's signing autographs too and judging by that super smug look on his face, he's loving every single moment of it.

He catches me looking at him, and waves.

I instantly dive back into the kitchen. I sense he wants to talk to me. I don't want to talk to him. He's so full of himself.

Frankie fixes me with a stern gaze. "Who are you hiding from this time?"

"Who? Me?" I look up at her, as I pin another few orders on the board. "No one."

"Ummm hmm." She folds her arm and sets down the crossword puzzle she'd been doing. "Then shouldn't you get back in there?" she tells me. "It's starting to fill up again."

I look out. She's right, but I suspect it's become busy so quickly because word must have spread quite quickly that the big-headed actor guy is here.

Luckily, I've managed to avoid waiting on him, and Joni ends up taking his order. It will probably be the highlight of her day. A quick glance in his direction and I see him surrounded by a group of pretty young things who are huddled around him taking selfies. I turn my back to him and continue waiting on other tables.

"He's so gorgeous!" Joni whispers in my ear as I pin another order on the board. "I could sit across the table from him and stare at him all day long."

"He'd love that, I'm sure," I mutter under my breath.

"Hey," he pulls at my apron as I walk past. I turn around, because nobody does that. Nobody has ever done that to me in all the years I've worked here and I'd like to know what makes this guy think he can. I cock my head, and shoot him a stern stare. Matronly, is the effect I'm going for, but I don't have that kind of air about me.

"Can I get a—"

"I'm serving someone else," I tell him, not giving him a chance to finish his sentence, "and you already have someone waiting on you."

"You've got your hair up," he comments.

"Food hygiene dictates it. I'll get your server."

"Can't you take my order. I just want to order another milkshake. This place does great milkshakes. Their Key Lime Pie looks good. Do you recommend it?"

"I'll get your server for you," I say, turning to go.

"Why are you avoiding me?" he asks, lowering his voice. I'm not the kind of woman who bats her eyelashes at anyone, and least of all him. I suspect he's not used to this level of indifference. I look around and see a table of tourists ogling him. They're already taking photos of him, without his consent.

"Doesn't that bother you?" I ask him, genuinely shocked.

He looks at them. "Nothing I can do about it. I should have come in disguise."

I remember the beard hanging off his face on the night he got robbed. "You should have."

Joni comes rushing over. I'm surprised she didn't come sooner, because she's territorial and obviously this is new for her, to have someone be interested in her for a change, instead of me. "Is there anything else I can get you?" she asks, her voice soft and sweet.

"Just the bill, thanks."

"Coming right up."

"I believe the gentleman also wanted another milkshake and a slice of Key Lime Pie."

"To go, please." He smirks at me.

Joni gives him a huge smile before leaving. She'll also be expecting a huge Hollywood-sized tip.

"Nice milkshakes you do here."

"Frankie's is known for them."

"Nice food."

"You should tell Frankie."

"I'm telling you," he says.

"Well," I turn to go.

"Don't go. Please." Is that a hint of pleading in his voice. Surprised, I stop and listen. "What is it you want?"

"You saved my life the other day."

"So you admit to it now, because you didn't admit to it so easily at the hospital."

"I wasn't thinking straight. You came to my aid. I'm grateful to you for that."

"I was in the wrong place at the wrong time." But I wonder why he feels the need to bring this up now. I haven't told anyone anything about that night, and his secret is safe with me. "Is that why you're here?"

"I wanted to thank you."

That doesn't quite ring true. I scoff.

"What's so funny?" he asks.

"You, pretending you came here to thank me. You could have thanked me the night you got beaten up—"

"Shhhh," he says, putting a finger to his lips and looking around. And that tells me everything I need to know about him.

"So, what is it? The real reason you're here?" I nod, waiting for it. The thing he really wants. The real reason as to why he came. He didn't come here for Frankie's famous milkshakes either. I may not be very man-savvy but I know people usually want something when they appear out of the blue for no reason.

He laughs. "There's no reason. I genuinely wanted to thank you, and I'm curious to know why you didn't tell anyone."

I shrug. "Because I can keep a secret."

"But you didn't have to do that for me."

"I didn't."

"So why did you?" he asks. It says a lot for his industry, and his life, if he thinks that me withholding what happened that night is such a big deal.

"I figured you had your reasons. You had your reputation to worry about, and with your friend trying to pay me off, it wasn't hard for me to understand."

His face and body are pure hunk and yet his eyes are dark, and wise and ageless. I feel as if he's appraising me. Trying to work me out. His expression isn't so much brawn, as something altogether deeper. Strange how I would have missed it if I'd walked past him. He's not the type of guy I would notice let alone whose picture I would drool over, but talking to him makes me a little self-conscious. This isn't like me.

"You're different to everyone I know," he says.

"That doesn't say much for the people you know." He's so cheesy. A man with that face and that body doesn't need to use such lines. In any case, he's wasting his time trying them out on me.

"You didn't even tell your brother or his girlfriend."

I blink, then blink again. "How do you know about my brother?" But I already know the answer to that as I ask the question. I realize then that this is the reason he's found me.

"I met them at the gym. How do you think I found out where you work?"

"You went to the gym?"

He nods. "I wanted to thank you."

I remember what Elias said about this guy wanting to spend time with him. "It's unforgiveable that you told my brother." The other reason I didn't mention it to them was because Elias would have scolded me.

"Sorry," the actor says. "I didn't know that your brother didn't know."

"He's going to be so mad at me."

"He was mad at me," Callum says.

"I fully understand that." Right now, *I'm* mad at him. Elias and Harper are going to interrogate me when I next see them.

He raises an eyebrow. "You're nothing like how I thought you'd be."

"You're exactly like how I thought you'd be."

"Is that a good thing or a bad—"

But Joni returns and looks at me as if I'm stealing her customer, so I shake my head as I walk away.

Callum Sandersby told me exactly who he is just now. People always want something. No one does something for nothing. If he wanted to thank me, he could have sent his assistant the day after, instead of waiting three days before showing up.

CHAPTER EIGHT

CALLUM

Well, this is a first. This woman hates me. She deliberately ignored me when I walked into the diner, and even when I waved at her, and she could see who I was, she didn't come over. I ended up having another waitress waiting on me.

Later I pulled Cardoza's sister's apron as she walked past, but she didn't like that either.

I'm beginning to hate Chicago. First I get mugged, then the city's golden boy looks at me as if I'm his opponent in the ring. Then his sister acts as if she's had a vaccine against my charm.

I leave a huge tip for the waitress who served me. "Thank you!" she squawks, seeing the huge tip I've given her.

"You're welcome." I reach for my jacket and survey the door.

"Do you need to leave from the back entrance?"

I turn around and stare at the waitress. "The back entrance?"

"To avoid the crowds."

I laugh. "That's not necessary." I've called an Uber.

"But won't you get mobbed by fans?"

"I won't get mobbed," I assure her. There are people here, and I've been recognized. A few have had their selfies taken with me, but it hardly constitutes a mob. "I try to maintain a low profile."

"That's not possible. You're Callum Sandersby!"

I slip on my jacket. "Believe me, it's possible."

"Any chance I can get a photo with you?"

"Uh, sure."

She whips out her cellphone, primps her hair, and pouts as she comes to my side, then she raises her cell in the air and snaps away. She looks at her photos, as I survey the door, checking to see if my Uber has arrived.

"Oh no!" she whines. "I had my eyes closed. Can we take another one?"

I stifle my breath of exasperation, smile sweetly and oblige. We go through the same rigmarole.

"Have you worked here long?" I ask, as she looks through her phone.

"*Too* long." She smiles. "The photos are great. Thanks".

"Say, what's with your friend?"

"Elias's sister?"

Interesting choice of words. "Yeah."

"Don't worry about her. She's stuck-up. She thinks she's too good for everyone." I wasn't expecting this woman to talk of her colleague in those terms. But I'm curious. "She's not as friendly as you," I tell her and give her one of my best pantie-melting smiles. Her eyes widen and she flashes me a smile. "I have a boyfriend," she says, probably without thinking, because she suddenly looks embarrassed. "I don't know why I said that."

I laugh and dismiss it. People sometimes say the stupidest things to me and I have no idea why. "You were saying about your friend?" My curiosity gets the better of me.

"Nina's never friendly. She gets a lot of attention just because she's Elias's sister. It's gone to her head."

"Gone to her head?" Somehow, I find this hard to believe. If she had told everyone the truth about how she met me, I might have been more inclined to agree, but Cardoza's sister remained silent when it wasn't in her best interests to do so. I can't believe she did it for me, because most people aren't wired like that—doing things for the benefit of others. I'm already intrigued by her and I didn't expect to be.

"A lot of guys hit on her. She's never interested."

"No?"

"She's only getting that attention because of Eli."

I glance over the waitress's shoulder and see Nina going about her business. Unlike almost everyone else in this diner, she's not even remotely interested in my presence. Not once does she look my way.

"You probably have that effect on most women, huh?" The selfie-taking waitress refuses to budge.

"You think so?" I lean towards her an inch and give her one of my I-dig-you-looks. Acting has so many advantages.

She exhales and seems unable to say anything back.

"Shame your friend isn't as nice as you," I add.

"Her loss."

I nod. "Thank you for the service."

"Anytime."

It takes me a while to get out of the door because in the

few yards between where I am and the door, a whole heap of people want to take pictures with me, or get me to sign their T-shirts, their hands, their arms.

I willingly oblige. I should have known better and worn a disguise, but since I didn't, it's clearly my fault I'm getting accosted. I'll be back here again, soon. It's not that I'm taking Nina Cardoza's disinterest as a challenge, well, maybe I am a *little*, but I'm still eager to get a meeting with Elias. Cardoza obviously sees me as a threat, but between his sister and his girlfriend, I'm sure I can find a way to worm myself into getting something set up.

Anything that can help turn my performance.

CHAPTER NINE

NINA

"Are you seeing someone?" Harper asks.

"What?" I cry out in exaggerated surprise. I expected her to say about the actor guy, and here it is.

"You're obviously too busy to come over for dinner these days."

I've made too many excuses in the past few weeks, but that's because I have been genuinely busy with work and night school. Definitely not because I've been busy with a date.

Harper continues. "I wondered if you were hiding someone from us."

I scoff, even though I know full well what she's getting at. It's no surprise that she insisted I come over tonight—the same day that Callum Sandersby couldn't keep his mouth shut and came to the diner after going to Elias's gym. "I'm not hiding anything from you. Unless you want me to tell you what I've learned about selecting color palettes for your bedroom."

"Hardly." She sniffs. She doesn't usually pry into my private life, but Callum Sandersby has given her something to sniff about and this is her way of slowly getting to the point.

Only, there is no point.

I inadvertently stumbled across the actor guy getting beat up.

The muggers ran away. He was hurt, I wasn't.

End of story.

But this is Harper, and she will ask me every single question she can think off. I got to know her better last summer, around the time of Elias's fight with Garrison. I like her and trust her, and she's good for Elias.

Back then I spent the weekend sharing a hotel room with her, and I owe her, because she convinced me to go to the fight and watch. I don't ever like to watch my brother fight, but Harper sensed that my brother needed support. Garrison was the reigning heavyweight champion of the world. He had the whole crowd rooting for him. Elias was no one, and he had only Lou, his manager, and the guys from the gym. Thanks to her, I got to sit in terror as my brother stepped into the ring to fight a man who everyone expected would knock him out in the first round.

Except that's not what happened.

I witnessed history in the making that night and my brother became an overnight sensation and the boxing world's newest darling.

I trust Harper, but I don't like her asking about my boyfriends, or lack thereof. We might still be getting to know one another, but that stuff is off limits.

Even Elias has never pried into that part of my life.

"Are you sure you don't have anything to tell me?"

"Nothing." My denial is probably killing her.

"Come over tonight, have dinner with us, like in the good old days."

"I have assignments to finish." This is the truth. I always have assignments, and Joni wants me to come to a party at her boyfriend's house one night this week. I don't have time for these things.

Harper groans. "I knew that would be your next excuse."

"It's not an excuse," I wail. I do have stuff to do. She's being especially insistent and refuses to take no for an answer.

"Come on," says Harper. "Your brother's getting antsy about the fight. The papers are saying his win was a fluke, and that he's a one-time wonder. It's starting to get to him."

"Why didn't you start with that?" I would drop everything for Elias, in a heart beat, and that's exactly what I do now.

Even though I will have to stay up late tonight and finish off my homework for tomorrow, I start to make my way over to Elias's place. Harper pretty much lives there, even though she has her own luxury apartment nearby.

The fight is still months away, but Elias can get uptight when he's stressed, and this fight has stressed him out bigtime.

When he beat Trent "The Tank" Garrison it caused one of the biggest upsets in boxing history, because Garrison had been the favorite and Elias uprooted him. It catapulted him to fame overnight. The city gave him a Welcome Parade, and he was invited on talk shows, and he was in all the papers and magazines.

It was around that same time that the other stuff came out.

Things I had no knowledge of. The past suddenly thrust into my future and before I could save myself, I was at it again. I glance at my wrist. The cuts had started to fade away. Little white markings that weren't so noticeable, but ever since I started cutting again, the scabs and ugly marks have come back.

I should stop. I know that. I *plan* to. But when I cut, it makes me *feel* better. It relieves the pressure that builds up, especially after I've had a bad dream again. I'm back in the children's home, in Grampton House, and I'm being chased again. Not by the other kids, not by Elias, but by a grown man.

The janitor.

He's chasing me. *Again.*

He's counting to one hundred. *Too fast.*

I wake up from those bad dreams with my heart pounding in my chest. The only way I can deal with the pain of my remembrance is to cut.

Nobody will understand, which is why nobody will ever know. Seems like Elias lifted the lid on his demons when his news came out, and I've been trying to put myself together ever since. But it hasn't been easy, and it's especially not easy being alone, trying to deal with it, but I barely allow anyone to get close to me, so there is no simple solution to all of this.

I pull the cuff of my sleeve lower, to hide the scars.

Soon, I'm on my way to Elias's place. This is upscale Chicago. A world away from my small place. Elias is always threatening to buy me a place, but I won't ever take him up on it. Where he lives now is beautiful, it's like the kinds of places one only dreams about or sees in magazines full of rich people. It is a million miles away from the types of places we are used to living in.

But this is a good thing because we have moved on. Elias has moved on. He was always such an angry young child, always ready for a fight. Growing up I used to worry that he would get in trouble or end up in a fight killing someone. He joined the underground fight clubs, so that we could keep a roof over our heads once we left the foster care system, and I used to worry about him even more. I was always frightened that one day the cops would be at the door, to tell me that he had been killed. I lost track of the number of times he would come home with his face messed up, rearranged, more like, and covered in blood. I'd see the bruises all over his chest. I'd get him cleaned him up and pray that he would be okay, because he was all I had.

Now he has Harper, and she's the best thing that could have happened to him. Winning the belt is right up there with his achievements but success can be fleeting and real love, well, I like to believe that that's for life.

Out of all the girls he's been with, Harper's the one. I can tell from the way she is with him, the way they are together. They're in love, and I am happy for him. Sometimes I feel like a complete gooseberry when I'm around them.

"Hey," Elias opens the door. "This is an honor," he says, sarcastically, though with a smile.

"How are you doing?" I ask, observing him carefully.

"Good, great. How are *you?*"

I have my suspicions about what he's alluding to. This is the real reason they wanted me here.

"We're getting take-out," Harper announces, as she joins us on the couch with two glasses of wine in her hands. She hands one to me. "What do you fancy?"

"I don't mind. Whatever you guys want, but I can't stay late. I've got my—"

"Assignments to do," says Elias.

"How's the training?" I scan his face for signs of worry and upset over that article Harper mentioned.

"It's going according to plan." He doesn't look unduly stressed out to me. I wonder if Harper lied just to get me here. I open my mouth to say something but she comes out with it. "But first, tell us about Callum Sandersby and your little rendezvous in the alleyway."

I narrow my eyes at her.

"How come you didn't tell us?" Elias says, accusingly, as if I have underhanded reasons for this.

"How come we heard it from Callum first?" Harper takes a sip of her wine.

"Callum?" I nod my head at her. "Since when have the two of you been on first name terms."

"He came to the gym, we got talking."

Elias sighs out heavily. "*She* got talking. I had to go over and make sure that he wasn't hitting on her."

Harper nudges him lightly in the side. "He and Alyssa Watts fell in love while making this movie."

"Who?" I ask, but not really caring.

"His co-star in 'Death of a Legend'," Harper announces.

"See," Elias thumbs in Harper's direction. "She knows all about him, even who his latest girlfriend is."

"It's in the papers," Harper cries defensively. "Haven't you read the papers?" she asks me. "He's all over them. I'd say he and Elias are competing for front page real estate."

Elias looks incensed. "What were you doing walking down an alleyway at that time of night, Nina? Are you stupid?"

I can tell he's angry, because he never uses that word

when talking to me or about me. "I wasn't walking down the alleyway. I walked *past* it."

"And yet you somehow ended up *in* it, and breaking up a fight?"

I guess now is not the time to tell them that I accidentally took a photo of the robbers. My actions were truly stupid. I see that now.

"Why didn't you tell us?" Harper cries. "You let us believe that phony news story instead."

"You don't have any loyalty to him," Elias points out. "Why were you protecting him?"

"Protecting him?" I snort. I wasn't protecting Callum Sandersby. I wasn't doing it to save his hide. I just didn't want this FBI level of interrogation which is what I've ended up having anyway. "It was done. It was over. I didn't see the point."

"You didn't see the point?" Harper echoes, "He's *Callum Sandersby*, for goodness sake. One of the biggest actors around."

I'm not into worshipping celebrities, and I couldn't care less. "He's only a guy."

Harper's about to say something, then seems to think better of it. "But he's famous," she says finally.

"I don't care! He's a guy to me. A selfish, vain, self-obsessed guy."

"He is not. I found him to be quite nice," she replies.

"I agree with you," Elias says to me, raising his bottle of some red colored liquid. I grimace. "Tomato juice," he replies. "Vain and self-obsessed."

Harper frowns. "How can you say that? You were barely civil towards him."

Elias takes a huge gulp of his juice. "I can tell."

"So what exactly happened that night?" my brother

wants to know. I regurgitate a quick version of the story. "And then we went to the hospital, I made a statement to the police, and the guy's agent tried to give me money."

"For what?" Elias asks suspiciously.

"He didn't want me to run to the press and spill the real story about this big hero boxer guy getting beaten up, I suppose."

"I can see why. It wouldn't look good for his upcoming film," Harper adds. "Did he come to the diner? He said he wanted to thank you."

Thank me. Three days later? "I don't know why he came looking for me."

"He wanted to thank you," Harper insists, "On account of you coming to his rescue. That was brave of you, doing something like that."

"I call it stupid." Elias's face is still hard set.

Harper runs to the actor's defense. "I think it was sweet of him to make the effort to seek you out."

I disagree. "I don't think it's that simple."

"The dude wants my time. I know, and *you* know," he points his bottle me, "but you," he points his bottle at Harper, "you seem to have other ideas."

"She saved him," Harper retorts defensively. "He wanted to thank her; I don't understand why you two are always so suspicious of people's good intentions."

Elias and I share a knowing look. Harper wouldn't know of these things. She has no idea about people's intentions, and how they make you do things, how they trick you.

Elias lowers his head and a crease appears on his forehead. What happened to him breaks my heart. But there is another story about our childhood; one I can't ever change. One that Elias doesn't know about. I just have to make sure that he never will.

"Not everyone is out to get you," Harper insists.

"The actor dude wants something from me. He wants to talk to me, get a feel for the character, and check out the gym. 'Get into character'." Elias air quotes the last bit. "That's what Lou was told when someone called him asking if we could get together. That much I get."

"Guys," says Harper, obviously not stopping. "You saved him, one dark stormy night as he walked around the streets of Chicago."

I point my finger at her. "It wasn't a stormy night."

"But what a story," Harper says, breathlessly, for effect. "*That's* the one they should have printed, except he's gone and fallen for his co-star."

I shake my head. She is such a romantic airhead. "You're always looking for a story."

Elias snorts. "It's a shame we're not getting the real story about that dude, 'cause it would be damned embarrassing." He motions with his hand, as if he's writing the headline in the air. "Hero boxer beaten to a pulp."

Harper gets up. "Leave the poor guy alone. We should order."

"Good idea," I agree, not wanting to continue with this conversation. "I'm starving."

CHAPTER TEN

CALLUM

"Milkshake and one of your wraps with extra salad on the side." I'm talking to the owner of Frankie's Kitchen.

Filming resumes in a few days' time, and I've come in again, hoping to see Cardoza's sister. She's not around, and neither, thank heavens, is that other waitress.

I order my food and because I'm in disguise, a wig, a hat, and a moustache, nobody bats an eyelid. The owner doesn't either. I ask her if they do deliveries. They don't. She stares at me, then stares at my moustache. "You look familiar?"

"Yeah?"

She stares at me suspiciously then touches her upper lip. "And your moustache is hanging off." I raise a hand to my face and see that half my moustache is hanging off. The glue hasn't done its job well. I pull it off.

"I thought I recognized you."

I smile at her.

"This place was mighty busy after you left the other day. I guess word got out."

"Sorry about that."

"Oh no. Don't apologize. This place needs to be busy. You come here all the time you can." She laughs, a big, hearty laugh that seems to come from her soul.

"I will. I like your milkshakes and the Key Lime Pie is great."

"There's always plenty of that to go around. I'm Frankie."

I shake her hand. "I'm Callum.

"I know exactly who you are, young man."

I smile at her. "I hear Elias Cardoza hangs out here a lot. You probably get a lot of customers on account of him?"

"I'm not complaining."

"I was trying to talk to his sister the other day. She seems shy."

"Nina?" Frankie sits down opposite me.

"Yeah, Nina." I wait for her to offer up more information, but this lady isn't saying much. "I needed to talk to her. Harper said I could find her here." I'm hoping that throwing names around might get me somewhere.

"You spoke to Harper?"

"At the gym. I met Elias, too."

"Uh-huh." She folds her arms and peers at me.

This conversation isn't going anywhere. The other waitress sounded jealous about Nina, this Frankie woman isn't giving me much to go on. Harper seems to be the only friendly face, but her boyfriend probably wouldn't hesitate to gouge my eyes out given half a chance. I can't rely on Rudy to get anywhere, so I have to take matters into my own hands.

"Can you keep a secret?" I have no option but to tell her, especially if I'm to gain her confidence.

"A secret?" Frankie nods, but still looks at me suspiciously.

This is a weird moment for me, and I expect it is for her as well. What am I doing here, sitting in a diner in the early hours of the morning, looking out for a waitress who interests me for reasons I don't understand? Oh, and one who happens to be related to a famous boxer. I've never had to work so hard for a date before, and while this is not a date at all, the principles are still the same, trying to win someone's attention. I lower my voice and tell her what happened in the alleyway that night. How Nina found me and came to my rescue.

She's surprised, and at first it doesn't look as if she believes me. I continue telling her everything, how Nina came to the hospital, and how the studio fabricated the story of my injury.

"You expect me to believe that?" she asks, when I finish.

"It's true, I swear to God. She swooped in like Superwoman and got me out of a mess." I tell her to ask Elias or Harper, or even Nina, if she doesn't believe me, and that seems to do the trick. "You can't tell anyone."

She makes a motion as if she's zipping her lips. "Why did you tell me this?"

"I like Nina, and I want to make it up to her."

"You like her? Why?" Frankie reminds me of an overprotective father, mother and grandparents all rolled into one.

This is harder than negotiating a percentage of profits for a film role. I breathe in slowly, thinking on the spot. "I like her because she's not like the others. She's just not interested. I came to thank her and she barely acknowledged me."

Frankie chortles. "That's Nina for you."

I lean towards her. "The papers made out a story about my injuries—"

"I know. All the waitresses were talking about you."

"And Nina, who saved me, didn't say a word. Did she? She didn't tell you the truth, did she? She didn't even tell her brother and his girlfriend about what happened. That kind of ... " I struggle to find the right word. "That kind of *uniqueness,* is rare. She's different."

"She is."

"I just want to get to know her."

"I'm not so sure she'll want to get to know you."

I've never had to work harder to get access to someone before. "How about you get her to deliver my lunch to the set every day?"

Frankie's brows push together and she cocks her head. "Why would I do that?"

"So that I can get to know her. She's not giving me a chance."

"She doesn't give anyone a chance," Frankie retorts. "What exactly are you doing this all for?"

"You know what she's like. She won't give me an in."

"Maybe she's not interested."

"I accept that. Just let me get to know her. I'm not going to do anything," I throw my hands up, for effect. "She's just got to come to the set and give me my lunch. It's hardly a date. It's just business."

"If you're looking to ask her for a date, don't hold your breath."

"So you will?"

"We don't usually do delivery, but I'll make an exception."

"I appreciate it, and of course, I'll make it worth your while."

"You'd better not hurt that girl. I shouldn't do this, but she's not going to make any friends just working here and going to night school."

I feel as if she's convincing herself that she's doing the right thing.

"I'll never do a thing. I swear. If she was easy to talk to, I wouldn't need to resort to this."

"Okay. We'll give it a shot. Let me think about it."

She still needs to think about it? "I need to check your story about you getting attacked. If I find out you lied, this isn't happening."

"Fine. Go right ahead." In a way, her protectiveness over Nina is endearing. "Thank you. This stays between you and me," I tell her.

"You bet it does. Nina would kill me if she found out I was in on it."

NINA

"We've had a request. Someone wants a lunch delivery every day to their place of work." Frankie's giving me an odd look.

"Ok-ayyy." I wonder why she's telling me, and not the other waitresses. "This is new. When did we start doing this?"

"As of today. It's your friend. He wants his lunch delivered to him on the set."

"What set?" *What friend?* And in that split second, I already know the answer to that question before Frankie replies. "Your actor friend."

"He's not my actor friend." My mind scrambles to figure out when this little plan was concocted.

"He said you swooped in like Superwoman." Frankie tries hard to suppress a grin.

I narrow my eyes. "He said what?"

"You heard."

Damn that guy. He's gone and told Frankie about that night as well. For someone who's supposed to be preserving his image, he's doing a bad job of it. Why did he need to tell Frankie?

"I need you to go."

"But I'm on my lunchbreak," I protest.

"You can take a break when you get back."

Over my dead body.

I'm about to protest, but the expression on Frankie's face tells me I have no choice.

Whatever Callum Sandersby has up his sleeve I won't be a party to it. "Why does it have to be me? Why can't someone else do it?"

"You never get out. You're either at night school or in here."

I fold my arms. I'm not buying this. "*That's* your reason? Can you get someone else to do it?"

"I want *you* to do it." She walks right up to me. "I can't trust anyone else. They'll end up on an extra hour-long break. You get a taxi there and back. Simple. Your security pass has all been sorted."

I frown. "My security pass?"

"To go on set."

"When did this happen?" I ask, suspicious.

"Don't you worry when it happened. Think of it as you helping me to spread the word about Frankie's Kitchen. Who knows, it could lead to more business for me."

We stare at one another. "Be a good girl, Nina and follow my orders for a change."

A short while later, I'm at the film set, and I've gone through security. I'm expecting someone to take Callum's take out from me, but instead I get told where his trailer is.

I knock on the door, and I'm surprised when he opens it. I'm not sure why I was expecting, or hoping, that it would be someone else.

"Hey." He flashes me a beautiful smile, one that reaches his eyes and lights them up, but I'm not falling for it.

"Your delivery," I say, holding his bag up in front of me. "Take it."

"Come in." He doesn't take the bag from me, but goes back into his room, and sits down on the chair in front of the dresser. I dump his food on the coffee table, then turn to leave.

"Hey, don't go!"

"I've done my bit; you've got the food."

"That's it?" he asks, sounding surprised.

"I have a real job. I have to get back."

"A real job?" he asks, obviously not liking my comment.

I cut to the chase. "Why am I doing this? Why did it have to be me?"

He looks slightly startled. "Uh, it's just easier having one person because of the security pass and all that ..."

"Is it that much of a bother to get a security pass sorted?"

He scratches the stubble on his jaw. "Yeah. You wouldn't believe what a pain those things are. Anyway, thanks for my lunch. I hope I didn't get you in trouble with your brother."

"He was mad."

"I noticed. He's never been happy when I'm around."

"I understand that," I reply.

He picks up the brown delivery bag, and looks inside, then takes a sniff. "Hmmm. Delicious." He pulls out the milkshake and slurps it. "Did you want to look around the set?"

"No."

I can tell that my response isn't what he was expecting. "Just in case you wanted to see what it's like, you know, being on a movie set and all."

"It's not something I lie awake at night thinking about."

"What do you lie awake thinking about?"

Ugh. My stomach churns at such cheesy lines. I'm out of here. I turn on my heels, and step towards the door, only, he rushes up and beats me to it.

"Don't go. I'm sorry. I didn't mean that."

I don't understand why this guy wants me to hang around. I'm not feeling anything. I don't give a hoot who he is, and I don't care to be on this set.

"Are you sure you don't want to look around?"

"Positive." Most of the women he meets must be so easy to impress. Though he also seems kind of desperate for me to stick around. I don't have him down for being a lonely guy, but he seems both desperate and lonely to me right now. Or he's after something. "I'll have to show you around the kitchen at the diner, when you're next over," I shoot back.

"I look forward to it."

"Just to get this out of the way," I brace myself because it's hard to say but he gives me no choice—this guy is so in my face. Office Guy is restrained by comparison, and Joni's boyfriend is a jerk, but this actor guy, he's too much. "I don't know what you're playing at, but I'm not interested in you."

"In me, as a person? Or are you talking about the actor population in general?"

"I would never date an actor."

"Ever dated one before? We're not such a bad species."

I shiver with exaggeration. "I'm really not going there."

"You never know, you might like it."

"You're unbelievable."

I rush away before he can stop me.

On the ride back to the diner I contemplate what happened and how transparent this guy is. I hate that Frankie's making me do this, and I hate him even more for asking her to do this.

CHAPTER ELEVEN

CALLUM

"Today's lunch." Nina hands me the food takeout bag and hovers around the door as if she's too scared to come into the trailer.

"Thank you." I reach for the bag. "This is my personal assistant, Dottie. Do you remember her from that night at the hospital?"

"How could I forget that night?" she says, not without a touch of sarcasm.

"Hey," Dottie waves at her, then rushes out with her ear glued to her cell phone.

"Care to come in?" I ask, expecting to be turned down. To my surprise, Nina steps inside and I move back, wary of scaring her off.

"I'm curious about something," she says slowly, taking in the contents of my room and examining it carefully. She does all this without moving an inch.

"What?" I'm all ears, and I'm puzzled by her slight

change in temperament. She doesn't seem as eager to rush away today.

"Why did you wait until the end to throw your wallet to the guys who mugged you?"

I suck in a breath. My sudden elation at the fact that she's stayed out here, as opposed to running away from me, suddenly deflates. I want to tell her the truth, but I also don't want to talk about it. "I didn't want to give it up."

"Designer label?" she asks, with a slight sneer.

I shake my head slowly. "That wasn't the reason."

"Was it made out of some hideously expensive animal hide?"

I'm surprised by the aggression in her voice. It's almost as if she hates me. "I'm not into stuff like that."

"So, why didn't you give it up? It would have saved you the black eye and bruised ribs."

"I didn't want to." I'm struggling for an excuse. "It had sentimental value." Every time I think of Ben, I tear up.

"A present from a girlfriend?"

"Something like that."

She's asking a lot of questions, it's almost like she's testing me. I don't like telling others about Ben, but if I back away, and don't answer, she'll think I'm hiding something, and this is the longest we've talked.

"But you gave it to them eventually."

"I heard your voice, heard it was a female, and I was scared, even in my bloodied state lying on the floor, that they might go for you."

She squints at me. "You did it to save me?"

"I didn't want those jerks to do anything to you. So, I tossed it at them."

"*After* they had beaten you silly? You should know the

first rule of getting robbed is that you give them what they want."

"I wasn't planning on getting robbed."

"It's not exactly safe, especially where you ended up. I'm surprised you didn't know better."

She could be Rudy, for all the advice she's giving me. "You're just like Rudy. Freakily like him."

"Who's Rudy?"

"My publicist. The guy at the hospital who tried to pay you off."

"That jerk," she mumbles, loud enough that I hear it.

I chortle. "He was rude to you. I apologize for that."

"He was, and it's not your place to apologize for him. Don't you have bodyguards or something?"

"I avoid them as much as possible. I have to have them in large crowds, and when we're going to film premieres and stuff like that, otherwise I try to live as normal a life as possible."

"Is it hard? Trying to be normal?"

"It's not easy. People flock around me wherever I go. That's why disguises are my best defense. It's either a disguise or a bodyguard, and I'd rather have a disguise any day. A bodyguard just ups the ante, whereas a disguise gives me anonymity. If I could be invisible, that would be the best."

"You want to be invisible?" she asks, as if this surprises her.

"Yes."

"And yet you're an actor. You want to be on screen, everywhere, worldwide. Isn't that the aim?"

"But in my private life, I want to be left alone."

"I expect your brother's probably experiencing some of that, what with being thrust into the limelight so suddenly?"

I'm proud of myself for moving the conversation so seamlessly to Elias. Let's face it, he's the reason I've gone to all this trouble.

"He hates it."

"The fame?"

"The spotlight. Being a boxer is a lot different to being an actor. Elias doesn't court the publicity."

I'm about to tell her that I don't either, but I don't want to end up in a disagreement for no reason. "He's hard to get a hold of," I venture.

"He has a lot going on."

"With the rematch, I guess."

"It's a big fight."

"The biggest. Is he scared?" I ask her.

"We don't talk about it much."

"No?"

She stares at me, as if she's appraising me and trying to figure me out. I'm getting mixed signals from her, as if she's interested in my story, but not *me*.

"Why do you always push me away, Nina?"

"Because I'm not interested in you. I guess that must come as a shock even to your Mount Everest sized ego."

I'm about to tell her that I have something that's Mount Everest sized, but I stop myself before I say something that might make her blush. Smirking, I tell her, "If you're too proud to ask for my autograph, I can sign your hand."

She makes a face as if I've asked her to eat vomit. "I don't want your autograph. Why would I? I didn't even know who you were when you got attacked that night." Her attention diverts to something else. "Leanne Rose," she says, moving towards a card I've got on my dresser. She peers at it, but doesn't pick it up. "I like her. You were in a film together."

"Amazonian Adventure," I recite the title. That was one of my earlier films.

"I like the way she put you in your place. She had a badass role in that film."

I grin, remembering. "She was good, and she's good at putting me in my place, on screen and off."

"Yeah?" I wonder if Nina is trying to find out if I'm single or not. This surprises me. It's good that we seem to be getting on fine. I just hope she doesn't think I'm hitting on her. Some Sandersby and Elias Cardoza interaction might be good for my reputation. I wouldn't want Nina to think that I was making any moves on her.

"That picture was taken many years ago and we've been good friends ever since." Leanne is a sweetheart, and she sent me a Good Luck card, with a picture of her and me taken on set during that film.

"Interesting," says Nina, gliding over to the door.

"This has been interesting," I agree. She was almost friendly towards me today.

CHAPTER TWELVE

NINA

I hate Joni's boyfriend. I've passed enough veiled comments to Joni about him when she gushes about what a misunderstood guy he is, and how he has a nice side to him. I can see him for what he is; an abusive, controlling pig, and I hate myself for letting her convince me to come to this party.

The music is loud, but it's not that loud that I can pretend I didn't hear him. Scott is saying something to me, and I smile at him every now and then, making him think I'm listening, or interested.

We're in the kitchen which is overflowing with people. The smell of weed and alcohol permeates the air. I'm seriously considering going home in the next half an hour.

"Don't look so miserable," Joni wails, shoving a glass of something in my face. I take a sniff. It smells like paint stripper. I decide not to drink it.

"I shouldn't have come out tonight. I had an assignment to finish."

"You and your assignments," Joni cries. "That's all you ever do."

Scott comes over to us, with a bottle of beer in his hand. "How about you and I go for a drink sometime?" he says to me.

"You're not going to have any luck with her," Joni giggles. She's already had a glass of that paint stripper-like liquid and she's on her second one. "She's set her sights higher."

When her tongue is loose, I forget how easily she talks. Scott looks visibly shocked. "You're seeing someone?" The laughter and noise around us suddenly seem to lessen.

"Someone's seeing her," Joni doesn't make sense and she's not trying to.

"Who?" Scott asks.

I rush to put the facts straight. "I'm not seeing anyone."

"That's not what she said," he nods his head in Joni's direction. I stare at Joni and pray that she'll keep her mouth shut. "She's had a lot to drink. I wouldn't trust what she says."

"I want to know. What does she mean?"

"Callum Sandersby," Joni drawls out slowly. "That gorgeous actor guy. You know the one. He always making those action movies. The guy with the dark hair, sexy eyes."

Scott looks confused. "As if I'd ... oh, *that* guy?" His mouth falls open. "He's in Chicago filming his latest film? You're seeing *him*?"

"She turned every other guy down, but not him." Joni can't help adding more fuel to the fire. Scott's face hardens.

"It's not true," I say, trying to reassure him. I don't even know why I'm trying to reassure him. This news isn't true, but he looks crushed.

"What isn't true?" Rhys comes up behind Joni and puts his arms around her. "I'm honored you came," he says.

"Joni insisted." I hate his pose, and the way his hands move lower down. I can't see, because the kitchen island is in the way, but from the way she's sighing, it doesn't leave much to the imagination. He drops little kisses along her neck.

I was about to tell Scott that there's nothing going on between me and the actor, but I don't want to say anything in front of Rhys. Why the heck did I come here at all? I hate that I've hurt Scott, and I wish Joni would keep her mouth shut. Ever since she found out that I go to deliver Callum's lunch, she's been in a pissy mood with me.

Rhys continues to nibble on Joni's earlobe, and she continues to sigh. He stops and stares at us. "Aren't you drinking?" he asks me. I'm the only one not holding anything in my hands.

"I'm fine."

"You're not fine. You're kinda uptight. What say you loosen up a little?"

"I got her a drink!" Joni says, then giggles. I can only assume that Rhys is doing something to her below the waist that we can't see.

"Are you girls staying over?" Rhys asks.

Staying over? Heck, NO. No way.

"I can't. I'm going to have to leave soon." That was sneaky of Joni, not telling me.

Rhys doesn't seem to want to drop the subject. "But you only just got here,"

"I didn't know it was an all night party."

"Does it matter? You said you've been having trouble sleeping," Joni counters.

"Why don't you let your hair down tonight instead of being a goddamn goody two shoes, and going on about your assignments and night school and shit," Rhys says.

I look at him. This guy hates me as much as I hate him.

"Rhys," Joni says, laughing nervously. "You're not the one going to night school, and you don't have to do those assignments. Why are you so worried?" He eyes me with something bordering on contempt. "If I'm worried, it's because your friend here doesn't seem to know how to relax."

"Oh, I know how to relax," I say, "But I choose who I want to go to relax with."

"Ouch," I hear Scott say. I haven't figured out if he is Rhys's sidekick, or friend. He's a nice guy, seems decent enough, and I don't understand why he hangs around with someone as nasty as Rhys. I still don't understand why Joni is with someone like Rhys. He's not bad looking—he's not my type, though I don't have a type. He's appealing enough that most women would notice him what with his square jaw, and muscles, and menacing look. Some call it a brooding look. I say he looks threatening.

A real bad boy. He's the type of guy someone like Joni goes for. She needs validation from a big, strong guy, she thinks she's in love because he's with her.

I don't like him, and I can't hide it.

Rhys lowers his face onto Joni's neck. It looks like he's giving her a hickey. Gross.

"Get a room," Scotts growls.

"Luckily I have one." Rhys lifts his head and stares directly at me, before reaching for Joni's hand. "Come on, babe."

"Can't we stay here?" she whines.

"Upstairs," he tells her, then drags her off with him. I watch her follow him up the stairs like a lamb to slaughter and my insides hollow out. It's not even me inside that room this time, but I know what it's like to feel helpless.

"*Are* you seeing that actor guy?" Scott asks.

"No." I hate that Scott isn't letting go of that conversation.

"What's Joni on about, then?"

"Since when does Joni know everything?" I snap. I catch myself quickly. "Look, it's not like that. He likes our food, and he's got an arrangement with Frankie to have his lunch delivered to him on the set."

"Oh."

We stand in silence and listen to everyone else having fun. I look at him, but my mind is on another planet in a faraway galaxy. I don't hate Scott. But I don't like him either, not in that way.

"We should go for a drink sometime," he says again. "You and me and no one else. What do you say?"

I try not to groan too loudly, the guy needs an answer, and I might just have to spell it out if he can't get the hint. "I have too many assignments to do."

He laughs a short false laugh. "Surely you can spare me a few hours?"

My mind wanders to Rhys and Joni being dragged up the stairs. She's had too much to drink, and she's not going to know what's right or wrong, and Rhys isn't the type of guy to pay attention to what she wants or doesn't want. I feel sick in my stomach thinking about it. "Yeah," I say, because Scott is looking at me as if he needs answer.

"You're not really here, are you?" he guesses.

"Not really."

"Want another drink? You haven't touched that."

"Lemonade," I say.

"Back in a mo."

He swerves through the swathe of people, and I take my chance. My head isn't here in this room full of people making out. Music blasts out from the speakers, but I keep looking at the stairs.

Joni. With Rhys.

Panic rolls up my spine.

I know what it is to be dragged against your will. Only, Joni is a grown woman now. She can say 'no'. She doesn't have to pretend with Rhys.

I go upstairs. There are a few doors on either side of the hallway, and I don't know which one to try first. The door to the bathroom is wide open and a couple are making out on the toilet seat. I sure hope the seat is down.

I listen outside the other doors, and I can hear something that sounds like Rhys. Some type of grunting.

I know I shouldn't, but I need to see if Joni is okay, so I slowly, and quietly, open the door a little.

Joni's bent over the desk, and Rhys is thrusting into her. She's making noises, but I can't tell if they're the good type or the bad type. My heart crashes to the floor, and lies like a deadweight around my ankles.

I'm going to be sick.

This is wrong. So very wrong.

Rhys glances over his shoulder, sees me looking, then thrusts into Joni hard. He smiles as if he's enjoying the look of disgust on my face more than what he's doing.

I hear her whimper. Bile climbs up my throat. The bitter taste of it making me want to retch.

I close the door and run downstairs, pushing my way through people. I see the front door in front of me, and I struggle to reach it. My fingers finally clasp around it and I twist it and pull back.

And then I escape.

I run like mad.

Run, run, run away.

Like I used to try to.

It's not until I'm at the end of the street that I realize that I'm okay. It's just me, and I've made it.

CHAPTER THIRTEEN

NINA

"Look what I got for you."

That nasty man holds up a sweet. I hear my breath, but my body freezes. I can't move my neck. He creeps closer to me. I feel the urge to move back but my legs aren't working.

"Nina." He waves the sweet at me. It's in a shiny pink wrapper, and my mouth already feels weird. My stomach empties. I move my eyes, looking for my brother. He won't touch me if Elias is here. It's when I'm alone that I'm in trouble. I try not to be alone, but sometimes it happens, when I'm walking around looking for Elias, but this man always finds me first.

I don't know how he does it, comes out of the air. It's like he's always watching and waiting for me.

He takes another step closer to me and I want to throw up. I need to run, but I can't. I can hear my breath even louder now. It sounds like it does when I've been running.

When me and Elias play hide and seek around the house. It's a fun game when I play with my brother, but it's not fun when this man makes me play it with him.

And now he's got me.

"Do you want this, Nina?" He waves the sweet again.

I nod my head, because my voice has stopped working.

"Come on, this way, pet," he says, turning around to leave.

It feels as if my stomach has fallen to the floor. I don't want to follow him. I want my brother. I want the other kids, and the other grown-ups to be here. It's safer then.

I wish I could disappear.

"Neeee-naaaaaaaaaa." I hate the way he says it, like he's singing it. Like he's in a happy mood. But I'm scared, because he's taking me to his room, and he will do things that make me cry.

"Tell you what," he whispers, bending down. He has holes in his skin. His face is sweaty, and when he smiles, his teeth are crooked and yellow. "I'll make it easy for you this time. Just this time, mind. If you can find even *one* sweet, before I stop counting, then you can have *all* the sweets and go."

One sweet out of five? That sounds easy. I should be able to do that. He'll let me go, and he won't do anything to me.

I don't move.

"Or..." he smiles, showing those ugly teeth again. "Or I could play this game with your brother."

My lower lip starts to wobble, and I start to cry, but I don't make a noise. Big fat tears roll down my cheeks and I shake my head.

Not my brother. Not Elias. He's all I have.

"You want me to leave Elias alone?"

I nod.

"Good girl. Come on, then."

I follow him, sniffling as I wipe away my snot with the back of my hand. We're going down to his basement again. "Close your eyes, so I can hide the sweets."

I do as he says but I strain my ears for the tell tale clues but the thumping of my heart is louder and gets in the way.

"Go! Find them before I get to a hundred."

He starts counting, and I run around the room. It's not a big room, there's some furniture, a table, a chair, a sofa and a TV. I run around, terrified. Something inside me flips. I want to scream, but no one will hear me.

I'll play with your brother instead.

He can't do that to Elias. I am desperate to find a sweet. Just the one.

"Fifty-seven, fifty-eight."

I feel like I'm going to pee myself. He's halfway through and I haven't found anything. I look under the sofa cushions, and crawl under the table. I search everywhere I can think of, but the sweets are nowhere.

He's counting quickly. I try not to listen as he gets closer to ninety. My heart feels like it's going to burst.

"Ninety-eight, ninety-nine, one hundred."

I haven't found a single sweet.

I've lost the game.

I *always* lose the game.

I start crying again because I know what comes next.

He will punish me. I close my legs together, and I try to lift my head, but I can't look at him.

"Naughty girl, Nina."

I cry silently.

"Do you know what happens to naughty girls?"

I nod. I do know.

I want to throw up.

I want Elias.

"Come along, then, pet," he says, lifting up my dress and pulling down my panties.

It feels like the world has slowed down. It feels like I'm underwater, like I can't breathe. Like I can't hear, or see properly.

Like everything around me is blurry.

"Get up."

He pulls my hand roughly, and yanks me up. It hurts down there. It always hurts, but not like before, like that first time.

"Remember, this is our little secret," he says, pulling up my panties. He smooths down my dress. "Not a word to anyone. You know what happens if you tell?"

I stare back at him.

"You know what happens, don't you, pet? Answer me."

I open my mouth but no words come out.

"Answer me," he barks.

"Elias gets hurt." Somehow I manage to say those three words.

He nods. "That's right. If you want me to leave your brother alone, you keep your mouth shut."

I nod.

"Off with you then. Go on, get lost."

I run to the door, and then I run up the stairs, then out and into the hallway. The smell of disinfectant is so strong, and I almost trip in my rush to get away. I run and run, even though we're not supposed to run inside.

"Where you been?" Elias shouts, as I see him in the hallway. It feels like my lungs are about to burst.

I run to him and throw my arms around him, because he is my world, because I'm so happy to see him. I hold on tightly.

"Ewwww," he cries, pushing me away. "What did you do that for?"

I shrug. "Dunno."

He's lost one of his big upper teeth and two of his bottom ones. His dark eyes flash at me, he's not angry, but he thinks hugging is girlie stuff.

There is a pain between my legs, but I'm so happy to see him, that it doesn't matter.

CHAPTER FOURTEEN

NINA

Joni's been quiet all morning. I seek her out when she disappears outside for a cigarette break.

"Why did you let him drag you upstairs with him?" I ask her.

"Who?"

"Rhys."

"He's my boyfriend."

"You didn't look like you wanted to go upstairs."

She inhales deeply, then blows out smoke rings.

I persist. "He forced you to do something you didn't want."

"It's foreplay."

I freeze up when guys try to feel me up—the few guys I allowed to get near me. When I couldn't put out, they didn't stick around. But even at a young age, even at eight, I knew that a 'no' was supposed to mean a 'no'.

"But still, no should mean no." The janitor was evil. I

was a child. He was bigger than me and I couldn't escape him. What Joni has with Rhys is supposed to be consensual. It's a relationship between two adults. It's supposed to be different. I don't understand how a grown woman like Joni can let a man who is supposed to be her boyfriend, treat her the way he does.

Joni's expression turns coquettish. "When I say no, I don't really mean it." Her words horrify me, especially because I don't believe her.

"I'm just playing hard to get. I'm being a prick tease," she continues.

That's not what it looked like to me. She didn't look like she wanted to go upstairs with him. "What if one day you do mean it?"

"He's my boyfriend. Just because I don't feel like it then, doesn't mean I'm not going to enjoy it later."

"That's not right."

She throws the stub of her cigarette on the floor and presses her shoe over it. "Rhys is right. You're too uptight, Nina. When was the last time you had a boyfriend?"

I fold my arms. "I don't have a time for a boyfriend."

"What's wrong with Scott? The guy is crazy about you."

"I don't feel the same way."

"What about Office Guy? He's cute, nicely dressed. Seems smart. What's wrong with him?"

I shrug.

Nothing.

Nothing is wrong with any of them.

It's me.

I'm the one who's not wired right. I'm the one who is damaged and dirty and broken.

"Have you considered that you might be gay?" Joni asks.

"I'm not."

"Then why do you hold back? What are you waiting for?"

I turn to her in anger. "Life isn't about getting laid all the time."

"Getting laid all the time?" She laughs. "I don't remember you ever telling me about you getting laid at all."

"I'm not like you. I don't go around bragging about it."

"I don't brag. I tell you because you're my friend. I've never heard you talk about a date. You've had plenty of guys showing an interest in you, but remember, guys wouldn't hit on you if your brother wasn't famous."

Joni's jealousy blinds her. They did hit on me before, just not as much. I say nothing, because I'm too shocked by the vitriol in her voice.

"You're too stupid to even realize when someone like Callum Sandersby shows an interest in you. But don't forget, he's only interested in you because you're Elias's sister."

She's right. She's also pissed off, but it's with her boyfriend, and not me. She's just too stupid to see it.

I go back inside, annoyed by Joni and having had another bad night's sleep last night. That has been happening more and more since the summer. When I can't sleep, I cut myself. It's addictive, like scratching an itch—it feels so, so good. I try not to, but on those restless nights, after hours of tossing and turning, I often give in to the blade.

When I cut, I feel the pressure lift off. I become calmer. I feel at peace. I *feel*.

I stay away from Joni for the rest of the morning, but my mood is no better by the time I head off to the film set to deliver lunch for the golden boy. I hope he's shooting instead of being in his trailer, so that I can dump his lunch on his table and make a fast exit. Yesterday he was in makeup, and his assistant took the food from me.

However, my day worsens after I knock on his door. Callum tells me to come in. He holds up a book for me to see, presumably its something he's reading. To my dismay it's a biography about Elias.

"Find anything interesting?" I ask, only because he's put me on the spot.

"Quite a lot of things, actually. I'm only halfway through. You guys spent some time at Grampton House. It's still here, right?"

The reminder of that place is like a kick to my belly. "It closed down years ago," I reply as I walk towards him. "Your lunch."

"What was it like, growing up?"

Oh, heck, no.

I shouldn't have started this. Delivering lunch, agreeing to do it just because Frankie asked. I shouldn't have been so chatty last time. It's given him the wrong idea that he can ask me whatever he wants.

"Sorry, I have to rush back. Things are crazy hectic back at the diner."

"And you returning will make all the difference?"

"Yes." I will not talk about Grampton House to him. Even Elias and I don't talk about that time.

"Thanks for lunch.

I rush towards the door, and before I can say, "You're welcome," I run bang into his assistant.

"Ooops, sorry," she says, as we bump arms.

I can't get away fast enough.

CALLUM

. . .

She's not in the mood for talking today. I watch as she leaves, then crashes into Dottie who's on her way in.

"What did you say to her?" Dottie asks, handing me over the vitamin supplements I asked her to get for me.

"I didn't say anything."

"Tell me again why she's delivering takeout here every day?"

I pull out my wrap and the milkshake from the bag, and set myself down, ready to eat. "Because Frankie's has the best food in Chicago."

Dottie raises an eyebrow. "Is that the only reason?"

"That's the only reason. Can I eat my lunch in peace?" I pick up Elias's biography and start to read it while eating my wrap.

CHAPTER FIFTEEN

NINA

I've finished my assignment. It's late evening, and the place isn't particularly busy.

I bite my lip, as I see Frankie wiping down the tables. I should be doing that, but she knows I've been stressing about finishing my assignment, and she ordered me to sit in the corner and get it done.

So, I did.

I close my books, and yawn.

When I look up, Frankie's at the table, looking down at me with disapproval written across her face. "Looks to me like you need to get to bed."

"I've got a class tonight."

"You and your night classes," she spits the words out with contempt.

Yawning again, I glance at my watch, and see that I'm late. I've got twenty minutes to make it to my class, and I can do it if I run to the train station and run to my class at the other end. I might be a few minutes late.

"I have to hand in my assignment," I say, yawning again as I start to I pack my things away quickly. I hope I sleep better tonight.

"I shouldn't say this, as the owner, but you're too good for this place. I don't understand why you've never taken up your brother's offer to go and work for him?"

"Work for him and give up this?" I sweep my arm around the diner.

Frankie waggles her finger at me. "You come here for the company; don't think I don't know."

"I love working here, Frankie. This place is like my second home."

"You've got a job here for life, but what are you doing all these night classes for? You've been doing them for as long as I've known you. What are you doing, a Phd?"

"I wish," I mutter. I'd like to be a doctor of something. Dr. Nina Cardoza. It has a nice ring to it. I wonder if that will fix me? If it will miraculously make me feel worthy.

"Then do that," Frankie insists. "Elias is in a position to help you. Let him."

"I don't want his help."

"You're too damn stubborn."

I turn my back to her as I zip up my bag.

"Well, hello there," I hear her say, in a voice that hints at flirtation. I wonder who she's talking to and I turn around to the tall and muscular form that is Callum Sandersby standing in front of me. What's he doing here at this time of night?

"Hey, Nina." He looks directly at me.

"Hey," I reply, and at the same time I'm relieved that I have a night class I can escape to.

"You're leaving?" he asks, when I put my bag over my shoulder and get ready to leave.

"Night school," Frankie tells him.

"Night school?" Callum echoes, as if it's the greatest surprise. "You go to night school? I had no idea."

I move past him. "Why would you?"

"Because we're friends? Because we see one another every day." He grins and it annoys me, so I walk away, towards the door, and shout out a "Bye' to Frankie. I glance behind to find that he is following me. "We're not closing," I tell him, as I catch his reflection in the door. "Frankie's still here. She'll serve you." I push the door open and leave, then speed up my footsteps as I note the time on my wrist watch again. This little interruption has cost me precious moments I didn't have.

"Hey, wait up."

Ugh. No. Callum's following me. I start to run.

I hear him chortle, then break out into a run. Soon he's jogging beside me. "Where are we running to?"

"I'm late."

"Are we running all the way?"

We're still jogging, and he's not out of breath, he's managing to keep up with me. This is ridiculous. I stop, and it takes him a few strides before he realizes he's running alone. "Don't you have a class to get to?" he asks, circling back towards me.

"What. Are. You. Doing?" What? I don't have time to deal with this, I *shouldn't* be dealing with this, and yet he has given me no option but to stop in the middle of the street on the way to my already-late-class.

"I'm going to night school with you."

"Why?" I almost yell at him.

"Because ... it's something I haven't been to before."

That does it for me. Who does he think he is? "Why? Look, I don't like you. I'm not interested in you. I don't wish to spend any time with you."

He walks over to me, and now he's a little breathless as he stands in front of me, with his hands on his hips, breathing in and out a little heavily.

Then he says something that grabs all of my attention. "I was just checking up on you."

"Checking up on me for what?" Irritation gnaws at me. I don't have time to waste, yet here he is, Mr. Hotshot, taking up every precious minute of my time.

"You looked a little upset when you came to drop my lunch off earlier."

"If I was upset, it's because you have that effect on me."

His signature grin breaks out. "At least I have some effect on you."

I squeeze my eyes shut for a second, and when I open them again, he's still there. I rush off. I hear him whistle, and when I turn around, he's hailed down a taxi. "Get in." He waves me over.

I hate that he is so persistent. I hate that he thinks he can do what he wants.

But he's hailed a taxi, and I could be at my class within ten minutes.

I hop in, because, really, what choice has he given me?

CHAPTER SIXTEEN

CALLUM

She jumps out of the cab and rushes off.

I wait for her.

Like a doormat, I wait for her in the cold. Pacing around outside the school building before realizing that I can wait inside. The security guard at the front desk strikes up a conversation as soon as I take off my beanie hat. We end up taking selfies and he gets me so sign some autographs for his daughters.

Then I walk around the corridors waiting for Elias Cardoza's sister to notice me. This is insane, I realize that, and I can't imagine what Rudy or Dottie would make of it, but it's a tiny challenge for me. Something to do instead of sitting around in my hotel suite.

Nina wasn't expecting me to do this, accompany her to night school, and to be honest, I wasn't expecting to go with her.

We finished shooting early today, so I took a chance in

going to the diner. It beats going back to an empty hotel suite. Except tonight it wouldn't have been like that. The guys would have gone on to a club, or a party and I'd have gone along. I only went to Frankie's to get a milkshake and because I was curious. I could tell that something was up earlier when Nina delivered my lunch. I'm hoping to get into her good books with the idea that she might consider me a good enough friend to introduce me to her brother. The biography I'm still reading talks about how close the two of them are. That's what I'm banking on.

Also, she's cute in the way she doesn't invite my interest. I am so used to getting attention, to having women fawning over me that I can't understand what's wrong with this woman. Still, it's access to Elias that I need, and why not chase a bit of skirt in the process? I'm not looking to sleep with her or date her, yet while she's not attracted to me, there is something about her that intrigues me. Something about her that isn't quite what it seems. She's like a cryptic puzzle. I just have to look deeper to solve it.

She comes out of the classroom and looks surprised to see me again. "You're still here?"

"I'm not looking to go on a date with you or anything, okay. Let's just get that out of the way."

"You're not?" Her exaggerated disappointment is laid on extra thick.

We walk along the hallway. Even though I've put my beanie hat back on, I can sense people around us whispering and looking at us. I have a feeling they've seen through my disguise. I try to ignore them. "Two people can be friends. It doesn't have to be anything more than that."

"What makes you think I want to be friends with you?" she asks.

I lift my eyebrow and smile at her, not because I want

her to swoon over me, but because I know it will annoy her. "Because we're bound together. You saved my life, and I saved you right back."

She groans loudly. "If I could get that night back, I'd do things so differently. I would have walked right past the alleyway."

"But you didn't, and I don't believe you would. *Normal* people would, but not you." I smile as I say it, but she doesn't find it amusing.

"Why do you keep showing up where I am? Are you that lonely that you don't have any friends?"

"I'm on the set for most of the day. Dottie and the film crew are the people I see all day long. You are something different."

"You are lonely."

"We met in highly unusual circumstances. You're not easy to impress—not that I've tried," I add quickly. "You're not like other women. Being an actor, I'm surrounded by people who think I'm this amazing guy. They want to get close to me. They think they know me."

She frowns in disgust. "It must be an occupational hazard?"

"It is."

"It's a wonder your head can fit through the door," she says, as we go through a pair of double doors.

"You might be joking, but people's brains sometimes turn to mush when they meet me. And when they realize they've seen me in a film, they treat me like I'm some God-level deity."

She smirks. "Luckily, I don't suffer from the same delusions."

"And that's why I like you, in a non-girlfriend kind of way."

She opens her mouth to say something, then pauses. "You're very annoying."

"Be nice, and I'll play nice back."

"I don't want to play."

That's a line I've never heard from a woman I've invested time in.

"I'm going home," she says, adjusting the straps of her bag. "Are you going to follow me home?"

"It depends, are you going to invite me in for coffee?"

She doesn't answer that question.

"What is it that you're studying?" I ask her as we leave the building and walk down the street. A couple walking past do a double take, which I notice, but ignore.

"Interior Design."

"Interior Design? That's interesting. You're looking to change jobs?"

But she seems busy watching people's reactions as we continue to walk. It's like a whispering campaign suddenly started, and now everyone around us knows that it's me.

Suddenly, two girls come up to me and ask for my autograph. They're shy, and hesitant at first, but they're blocking our passage, and they want what they want. "You're Callum Sandersby?" says one.

"So cool!" shrieks her friend. "Could we have your autograph?"

This is one part of my career that I'm beginning to hate. I don't mind doing this when I'm out promoting my films, but not when it's a private moment, with friends. Like now. I hate that people think they can interrupt all the time and I'll be okay with it.

I take the notebook one of them shoves in my face, and scribble away. Her friend whips out her cellphone and asks if we can get a selfie. I don't have a chance to say anything when she takes a few shots.

By now, a small crowd has gathered around us. I've done it again, gone out and attracted attention.

But tonight, I have no intention of ending up in an alleyway.

I see a cab, then hail it down.

"Jump in," I tell Nina. "Now!" I yell, when she appears to hesitate. She jumps in, and I do too, but she doesn't like this one bit. Most women would die to be in the back of a cab with me, but not this one. Nina looks like she'd rather be roasting in hell than in here with me.

"Where do you live?"

She mumbles an address. We don't even live in the same direction. It makes sense for me to get off first, but that would give me less time with this woman, so I tell the driver to go to where Nina is first.

"Fans," I say, with contempt, trying to break the ice and make conversation. It seemed easier when we were outside. Here in the closed confines of the taxi, she seems to have withdrawn into her shell again.

I seriously have no idea why my charm and my good looks, and my status are having exactly zero effect on this woman. She's looking out of the window, her head turned away. I catch the taxi driver looking at me in the rear view mirror. I can't tell if he knows who I am yet. Maybe he can't figure it out yet, after all, this isn't LA, and I shouldn't feel too down about it.

I shift my body so that I can angle my body and see her properly. "You've had a really long day," I say, hoping to have a simple conversation. "You worked all day at the diner, delivered my lunch, and now you've just been to night school."

"Why did you want lunch delivered?"

I blink. That came out of nowhere. "I told you. I like Frankie's milkshake and wraps."

She fixes me with a stare, that even under the dim light in the taxi, I can feel the intensity of. She doesn't believe me, that much is obvious. She also isn't easy to win over. "I don't understand why you hate me so much when we barely know one another."

Her brows push together, as if she's trying to find a diplomatic way of giving me an answer. "I don't hate you. I just don't understand why I'm seeing so much of you."

"Because we're destined to be together?"

"Did you pick up those tacky lines from your scripts?"

That's a hell of a put down. "I might have. You should see some of the things I've had to say."

"You've mistaken me for a celebrity watcher. People like you don't interest me."

Our conversation is like barbed wire, hard, and prickly, but at least we're talking. "None of my lines have any effect on you," I comment. "And your armor's bullet proof." I'm curious to know why. I don't have an extraordinarily large ego—not compared to some of the people I've met in this industry—but this woman is completely unaffected by my charm. By me. I don't want to be rude and ask if she bats for the other side, but maybe she's bi? Yet I don't think it's that either. I can tell these things, and I'm not getting that vibe from her. "You think I'm wasting my time getting to know you?"

She does one of those exaggerated eye blinks, as if she's indicating extreme surprise at my question. "Is that what this is?"

I shrug. "You can't knock me for trying."

"That stuff doesn't work on me"

She's hard work. I've reined in my charm, and I'm not flirting with her, much. I only want to figure out why she dislikes me so much. "Is there really no chance of you ever being nice to me?"

She groans. "Don't you ever let up?"

I level with her. "Talking to you is a nicer way to spend the evening than going back to an empty hotel room."

For the first time this evening, the corners of her lips turn upwards. The ice maiden might be starting to melt. It also makes a difference that we're not sitting at a club, or at an after party. Talking to her reminds me of the down-to-earth conversations I used to have with women before I became famous.

I miss those days.

I miss people being honest, and liking you for who you are, instead of your fame. I don't want to let this opportunity pass. "How about a drink tomorrow night?"

"No." She tuts, and then turns and looks out of her window. Her reply is so final, the tone behind her words so strong, that I am temporarily wounded. It's a surface level wound only, but it's there. "Why not? You're not seeing anyone."

Her head spins around so fast I'm scared she might have given herself whiplash. "How would you know?" I wasn't sure, it was just a hunch based on what I've heard about her, but she's confirmed it now.

"It was a guess."

Nina's eyes narrow. I feel sure that if she had anything on her, like a bow and arrow, she'd hold it up and take aim at me.

"Is it women?" I ask, trying to figure her out. "Is that what you're into?"

The look she gives me, freezes me in place. "It must

fracture your wafer thin self-esteem, to meet someone who doesn't fall at your feet. *This* is the only reason you have for it?"

Now we're getting somewhere. "Wafer thin." I scratch my head. "One thing you should know, there's nothing wafer thin about me." I raise an eyebrow, in jest.

She looks disgusted and makes a noise as if she's about to gag. "Most women might throw themselves at you, but I'm not one of them."

"I can see that." I try again one last time. "That's a no to my offer of a drink?"

"That's a definite 'no'."

The taxi grinds to a stop and the driver turns the light on. "Is it safe around here?" I look out of the window and find it hard to believe that for a guy who's just won millions, Elias is okay for her to still live in this neighborhood.

She winks at me. "If you stay off the streets, you'll be safe."

"Funny."

"I wasn't trying to be. I meant it."

"Ha ha." I croak, my face deadpan.

She looks up. "I don't understand why we came to my place first."

"I'm a gentleman, and I wanted to see you home safely. I guess there's no chance of me coming in for coffee?"

"No chance at all."

She opens her purse and starts to take out some dollar bills.

"I've got this," I tell her.

"I want to pay for my share." She pulls out a few dollar bills from her purse.

"Please, Nina. I can get this."

"I wouldn't want to be beholden to you," she says,

thrusting her arm out to hand the money to the driver in front. "That should take care of my share."

I grab her wrist, a little harder than I intended, and I catch it further up along her forearm. She winces, it's audible, and it sounds painful enough that I snatch my hand back as if I've touched fire. She drops the dollar bills, and quickly apologizes to the driver who snatches them up from the floor just as quickly.

"Did you hurt yourself?" I'm certain that I felt something bumpy, like scabs, on her skin. She moves her arm away quickly and out of the way, almost hiding it out of sight behind her back. "I burned myself at work by accident. 'Bye," she says, before I manage to mumble a 'See you around.'

As the taxi drives away, I twist my neck, and see her walking towards her apartment building. I'm worried for her. "Wait," I order the driver. "Let me see her get in."

When I see her step through the door, I tell the driver to go. A part of me knows I should have walked her to the door, but that would have annoyed her even more.

I wish I'd done that.

CHAPTER SEVENTEEN

NINA

I'm taking a pitcher of water to a table, when Harper walks into the diner. I see her placing an order at the counter, and when I'm done, I walk over.

Joni is floating around somewhere. She flits in and out taking a cigarette break.

"Hey," I say, "Are you eating in or getting a takeout?"

"Takeout. I've ordered the usual for your brother, a jacket potato with tuna and salad, a double portion of it."

We grin at one another. Elias has a huge appetite. We go and sit at an empty booth while she's waiting for her food. I don't smoke, so this is my way of getting my little breaks in.

"How's the actor?"

I give her a blank look.

"Have you seen him lately?" she asks, when I fail to answer. I have seen far too much of Callum Sandersby than I want, but I don't want to lie to her.

"Why do you ask?" I also don't want to tell her the truth, and then I wonder why that is. It's not like there's something going on with me and him. "Are you working an angle on him for your magazine?"

"My tech mag?" She laughs. "I'd get fired if I wrote about this superstar when I'm supposed to be looking at this new gaming software." She makes a face, clearly not enthused. Tech isn't her thing. She used to work for a local paper before. This is miles away from her safety zone, but she wanted to prove that she could get a job without her dad helping, and this was it. I have a feeling that she and Elias are going to get married in the not too distant future. I can't see Harper working for this magazine for long. Hopefully she'll end up working for Elias instead, and that will get him off my case.

I try to think of what to say. Does she need to know that he's somehow managed to get me to deliver lunch to his set every day? I think not. I myself don't fully understand why he did that; it's not like I'm some raving beauty, with a voluptuous figure, a happy childhood and no extraneous baggage.

I'm just me.

Insignificant and damaged Nina Cardoza.

"I'm sure he's been here a couple of times," I say, deliberately being vague. "Why do you need to know his every move?"

"Why?" Harper parrots. "Because he's a famous movie star, Nina. I can't believe I have to spell it out to you. How do you not see what I'm seeing?"

"He's just a normal guy."

Harper shakes her head. "I don't get you, Nina."

"Get what?"

"It's not every day that a Hollywood heart throb lands

on your doorstep, and this kind of stuff only happens in films. This is a big deal. *Huge.*"

"It's not a big deal."

"It so is!" she cries.

"I can see why you're a journalist. You find headlines in the unlikeliest of places."

"The man is gorgeous!"

"Should I warn Elias?" I ask her.

"I'm not interested in Callum, but he's interested in *you.*" She points a finger at me as if to drive the point home. "When was the last time you had a boyfriend? I've never known you to have one, and when I asked Eli, he said he didn't remember either."

My stomach hardens, and I hate the direction this conversation is going in. "Why would you ask Elias about something like that?" I rub the back of my neck, my mind still fixated on that part of the conversation. I've never discussed anything with my brother. The few relationships I've had—if they could be called that—were short-lived.

"I've never seen you with a guy, and I don't understand how someone like you can be single for so long."

"It's not a sin."

"I never said that. "I like to think that we know each other well enough by now for you to tell me. Mark my words, Nina, Callum Sandersby is interested in you."

"That's what I think, too," says Frankie. Her ultrasonic bat-like hearing never ceases to amaze me. She stands, with her arms folded and eyes me like a hawk. I momentarily brace myself for a telling off because I'm sitting at a table chatting to my brother's girlfriend as if I'm one of the regulars.

"Did you know he came by the other night and went

with her to night school?" she tells Harper, and nods slowly, as if she's disclosed some huge secret.

"He did *what?*" Harper asks.

"Went to night school with her."

"Look at that juicy piece of news you conveniently forgot to mention." Harper narrows her eyes at me. "Then what?"

"He waited."

"He waited? He's persistent. Definitely interested, I'll give him that."

"That's what I think," says Frankie.

"And then?" A waitress puts Harper's takeaway bag on the table.

"Shouldn't you get that to Elias while it's hot?" I ask her, desperate for her to leave.

"He's sparring with Jake and Santos. Go on."

"Go on what?"

"What did you do after the class?"

"We were walking, and he attracted attention and so he called a cab and we jumped in. He dropped me off first."

"He dropped you off?"

I nod.

"Did you not invite him in for coffee, or something?" The way she says 'something' makes me uneasy. I scowl.

"How are you not reading the signs this guy's giving off? He has the feels for you, Nina. He's *interested.*"

"He is *not* interested." Someone like him isn't going to be interested in someone like me. "He's surrounded by gorgeous women."

"Maybe he's realized that he wants something different now ... someone kinder, softer, genuine." She backtracks immediately, but it still leaves me feeling shitty. Unperturbed, Harper continues. "Maybe he doesn't want the brash overly confident type of woman. He's seen something different in you."

I snort with derision. He has seen something in me. Something dark and damaged.

"Give him a chance, Nina."

I don't think so. I can't shake Joni's words out of my head.

He's only interested in you because you're Eli's sister.

While I'm revisiting my dark hole and remembering that conversation, Frankie tells Harper about the daily delivery of Callum's lunch.

"You lied to me." Harper looks at me accusingly. "You said he's been here a couple of times, like it was no big deal."

"I didn't lie. I just didn't tell you the truth."

Harper protests. "Just like with the mugging."

"She kept that quiet, too, huh?" says Frankie.

"It almost makes me think she's living a double life." Harper and Frankie laugh at my expense, though Harper suddenly sobers up when she sees my somber reaction. "Look, Nina. I don't think you understand what's going on."

"Oh, I understand it just fine, thank you."

"Callum Sandersby sought you out, came here to thank you, then he's got you delivering lunch to him every day—"

"I wonder why," I say, tardily.

Harper ignores me. "Then he went with you to night school." Her eyes light up like sparkling crystals. I imagine any time now she'll whip out a notepad and pen and start scribbling notes. "You shouldn't be drooling over another guy," I remind her. "You're with Elias."

"I'm not drooling over Callum Sandersby, but I am *so* happy for you!" She claps her hands together, as if I've announced my engagement to him.

"Me too," says Frankie, looking pleased with herself.

"One of the hottest hunks in Hollywood is interested in you and you're still acting so blasé about it."

"I don't care who he is, I'm not interested in him." I get up from the table. "Did you come in here to get Elias's lunch, or to quiz me on Callum Sandersby's comings and goings?"

"I'm on your side. You're gorgeous, and cute, and sexy."

I make a face, hating the praise and the flattery.

"It's true, and he's interested in you."

I shrug. I still have my suspicions.

"It doesn't matter who he is," Frankie says. "Between you and me, she's working through the A to Z of night school courses. She's got no time for romance."

Harper laughs. looks at her watch, gasps that she didn't realize she'd been talking for so long.

"You didn't realize?" I say, sarcastically.

"You are a dark horse," she points an accusing finger at me. "It makes me so happy to hear about you and Callum Sandersby."

"Shush!" I put my finger to my lips. "There is no me and Callum Sandersby," I insist, standing up and smoothing down my apron.

"There's no anybody, knowing you," mumbles Frankie as she walks away.

I have my own suspicions about why Callum has taken a vested interest in me, and it's not because of *me*.

"I have to go. Eli will go nuts that I've kept him waiting so long for his food." Harper grabs the bag, kisses me on the cheek, and rushes out.

I spin on my heels and pick up a coffee pot, ready to take it over to a table. I hate that all of a sudden everyone is fixated on my love life. Or non-existent love life, more like it.

I head towards the table in the corner and refill everyone's cup of coffee.

No way is Callum Sandersby interested in me. He wants something, but it's not me.

He's annoying, and persistent, and right now he's like a leech, although he's not like Office guy. This doesn't feel like it does when Office Guy hangs around the diner. I don't feel claustrophobic. I don't understand it either. Maybe Callum is right, we're bound together, for now, for this phase, while he's here, because of how we first met. There's nothing romantic about it, that's for sure.

The reality of it is that we are worlds apart and Harper lives in cloud cuckoo land.

CHAPTER EIGHTEEN

CALLUM

"Good book?" Dottie walks in with a bottle of water for me. I'm taking a break from shooting. Elias's biography rests on my lap.

"It's a very good book." I've ended up reading this more often than not during my breaks. Elias's life story is bleaker and sadder than I imagined. Reading his biography gives me a better insight into the man, but it also helps me to better understand Nina.

Even though I see her daily, and we got to talk for longer than usual the other night, I still don't feel as if I know her. I sense that there is something vulnerable about her, something in her eyes that I can't reach.

Worse, I find myself thinking about her more often than not. It's becoming less about finding a way to meeting Elias, and more about wanting to meet with her. That's not something I expected to happen.

She's not my type.

And yet, she's everything new, and fresh and alluring. She's the breath of fresh air that I need. Someone who doesn't pander to me but puts me in my place. Someone who treats me like a normal person instead of a demigod.

Is it weird that I think about that night in the alleyway, and giving up my last photo of Ben.

It saddens me, to have lost such a precious thing. I have many photos of him. But that was the last one.

It was a decade ago, and yet it seems like yesterday.

"You're reading that book, you have his sister come here every day. Is there something you're hiding? Rudy will be onto you before you can--"

"Dottie, Dottie ... " I say, closing the book. "There's nothing going on."

"She's here everyday."

I sigh out in exasperation. Seems like I have to explain this to every single person. "I like the milkshakes and food from that diner."

"I could have picked that up for you. God knows you have me running around after you like a headless chicken." She walks around my room tidying up, like a mother, even if she's a good couple of years younger than me. The main reason I picked her was because she was efficient.

"Does it matter?" I cry out, unable to find a good enough answer to that.

Dottie cocks her head. "Do you know how many column inches have been devoted to your and Alyssa's new romance?"

"Jesus, Dot. You're beginning to sound a lot like Rudy. It's scary."

"I'm only looking out for you."

I glance at my watch. Nina should be arriving here about now.

"Look, why do you think I'm pursuing her?"

"I have no idea. She's not really your type."

I stop myself from rolling my eyes. "Exactly. She's not my type, but what she is is Elias Cardoza's sister. You do know who he is, don't you?"

"Yes. I know who he is. My boyfriend won't shut up about him."

"There you go. That's my plan. Rudy can't get me a meeting with Elias, but maybe his sister can." I wink at her and nod.

"You should have left it to me to set up a meeting with him," Dottie says.

"Well, I'm taking care of it. Now, can you get me another two bottles of water? I'm really thirsty today."

CHAPTER NINETEEN

NINA

I knock on the door to Joni's apartment. We're going out tonight, on a rare girlie night out. A movie, then pizza.

We used to do this a couple of times a month, but then Rhys came onto the scene and she suddenly didn't have time for anyone else. It bothered me at first, when she shoved me to the side, but I have enough to keep myself busy, so I let her live in her little bubble with Rhys.

But today we both decided to put our recent disagreements behind us and do something fun. Besides, it's been a lousy day. A god awful lousy day. I need this night out with a girlfriend.

I went to deliver Callum's lunch as usual, but just as I got to his trailer, Harper sent me a text with a link to a write up about him in a magazine. I was just about to put my cell phone away when I overheard Dottie and Callum talking. The trailer door was slightly ajar, and I'm not usually the type or person to eavesdrop, but something Callum said stopped me cold. He said something about me not being his type.

'She's Elias Cardoza's sister. You do know who he is, don't you?'

I froze. Couldn't breathe. Couldn't move. And then I heard him talk about his plan and it sickened me to my stomach. I had been starting to entertain the remote possibility that Callum might be interested in me. Deep down, I've always believed that it was because of Elias, but it was nice to be able to dream about an alternate reason for his interest.

And now he's gone and confirmed it. Of course Callum isn't interested in me. It's Elias he wants, so that he can perfect his role, get into character, get some publicity with a real boxer. I'm just a means to an end, to help him get close to him because my brother isn't so friendly, especially with people who want something, like Callum does.

Hearing Callum say it out loud hit like one of Elias's punches. I've always known that I'm not beautiful or worthy. I am unlovable. Hearing him explain to Dottie smacks into me like an unexpected left hook. I rushed away and couldn't bring myself to walk into his trailer, pretending that I hadn't heard a thing.

I can hide my emotions well, but I was too shocked. His words had slapped me too hard and back to reality. I hovered around nearby, wondering how to get his lunch to him when Dottie walked by and I told her I was in a rush and handed it to her.

That's why I need tonight, with Joni. To get away from everything.

"Hey," I say, when she opens the door. She's got two curlers in her hair.

"Why are you...?" I raise my hand towards her head. It's

only the two of us, and I don't understand why she's making all this effort. I place my bag on the table, and follow her to the bedroom. "Why are you going to all this trouble? We're only going to the movies."

She pulls her curlers out and primps her hair. "It's nice to make an effort. I'm sick of always hanging around in the diner."

But she doesn't always hang around in the diner. She goes out a lot, especially now that she's with Rhys. She socializes much more than I do. That's more my fault, because I'm a hermit. I prefer my own company.

"I don't have those lovely job perks like you do."

"Job perks?" I ask, not understanding.

"I don't get to drop lunch off for Callum Sandersby. *You* do." She waves her hairbrush at me. "Can you at least put some lipstick on before we go?"

"I didn't bring anything with me."

"Don't you carry make up with you?" She looks at me as if I've killed someone.

"No, I usually go home."

"Here," she rummages around in her make up bag and throws me a lipstick. I open it up, see that's is a gaudy red color and swivel it back down again. I'm not putting this on.

"What do the two of you talk about?" she asks.

"We don't talk about anything much." Not that its any of her business. "I drop his food off, and I leave."

"Why do you think he asked for you?"

If she had asked me yesterday, I might have considered my alternate wishful reason behind Callum's request. I might not have said it out loud to Joni, but I would at least have considered it. But now I know the truth, and still, I'm not about to tell her. "I don't know."

"For someone who's meant to be clever, going to all

those night classes like you do, I'm surprised you haven't worked it out yet."

"What's that?"

"Don't you see the connection? Elias is the boxing heavyweight champion, and Callum's making a boxing film."

"Right. That's what it must be." How can I so easily forget that Joni isn't a good friend?

"Scott's crazy about you and you don't give him the time of day."

"I don't have those feelings for him."

"You've always thought you're better than everyone else."

We've had this argument many times, and I'm not going to get into another row with her about it now. "I see Scott as a friend."

"How do you know that when you haven't given the poor guy a chance?"

Because I'm not interested. Because I haven't felt any remote hint of attraction. I have no interest in trying to get her to see my point of view because she won't understand. If I'm overly picky about who I allow into my life, she's the total opposite. She's never turned down a single guy who's asked her out.

"Callum's way out of your league," Joni tells me.

"Thanks for pointing that out."

"I don't mean it like that. I mean that Scott is more on your level. I'm just doing you a favor. Someone's got to tell you."

"I can figure it out myself, thank you."

She opens her mouth as if she's realized she's being overly malicious—even for her. "I don't want you to make a fool of yourself."

"Thanks for watching my back." I'm taken aback, not by her words so much, as by the venom in her voice. "Even Rhys agrees."

"He would."

"I'd hate to see you making a fool of yourself, Nina."

"Nice of you to be so concerned but we both know Callum isn't interested in me. He's just using me because of Elias, remember?" My sarcasm is lost on her as she applies her red lipstick slowly, "I was worried that you might think he's into you. Chasing you ..." She presses her lips together and carries on talking but I've stopped listening.

Chasing me.

The words send fear shooting through my veins. I can almost hear the janitor counting to fifty real fast.

"But," Joni turns to me. "A guy like him, he probably sees you as a challenge only because you play so hard to get."

"Thanks." *What a great friend to have.*

I lower my head, and instinctively tighten my stomach. Like the way I used to when that man used to tell me it was time to go down to the basement. I didn't know it then, but I was putting up my own human shield, made out of my own skin and muscles, tightening, bracing my body against his invasion.

"Hey. Don't look so upset." Joni touches my arm.

"Huh?" I jerk my head up. Force myself back to normality, like I used to when I'd emerge from the basement, feeling like a dirty little rag. When Elias would ask me where I had been. All I could think was that I had done something that would keep him safe from that evil man, and that he would never do to Elias what he had done to me.

"I don't want you to get hurt, Nina."

"I won't." I think about the blade against my skin. Slicing into my flesh gives me a release. I tell myself that it's all the badness. All my sins, and dirt seeping out.

"Are you okay? You've been acting really weird, lately." She lifts my chin up with her finger. "I'm sorry if it's not what you want to hear, but I don't want you to go around thinking that Callum Sandersby is into you."

"I don't need you to tell me." The evening has suddenly gone from a supposed fun night out, to something else. When the doorbell rings, I glance at her, startled. "Who's that?"

"Probably Rhys." She slips on her jacket.

"What?" No wonder she's getting all dolled up. "Is he coming? You said it was only you and me."

"It was, but Rhys wants to watch the movie."

"But I don't want to watch it with him."

"Scott's coming too. He's meeting us there."

"You invited him?" "

"He's meeting us there."

"Really?" I scoff.

"Why are you so angry?" she asks, then, without waiting for my answer, "I need to go to the loo. Could you get that?"

My stomach churns when the doorbell rings again.

"Can you get that?" Joni cries, as she disappears into the washroom. I want to run the heck out of here and go home.

"It was supposed to be you and me," I groan to myself as I walk towards the door.

"Joni's getting ready," I say, as soon as Rhys walks in. I can't get it out of my head, that indelible image of him with Joni at the party.

"Scott's gonna be happy," he says, grinning at me like a predatory shark. I take a step back, and I must have moved too soon, because it's given him the advantage. He can smell my fear.

He sniffs, as he walks towards me. "Do I smell?" he asks, ducking his head under his arms, not unlike a Neanderthal. I glance towards the hallway, willing Joni to hurry the hell up and get over here.

His face is close to mine, and my back is flat against the wall. I can smell his body odor, and his breath.

It takes me back, way, way, way back, and I feel like my eight year old self again. Helpless, and lost, and so, so scared. I feel as if I'm going to pee myself.

Rhys smiles at me, then lays his hand flat against my belly. I am terrified that it will slip lower, like the janitor's hand used to. I clench my legs together.

"You want some?" he whispers.

I manage to exhale, but I can't find my voice. I know, at some deep, low, survival level, that I am not supposed to talk back.

"You want some of what I gave Joni? She squeals like a pig when she comes. I bet you don't make that noise. I bet you don't even sweat. I bet you sparkle, or some shit like that. You've got a little more class."

I release a breath.

"Is that the noise you make?" he asks, grinning. "'Cause it gave me a stiffie." He tries to thrust his hand between my legs, but I grip his wrist super tight. His eyes widen in surprise. "Gotta lotta strength in you, given that you're so tiny." He licks my neck. I recoil in disgust and I turn my face to the side, squeezing my eyes tightly shut. I can feel his hand resting on my body and I'm thankful that I'm wearing jeans.

"Baby!" Joni's voice floats over from the distance. In the time it takes for her to appear into view, Rhys strides towards Joni and clamps his mouth to hers. She makes a moaning sound. I flinch at the sight of her with him. Moving away, I suddenly have trouble swallowing. My throat feels like its burning and suddenly, I don't feel so great anymore.

"I don't feel so good," I announce, in a shaky voice. My heart rate rockets and I think I'm going to have a heart attack. Joni looks annoyed. "Are you upset because of what I said about Callum?"

"That actor dude?" Rhys asks.

"I don't feel well," I answer. She has no idea. She never will. She can't see the pig of a man she's with for who he really is, and she will never understand the scars I have to live with.

"You're upset." Joni tries to put her hand on my arm, but I shake it off.

"I'm not. I really don't feel too good." My stomach twists and heaves as if I've eaten something well past it's best before date.

Joni won't give it up. "All of a sudden you don't want to come? Is it because of Scott?"

"Give the poor guy a chance," Rhys drawls over her shoulder. I can see him grinning at me behind Joni's back.

"It's not Scott that's the problem," I fix him with a pointed stare. I grab my bag and walk out, just in time to hear Joni say, "She's upset because I told her that Callum Sandersby isn't into her."

The last thing I hear as I close the door is the sound of Rhys laughing.

CHAPTER TWENTY

CALLUM

We're in a fancy restaurant with a group of people from the set. I didn't really want to come but it's someone's birthday, which is the only reason I'm out.

We've ordered dessert, and I stick around for it, but don't order anything. After this they want to go for drinks in the bar. I want to get back to my suite. We shot some brutal fighting scenes in the ring earlier and I got beaten to within an inch of my death. My ribs started to hurt and I've got a slight cut on my upper lip. I'm exhausted and all I want to do is sit in a salt bath.

"Try some of this cheesecake," the girl to my right says, lifting the fork to my mouth. I push her hand away.

"I need to maintain my physique," I explain.

"You're looking pretty good to me, Cal." She smiles at me, and there's a world of suggestion on her lips.

I sat through dinner eating salad and tuna. How boxers

eat this forever, beats me. It would be enough for me to want a change of career.

I yawn. It's odd how that happens. I'm not even tired, but I need to make an exit otherwise I'll end up going to the bar with this bunch of guys, and as nice as they are, I see them all day long on the set. I want a break. I consider talking to Nina, because having a conversation with her can be a challenge, and I'm sick of being surrounded by 'yes' men, and women.

"I'm going back," I announce fully yawning now.

"Already?" The girl to my right whines.

"He's a lightweight," the girl on the left states, jabbing me lightly in the ribs.

"I *am* a lightweight," I say, nodding. We're sitting around a circular booth, and I get her and the person next to her to move out of the way.

"Are you leaving, Cal?" someone shouts.

"I got beat. Can't you see?" I point to my lip. I yawn again, as if my built-in radar needs to get the message home. "I'm outta here. See you guys tomorrow."

"Bright and early. We have extra scenes to redo."

I wave as I walk out.

Milkshake from Frankie's Kitchen. That's what I suddenly develop a thirst for. My cell phone vibrates in my pocket and when I fish it out, I smile, but I'm also puzzled.

It's Harper, and I wonder how she got my number.

"Am I disturbing you?" she asks.

"No. We were having dinner, well, dessert, really."

"We?"

"The guys on set."

"Oh, okay. I called to let you know that you've been invited to a party at City Hall."

"A party?"

"Eli's promoter is putting on an event, for Eli, publicity and all that. You know how these things work."

I've seen posters going up about the rematch next month. A couple of the guys on set were talking about it. But to be at a party where Elias will be? I'm beyond ecstatic. Maybe I should tell Rudy? He needs to know about all possible publicity events, even though this is a private event. I'm going as a guest of Elias, not as a means of promoting 'Death of a Legend.'

"I know all too well, unfortunately."

"Can you make it?"

Can I make it? Hell yes! "Sure." I'll get a good opportunity to talk to Elias. He might even be civil to me this time. "Thanks. But will Elias be okay with me being there?" I laugh to make light of my hesitation. "Because I remember that he wasn't so friendly last time we met. "

"He was the one to suggest I invite you."

Now that's interesting.

"The only reason I'm calling you instead of Elias doing it, is because he's not the type of guy to pick up the phone and make small talk."

"And, he's obviously got more pressing concerns," I add.

Harper laughs. "That too."

I'm not fully convinced Elias is entirely behind the invite. My gut tells me it's Harper. "I'm thrilled that you called."

"It will be nice to see you again," says Harper, and I'm suddenly not sure of her motive for asking me. People are always nice and courteous towards me. Women can't seem to do enough to please me. It's only the Cardozas that I can't get to like me.

"Well, thanks. It will be good to see you guys." I reply.

"I'll text you the details. Oh, and in case you're wondering, I got your number from Frankie."

"Cool."

"There's no formal invite. It's all word of mouth, and only a few select people are invited."

A few select people. I'm honored to be counted among such company, especially given the fact that this is Elias's event and his crowd.

"As long as you're sure that Elias isn't going to be pissed off when he sees me."

Harper laughs. "He's really not that bad."

"Easy enough for you to say."

"Did you want to bring a friend?"

"A friend?" Now I'm getting really scared. Is she fishing for information about my status? It would depend on who's asking. Harper's pretty friendly but I really don't want to get involved with the girlfriend of the current world heavyweight champion. I never want to get involved with *anyone's* girlfriend, but least of all a boxing champ. The guy would kill me if he ever suspected anything—not that I have any interest in her. At all. Or will, ever.

"I have to let security know so they can let you both in."

"It will just be me," I tell her. "Will Nina be there?"

"I hope so. We asked her."

"But will she turn up? It's not a night school night, is it?"

"You seem to know a lot about her timetable." There is a touch of amusement in Harper's voice.

"She's the only person I'll know there."

"She'll be there," Harper tells me, "and she also doesn't have anyone to bring along, so..."

This reassures me on two levels. First of all, I'm relieved to hear that Nina doesn't have a boyfriend, and secondly, I think Harper might be trying to get me and Nina together. Maybe Nina hinted to her that she likes me, and this is Harper's way of getting us together. Maybe this is it. Nina likes me and this is her way of letting me know. I have to admit our daily meetings at lunchtime are getting more relaxed now, though I didn't see her today. She gave my lunch to Dottie. I'd say I was making progress. Slow and painful but it's still progress. "I'm looking forward to it."

"I'll text you the details and time."

"I'll be there."

I hang up and my brain goes into overdrive.

Nina is one of those women who doesn't want to show that she's got the hots for me. Now I get it. I understand her game. I'm so used to women throwing themselves at me, and their over-the-top admiration for me often leaves me feeling embarrassed, more for them than for me.

Nina isn't that type of woman. That's not her style. She's more subtle.

I can hardly wait.

I leave the restaurant and get a cab straight to the diner. I want to see Nina's reaction when I tell her I'm going to Elias's event.

I've got on my baseball cap and shades, which I guess look conspicuous given that it's dark outside. The diner is quite empty as I look around and see different waitresses here tonight. No sign of Nina, or her friend. But Frankie is here. A few heads turn as I glide into a booth at one end of the diner and order a milkshake. A short while later, Frankie comes over looking all smug and cheery. "Are you looking for anyone in particular?"

"Me? No."

"Can I get you anything?"

"Thanks, but I've already ordered."

"The daily lunch delivery not enough?" she asks, with a smile.

"The daily lunch delivery is working out very well. Thanks for arranging that."

"Happy to help."

A waitress brings me my milkshake. "You decided to come here at this time, for only a milkshake? Don't you want to eat something?"

I explain that I've already had dinner, then I take a loud slurp of my milkshake, and sigh in contentment. "It's damn good. Worth taking the cab to get here."

Frankie is still hovering around my table. "Sit down, please. Join me." I motion for her to take a seat.

She obliges, then says, "She's not working tonight."

"I never asked."

"Your eyes did,"

"You don't miss a thing, Frankie."

"It's my job not to. Tonight, isn't a night school night," she continues, "in case you were thinking of following her there."

I change my expression to one of disappointment. "You make me sound like a stalker."

"But you're not, are you?" She lifts an eyebrow.

"Obviously I'm not."

"Why are you looking for her?"

The question confuses me. "Specifically tonight, or do you mean generally?"

"Both."

"I meet a lot of women, but Nina sticks out because she's nothing like them."

"I care about that girl, so if you hurt her," Frankie doesn't need to lift her finger, or change her tone, or narrow her eyes, but I sense the warning in her words.

"I would never do that. What you see of me on the screen is nothing like the real me."

Frankie chortles. "I haven't watched a single movie of yours. I only know who you are because the waitresses here keep showing me all the magazines you keep appearing in. You're everywhere."

"Because of the new film."

"And with different women."

"Because of the new film."

"And your co-star, too. Is that for real?"

I put a finger to my lips. "Because of the new film."

"It's not true then?"

I put my finger to my lips again. "Because of the—"

"Okay. Okay. I hear you. Like I said, if you ever so much as harm a hair on her head." Frankie looks daggers at me.

"I heard you loudly the first time."

"Talking of Nina, I'd like to call her but I don't have her number," I say. "You wouldn't happen to have it, would you?"

"I'm not supposed to give out the phone numbers of my employees."

"I shouldn't really expect you to do such a thing, should I?"

"Then why would you ask such a thing?" she shoots back.

I suddenly sit up taller. The matron in Frankie comes out, and I sense her mother bear protectiveness about Nina. I wonder if I am being vetted. "I wouldn't do anything improper. I like her, and she's not even remotely interested in me."

Frankie snorts as if she finds this amusing. "That sounds about right for Nina. You're probably not used to this."

"I'm not. It's something I've never experienced before. I

like her, and I don't understand why she doesn't like me back."

She laughs and slaps the table. "A lot of folks here like her, and many more of them seemed to like her once Elias won that belt. Word gets around, you know."

"I'm sure it does."

"I can't complain. Elias coming here every so often helps my business. People come here hoping they'll see him, but they also know who she is because word gets around. I have some folks who hang around here, sniffing around Nina hoping they will get some juicy gossip about him. Hoping he might come in here one day and give them something, an autograph, a photo, even a ticket to his next fight. She gets good tips out of it. It's natural of her to be wary of people like you."

"I'm not hanging around her because of Elias." Nina Cardoza doesn't think anything of me. She doesn't fall at my feet, she doesn't want a photo of me, or an autograph. She's so different to anyone I've met, and that is enough for me to take an interest. She's like a fragile injured bird who is running from something, or hiding, and I can't work out what.

What I said to Dottie, about pursuing Nina in order to get to Elias, I said in order to get Dottie off my back, and that was the only way to do it. My pursuit of Nina now has nothing to do with getting onto Elias's good side, and everything to do with wanting to win her over.

"She doesn't care much for you being an actor. She's not into status and wealth."

"I know."

"I don't know if she'll ever notice you. I've watched countless guys try, and she hasn't given them a look in."

This tallies with what her friend told me, and it further

piques my interest. I pick up my milkshake to take a sip, but suddenly don't feel like it. "I guess I shouldn't take it too hard then, that she's always pushing me away."

"I'm not doing this because you're famous." Frankie pulls out a pen, then leans over and grabs a clean napkin from the table. She scribbles something down. "I'll leave this here for you. You didn't get it from me."

I pull the napkin towards me and see a number on it. "Frankie, it doesn't work like that," I try to suppress a smile. "You're the only one who has access to everyone's numbers. She'll know I got it from you."

"I have a feeling that girl will be so shocked to hear from you that she won't even worry about how you got her number."

I disagree. "I have a feeling she quite likes her privacy, and it's going to be the first thing she'll ask."

"We'll see."

I might not have known Nina properly or for as long as Frankie has but I'm certain that I'm right on this point.

I get out my cell phone and call her.

CHAPTER TWENTY-ONE

NINA

This feels good.

At least I feel *something*.

Relief mostly.

At least I *feel*.

It's usually numbness that comes over me. Remembering the janitor and the things he did, and now the encounter with Rhys—another sexual predator I have to deal with—it sets off something inside me, dredges up the dirt.

My insides close in, and at the same time my stomach turns to concrete. It's a horrid sensation, not being able to breathe, or move. No matter what I do, I can't seem to put my past behind me and have it stay there forever. This is a hellhole I cannot escape.

I'm stuck in a vicious cycle, like Groundhog Day, only this isn't a movie. This is my miserable life.

The marks are ugly, sometimes gnarly, sometimes blood red. It depends how deep I've gone. A drop of blood oozes down my skin where I cut deeper than I intended.

I wipe away the blood with my finger, letting it spread out thinly until it almost disappears.

Joni hasn't called. I'm relieved. I don't want to deal with her questioning about why I wimped out and refused to go to the movies with them. The thought of Rhys makes me sick to my stomach. I decide that I can never be in the same room as Rhys. The guy is a snake. I can't even tell Joni how evil he is, because she won't believe me.

My cell phone rings, pulling me out of my dark thoughts, and I stare at the number. It's one I don't recognize, so I don't answer it, in case it's Rhys or Scott, in case Joni has asked them to call me. I'm not in the mood to talk to anyone, and I'm definitely not in the mood for hanging out with any of them.

I've also decided not to go to the event at City hall that Elias told me about last week. Harper reminded me about it a few days ago. She wants me to come. It's not a fight, which she knows I can't handle, but a party, so I need to come up with a good excuse for missing it. I'll call her tomorrow.

My cell phone beeps, and whoever called me has left a message. I hit the voicemail button along with the loudspeaker button.

'Nina?'

It's Callum. Why's he calling me?

*'I ... uh ... I uh ... I didn't see you today at lunchtime. Dottie
said you had to rush off'*

His voice reverberates inside me, filling me with
something warm and comforting. I don't answer
straightaway. Instead I close my eyes, and allow this one
sliver of goodness to sink in. And then I remember what he
said to Dottie, and my eyes fly wide open. Now I'm caught
in a dilemma between wanting to listen to him and cutting
the message dead. Sometimes Callum seems genuine, and
nice and caring. These are words I never thought I would
use to describe him. But maybe my guard is starting to come
down. When you've been battered and bruised by the bad
things, you'll take any grain of good.

Remember what he said.

And so I harden myself again.

How and from where did he get my number? It's either
Harper or Frankie, because they're the only two people
both he and I know who might do such a thing.

He coughs, and in the silence it sounds as if he's
uncomfortable. Then I hear a slight laugh. He comes across
as clumsy and inarticulate, which is nothing like how he is
in real life, but more than the clumsiness, I wonder why he's
calling me when he surely must have an address book as big
as his ego.

*'I was hoping you would pick up. I um ... I ... 'I'll try again
some other time'*

Try again another time?
I think not.
I heard him loud and clear today.

I make a face and replay the message, putting down my blade and wiping the new trickle of blood away again.

It's as if the universe wanted to leave me in no doubt of who I am and why no one will ever be attracted to me. I seem only to draw the cockroaches. Men like the janitor and Rhys.

CHAPTER TWENTY-TWO

CALLUM

I get out of the car and start to walk towards the entrance to City Hall. This is a private event, and I'm attending as a private guest. I hope Rudy doesn't find out about this otherwise he's going to be pissed at me again. He screens the events I attend, and no doubt he will have something to say if he finds out I've been here.

A low roar erupts and ripples around the crowd outside. People are lined up about ten deep and they're all waiting for Elias, but then I hear something which takes me by surprise.

"Callum! Callum!" I turn and stare and the roar grows louder. Maybe I should have turned up in disguise. I don't want to steal Elias's limelight. It's too late now, so I lift my hand and wave, and another loud roar starts up. A couple of guys come to the door, and I catch sight of Harper who quickly motions for me to get inside.

She kisses me on both cheeks. "You've caused quite a

commotion." She looks over my shoulder at the crowd outside. "Not that I'm surprised."

"You look stunning." I marvel at her choice of outfit and her figure.

"She sure does." A heavy hand lands firmly against my back. The thick voice, full of confidence, and laced with a hint of possession, warns me off.

"It was a compliment," I say quickly, turning to face Elias, while hoping that my face doesn't turn bright red.

"Relax," says Elias, grinning. I look at Harper, then back at Elias. He unnerves me and that in itself is something else I'm not used to. My ego is huge. Nobody unnerves me, but Cardoza seems to have made an art of it. It could be his physique. He is the epitome of strength. A powerhouse of muscle. There's something else about him that surprises me tonight; he's wearing something that could easily pass for a smile. It's the most relaxed I've ever seen him.

I can't relax as easily, but I smile, because he is.

"You don't have to be scared of Elias," Harper says. "Despite what he'd like you to believe, he does have a heart, buried somewhere beneath all that muscle."

Elias turns to me. "Harper said I have to be nice to you."

I raise an eyebrow at Harper. "You did?"

"I want you to have a nice time here. Anyway, how's your filming going?"

"It's going." I reach for a glass of juice when a server goes past, as does Elias. Harper reaches for a glass of champagne.

"Yeah?" Elias asks. "How much filming is left?"

"About a month. It depends." I wonder if he's eager for me to leave town.

"Need some tips and pointers?"

Did this guy ask me that? Now I grin. "If you have any

time to spare, I'd appreciate it. I have a boxing coach, and I've been watching fights of all the legends, but I still don't know if I have it right, you know?" My eyes laser in on Nina as she walks through the door. "Nina's here," I say out loud, when I should have kept that to myself. At least then so that I could have carried on checking her out from afar.

Elias raises his chin. "Well there's a surprise. I didn't think she'd come."

"She had to," says Harper, taking a sip of her champagne. "I insisted. Nina can be hard work sometimes."

"Funny how you noticed her right away, huh?" Elias asks me. His comment makes me stop instantly. Standing next to her protective brother I suddenly feel wary.

"I uh, ...yeah." Because I have no excuse. She's on my radar now, the way something of interest suddenly becomes. Like when you buy a red sports car and suddenly everyone is driving red sports cars. I can suddenly sense when Nina is around. What's telling is that I usually only get this when I'm sufficiently interested in someone, in a romantic way, in a get-you-in-my-bed kind of way. I don't think of Nina like that, which is new for me. There is something, an interest, but I don't know yet how much of an interest because she gives nothing back. I don't even get the slightest signal from her, much less the chance of any flirtation. She's hard to read, impossible to gauge, tough to pigeonhole. What confuses things further is that I'm drawn to women who are tall, and voluptuous, and she is neither.

She disappears, then re-appears a few seconds later without her jacket. She's wearing a long sleeved black top, and wide legged trousers, which only someone super slim like her could carry off.

It's so *her*.

I've only ever seen her in a waitressing uniform, and this

first time of seeing her in something else, seeing her all done up, takes my breath way. When she stands around, looking a little unsure, a little hesitant, I'm tempted to break away and go to her—and not care what Elias thinks—but Harper beats me to it. She excuses herself and walks over to her.

"She was silly for getting involved that day, and coming to your rescue," Elias remarks.

"Are you still holding that against me?"

"It's not your fault. It's Nina all over. She doesn't look at her size or the risk she could be in, she just wants to protect people."

"She was very protective of you, back in that children's home," Reading his biography has been enlightening. With his kind of difficult past, I can see why he and Nina are so close. Coming up through the foster care system, they only had one another. Their childhood is so different from mine, and what surprises me is how different they are. Elias is strong and self-assured, and wild; he has that air about him. Nina is so much the opposite.

He moves his glass, and the one quarter full amount of juice swirls around. He stares at it and nods, but doesn't say a word. Then, "I love my sister. We've been through a lot. I would hate to see her get hurt."

My heart jolts unexpectedly, and when Elias looks up, his brown eyes flash a warning to me. I'm not sure what he means. Is it that obvious that I have some interest in Nina?

"How about you come over, say maybe tomorrow, and we can talk about things?"

The invite suddenly sounds ominous. "Tomorrow?"

"I don't have many free days left. The fight is coming up fast, but Harper's been on at me to be nice to you."

"So you're doing this because Harper asked you, and not because you want to?"

"I can spare you an evening. Do you want it or not?"

"Yes, sure, I mean, of course. That would be great. Thanks."

That explains it. Harper has been the architect behind everything, me coming here tonight, and Elias suddenly changing his stance towards me. I had felt honored because I thought he liked me enough that he's invited me to his place, and that he's willing to give me some of his precious time. But I have what I wanted from the start, though now it feels slightly hollow.

It's also too late to use anything I glean from him towards my role, though I've watched as many of his interviews as I can, and I've watched and re-watched the Cardoza vs Garrison fight. And I'm almost finished with his book.

I try to look upon it as something positive because if Harper's behind all of this, chances are that she'll invite Nina over at the same time.

CHAPTER TWENTY-THREE

NINA

I'm only here because Harper didn't stop hounding me until I agreed to come. She knows how to get me to do things. 'Do it for Elias. Think how much he'd like you to be there,' and of course, when she puts it like that, what choice did I have?

It took me ages to find something to wear. What do you wear to such an event? After much deliberation I settled on some wide palazzo pants and a long sleeved top.

I look around at the large room full of people all dressed up. There was a huge crowd outside, and it scares me, that all of these people are here for Elias. He seems to have taken to the limelight so easily; doing interviews on TV and for the papers and magazines. He's in the papers or on TV almost every week, and with his next fight with Garrison looming on the horizon there seems to be a sense of growing hysteria.

I couldn't do this.

I could *never*.

Anxiety twists in my belly as I scan the room, desperately trying to find Elias or Harper.

"You came." Harper appears out of nowhere and kisses me on the cheeks. She's wearing a short cocktail dress with her hair in a slick updo, and I suddenly feel like a boy standing next to her feminine gorgeousness.

"You didn't really give me a choice." A sneaky thought flickers across my mind. I wonder why Callum called and left me that message.

She grins. "Isn't this nice? Getting out in the evening instead of working at the diner or going to night school? You need to live a little, Nina."

"I do live a little." I counter, not pleased with the preconceived ideas she has about me, even if she is mostly right.

"You look lovely." She stares at my trousers in admiration.

"Your dress is pretty."

"Thanks."

I glance casually around the room, tracking a server who is nearby, and that's when I see him.

Callum Sandersby, with my brother.

My heart lurches,

"What's he doing here?" I'm annoyed to see him, even though my chest feels light and fluttery. Why does he seem to be everywhere I go?

"Eli invited him."

They are both surrounded by a group of women. Elias has begrudgingly gotten used to the attention of his female fans, and he has plenty of them. I imagine someone like Callum thrives on that type of adulation. That's exactly the type of thing I expect from someone like him and the sight of it makes me sick.

I stare at Harper, and I smell something. "Did you have something to do with this?" I remember that she was adamant that I came, even though I told her that I wasn't in the mood.

"Me?" she asks, smoothing back her hair, and her tone implying complete ignorance.

"Yes, *you*." Elias wouldn't care about Callum Sandersby being here. But Harper would. She refuses to meet my gaze and instead reaches for another drink. I have a sneaky suspicion that she's playing matchmaker.

I can't see Elias being too bothered about whether some actor guy comes to this event or not. I'll venture a guess that Elias probably didn't want to come tonight either, but he had to. I've met his promoter, he's a big show-offy type. He and Callum would get on fine.

"Why do you hate Callum so much? He's a nice guy."

"As if you know."

"The way you met, it's so romantic," says Harper, with a sigh.

I stare at her in disbelief. "He got mugged. I happened to walk by."

"But still. You go and deliver his lunch every day."

"He likes the food at Frankie's," I counter.

"He likes *you*."

"Shhh." I hiss, and put my finger to my lips. "Not so loud."

"Why? Are you afraid he might hear me? The poor guy's trying every trick in the book to get near you."

"It's not like that," I insist.

I flex my jaw and reach for the first glass of champagne from the server's tray. I take a big swig of it. I'm going to need it. I wasn't expecting to see Callum Sandersby tonight of all nights, and it's only been a few days since that episode with Rhys. I've not been in a good place lately.

I wish people would leave me alone. It's bad enough Frankie worrying about me, and Joni trying to fix me up with Scott.

"Come over and say 'hi'," Harper grabs me by my wrist, making me wince. I manage to stop myself from crying out. I cut deeper than I intended, and it still bleeds a little.

"What's wrong?" Harper asks, catching me in pain.

"Period pain," I lie.

"I have some tablets if you want."

I shake my head. "I'd rather not take anything."

"Come on." I dutifully follow her before she grabs my wrist again.

Callum is by himself now, though still surrounded by a harem of women. Elias has disappeared. I won't be surprised if he goes home at the first chance. He doesn't care for such events, and his focus is on the fight. It's been billed as a huge event. Posters are going up everywhere in Chicago, only because Elias is from here. The fight will be in New York, at The Garden like last time. Harper keeps asking me if I'll come with them to New York to watch it, but I keep turning her down.

"Where did Elias go?" I ask Harper, as she waits for Callum's harem to finish taking pictures. He's having a photo taken with a woman who's squashed up so close against him that they could almost be Siamese twins. Then he sees us and his eyes flit from Harper to me before settling on me. His smile widens. I expect him to look at Harper again, but he doesn't. He excuses himself from everyone and walks over to us. "Hey."

"I didn't expect to see you here," I say stiffly.

"And it's nice to see you, too," he tosses back, casually. He's grinning again, brightening up the room with that mega-watt Hollywood smile. When he and Harper exchange looks, I suddenly don't trust them. I think back to the phonecall the other day.

"Did you give him my number?" I ask her.

"Uh...no, she didn't," Callum interjects.

"What are you talking about?" Harper wants to know.

"I called Nina to ask if she was going to be here tonight, but she didn't pick up," Callum explains.

"I was busy," I answer.

He turns to me. "Would have been nice to get a text at least."

"You didn't leave much of a message."

He smiles and his tasteless grin irritates the heck out of me. "My mistake. I'll make sure I leave a longer one next time."

Harper excuses herself and leaves me with Callum.

"Why didn't you call back?" he asks.

"I was busy." *Cutting myself.*

"You're here now. I'm pleased you are," he tells me, as if it somehow matters to me.

"Why?"

He angles his head, as if he's unsure what I'm asking.

Knowing what I heard him say to Dottie, I decide to have some fun. "Why is someone like you trying so hard to be with someone like me?"

"What do you mean by 'someone like you?'"

I'm won't dignify that with a reply. He wants me to shower him with compliments, and I'm not going to. He's a Hollywood star, and I'm ... no one. I know what I see when I look in the mirror. I know how ugly I am inside, how tainted and messed up I am, but he doesn't need to know of the things which keep me up at night.

"You don't need to pretend to be nice to me anymore. I see you've gotten what you wanted."

He laughs uncomfortably. "Who's pretending? I'm happy to see you here tonight."

"Why are you here? Don't you have some scenes to shoot?"

"I've finished for the day. We don't shoot all day and night."

"Don't you have lines to learn?"

He cocks his head at my frostiness. "Don't you have an assignment to hand in?"

"I've finished it."

"At work? Like last time?"

"Frankie doesn't mind. She knows I come in early and cover when anyone's off sick. So I get to finish my assignments at the diner. So what?"

"Next time you're doing that, give me a call. I'll sit by you and keep you company while you do."

"Why would you do that?"

"Don't you find this fun? This constant love-hate thing we've got going on." He gives me another one of his grins. "You like ripping into me, with your clever little digs, and your subtle little put downs."

"They were never meant to be subtle."

"What's wrong? Why are you like this?" he asks. He's noticed that I'm not friendly, and yet it doesn't stop him. It doesn't stop Rhys either, but that guy creeps me out. He and Callum are different. I finish my champagne and swap my glass for another one when a server goes by. A sip of champagne makes me brave. "At least now you don't have to fake interest in me to get to Elias."

He looks genuinely surprised, then wipes his hand across his chin. "How could you say such a thing?"

"Because I overheard you saying it to your assistant."

His mouth falls open. It looks like his cheeks are burning, because I've never seen his face turn so red so fast. I enjoy watching him squirm. Does he feel guilty, or is he that good of an actor? Is someone like Callum even capable of feeling guilty, or does he move on from one conquest to the next? He stares at me in silence and I can almost hear his brain ticking, trying to work out when this happened. I decide not to put him out of his misery yet, and I continue watching his face, and seeing him squirm in discomfort. "Overheard what? When?"

"You really don't remember?"

He peers at me, and his beautiful green eyes narrow to raisin size. It's so satisfying, watching his discomfort. "You said you were only getting me to deliver your lunch to you because I'm Elias's sister."

"You heard that?"

"Loud and clear."

"No wonder you're so aggressive tonight. I don't blame you for hating me."

"I don't hate you Callum. I'm just not interested in you the way you thought I'd be. I'm not like most of the women you meet."

"I can see that, and please believe me when I say I didn't mean it, what I said to Dottie."

I shrug. I know what I heard and he can make out like he didn't say it or mean it. No amount of him trying to back peddle his way out of this is going to make me think I heard wrong. I'm done with this conversation

"I said it to deflect her attention. I had to cover up the real reason."

"And what's the real reason? Spin me another lie."

"Nina..." He lets out a sound deep in his throat; the sound of defeat, of someone getting caught red-handed. "I'm sorry. I didn't mean to hurt you."

"You didn't mean to get caught, is what you really mean." I shrug. "You don't have to try to worm your way out of this situation. I don't care what you think of me, Callum. I've seen you for who you really are. And my suspicions were spot on from the beginning."

"Okay," he lifts his hands as if to signal surrender. "I admit, in the beginning, yes. Wanting to get to know Elias might have been my motive for pursuing you."

I knew it. I take a huge sip of champagne. The bubbles dance down my throat.

As he starts to say something, the promoter takes the mic and addresses the guests. He cracks jokes and thanks everyone for coming, then he talks about Elias and the fight. He calls Elias over, and my brother goes up to him. There's a back and forth between them, and someone from the crowd asks a question. It's all light hearted stuff.

We watch, and listen, and I look around and see that everyone is completely wrapped up in what Elias has to say. I'm so proud of him. I'm so happy for him, and I'm glad I came here tonight.

"Come outside," Callum whispers in my ear. "We need to talk." I flinch, but not before I get the subtlest hint of his aftershave. It's zingy and fresh, and it startles me. I pull back, and stare at him. I don't want to be mesmerised by Callum Sandersby, but against my better judgment, I am.

"I've got nothing to say to you."

I don't want to go anywhere with him. I don't want to be someplace where it's me and him. I don't want to give him the chance to explain himself, or say something to make himself feel better.

I don't want him to feel better.

"I need to explain. Can we go outside and talk, please?" There is a hint of pleading in his voice. Another woman comes up and asks for his autograph, and then some more photos.

I stand back and watch. "Please," he says again, when the woman leaves. "I don't bite, Nina."

Can this really be happening to me, that one of the biggest movie stars in the world wants me to come outside with him?

News about the janitor and what he did to Elias broke me. I have spent the past few months trying to build myself back up again, and I was almost there. I managed to keep guys at bay, guys like Rhys the creep, and nice-but-boring Scott. Then along comes Callum Sandersby, the man with a smile that could melt the clothes off a woman. He takes an interest in me. Despite my gut instinct, I sometimes allowed myself to believe that his interest might be real. Until I heard him say it, loud and clear. What am I even doing talking to him, allowing him to follow me around?

I don't want to give him that chance. He hurt me, and I can't forget it. I need to get better again. I need to build myself back up again, and this man is only going to get in the way.

I don't need Callum to take me someplace quiet so that he can entice me into believing that he didn't say what he meant. He meant it, he didn't intend for me to overhear him.

I shake my head and walk away silently, heading towards the front of the stage, next to Harper who's standing there looking up at Elias with her face full of pride.

CHAPTER TWENTY-FOUR

CALLUM

I had no idea she heard me say that.

I watch her walk away, while some woman hands me a pen and a notepad and asks me to sign it. Her husband, or boyfriend or whatever, gets ready to take a selfie of her with me. I find that odd. I smile and make meaningless small talk but my mind is on Nina. I hate that she heard me say what I did to Dottie.

She wants to know why someone like me would be interested in someone like her. I can't give her an answer because I don't know myself. I did start out using her, thinking that she was my ticket to Elias, but something happened along the way.

Now I see her talking to a couple of guys who I vaguely remember from Elias's gym. I watch her laugh and talk to them and I don't like it.

"Why don't you go and talk to her?"

Harper's standing next to me with a glass of champagne

in her hand. Before I can say anything else, she says, "Nina's quite shy, even if she gives off the vibe that she's feisty."

I see it all so clearly now, Harper working behind the scenes to get us together.

"Do one of those guys like her?"

"Jake and Santos?" Harper laughs, as if the idea is a crazy one. "They're Eli's sparring guys from the gym. They'd be too scared to start anything with Nina."

I take heed of her warning. Having Elias Cardoza as an enemy is the last thing I need. "I've noticed he can be quite protective of Nina."

"He's always been like that ever since I've known him, but that doesn't mean you can't go and talk to her. Jake and Santos are more like her brothers. You're not."

I continue to watch Nina while I try to work things out. This isn't right. This isn't how things go for me. I don't have to work this hard to get someone's attention. "Where's she going now?" The three of them leave the room and slip out through a side door.

"They're going outside. Come on. I'll show you."

I follow Harper, and soon we are outside the hall. There's a man-made garden area at the back, and a few people are milling around. Nina and the two guys are sitting over on a bench. One of the guys stands up and starts to smoke.

"You're going over to them?" I hiss, when Harper starts heading their way.

"Are you planning to shout to her from here?" I don't miss the eye roll Nina gives us as soon as she sees us approaching.

"You left Eli all alone in there?" one of the guy's asks.

"He can take care of himself." Harper introduces me to Jake and Santos. They start asking me all sorts of questions, about the film, about Hollywood, about some actresses. I answer, but even though I avoid looking in Nina's direction, I can sense she's mad at me for coming out here.

"It's 'Legend' something or other, right?" one of the guys asks.

"The film? It's 'Death of a Legend'." I can't remember if it's Jake or Santos, because most of my concentration is on Nina. At the same time, I find myself in a position that is completely new to me. How is it that I feel like a gangly teen, instead of the self-assured and confident guy I usually am around people. Wanting to impress, I make a suggestion. "I can hit you guys up with tickets to the premiere if you want."

"You'd do that?" Harper asks, beating Jake and Santos to it.

"Sure. It will be in LA." I can do that, for sure.

"Red carpet and everything?" Harper seems the most excited, while the guys barely make a comment. Nina is too engrossed in her cell phone and makes it clear that she's not impressed or interested.

"The whole enchilada."

"Cool, thanks, man," one of the guys says.

"Let me know how many you need." I make it a point to stare at Nina.

"Thanks." Harper squeezes my arm. "Oh, shoot. Eli wanted me to send some tickets for the fight to some guys who crashed into him a few days ago."

One of the guys perks up. "I heard about that. It was in the limo, right? When he was going for an interview?"

"Did he tell you to send the tickets?" Harper asks.

The guys look at one another. "He didn't ask me."

"Or me."

"Come on. Let's go and get this sorted out now." She beckons for the two of them to follow her.

Nina sips her drink, then gets up, ready to follow them.

"You're going back inside already?" This cat-and-mouse game is seriously doing my head in.

"Why? Are you going to follow me back inside?"

"We never got to finishing off our conversation earlier. You left me with those women."

"Your fans. They're everywhere. It must be a nightmare living like that."

"It is."

"'I'm sure you thrive on it."

"I don't. It's just a by product of what I do. I can't have my career and not the fame." She sits back down, which surprises me because it seemed as if she was ready to bolt along with the other guys. I cannot for the love of god work this woman out.

Does she like me?

Does she hate me?

I want to believe that she likes me, but she's fighting it real hard, almost as if she doesn't trust herself. What she overheard doesn't help either.

I want to level with her. I see Ben's image flash before my mind, and I feel as if I can tell her the stuff I've kept from her. "You asked me once why I didn't give up my wallet as soon as I got mugged."

She throws me a what's-that-got-to-do-with-anything look. "And?"

"Is that blood?" I ask, pointing to her wrist. Her champagne glass is lifted in the air, and she pulls her sleeve cuff down but I have already seen the trickle of blood that slid down.

"I cut myself in the kitchen. Those pesky potatoes," she

murmurs, pulling her cuff down even more.

"Nina," I reach out to touch her, but she pulls her hand away, tucking it behind her back. In my mind I'm trying to figure out how she can cut that high up on her arm. Cutting potatoes? I don't believe her.

I try to reach out again, but this time she steps back and sets the champagne glass on the bench. "I've remembered. I have an assignment to hand in tomorrow." She makes her announcement with such conviction that I'm left wondering who she's trying to convince. She starts to walk away, but she doesn't go back the way she came.

"Nina, wait, stop." I follow her. "Don't you want to tell the others that you're leaving?"

She spins around. "Don't follow me, Callum. Please don't make a scene. *Please.*"

There it is again, the pleading in her voice, pushing me away.

I can't *not* do as she says, but I also can't let her go with so many unanswered questions flying around in my head. "Your wrist," I say, quietly.

"I told you," she says tightly. "I accidentally cut myself when I was cutting the tomatoes."

"Potatoes."

"What?" She looks and sounds annoyed.

"You said potatoes before."

She exhales in annoyance. "I'm always chopping things. I can't remember what it was."

"You're a waitress, not a cook," I remind her.

"What are you? A detective?"

"A guy who cares."

"A user, more like."

She marches off, and even though I want to go after her, I know it will only make things worse.

CHAPTER TWENTY-FIVE

NINA

I hate that Callum is nosey. I hate that he saw the blood on my wrist. I blame Harper for that because when she grabbed my wrist, she made it bleed again.

I wanted to curl up and die when Callum called me on it. He's more perceptive than I thought and I can't throw him off as easily. He sees things. *Senses* things. This is unusual for a guy.

My brother is nothing like that. You'd have to hit Elias over the head with something if you want him to take notice. He lashes out first, then asks questions later. That's probably not a bad thing, given the career path he's chosen.

Callum has more of a sensitive side than I ever imagined. As annoyed as I was that he seems to be closing in on me, I was still curious enough to look him up online. It startled me, seeing the countless pictures of him with all those women. He seems to have a new girlfriend every few weeks. They're all so pretty. So glamourous. So *together*.

I didn't like seeing him with all those women. There are rumors of him and his co-star on this latest film. She's pretty too. Tall and leggy with tumbling auburn hair. I found a few photos of him and her walking through the park. I couldn't bear to keep looking.

I had to tell myself not to feel too down about it, because this guy isn't really into me.

But, I wonder, am I into him?

I don't want to think about it.

Harper has invited me over to dinner, and I really shouldn't go. I don't have the time as it is. Going to that event at City Hall was a waste of my entire evening. I hadn't planned on staying too long, but I left much sooner that I had intended. I have another assignment to turn in, and I could do with staying in today, but Harper told me that Elias didn't like it that I left so quickly, and without saying goodbye. We didn't get much time to talk that night, and his schedule is getting busier.

So I have to go and see them tonight.

But when I turn up less than an hour later, Callum Sandersby is sitting on the couch with a bottle of beer in his hand, talking to Elias as if they were old time buddies. He's the last person I want to see.

"What he's doing here?" The words tumble out of my mouth before I can stop them. Harper takes my jacket and hangs it up, while giving me a disapproving look.

"Be nice. Elias invited him."

I frown. "They're best pals now?"

Harper shrugs. "They hit it off the other night. How come you left so quickly?"

"I had an assignment to do."

"You and your assignments." Harper leads me into the main living room.

"I still have to finish it, so I won't be staying that long tonight." I drop the hint now so that she won't be too surprised when I eat and get out quickly. I don't need Callum eyeballing me all evening. He's not stupid, but I don't need his questioning any more than I need to have anything to do with him. Unfortunately, the guy is like a leech; stuck to my side, and impossible to shift.

"Hey," Elias gets up to greet me as I walk in.

"Great to see you again," Callum says, getting up and extending his hand. He flashes me that blinding smile of his which I'm sure works on many women, but not on me. "I didn't know you'd be here tonight." I shake his hand quickly, it's more like a touch than a shake.

"Your brother invited me over."

I look at Elias as if he's suddenly grown three heads.

"We were just talking," my brother says, sitting back down again. Callum does the same. Harper sticks a glass of wine in my hand, and I'm suddenly conscious of my arms and Callum's scrutiny.

"Sit down," Elias says. I can feel the heat of Callum's stare on me, and I don't dare to look at him. I'm paranoid that he's looking at my wrist, that he must have questions. I sit down but I'm uneasy. My emotions are all over the place when it comes to this man. Is he being real, or is he playing a part?

"I'll leave you guys to it," I say, and get up again. I don't want to be anywhere near Callum. "I'll give Harper a hand in the kitchen."

Elias gets up quickly, "Hey, no. Sit down. *I'll* give her a hand. Making tacos is my specialty." He leaves before I can protest.

This is new, too. Elias's culinary skills are hardly legendary. I smell a big fat rat.

It's just me and Callum in the living room. He's sitting back on the couch, and I'm standing awkwardly, suddenly not sure what to do with my hands, or my face, and I forget how to make boring, insignificant conversation. So I dive right in. "You're best buddies with my brother now?"

"Is that a problem for you?" He eyes me for a split second before lifting the beer bottle to his lips.

"It's a problem for me that I have to run into you everywhere I go." I don't want to hear any cheesy comments from him so I add in, "Elias doesn't have time for the likes of you."

"The likes of me?"

"Actors."

"Your brother is a friendly guy, once you get to know him."

I frown. "What is it that you want from him?"

"Some words of wisdom. Anything that might deepen my understanding of what it takes to be a boxer."

"Isn't it too late for that? You've almost finished shooting the film."

"It's never too late," he says, sitting up straighter. "I was going to call you. I've been worried about you."

"You shouldn't waste your time worrying about me." I fix him with the meanest stare I can find. "You've managed to snake into Elias's life, so you can quit the trying-to-be-friendly-to-me thing."

"Snake into—?" he looks genuinely surprised. He's obviously good at acting, but I have no doubt that he knows exactly what I'm talking about.

"You got what you wanted, my brother's time. Good luck. Now please, leave me alone."

"You push people away, I see that about you now. You

don't mean what you're saying." His voice is still low. He's in my personal space, and I hate it.

"I do mean it." I grit my teeth together because I don't know where this is going. I know only that I've caught a hint of his aftershave, and for some strange and bizarre reason, it sends a tingle along my spine.

"You're angry because I saw something you didn't want me to," he whispers. "I'm worried about you, Nina. Why was there blood on your wrist?" I glance over my shoulder, aware that Harper and Elias are only a stone's throw away.

"I told you. I cut it at work."

His eyes, filled with concern, stare back at me. Disbelief is written all over his face. "That's not the place you'd cut your wrist."

"Dinner's ready," Harper calls out, and we spring apart, but it's not soon enough, and she's got a smug smile on her face when she sees us. There's a glimmer in her eyes which I don't like. "Come on into the kitchen," she tells Callum.

I lead the way into the kitchen where Elias is sitting at the table. Harper sits next to him.

"This is a treat," says Callum, sitting down opposite them. "Home cooked food. Thank you, both of you."

"Don't mention it," says Elias.

"The food at the event was quite good, wasn't it?" Harper asks enthusiastically.

"It was good," adds Callum.

"You left early," Elias says to me, completely changing the subject. I'm sitting next to Callum because that's the only seat that makes sense to. I could sit at a few seats away, because the table is big and can easily seat ten people, but it would draw more attention if I did that.

"Why did you leave?" Elias persists, and I'm aware that everyone's waiting for me to answer.

"I had an assignment to hand in."

He heaps salad onto his plate. "Your assignments are never ending." He glances at Callum. "When my sister isn't working at the diner, she spends the rest of her time at night school, or studying. You must have noticed that about her."

"Why would he have?" I ask my brother. I deeply abhor the way he's suddenly become so friendly with Callum, but I'm relieved that he's talking about something else now.

"Because he told me that you were delivering lunch to the set every day."

It's on the tip of my tongue to say that this was Callum's plan in order to get access to Elias, but I don't have the heart to.

"You kept that quiet," Elias says, making my job of keeping my mouth shut almost impossible.

"I didn't realize it was an event I had to report on," I say tightly, reaching over for a taco.

"How long do you have left to shoot?" Harper asks.

"Another month or so, followed by a whole round of promotion and marketing, and lots of parties to attend to, in order to hype up the buzz. Not unlike your event the other day."

"I've never been one for parties and mixing with people," says Elias, grabbing a taco for himself. "I like to keep myself to myself and focus on the thing that counts, the boxing."

"He's done more socializing these past few months than in his entire life," Harper says.

Elias takes a huge bite, then chews thoughtfully. "That's because I met you." Harper smiles brightly. Her plate is half full of salad, and an uneaten taco.

"These are good," Callum says, making an approving noise in this throat. He's almost devoured his taco.

"Thanks," says Harper. "They're not all that difficult to make."

"I thought it was your specialty?" I ask Elias. He left me and Callum alone for a reason, and I knew that making tacos wasn't the reason.

"It needs the right blend of herbs, and the best lean ground beef."

"These are good, really good," Callum insists, as an uncomfortable hush fills the room.

"They heard you first time." I can't help myself.

"How long have you two been together?" Callum asks, expertly trying to smoothe things over while I fight the urge to let out a groan. I wish I hadn't come tonight. I hate that I'm here, and I hate that Callum can see through me. I don't want his pity. I don't want this interest. I don't want him.

People like Rhys and Scott are easier to push away.

This guy, not so easy.

CHAPTER TWENTY-SIX

CALLUM

Nina seems on edge tonight. I've been looking for the right time to explain myself, to apologize for what she heard me say to Dottie. She's not giving me a chance though. It's probably better if I talk to Elias and Harper more, and hope that I find time with Nina alone later.

"What?" says Harper, when she catches me looking at Elias.

The guy himself stops taking a bite out of his taco and looks up at me.

"You guys seem really tight, really good together," I say, putting down my cutlery. I pick up my napkin then wipe my mouth. "How long have you guys been together?" This seems to be a safer conversation to have. For the fighting machine that Elias is, he seems all soft, and different when he's around his girlfriend, and he seems completely taken by her.

Harper proceeds to tell me the story of how she and

Elias met, while he interrupts occasionally, embellishing things further.

He was an angry young man who had issues while growing up, and that he'd often get into lots of fights. Elias Cardoza had the right background and mindset to become who he is—the guy who took on Trent Garrison and won against all the odds. The person I see before me right now doesn't seem at all like the man I've read about.

I have a chance to delve deeper, to get into his head, but I find myself holding back. I sense, at some level, that Nina doesn't like this. But it's my chance, so I grab it. "Looking at you now," I nod at Elias, "You have world success, and wealth, and the respect and adoration of so many. It's hard to reconcile your past with the man you are today."

"Which part are you having problems with?" Elias asks, and thankfully he has a wisp of a smile on his face as he says it.

"Just ... you know...the angry young man. The guy who fought in fight clubs. I guess, you've earned it, and achieved all you wanted, and here you are. But, is it really that easy to forget the past and move on? Sorry, man, I don't want to rake up your past."

"Then stop asking such nosey and personal questions." It's the first time Nina's had anything to say.

Silence falls and while I don't want to make her look silly, I feel compelled to stand up for myself since they're all looking at me. "I'm sorry. Maybe I'm crossing the line. As an actor, these things fascinate me."

Nina shakes her head, as if she's having an internal conversation, as if she's irritated by me.

"Uh...so...uh," Elias also seems caught off guard. He glances at Nina, before attacking the food on his plate. It's not only me who senses the tension in the air. "What did you ask?" Elias seems to have completely lost his train of thought.

"I wanted to know how you were able to overcome your past and move on the way you—"

The sound of something hitting the floor clanks and reverberates through the air. Nina bends over and picks something up. "I dropped my fork," she says, and puts it to the side.

Her face is ashen, indicating that she's even more agitated than I first assumed.

"We're going to Dwayne's place in the mountains," Elias says, matter-of-factly.

"Dwayne Banks?" The name rings a bell. "Wasn't he the middleweight champion years ago?"

"You've done your homework." Elias sounds surprised.

"Yes," I announce proudly. "Had to. I didn't know anything about boxing, apart from watching the fights. Saw yours against Garrison. Epic. Great fight. The best boxing match I've ever seen."

"Thanks."

"We can go through some old fighting footage, if it might help you?" he suggests. "I look at that stuff all the time, seeing how the legends used to move around. Studying their signature punches." He shrugs. "I don't know if something like that might help?"

"It will help. Most definitely. Thanks." Me, sitting down with Cardoza and looking through footage of boxing matches? Yes it will help, and it will be something cool to boast about in future film interviews.

NINA

. . .

I can't get this food down me. They're all sitting around talking as if they've been best friends for decades.

"It's a cool place, Dwayne's mansion in the mountains," says Harper, obviously eager to reset the mood. "I went there when I was covering the life of Elias Cardoza before he was catapulted to fame." She and my brother look at one another, and I know something happened on that training exercise.

"You should come along," my brother suggests to Callum. To my horror, he seems to consider it. "Thanks for the offer. I'm honored that you would even ask me." He refuses to meet my stare. "I would love to, but I can't get any time off."

"It's a shame we can't make a weekend of it," Harper adds. "The four of us could go up, for a few days. You get weekends off, don't you, Callum?"

I don't even hear the reply, because my blood is boiling. Who the hell does Harper think she is. *The four of us?*

There is no *four* of us.

"Couldn't you try and come for the weekend?" asks Harper. "We must go back to that nice little Italian restaurant we went to last time." The muscles in my stomach tense. Why won't she drop the subject?

"He says he doesn't have a lot of time," my brother reminds her. I want to shout out that there's no four in this group. There's no *two* in me and Callum, only what exists solely in Harper's brain. That woman should switch from writing tech articles to writing fantasy fiction because she seems to be good at making stuff up.

Callum looks at me quickly, as if he's trying to assess my mood. I'm already pissed off with the conversation, so I play around with the food on my plate. My appetite vanished before I'd even sat down.

"Lou and Margrit are going," Elias reminds her. "Lou's my trainer, and Margrit his wife does all the cooking when we go there," he tells Callum.

"We had a great time, didn't we?" says Harper, grinning.

Elias nods in agreement. "There's a cinema room, and jacuzzi and sauna and a pool, in case you get bored of being stuck inside the whole time."

I listen to this exchange and try to chew on my taco, which suddenly tastes like cardboard.

"You probably have all those things in your place?" Harper asks Callum suddenly.

"In one of my houses."

I shift in my seat.

"In *one* of your houses? How many do you have?" Harper the Fangirl asks.

Callum scratches his ear and seems hesitant to reply. This takes me by surprise, he's being careful with what he says. He's being careful on account of me. I know this, but I don't know how I know it. "A couple."

Harper's eyes widen. She's trying to rein her excitement in and failing. "A couple? Where?"

Callum winces. "Here and there."

"Leave the guy alone," my brother says, with a grin. It strikes me that Elias is a lot more relaxed these days. Come to think of it, he's been jovial and relaxed for a long time now. Clearly, his counseling sessions are helping him.

"Do you have a private jet?" Harper asks. I hang my head, in fact, I have the strong urge to bang it on the table.

"You bought a jet?" Elias asks.

"Not me. I know a lot of people who move from houses, to buying yachts and planes, but I'm not one of them."

I play around with the taco in my plate, while Elias and Harper grill Callum on his movie star lifestyle. It's more Harper than Elias, but listening to them all talking it quickly becomes obvious to me that Elias likes Callum. Harper liked him from the start, but I can tell that Callum has wormed his way into my brother's good books.

I despise this fact.

"Your life must have changed drastically since the win?" Callum asks.

Elias nods. "You have no idea."

Harper is all smiles. "He's handling the fame better than I thought he would."

"That shit takes time to get used to," Elias mumbles. "I'm not sure I'll ever like it."

"I read somewhere that you've lived in foster homes before. You were at Grampton House for a while, here in Chicago."

"Oh, right, we were talking about that before the conversation side tracked," says Elias.

Thanks, Callum. Thanks a hell of a lot.

"We were at that place." Elias's reply is short, thankfully. I wish the floor would open and suck me up. It's pin-drop quiet again. Then Harper puts her hand over Elias's. "It's all good now though," she says softly.

My brother nods. "Harper helped me. Talking about it to her and getting therapy helped."

"You're getting therapy?" Callum asks. I look up. Callum appears surprised, and then he looks embarrassed. "That's cool. It's not something I realized about you."

"I don't tell the press all my business. And I pay my therapist good money to keep the news quiet."

"She wouldn't say anything anyway," I point out. "There is such a thing as patient confidentiality."

"Is that what your therapist told you?" Elias says jokingly. He's trying to be funny, but it still hurts. Not because I have a therapist—I don't right now—but that he can suddenly make jokes about our past.

"You have a therapist?" Harper echoes.

"No I don't." I'm so freaking pissed off now that my voice is hard, like lead. I force a smile. "It's obviously helping you," I reply to Elias. My brother lifts his napkin to his lips, before pointing it at me. "Having a therapist has helped me deal with all that shit we went through."

My muscles tighten. If I could close my ears and not hear this, I would. His voice is calm, his expression peaceful. That pent up hatred fueled his fighting, and now I worry that he won't be tough enough mentally to fight against Garrison. I'm worried that he's lost his edge. He has suffered the most horrific abuse and at such a young age, but you would never think so looking at him now.

He could never talk about it before. Would never talk about it. We had a code, he and I. We never spoke about our past. And here he is, sitting with a world-famous star and telling him everything.

I force myself to take long, slow breaths because I can't listen to this and pretend to be calm.

Let it go.

I've been trying to, but these three are suddenly best friends. The more they talk, the more I retreat into myself.

"Dennis Swain." Elias smiles as he looks at us in turn. "See, I can even say his name without putting a hole in the wall."

Elias said that name without flinching. My chest

tightens. Like someone just skewered my coronary arteries. Soon I'm going to stop breathing. Or bleed out.

Their voices fade away, and all I can hear is the pounding of my heart. I place my hand on the table to steady myself and I accidentally knock my glass over. Luckily it's empty.

"What's the matter with you today, Butter Fingers?" Elias asks. I set it on its base again and when I look up three pairs of eyes are staring at me. I fan my face. "Excuse me. I don't feel too good."

I rush out and head for the washroom.

CHAPTER TWENTY-SEVEN

CALLUM

Nina hasn't been interested in this conversation much, and she's been looking down at her plate and eating quietly. I've sensed her uneasiness the whole evening and it's because of me. If anyone should be feeling uneasy, it should be me.

Elias has been a good host, and tonight he's been really easy to get on with, but I'm certain that Harper is a steadying influence on him. He's a wild card, and I never know quite when his mood might turn.

When Nina suddenly gets up and leaves the table, I'm torn between running after her, and staying here, listening to Elias. Luckily, Harper gets up, beating me to it, and then Elias continues, talking about his past, how difficult it was to fit in with new families, and schools, and not feeling as if he really belonged anywhere.

When he talks about his stay at the children's home, he thankfully doesn't give any specifics. I don't want to hear about the details. Reading about a seven year old child being abused was bad enough.

For me, his winning the heavyweight title the way he did is nothing short of a miracle. He overcame the horrors and became a champion. His victory is well-earned; a well-deserved crowning glory given the ugliness of his past. I don't know if I admired Cardoza more when he won the fight, or after I read about his troubled past.

I'm simply honoured that he's allowed me into his inner circle, because that's what this is, given that I am in his apartment, having dinner with the man, and the people closest to him. I feel lucky to be here.

Harper comes back, and lifts her glass of wine. "She's okay."

Elias puts down his glass of water. "She needs to slow down and chew her food."

"She seems to be in a rush," muses Harper. "Has she got a class tonight?"

"Not tonight." They both look at me as if I've said something completely inappropriate.

"How would you know?" Harper asks, smiling.

"I overheard her talking at the diner," I mumble.

Elias stares at me. "That would freak Nina out, you knowing her night school timetable."

"He didn't say he knows her timetable, Eli." Harper squeezes his hand. "Leave the guy alone." Something about the way she says it tells me that they've been talking about things. About Nina and me, maybe. It's a hunch. Or maybe it's wishful thinking on my part.

"I appreciate you inviting me to your home," I say, "you have a huge fight ahead of you and you have a lot going on at the moment."

"Glad to help, though Harper kept going on at me and I

figured this was the only way to shut her up." He says it with a smile, while Harper shakes her head and takes another sip of her wine.

I nod. "But I appreciate you talking about your past."

"You never forget the things that were done to you," says Eli slowly. "I thought I had pushed them away, thought I'd blocked them out. Thought I'd forgotten them, but as soon as I started to talk about them, they came back, like they were new, like I was going through that shit all over again."

"You're not going through it all over again, you're dealing with it, accepting it and putting it to bed forever," Harper tells him. She leans in and kisses his face. I catch his expression and in that second, it's unguarded. There's something sad about it. I feel as if I'm eavesdropping on a private conversation. "I promise it won't go anywhere," I tell him, in case he's worried. I know what it's like to trust people and have that trust betrayed.

Elias swats his hand in the air. "I don't care about that. My past is now out in the open. I can handle it. It's when that stuff is inside you, when it's a dirty little secret that's gnawing at you, *that's* the cancer. It eats and eats and eats away at you."

"Well, I appreciate you being so open." I get up. "I should go and check on Nina." I don't fail to miss the look of surprise on Harper's face.

"She feels guilty," Elias says in a low voice. He doesn't look at either of us.

"Guilty?" I ask.

"She fell to pieces when she heard what happened to Eli when they were kids," Harper explains.

This is a surprise to me. "She didn't know?"

"She found out when this asshole at my last workplace

printed it without me knowing. That's when the world found out. Gerry was such a jerk."

Elias clutches his glass so tightly that his knuckles are white. I'm worried that he might break the glass. "Nina didn't know about that shit. It broke her. She always tried to protect me. She's always taken on the mom role, wherever we were, at the children's home or a new foster home. She's only a year older than me."

"The washroom's down the hallway," says Harper, "The last door on the right."

I head in that direction, but I don't need to walk far because I find Nina leaning against the wall. Her eyes are shut, and she's breathing heavily.

"Hey," I rush over to her side. This startles her, and her eyes fly wide open. She stands up straight. Her sleeves are rolled up slightly, and I wonder if she's been sick. That's when I see them. Scars, red, and ruler-straight. I've caught her unexpectedly. I've seen something she didn't want me to see. She pulls her sleeves down.

I'm too shocked to speak. Now I understand. The muscle along her jaw twitches. She hates me more than ever now because I've seen something she never wanted me to see. A new realization dawns on me. *Guilt.* That's the poison that's killing Nina slowly. She feels this much guilt for what happened to her brother.

"Nina," the word hangs in the air, as she marches off, back towards the kitchen.

I follow her back to the others, but I'm unsure how to be and how to react. I don't know what to say. She sits back at the table, and lifts her glass of water to her lips. "It must have been something I ate yesterday," she says.

"Coming back to what you were saying." Elias wipes his hands, then clasps them together, under his chin, as if he's thinking about something. "It's not that you ever forget. I'll never forget my past, there are things that will haunt me, but I've learned to deal with them." His voice doesn't waver, but it sounds oddly off, and when he takes Harper's hand and she clasps it, I sense that this man is still dealing with his demons despite the composed exterior that's on view for everyone to see. "This woman has been a great help." Harper lifts his hand and kisses it.

"You have," Elias says softly. This is a private moment between them but I'm also acutely aware that Nina hasn't picked up her cutlery and resumed eating. We are two gooseberries, who happen to be sitting opposite Harper and Elias, but now I'm also deeply mindful of how Elias's past has affected his sister.

"Talking is important," says Elias, clearing his throat. "I kept that stuff inside me, and it wasn't until I started telling Harper, that it dislodged, and started to come loose."

"She convinced me to get therapy."

Nina makes a sound and we all turn to look at her.

"I told you about that," says Elias.

"You did," Nina replies, but her face is still pale.

I want to change the subject, but I don't know how to without sounding rude to Elias, yet it is Nina I'm concerned about. She coughs, and it suddenly turns into something bigger, louder, that goes on. I get up, and move over to her, and I'm about to give her the Heimlich maneuver when she pushes back on her chair, elbowing me in the balls. I'm not sure if that was deliberate or a mistake. She flaps her hand about as if she's struggling to breathe. I'm flailing around in pain. My balls are on fire but I'm trying to act cool, and I'm still debating whether to do the maneuver since she's still coughing.

"Did it go down the wrong pipe?" Harper asks, and

starts to refill Nina's glass with water. "You look like you're going to be sick."

"I think...I think..." Nina coughs. "... it went down the wrong pipe." She takes a huge sip of water.

"What is up with you tonight?" Elias asks, his brow furrowing.

"I shouldn't have come tonight. I have a ton of work to do. I need to go. Thanks for dinner," she announces suddenly rising from her chair.

"At least finish your food," Elias tells her. "You've barely touched it."

"She's not feeling well," Harper says.

Nina coughs lightly. "I've lost my appetite."

"I should go too," I say. They can't blame me for not eating. I polished off everything on my plate and had second helpings. I can't let Nina leave like this. It's not that I need answers, I'm genuinely worried about her. This is another first for me. How can I care so much when I barely know this woman?

"Don't you want to see the old fights?" Elias asks. "I was going to show you some key punches and moves. It would add some realism to your fighting scenes."

That would have been great but I've made my mind up. I can't let Nina leave alone. She catches me staring at her. "You should watch those fights," she says, getting her jacket and bag together.

"We could get a cab back together," I offer, even though it sounds pathetic because we're on opposite sides of the city.

"That's a good idea," says Harper.

"Watch the fights," Nina insists.

"But then again," Harper puts her arm around Elias's

waist and leans in towards him. "We could skip the boxing fights tonight."

Elias runs a hand through his hair. "It was only a suggestion. Maybe another time."

"That would be great," I answer. I'm genuinely humbled by his willingness to spend some time with me. "But, I've taken up enough of your time tonight. Thanks for dinner. It's been great." I take my cell phone out and call an Uber.

Nina looks pissed off. "You don't have your disguises on you."

"Disguises?" Harper asks.

"He has to wear a disguise otherwise he can't go out. Such is the price of fame," she mutters.

"How do you know?" Elias asks her.

"It's surprising what you find out when you have to deliver takeout to set every single day."

Harper's grinning at me.

"I like their food," I say with a shrug. "Five minutes?" I say to the guy at the other end of my phone.

"We live in opposite directions," Nina protests. I can hear the undercurrent of anger in her voice, but I know what I've seen. She wants me to get lost, but she can't push me away that fast.

"That's not a problem," I reply. "It should be here in a matter of minutes."

She's running from something.

She's hiding something and, worse than that, she's hurting, and no one knows. Despite how close they're supposed to be, I'm certain that Elias has no idea about what's going on with Nina.

"Thanks for dinner." She leans in and kisses Harper on the

cheek, then her brother, and when she turns around to look at me all I get is a hardened stare, full of loathing and disgust. She makes me wish I hadn't come tonight. "I don't get a kiss?" I ask, and put on a smile I don't feel. It's supposed to ease the tension coming off Nina in waves, but it serves only to heighten it.

From my peripheral vision, I can almost see Harper grinning.

Nina doesn't even bother to reply.

"Aren't you both getting a cab together?" Harper asks. Nina is out of the door.

"Yes, we are." I follow her out.

CHAPTER TWENTY-EIGHT

CALLUM

She's doing that thing again, avoiding eye contact and staring out of the window and I'm at a loss for how to start a conversation.

"What was that all about?" I ask.

"I don't want to talk about it."

I can't force her to, but it's obvious she's hurting. The more I think back to all my previous interactions with Nina, the more I see the signs. She hides it well, the guilt she carries. I can now see the sadness in her eyes, the plastered-on smile for customers, maybe even the reason why she pushes me away.

I don't understand it all, and it seems extreme to still be affected about something that happened so long ago, but what do I know? I've never experienced what she has. My upbringing has been safe and secure, in a family home with good people. My parents have always been supportive, and they have always loved me unconditionally.

My life would have been so different, I would have been so different, if I'd been tossed around in foster care like Nina and Elias.

I want to help her. She's struggling, and any idiot can see that. "Your brother said that counseling helped him."

She turns to me with blazing eyes. "Can't you butt out, even now? I don't want your advice. I don't need you to tell me what I should or shouldn't do."

She's doing it again, pushing me away. It makes sense, and it doesn't. It surprises me that she's still carrying the scars of her past, but she needs to know that what happened to Elias wasn't her fault. He was a kid, and so was she.

"Don't push me away, Nina. I want to help."

"I don't want you to help. I don't need your help and I never asked for it. You've been on my back ever since we met."

"I owe you for saving my life." Those guys could have pulled a knife on me. I get that now. Rudy reminds me of that often enough.

She heaves out a breath and runs her hand over her hair. It brings my attention to her wrist again, only her jacket is thick, and the sleeves don't ride up, so I don't see those wounds even though I know they're there. I know she does this to herself. I want to take away her guilt, bury her pain, and make her see that she did the best she could for her brother.

She was only a kid, for Christ sake.

"You know what I would love you to do for me?" she asks softly, her eyes turning glassy, making my spirits rise in hopeful want.

"What?" Anything. I'd do anything she asked.

"Leave me alone."

I sink back in my seat as I stare out of the window. In

the past, on the rare occasions it's happened, I've been able to walk away when a woman hasn't been interested. Twice it's happened. Why can't I do what Nina's asking me? I feel a pull towards her that I cannot for the life of me understand. The attraction is nothing to do with looks, nothing surface level. It goes way deeper, and I don't get it. I can't walk away, and that's what I tell her.

"Why not?"

"I don't know. You're different, and this is different, and I can't walk away."

"You're a movie star. I'm a waitress. People like us don't get together."

She's worried about demographics? Somehow, I don't believe her, because if that were the case, it would be so simple.

"I'm not interested in people like you," she tells me in that warning voice of hers. "You're not my type, just like I'm not your type." She throws back my words to Dottie.

"You don't have a type," I say foolishly, without thinking.

"How would you know?"

"I've spoken to your friends."

She fixes me with a gaze that could shoot bullets. "Butt out of my life."

I'm not falling for her tactics. "What happened to Elias wasn't your fault, Nina. I wish I could make you see that."

She scoffs and I start to wonder if I've got all this wrong. "Elias must never know," she says. "Don't go shooting your mouth off about it, like you did with the mugging."

If Elias found out, he would only want to help her, surely? Her dark eyes are pinned on me, and she's waiting for my answer.

"I promise. I won't say a word to anyone. I can keep a secret."

The cab comes to a stop outside her place, and she mumbles a goodbye and leaves.

NINA

When the cab pulls up outside my house, I don't even bother offering half for the ride. Callum would only refuse, and I would have to end up talking to him, and I don't want to.

He thinks I'm like this because of the guilt I'm carrying for what happened to my brother. Somehow that fills me with relief. If that's what he wants to believe, it's for the best. It would kill me for him or Elias, or anyone I know, to find out the truth.

I manage a 'Bye', then rush away.

Once inside, I change into my pajamas, brush my teeth and climb into bed. I think about the razor blade in the cupboard. It's like a drug. Cutting makes me *feel*. Somedays I'm so numb inside, I don't even know if I'm alive. I stare at the blade and it's like a terrible itch I need to scratch.

But a part of me wants to hold back. I don't want to give in. I want to get better. I was starting to. How easy it is for Elias to talk about Grampton House and what happened to him, and to someone like Callum, a complete stranger. He has gone from an angry man who would have punched anyone who dared to mention this, to someone calm and at peace. He's so Zen-like now that I don't even recognize him as the guy he used to be.

Happiness must do that to people; being happy, finding joy, being in love.

I know nothing about those things.

CHAPTER TWENTY-NINE

NINA

I found a sweet.

I found a sweet, and then another and another and another.

I've found *four* sweets. This has never happened before.

But Swain is counting, and I start to panic.

I rummage around in the basement, looking for that last sweet.

How is it that I've never found any sweets before, and now I've found *four*?

I rush around, desperate to find it. If I do, he will let me go.

"A hundred!" he says. He always counts too fast. I want to yell at him and tell him, but I know it won't make a difference. He's the grown-up and grown-ups always get what they want.

My heart crashes into my stomach and everything in my body sinks. I start to shiver. I see the fifth sweet in his hand.

I start to cry because I know what's coming, and because it's so unfair.

My lower lip wobbles, because he's going to do that nasty thing to me again. I hear my breath hard and fast, and I start to cry.

"Stop your bloody crying," he says, pulling down his zipper.

I throw the sweets at him and I step back. It's the bravest thing I've ever done.

"Come here you filthy little swine," he cries. He looks so horrible with those rotting yellow teeth. When he turns the light off, I run away, trying to escape. But he's too big, and too strong. He grabs me with his big hands.

I scream.

And then I wake up.

I'm shivering.

It wasn't real.

It was only a dream.

I sit up and feel the sweat between my armpits. I run a hand across my neck, and it's wet. It takes a moment for me to come out of my stupor. My heart rate is thudding. I'm scared that my heart will burst out of my ribcage.

I hug my knees harder, and I cry, huge racking sobs shake my body.

It felt so real, being back in that basement. It used to smell. Like smelly clothes and cheese. And it was so cold that my teeth would chatter and I would get little bumps on my arms and legs.

I never even found one sweet, let alone four.

It was only a bad dream.

An hour later, and I'm still sitting in bed with my knees bunched up. I am aware that I need to get some help. Elias said that talking about it helped.

I need to get over this.

I lift my head and see the razor blade lying on my bedside dresser. Once again, I am so, so tempted. And then I look at my wrists and I see what Callum saw.

I wish he would leave me alone but I have a feeling he's not going to. He seems to think he owes me a debt of gratitude for saving his life that first time.

I lie back in bed and pull the covers right up to my chin. I decide that I will call in sick today. I've hardly ever called in sick, and Frankie will wonder, but I can't face customers today.

I can't face myself today.

CALLUM

"Where's Nina?" I ask, when her friend from the diner shows up.

"She called in sick." She hands me my lunch, then gapes around my room in awe.

Nina is sick? "What's wrong with her?" I watch as this woman walks around, running her hands over everything, my books, the clothes hanging on the rack, even the flowers in the vase aren't spared.

She shrugs. "She's sick, that's all I know."

"Sick? With what?"

"Jeez." She stops short of picking up Elias's biography which is lying on my dresser. She glares at me. "Why do you care so much?"

"She looked fine yesterday." She didn't, but I can't think of something to say to this so called friend.

She picks up a paperweight off my desk. I'm surprised by her forwardness. "She must be really sick, 'cause it's the first time she's ever done that."

I know what Nina is capable of, and I'm worried. I can't tell Elias or Harper because I promised Nina that I would keep her secret to myself, but right now she has no one to talk to about this. Except me.

Her waitress friend hovers around, and I don't know what for. I do know that she's irritating the heck out of me. I hope she's not expecting a tip. "Thanks for my lunch." I hope she'll take the hint and get the hell out.

But she stands there, with a smug stupid smile on her face, looking around my room like she's Alice in Fucking Wonderland.

"You can go now," I snap. She's gone too far. I need her out so that I can check in on Nina. I have one scene to shoot after lunch and then I'm free for the rest of the day.

Her gaze falls on the Leanne Rose autograph I managed to get for Nina. I was supposed to give it to her, but I keep forgetting to. Her inquisitive fingers lift up the sheet of paper.

"Don't. Do. That."

She looks at me guiltily. "Sorry. Any chance of you showing me around the set?"

"No." Not a chance in hell.

"You must have showed Nina around."

"She never asked."

"But you would have, if she had."

"I probably would." Heck, I *know* I would.

Her face falls, and she looks pissed. "She gets it all, just 'cause her brother's a boxing champ. That's why you're interested in her, huh?"

"That's not why."

Her eyes widen, as if she's picked up on my secret. Only, it's not a secret. Even Nina knows I like her, heck, she ought to by now.

She leaves, and slams the door as if to make a point.

Pathetic woman.

I open the lunch bag, and take a peek inside. It's my usual. Only ... it's getting boring eating the same old thing day after day. I want to call Nina and see how she is but my gut tells me she probably won't take my call.

I eat the wrap anyway, and figure out a way of getting into her good books.

And this time, I'll remember to take the autograph.

CHAPTER THIRTY

NINA

Callum Sandersby standing on my doorstep is the last thing I expect to see.

I'm wearing an old cardigan which is way too baggy for me. I pull it around me like a blanket. I also thank the stars the sleeves are extra long, in case Callum's hawk eyes try to take another look at my wrist.

We blink at one another for a few awkward seconds.

"How are you?" he says, at the same time as I ask, "What are you doing here?"

"I heard you weren't well."

"From who?" I ask suspiciously.

"You didn't come by the set to drop lunch off today."

"Is that all you ever care about?"

"I care about you. Your friend Julie turned up."

"Joni."

"What?"

"Her name's Joni." I'm surprised he doesn't know. She's

always managed to sneak in and get to his table whenever he's come into the diner.

"Is she really your friend?" he asks.

"Yes, why?" I can only imagine that she must have done something stupid, and desperate to try to get his attention.

"She said you were off sick so I came to check how you were."

But why? I wonder.

Why, why, why, why, why?

Callum is the last person I want to see. *Ever.*

"Didn't I make it clear to you the other night?" I try to keep the anger out of my voice.

"I'm not so sure you mean it."

"Oh, I mean what I say. No means 'no'."

He looks puzzled. "Aren't you going to ask me in?"

"It's daylight. You won't get attacked and even if you do I'll be right here to save you."

He smiles. "I can trust you to have my back, Nina."

"You didn't need to come all the way here."

"Is it so wrong that I'm concerned?"

"You have an ulterior motive."

"You came to my aid when—"

Not that old thing again. "Can you stop going on about that?" I cry. "I was just as stupid as you to go into the alleyway. You've already thanked me for it about a million times. Please, can you drop it now?"

"Okay, I will. But you did go into that alley, and you did come to my rescue."

"Unintentionally."

He gives me a smile that would probably melt most women's defenses.

Not mine, though.

"I have something for you," he says, clearly in no rush to leave.

"What?" He doesn't look like he has anything for me. But he's clearly not giving up, even though he has Elias, and he has what he wanted, he's at my door, allegedly to see how I'm doing.

"Can't I come in?"

"Come in," I say, reluctantly.

"Thanks." I head into my tiny living room, and quickly check to see if it's tidy. Too late, if it's not, but I am strangely relieved that my clothes aren't lying all over the place. Nor my blade.

"Here." I watch, confused and enthralled as he pulls out a notebook from his jacket pocket, and then he whips out a sheet of paper from it.

"What is it?" I ask. He didn't tear it out. It's been placed in there. Now I'm *really* curious.

"An autograph from Leanne Rose. You said you liked her."

The what? I try to remember when I said that. I never said I wanted an autograph. *Or did I?* I'm not a celebrity fan at all, and I must have been making polite conversation. I take the sheet from him anyway. I can't help but wonder why this guy has gone to all this trouble to get this for me.

He hands it over to me, looking very pleased with himself.

"Thanks." Another part of my brain reminds me that he's a superstar, and that he's probably good friends with Leanne Rose. He probably has her on speed dial. This is not as big a deal for him as it would be for us mere mortals.

I glance at the autograph.

This woman doesn't know me but she's written:

Hey Nina, Callum says you're one feisty woman.

From one badass woman to another,

Leanne

The message touches me in a small yet significant way because he must have said something to her in order for her to write what she has.

"That's...that's sweet," I say finally. I hold the paper in my hands, not sure what do to with it. I'm not going to frame it, but I'm also not going to throw it away.

I'm uncomfortable. I don't like people doing things for me and even though I let him in, I'm still questioning his motives, because I don't trust anyone. "Why did you go to all that trouble?"

"Because you said you liked her." He looks sheepish now, and I feel bad for him. He shakes his head. "You're one tough cookie to crumble, Nina."

"Tough cookie to crumble?" I repeat, finding that an odd metaphor. "Is that what you're trying to do? Break down my defenses in the hope that I'll fall for your moves?"

"I don't have any moves. Not with you."

"This isn't a move?" I wave the autograph at him.

"No."

"You think I can't see you trying to be extra nice to me for no reason?"

"How have people treated you that badly that you consider this to be *extra* nice?"

He might as well have punched me in my gut. I feel the pain of his words as surely as if he'd struck me. Feeling brave, I answer back. "Don't expect me to go falling for your seductive eyes and ... and ... that ... that ... " I lose my train of thought.

Seductive eyes. Did I actually say that to him? I remember reading something about him when I looked him up. Trust that to stick in my mind.

"Seductive eyes, huh?" He throws me a casual smile. "It's funny you should say that because in a women's magazine poll, ninety-five percent of women said it was my eyes and my smile they fell for."

I let out a loud groan. "I'm not like those women."

"Of course, you're not like the other women. You're something else. You stand out."

My belly stiffens. "I don't want to stand out." I don't want him to notice me, much less pay attention to me. But I have to be careful. Callum isn't stupid and while he's got the reason wrong for those scars on my arms, if I give him enough time, if I let him get any closer, he'll figure it all out. And I don't want him to.

"You stand out in a good way, I don't mean like a sore thumb," he says, as if he's realized I feel uneasy. I *am* different to most women. Most haven't had to go through what I did. Even Joni, with that asshole of a boyfriend. She wouldn't know of the horrors I've lived through.

No one does, and that's the way I like it.

"You shouldn't feel bad about your past." He speaks so softly that at first I think I've misheard. I pull the cardigan around me, as if it's a protective shield, insulating me from Callum's kindness, from his interest, and concern, all of which I don't have any time for.

"What were you supposed to do?"

I want to fight back, and ask him why he's asking me these questions. Why does he feel the need to make it his business? But, like always, I freeze up about my past. I can't face it, I can't deal with it, I can't talk about it.

He takes my silence to mean that I'm listening.

I feel like I should offer him something but I don't want him to make himself too comfortable. Maybe I should ask him to sit down, seeing that we're both still standing and warily facing one another, as if we're in an invisible boxing ring.

"Sit down," I say, but it comes out stiff and awkward and doesn't sound as if I mean it.

"I don't want to take up too much of your time. I only came to see if you were okay."

Damn it.

"I think you're awesome, Nina. You're brave, you're so much braver than you realize."

I frown, unable to get my tongue and lips working. He has no idea what he is talking about.

"You remember the wallet, the reason why I didn't want to give it up?"

I blink, unsure where he's going with this. "Because it had sentimental value, you said."

Though, knowing what I know now about him, I wouldn't put it past him to make up some bullshit lie just to get some female sympathy. In fact, it's the type of thing I expect from someone like Callum.

"It was the last picture taken of me and my brother."

It takes me a few seconds to let that sink in but I am determined not to lower my guard for this guy. "What do you mean it was the last picture?"

"He died of an aneurysm while playing basketball. It happened suddenly."

I open my mouth to say something, but nothing comes out. Any anger I felt for him dissipates in an instant. "What?"

"One moment he was here, and then he went. It broke us as a family. "

"I'm so sorry."

"I didn't want to tell you back when you asked about the wallet. The truth is, I don't talk about it much."

"But you're telling me now."

He nods. "I feel as if I can."

Oh, for the love of all things ... But my quickfire sarcasm melts away. I see a sadness in him that I've never really noticed before. I see another side to Callum, and this time it's like I'm seeing him anew. "I'm sorry for your loss."

"I've carried that photo around with me ever since. It was the last one taken of us together."

I wipe a hand over my cheek, then I sit on the couch, it's like the news has weighed me down. "I see now why you didn't want to give that photo up."

"That was why."

I look up at him, surprised by how much he's opening up to me. Now I wish he would sit down..

"How old was your brother when he died?"

"Thirteen. I was sixteen."

Taken so young. Something heavy crashes into my stomach. I'm not the only one who has known extreme pain. I look at him with new eyes. His face and body are pure Hollywood hunk, and yet his eyes are wise, and ageless. And now that I'm seeing it clearly for the first time, his expression isn't so much brawn, as something deeper altogether.

"I don't usually speak about Ben, but I felt I could tell you."

I didn't ask him to tell me, and I wonder why he did. "It must be painful, even now, carrying the weight of your loss."

"I carried that photo around with me everywhere. It's like I needed to remember that moment, that one bright sunny day when everything was just fine in my world. I miss him."

I feel as if a ball of sadness has gotten stuck in my throat. I know of that bond between siblings, and even though Callum and I are so different—in our backgrounds, and personalities, and past—we've both been touched by sadness in our earlier lives, and he is right. Stuff like that binds you together in a small way. Only in that way do we share something.

I feel like a cold-hearted bitch, the way I've been around him, and now, hearing this, I feel even worse. This man has been hurting as much as me, maybe in a different way, but his pain is no less significant than mine.

"Why did you tell me?"

He ruffles his hair up, as if he has no idea. "I don't know. I didn't come here with that intention. I didn't come to get sympathy, I honestly came to see you because..." He pauses, and there's a world of explanation in that silence. We have spent enough time together, have experienced enough uncomfortable moments, to fill the quiet.

"Because I've seen your arms, Nina. I know what you do." His knowing and saying it out loud, shuts me down again.

I hate this. Someone knowing my secret. I've lived with it this long and there has been a sense of safety in this being my secret. I can't untell him, no more than he can unsee what he has. It makes the fabric of our already frayed relationship even weaker.

I am at a loss for words. I have no idea what he wants me to say. I have no idea what I want to say.

"I'm drawn to you, Nina, and I have no idea why. Maybe because we both have guilt. Maybe because we both wonder why couldn't it have been me?"

I shiver. *Because it was me.*

I wish it had been just me, and not Elias, but if Callum thinks otherwise, I'm going to let him.

Callum Sandersby, the sexy and confident self-assured Hollywood hunk. Who would have thought he was wracked with guilt? That he wished his brother had lived and not him?

"I should go. Good to see that you're getting better. You look well."

"Stay a while."

"I should go."

He's going now? He comes in here, hands me an autograph, tells me about his brother and now he's going? I get up, not wanting him to leave so quickly now. He opened up and let me see his wound, and even though I won't allow myself to do the same, I want to try to be a better friend.

When he leaves, I'm left looking at the autograph from Leanne Rose. Callum went to the trouble of getting that for me because of something I mentioned in a conversation once.

I never allowed myself to believe that he could be nice, and honest and decent. If he wanted something quick and dirty, he could click his fingers and women would come running.

Maybe the reason he won't leave me alone is because he genuinely likes me.

CHAPTER THIRTY-ONE

CALLUM

I'm glad I told her about my brother. I don't talk about him to anyone, except my parents and serious girlfriends. Ben doesn't deserve to be used as a pity card, but seeing that Nina is neither a girlfriend, nor a close friend, I'm not sure why I told her, except that I had an urge to tell her the truth.

I harbor a type of guilt that Ben died and I didn't. Brain aneurysms are a freaky occurence. I wish it hadn't been once to visit my family. We had bereavement counseling. My mom and dad had it for longer than I did. I was still in high school when it happened. School, soccer, girls, drinks ... these things helped me to cope with my grief better than any counseling could.

While I will never know of Nina's pain, I've suffered my own. The loss of a brother, so young, fit and healthy, so full of life, being taken in the blink of an eye is something you never recover from. It shattered our close knit family.

Luckily, we've managed to put ourselves back together again.

I don't think of him every single day now, not like I used to, but I feel that he's a part of me. An invisible extension of me, somehow. At any one time I would be able to open my wallet and see Ben's face. His smile would make me smile. In that instant, I would feel that he was there. That's why I couldn't part with my wallet.

I don't know if Nina liked the autograph. It wasn't too hard for me to get since Leanne and I are good friends. There's no romance there, despite the press wanting to make one up. I helped her through a tough time. She'd lost her mom to cancer towards the end of the film we were shooting, and because this business stinks when it comes to empathy, nobody cared. Nobody cares what goes on in the background, it's all to do with breaking box office records and multi-million, if not billion, opening weekend sales.

But I was there for Leanne. I listened, and I held her. All those pictures that the paps managed to get, those were of me being there for her in her hour of need. That's all it was.

"Who is this Nina?" she asked me, when I called her up and asked her to mail me an autograph.

"Just a friend," I told her. But the truth is, I didn't know then who or what Nina is to me, and I am none the wiser now. I'm glad I went to see her. I was worried that she might have done something hasty, but she seemed fine. I tried to get a look at her arms, but she had them well covered.

My cell phone suddenly rings. It's Dottie. "Where are you?" She sounds anxious.

"I'm...out, why?"

"Everyone's looking for you. You have some retakes to do."

"Now? I thought we were done for the day."

"No, you're not. You need to come back quickly. How come you left the set so fast?"

I can hear the shock in her voice. I shouldn't have left straight after my shoot, but I didn't think I'd be needed. Murphy's Law. "I had things to do." I usually hang around until late evening, because it's not as if I have anything else to do. Nina has been my only distraction, and hanging out with Elias and Harper has helped me to pass the time. "I'm on my way," I tell her.

"Rudy wants me to book your plane and hotel tickets for Alyssa's premier."

Shoot.

"You *had* forgotten," Dotty says, when I don't answer.

I let out a sigh of relief. "That's why I hired you."

"Do you want to stay in LA one night or two?"

"Two." The jet lag will kill me if it's just the one night.

"Rudy wants me to remind you that this is a PR opportunity. He says, and I quote, "Don't forget to turn up the love factor.""

I groan. Two nights in LA? I'm not looking forward to it at all.

NINA

I go back to work the next day and as soon as I walk through the door I feel Frankie's eyes on me. I've never taken a day off sick before. "You okay?" Her voice is gentle, as if she's talking to someone sick.

"All good, thanks."

"If you need more time off ... "

I frown. "Do I look ill?"

"You look just fine to me, a little tired maybe, though you were probably working late into the night finishing off your assignments." She snorts. "You don't have to rush back if you need more time off."

"I like being here."

"I worry about you sometimes."

I laugh. "You worry about me all the time, Frankie."

She snorts. "Someone has to."

I go in the back to get my pen and notepad, and that's when Joni walks in with a badly camouflaged black eye because despite the inch of concealer she has plastered on, I can still see it. "What happened?" I worry about her more than anything. Her dating that psychopath always makes me worry about her, even though I know she wouldn't care about me in that way.

Joni gives me a pointed, stare, as if she's trying to hold back on telling me the truth. My hate for Rhys is harder to hide these days.

"How long are you going to put up with it?" I ask her.

I can see by the way the muscles along her jaw flex, that she doesn't like my line of questioning.

"What was wrong with you yesterday?" she asks, completely ignoring my question.

"I didn't feel well." It's vague, because there was nothing wrong with me, nothing physically.

"Your actor friend kept asking me about you. I don't get it, why he's so into you."

"He's not into me," I counter, but this time, even as I say it, I'm not so sure I believe that anymore.

"You wouldn't know it even if a guy smacked his lips all over you," she says.

"I'd hope the guy would have asked my permission before he did that." I look at Joni's face, at the badly disguised black eye, at the tight press of her lips. She seems to hate me, even though I'm the only real friend she has. I feel sorry for her. "Did Rhys do that to—"

"I walked into the door."

"You've been walking into a lot of doors lately," I push back.

"Mind your own business," she snarls, and walks off.

She doesn't want to face the truth. She and I are similar in that respect. Callum isn't such a bad guy. I've always pushed him away, and he's doesn't seem to take the hint. I've been used to lumping every guy I ever met with all the bad guys, but Callum isn't a bad guy.

My feelings for him have gone through a kaleidoscope of ever-changing emotions. This is strange for me, because where I once believed myself incapable of having such thoughts, I'm starting to see Callum in a different way.

It hasn't happened suddenly. It's taken a while. It might have even started when I began delivering his lunch on set.

I've learned that he is different from the actor guy he portrays on-screen.

He could have any woman he wants, but he's being extra nice to me. I find his interest in me scary, and exhilarating, and something that I don't completely understand.

A whisper swirls up from deep inside me, something I have always pushed back whenever a guy showed interest in me.

If this man finds you desirable, you can't be all that bad.

CHAPTER THIRTY-TWO

CALLUM

Nina turns up with my lunch the next day. I'm so relieved to see her instead of her friend, but more than that, I'm happy to see *her*.

"Your wrap, and salad and milkshake." She puts the bag down

"Thanks. I take it you're better now. You look well."

"I'm better."

"How are the assignments?"

"Coming along."

"Need me to attend night school with you?"

She laughs.

Holy shit. Did Nina just laugh? I sit up in shock, then try to slink back down in my chair, hoping she won't notice. It's the most magical sound I've ever heard, and I want her to do it again. Emboldened, I press, "I'll let you pick my disguise this time, how about it."

"Disguise for what?"

"For me to accompany you to night school again."

"Why would you want to do that?"

"I'm a lonely guy, remember?"

"You really want to accompany me to night school?"

"It beats sitting alone in my hotel suite, trying to learn my lines."

"I get to pick?"

I sit up. She sounds as if she's considering it. *Hell yes, I would.* "Of course." Her eyes grow bigger, as if she's game.

"Can it be anything?" She seems softer. Lighter. Now that I think about it, Nina's always had a halo of darkness about her, I never fully realized that until this moment.

"Anything." I don't want to push her. I sense that I have to take one slow step forward then wait it out to see what she makes of it before I can even think of taking another step. I can see that she's fragile, deep down inside, even though she makes out that she's as hard as nails. "You decide when you want me to come along."

"I'll think about it."

I wish it wasn't night school she wanted me to accompany her to. I wish it were something else. Dinner at a restaurant, or even coffee at any place but the diner. A good old-fashioned getting-to-know-you date.

I feel as if I know Elias and Harper better than I know this woman.

"I'll have a think," she says, walking towards the door.

"Do that." I wish she'd hang around and talk some more, but I feel as if our previous interactions have been more jovial. I'm scared that me asking her any questions will push her away.

Her visit has already lifted my mood. She walks away, leaving me smiling to myself. She turns and catches me grinning like a fool. "What?" she asks.

"Nothing."

"What?"

"I wasn't expecting this..." I pause trying to find the right word, but it's almost impossible because I don't even know what how to explain it. "You're being so ..."

"Different?" she offers.

"Nice?" I guess, and I wonder if this thaw in her demeanor has anything to do with what I told her about Ben. I want to ask her what changed, but I don't want to push her away. She's given me a little leeway, and I don't want to mess things up. I don't have long left here, and it's taken me this long to get to this stage with Nina. I don't know where we'll be by the time my stay here ends. Life is a rollercoaster with her, and I'm willing to let her take me along with her for the ride.

"You're not as bad as I made you out to be."

I snort in surprise.

She turns back around and pulls the door open while I'm still trying to decipher what she's said. Why did she ever think I was bad? I've never done anything to her that might make her think that about me. Her words confuse me, but I let it slide, for now.

"Oh, and another thing," she says, turning around again. "I ran into Dottie on the way in, and I asked her about the security passes. She says it doesn't matter who turns up. The passes aren't a problem."

She's caught me red-handed.

I can only flash her the smile that usually makes women forget whatever it was they were asking me. It's my get out card for tricky situations. Only, it probably doesn't work on Nina. "You lied to me," she accuses, but she's smiling, so it can't be all that bad.

I stand up. "It was a little white lie."

"Back when you wanted to get to know me on account of Elias?"

I throw my hands up in defeat. "You've seen right through me."

She hovers by the open door. "Do we have to continue with this lunch thing?" Her tone indicates that she doesn't like it.

"You mean delivering my lunch here?" Technically no. We don't have to continue with this, not if she's allowing me to go with her to night school, not if we're at the stage now where she's picking out what disguise I have to wear.

"Unless Joni or someone else can do it?" she suggests.

What would be the point of that? I frown, and she picks up on it.

"So, it was a set up?"

She's right. It was, but the reasons for it changed somewhere along the way. I don't tell her that though, because we are always taking one step forward and twenty steps back. "I like the milkshakes and your waitress friend is so needy, I figured it was easier to get you to come." I slip my hands into the back pockets of my jeans. "Don't forget, you get to pick my disguise."

She shakes her head without turning around, and then she disappears out of my sight.

CHAPTER THIRTY-THREE

NINA

I awaken with a start. I dreamt I was back at Grampton House. Every time I am reminded of that place I feel as dirty as when I lived there.

Some stains never fade.

It's cold, and it's takes me a few moments to fumble around and switch on my lamp. I sit up and shiver, and rub my arms. The shift at work was so hectic and I couldn't wait to get home and when I did I promised myself that I would lie on the couch for a few moments. But I fell asleep. Now it's nine in the evening and I'm still in my waitress's outfit. And I'm hungry and cold.

I get up and put on a thick cardigan, then put on the central heating. And still I shiver.

I wash my hands then open the cabinet. I open the cupboard door and stare at it. My fingers tremble with anticipation. I could slice into my skin with this and I would feel so much better. The razor blade lies on a small shelf, teasing me. It's been my go-to after bad days at work, on nights I couldn't sleep, after run-ins with Rhys.

I've often wondered if it's written on my face, that I am weak. If there's a note on my forehead that says I can be used.

Just as I go to pick it up, my phone rings, and I pull it out of my back pocket. An involuntary smile flickers across my lips when I see who's calling.

"Did you pick something for me?"

I roll my lips together in an attempt to stop myself from smiling. I had a feeling he might call. I've been thinking about our little conversation, and him wanting me to suggest a disguise for him. I was hoping he would forget and things would slowly peter away.

Surely his filming days are almost at an end? I don't answer, but I hold the phone to my ear, somehow reassured by the sound of his voice.

The silence rolls on.

"Nina?"

"Yeah?"

"The disguise ... you were going to call me."

I hadn't given it any more thought. I mean. I *had*. I had wondered what to suggest for him. A long-haired blonde wig, hippie style, but since he sometimes doesn't bother shaving, and has a dusting of dark hairs across his jaw, the blonde hair would look odd. But who am I kidding? Where is this going to lead? What is the point? It was easier before, when he was using me to find a route to Elias. This is ... this is something I can't deal with.

"You weren't going to call me, were you?" he asks, guessing correctly.

I wasn't. I talked myself out of it each time I started to.

But I should have known Callum better than that. He's a persistent guy.

I stare at the blade. My past drags me to it, and now I have Callum at the end of a phone, offering me a different future, a way out.

I could cut myself and feel better. Or I could give into Callum and lie some more, fake my way through this friendship, then push him away when he wants to get too close.

"I've been busy," I say finally.

"You don't have to go out and buy me anything. I've got an entire costume department at hand. Just tell me what you'd like to see me in."

Now he's put me on the spot and I can't think straight. "Uh..." I haven't given it any thought, and that's why I'm struggling.

"You were never going to call me back, were you?" He sounds more serious than I've ever heard him.

I let out a sigh. He meant this to be some sweet and sappy thing, but it's had the opposite effect on me. He is the one guy I haven't been able to push away. He will never understand why none of this is easy for me. I'm not like other women who would fall at his feet, swoon at his interest, go dizzy with delight at the attention he's giving.

Me? I can't let him get close to me, and yet, my heart seems to disagree with my brain.

"I tell you what. I'm going to surprise you. I'm going to walk into the diner and I bet you won't recognize me straight away."

"You're going to surprise me?" This sounds like a challenge, and one which I'm strangely up for.

"Seeing that you haven't picked anything out for me. You had three days, Nina."

"I was busy."

"Is that your excuse?" Maybe he knows me better than I think he does. "Do we have a deal?"

I can say 'No', but I'm curious, and because he's made me smile. "We have a deal."

"Good. I'll come by soon and surprise you."

I laugh.

"Did you just laugh?" He picks up on it lightning fast.

"It was a cough."

"Funny. It sounded like a laugh to me."

"I'm curious to see what you might transform into."

"You'll find out soon enough."

"Where are you coming? To the diner, or my place?"

"I'm going to surprise you."

"When?"

"Again, I'm going to surprise you."

My smile widens. Callum is like a tiny light, and I'm the moth drawn to it amid all the blackness.

"'Bye." He hangs up.

All these things he's been doing—the autograph, the ploy to get me to deliver food to his set, him turning up on my doorstep to see how I was—that kind of commitment deserves something more than a trip to my night school and back.

Elias said talking to Harper helped him. I can see why. Having someone who cares is like having a security blanket, someone to cushion the heavy blows that life can throw sometimes.

Callum isn't my security blanket, but he's the nicest thing I've had around lately. I begrudgingly accept that my daily trips to deliver his lunch were something I had started to enjoy. Enjoy is probably too strong a word for it. 'Look forward to' is more like it.

I close the cabinet door and turn my back to the blade. I don't want to be a slave to it. I don't want to wake up sweating, with my heart thumping like it's going to explode just because the janitor sneaked into my dreams and turned them into nightmares.

I want to get over him.

I want to get over my past.

I want to get better, so that I can move on.

This unlikely suitor might just be the perfect distraction for now.

CHAPTER THIRTY-FOUR

NINA

I regret taking Joni up on her offer. I want to go home. It's been another long day at the diner, but at least there's no night school tonight. I have another assignment I need to make a start on when I get back. Only problem is that Joni wants to go out for dinner. I have a feeling that she wants to talk. With things being a little cool between us, I agreed, even though I'm not in the mood.

"Table five." Joni rolls her eyes as she walks past me.

"I've almost finished my shift," I moan. "Can't you get one of the others to do it?"

"They're all busy and he was getting snappy." I glance over my shoulder and see why she's happy to let me have him. The guy is old, and bald, and so not her type. Nor mine. "Hurry up. I'll wait for you outside."

I go over and take the order, and I'm not surprised when he orders everything fried and doubled in portion. Surprisingly, he doesn't make any conversation. I usually get asked about Elias, but this guy seems preoccupied with his cell phone.

I hand his order to one of the cooks, and beg them to make his food first. This isn't allowed, skipping the line, but it's early evening, and I really want to finish my shift. I want to eat somewhere fast with Joni and go home. I'm also annoyed at myself for agreeing to go out with her. It's not like I owe her anything.

Checking the messages on my cell phone while I wait, I see that Harper's called me a few times. She's probably itching to know about my cab ride home with Callum. I keep hoping she'll forget, but she, like Callum, is persistent. She and Elias are heading towards the mountains soon so I hope she'll soon forget to dip her nose into my business and focus on my brother instead.

I circle back to the kitchen. "The order for Table four, is it ready yet?" I ask one of the chefs.

"Five minutes."

I hover around. Joni's already got her coat on and tells me she's going outside for a cigarette. "You're making us late."

I narrow my eyes at her. "I wouldn't have if you'd passed my last order off to someone else."

"He asked for you," she says, sliding past me. "This is what you get for having a famous brother."

I walk around the diner, refilling water glasses and coffee mugs, in order to avoid having to deal with any more new customers.

"Table four!" The cook passes me the customer's plate just as I return to the coffee station. This order consists of everything fried. I hate to think what this guy's arteries must look like.

"Your order, sir." I put the plate down in front of my

customer. He's still looking at his phone, and grunts in acknowledgement. "Is there anything else I can get for you?"

"Nah," he says, gruffly. I turn around to walk away when he says, "Well, maybe you can."

I recognize *that* voice.

I spin around. My eyes grow wider as I lower my head and peer closer.

Oh.

My.

God.

My mouth falls open.

Callum laughs. "I told you you wouldn't recognize me." Even as I stare at him, I can't see the man I know. "Callum? Is that really you?"

He's balding badly, with a combover, and wrinkles, and saggy, baggy eyes, and he has the skin of an old man. He has age spots and jowls, and a saggy neck and chin.

"I got you though, didn't I?" he cries, thumping the table in glee.

I slide into the seat opposite him because even after all this intense staring, I still don't see the Callum I know. I put my hands to my face. This is a work of art. "I didn't realize you were going to enlist the help of your entire makeup department."

"Not the entire department. Just two make up artists."

I shake my head. It's him, it's his voice, and those are his eyes, but the rest of him is not *him*. It's jarring, hearing his voice, looking at him but seeing someone completely different. An old, and out of shape man wearing ill-fitting clothes. His body is misshapen, and large, and bloaty. I marvel at the transformation. "How long did it take?"

"Long enough."

"Are you coming?" Joni comes over and taps her watch impatiently. Her questioning eyes bore into me and she's clearly wondering what the heck I'm doing sitting and talking to this man.

I'm torn. I really don't want to go out with her tonight. I would much rather prefer sitting here talking to Callum. Even Callum looking like *this*. I'm touched that he went to these lengths. He picks up a greasy fry and examines it.

"Just give me a few minutes," I beg Joni, waiting to see if she recognizes Callum.

"Hurry up," she hisses, then walks away again.

"She didn't know it was you," I say, as if this is a surprise.

"*You* didn't know it was me."

I prop my elbows on the table, and take him in. It is so very strange to see *him* and have him be completely different to what I'm used to.

"I told you I'd surprise you."

"You did that, alright." I sink back against the leather backrest and smile. "You really did take that as a challenge."

He pushes his plate away. "You gave up on me. You didn't even want to give me a chance."

He says this like it's a question, and of course, I will ignore it and not answer. It saves me lying more. "So, tell me about your transformation."

And he does. He tells me how he asked his make up artists for help. As I sit there and listen, I'm still amazed by the transformation. I'm aware that I'm talking to Callum, yet he is buried beneath this huge, hulking shell of a man I would never look at. He went to all that trouble. Again. *For me.*

I had been expecting him to come yesterday, on a day

when I had my night school class, that I was completely blindsided by his appearance today.

"Shooting took forever last night. We had a long, almost twenty hour, day. Otherwise I'd have come here. There's no way I would have missed going to night school with you looking like this. It would have been the highlight of my day."

I shake my head, because his sarcasm is so obvious, and because I find that idea funny.

"Since you don't have a class tonight, how about we ... hang out?" he suggests carefully.

"Hang out?" My hopes deflate as fast as they've risen. I'm supposed to be out with Joni tonight. She's not been the best friend to me, but I'm not so callous that I'd ditch her in a heartbeat in order to spend some time with Callum. "I'm sorry but I've got plans."

"Oh." He looks as disappointed as I feel.

"I would have otherwise."

"Would you have? Or are you just saying that?"

"I feel bad that you went to all this effort." I mean it.

"Some other time, then."

I nod. I hardly ever go out, and trust tonight to be the night Joni asks me to come out with her. Now I find myself wishing that I could have been free to go out with Callum instead—maybe because that option isn't open to me any longer. I get up slowly. "Some other time. Call me," I say, surprising myself with that comment.

CHAPTER THIRTY-FIVE

CALLUM

Maybe I should have come yesterday, at least I'd have had a chance to escort Nina to night school. I push my plate away, the small victory I felt at tricking her so perfectly disappears. That said, I think she's warming towards me. Lately, we've been getting on much better. I guess I'm disappointed that she has other plans because I was sure we could have spent a nice evening together. Not doing the kind of stuff I'm used to doing with a woman I like, but something simpler, something that Nina would feel comfortable with. She used to always be so defensive, so angry and irritated whenever I was around. I'll take this new and improved level of our acquaintanceship.

I settle the bill and get up to leave when Frankie comes over. She asks if there was a problem with the food. "Uh, no, not really. I wasn't hungry."

She looks at me for a long time, as if she's trying to figure me out. "Callum?"

I nod my head and grin. "Clever woman."

She roars with laughter, then peers closer at me. "Unbelievable."

"I had a bet with Nina."

"I hope you weren't trying to impress her."

"I don't think she's easily impressed."

Frankie makes a disapproving sound. "She's not easy to work on, but that look is *definitely* not going to help you to impress her."

"This isn't the type of new man I'd aspire to be. I'm surprised you figured out that it was me."

"Nina doesn't talk to many customers, much less sit across the table from them. Besides, your eyes gave it away." She looks me up and down in wonder. "It's a miracle."

"It's a miracle that the make up department is at my disposal."

She hangs her hands on her hips. "You did this for Nina?"

"I wanted to surprise her."

"Boy, you are full of surprises." She looks over my shoulder. "Seems like your trick worked. Good luck." Before I can work out what she's talking about, Nina appears in front of me. "Joni canceled on me."

I silently thank the lord.

"I've got no plans, so if you're still free, we could ... hang out?"

"I've got no plans." I'm about to shoot her one of my genuinely heartfelt smiles, but I rein myself back. "We could hang out."

"Are you going out like that?" she asks, looking me up and down.

It's going to take me a while to take all of this gloop off my face, and the fat body suit I'm wearing. But equally, if I keep this on, it's going to be uncomfortable. Unless we go outside, for a walk. The upside is that nobody will recognize me. "Yes, unless you have a problem being seen with an old guy."

"I don't have a problem."

We walk out, and I don't even need to look over to see if Frankie's staring at us. I can *feel* her stare on my back. She wished me 'Good Luck'. I shouldn't find it odd—given what I know of Nina, but it serves as a good reminder.

I don't suppose she'll want to go and get something to eat, and I'm not in a position to do that, wearing what I am. I suggest we do the Chicago Riverwalk and she seems fine with that.

This is the kind of walk I could never do but disguised the way I am, no one bats an eyelid. I love being anonymous. Invisible. People who crave fame don't realize the huge sacrifice it is that giving away your soul entails. In letting your fans think they have access to you whenever they see you, walking outside, eating at a restaurant, trying to sit in peaceful solitude on a park bench.

So this, tonight, is a gift for me, not only because no one recognizes me, but because I'm with Nina. "What happened with your friend? The one you were supposed to go out with?"

"She got tired of waiting."

"Was it me? Did I mess things up? She sounded irritated when she came over."

"I wouldn't worry about it. Joni's always like that. Her boyfriend called her, so she's gone running to him."

"It sounds like you don't like him."

"I don't."

I wait for her to tell me why, but she doesn't. Instead she says, "He's a bully. He doesn't treat her well."

"Why's she with him?"

"You tell me. Anyway, we didn't come out to talk about my friend."

"No, we didn't."

We walk along and talk about my shooting, and she tells me more about her interior design course. The conversation soon switches to Elias and Harper, and then she's curious to know how I got the autograph from Leanne.

We talk in a way we have never talked before, for longer than we have ever talked before, and it feels nice. It feels easy.

There are plenty of picturesque spots along the way, and I can actually take them in slowly, and savor them, in a way I couldn't have undisguised. So much of my being outdoors, as *me,* is about rushing in and out of vehicles, or having a herd of photographers on my back. Or bodyguards in tow, if it's a public event. This rarely happens. People look past me and enjoy the evening. It's slightly chilly, but there is plenty of light coming off the numerous cafes and restaurants. A few live music performers are brave enough to perform outside. We walk over many bridges, admiring the many pieces of sculpture on display. We walk among families who have probably come from abroad, tourists enjoying the view, just like us, and lovers meandering hand-in-hand.

"Remember the last time we were out on the streets of Chicago?" I ask her.

"How could I forget."

"I bet you never thought you'd be going out with me like this."

"You said you wanted a friend, Callum." She startles me with that. It's as if she's making it clear what this is, what *we* are.

"I do." But equally, I wonder why she pushes back so much. I have never experienced such non-interest from a woman before. And it grates on me because I like her. My charm just doesn't work on her. I don't have any indecent intentions. I'm not the kind of guy who's going to stalk her and demand she goes out with me. That's not who I am.

But her reluctance for anything to happen, makes me curious. It's not that I can't take 'no' for an answer, it's that sometimes I catch a whisper of interest in her voice. Sometimes, I'll see a flicker of attraction in the way she's looking at me, in how her eyes settle on my lips, before she looks away. It's like a game of emotional tennis, we volley our emotions back and forth and keep the ball up in the air. This is why Nina captivated me, because she's unlike any woman I've ever met. "Why did you feel the need to remind me of that?"

"I'd hate for you to think this could be anything more."

I want to reassure her. I'm not the type of guy who would do anything untoward. "That wasn't a line, by the way." I need her to know that.

She looks at me, as if she can't work out whether I'm lying or telling the truth. "This is a nicer walk than going to my night school."

"I'm glad I came today and not yesterday. Then I would have ended up talking to that security guard in the lobby again."

"You know when my classes are?" She looks worried.

"I pay attention when you say something, Nina."

"Oh."

"I'm not stalking you, I swear."

"It would be the other way around, surely. Have you ever been stalked by a fan?"

"Not yet."

She laughs. "Must be scary."

"Unwanted attention is, yes."

"Are you hungry? You didn't eat much at the diner."

"That's not the type of food I like to eat."

"So you were in character today?" she asks, surprised.

"Of course. When I play a role, I get into character. You must be hungry, since you've only just come off your shift."

"I'm starving."

"We should get something to eat." I hold up my hands. "As good friends, not as a date or anything."

"Of course," she answers easily.

"Done." Even though it's going to be uncomfortable for me to sit down and eat, I'm looking forward to more time with it being just me and her. I suggest we sit outside. There are plenty of such places along the river. I'll be uncomfortable in my outfit, but it's worth it for this chance.

We find a place that looks half empty. It's cold outside, which explains it, but there are heaters. We order and talk some more. She tells me about how her day at the diner went, and about the different types of customers she encountered there today. And I tell her what happens next once we finish shooting the film.

Soon the conversation comes around to Ben again. I tell her about him, about his laugh which would fill the house, about the petty fights we'd get into over sports. I tell her the bits about him that come to me. Everything about him is preserved back at mom and dad's house. His bedroom is untouched. Mom won't let anyone lay a hand on it. His clothes are still in the closets, all his posters are still up on the walls. She dusts and cleans it regularly. I go in there sometimes, when I go back home to see them both.

Time has frozen in that bedroom, but all my memories about Ben are still as fluid and as colourful as ever.

"That must have been a huge shock for your family."

"It's like our whole world changed. The life we knew disappeared. We were broken. It must have been really hard on my parents, losing a kid." My voice breaks, and I clear my throat to keep it together. Nina puts her hand over mine. It shocks me like ice water thrown over my head, and then, I get used to the warmth of her skin over mine.

We've been not-flirting all evening, we've not touched hands accidentally, or bumped into one another, or given one another those long, lingering looks. It's never happened to me before, that I can be friends with someone I am attracted to, I'm not sure I can with her. The depth of my attraction for Nina has crept up on me like a climbing vine, twisting its way around me and ensnaring me. She has no idea how I feel. Worse, she's made it crystal clear that she wants us to stay as we are, nothing more than friends.

CHAPTER THIRTY-SIX

NINA

Joni avoids me the next day. She can be so childish sometimes, but now it irritates me more than ever. I don't have my usual patience for her, so I leave her to sulk alone.

I have nicer things to think about for a change. I rewind and replay my evening with Callum. We ordered dessert and coffee after dinner and talked long into the night.

I never knew I could talk for so long, or that I had so much to say to someone I barely know. Only, Callum is no longer someone I barely know. He's become a friend, this man who is so far away from my norm, and now he's fast becoming one of the people I look forward to seeing the most.

We agreed to meet up again. I'm probably going to go to his suite for dinner—he explained that he doesn't like eating out unless he's in disguise, and he didn't want to be in disguise all the time. It was either he come to my place, or I go to his. Going to his place works better because I can leave when I want.

He said he would call me when he was next free. We have agreed on no more night school for him, and no more delivering lunches to his trailer for me. Our daily interactions are gone, but it feels like something deeper, something more fulfilling might be blossoming instead.

"What are you looking so happy about?" Frankie asks.

"Can't I look happy?"

"You can, and you should, but it's rare. I like it."

My smile soon slips when I see Rhys. To my surprise, Joni doesn't run to him like a puppy. I avoid walking past his table, because I don't want to wait on him either.

Unfortunately, I forget to take a detour away from his table when I head back to the coffee machine to fetch a fresh pot of coffee.

"Did you put her up to it?" he snarls, grabbing my arm with his pincer-like fingers.

I frown in confusion. "What?"

"Don't pretend you don't know what I'm talking about."

I yank my arm away. "I don't know what you're talking about."

"She dumped me. The goddamn bitch dumped me."

Joni found the courage to split with this douchebag? My heart swells with pride. "That's the best news I've heard all day."

Something close to hate flashes across his face but is just as quickly replaced by a smug sneer. "The offer still stands," he says, his voice dropping dangerously low. "If you ever get lonely."

"I wouldn't come anywhere near you even if you were the last man standing." I spin on my heels and march off, almost colliding into Harper. It's a good thing that the coffee pot in my hand is empty otherwise I would have spilled it on her.

"You're impossible to get a hold of," she cries.

"I'm sorry. I meant to call you back." I know what she wants to hear. "Take a seat. I need to refill this." I refill my jug and go back to the tables I was waiting on, refilling all their coffee mugs, and then I slide over to the table where Harper is sitting. "Have you ordered?" I assume she's here to get the usual takeout for my brother.

"I have. Now, tell me what you've been up to. I came by this morning and Frankie says Callum turned up here in disguise last night."

"I didn't realize she was reporting my every move," I mutter.

"She said you both went out. Now I get why you're not answering my calls."

I tuck a lock of hair behind my ear and huff out a breath. "Aren't you supposed to be packing to leave for Elias's training?"

"That's the other reason I came by." She sits forward excitedly. "Eli's leaving in a few days' time, and I'm going at the weekend. Why don't you come along?" Her eyes glitter with mischief. "You *and* Callum could both come."

"He said he couldn't get any time off."

"He was probably just being polite."

"Or he was telling the truth," I reply. That night was a fraught one. There was so much tension in the air that I could have cut it with a knife and spread it.

Harper is like a pit bull with a juicy bone, she's not about to let go of this. "He's hardly going to jump to accept an invite from Elias, but if *you* ask him, he might ... "

Just as I'm about to dismiss the idea automatically, it sinks into my brain and I start thinking.

I *could* ask him.

Why would *I* do that?

A rush of heat spreads down my belly. Makes my heart flutter. What if I did ask him? Would his answer be any different?

But what would he take it to mean?

"You want me to ask Callum?" It's all I manage to say, as my brain whirls at full speed with the many possible ideas and outcomes. I feel excited in a way I haven't for a long time. My heart even skips a beat or three. I picture Callum and me going for walks in the mountains. Elias and Harper have said it's beautiful. I look up and see Rhys staring at me from across the tables. He winks, and I jolt, as if he's fired a crossbow at me.

This could be the break I need. Time away from here. From jerks like Rhys. From everything.

"I don't believe it!" Harper's fingers dance on the table. "You're actually thinking about it."

I seem to be. This is odd, because I would never do this. How have I gone from avoiding him, to going on the Chicago Riverwalk and having dinner, to thinking about *this?*

Harper sticks her neck forward and gapes at me. "You're seeing him, aren't you?"

I shake my head. Harper's idea of 'seeing someone' is very different to mine. I have a feeling that most women's version of seeing' someone is vastly different to mine. "We're just friends."

"That's how these things start. Me and Elias were *just* friends," she points out.

"Elias hated you," I remind her.

"And look where we are now."

Blissfully in love.

I swallow.

"Think about it," she tells me, as her cell phone rings. "Your brother's getting impatient. I should go. Think about it," she says again.

"I will." Elias turns into a monster the closer a fight gets. He turns inwards, and goes super quiet too, but it's not a calm rage. More like a volcano simmering and about to erupt at any moment.

Going to the mountains will be different. It could even be fun. And if Callum comes along, it could be so much more.

CHAPTER THIRTY-SEVEN

CALLUM

When I finally get a free evening, I call Nina over. I've prepared myself for her to decline the invite, because even though things are moving along nicely when we're together, I sense that it's when we're apart that she backtracks on everything and closes off towards me.

So, when she accepts my offer to come to my place and have dinner with me, I'm blown away.

I tidy up, get Dottie to get me some menus from some of the best restaurants in the city, and then I wait.

She turns up dead on eight o'clock. My hands feel clammy—something I've not experienced since my teens. This isn't even a normal date. There will be no first kiss, no touching, no holding hands.

Why am I so nervous? Who gets together with someone they've recently met—someone they have developed feelings for—just for dinner, and nothing else and no chance of it going any further? It's safe to say that Nina Cardoza has tested the limits of my patience. My curiosity has made me take these labyrinthine turns in a situation that is as unfamiliar.

I open the door with a beaming smile, that hides my nervousness. She's holding a bouquet of flowers. "I didn't know what to get you," she says, walking in and handing them to me.

I quirk a brow. Shouldn't I be the one to buy her flowers?

No, because she would take it to mean something.

"You didn't need to bring anything but thank you." They're in a bag of water. I'll get Dottie to put them in a proper vase later. Heck, I might even do that myself. Still, I marvel at Nina's thoughtfulness. She seems anything but nervous, and her sudden change in temperament throws me, because I'm the one who's feeling anxious while she's as cool as ice.

"This place is awesome." She looks around and does a complete three hundred and sixty degree turn, taking in the entire room. "This room is bigger than my apartment." This suite is huge, I don't deny that.

"Yeah?" I feel embarrassed by the opulence. I'm just one guy and looking at this sprawling living space with a balcony, it suddenly seems wrong that I have this all to myself.

We're standing in a huge room that doubles as my living room and eating area. The front facing side is a wall of windows, with two glass doors which open up onto a huge balcony which I've never stepped out onto.

"It's cheaper than me renting an apartment, and it's easier security-wise. I pretty much stay in my room, or I'm on the set."

"Or you're at the diner."

"Or there. I like their shakes."

She smiles, knowingly.

"Hungry?" I ask her and pick up the small stash of menus and hold them out like a fan, ready for her to pick one.

"A little."

"Take a look and let me know what you want."

"So much choice," she squeals, and rifles through the menus. "What do you like?"

"Frankie's food."

"We could get a takeout from there," she suggests.

"And risk your friend Joni bringing it over? No thanks."

We settle on Japanese food, and I order.

"You have a lovely place," she comments, walking around the room. "Sorry to keep going on about it."

"Thanks, but please don't apologize." It *is* nice, now that I take a moment and look at it. I've taken it for granted, just like I take most of the things in my life for granted. I would show her around, but I don't want her to think that there's a reason I'm showing her the bedrooms. So, I refrain from making the offer.

"Is that a balcony?" She stares at the floor-to-ceiling glass doors that open out to the balcony.

"I can show you around after dinner." Apparently, it has a beautiful view, according to Dottie, and out there, we can talk without her getting uneasy in case she thinks I'm planning any moves. I'm not. I'm happy that she's here. After all of our earlier interactions, who would have thought Nina Cardoza would ever come over to my place to have dinner with me?

I pour her some wine, and we talk.

She tells me that Harper came to see her, and that she and Elias are heading to the mountains soon. "My brother's going for a couple of weeks, for some intense training before the big fight, but Harper's going for a weekend, and—"

There's a knock on the door. "That was fast." It's the food delivery. I let the guy in, tip him, and then Nina comes over and takes the bags.

"Here?" she asks, putting everything on the main table. I nod. We've ordered tons. "This is too much," she says.

"You said you were hungry."

We sit down across the table from one another, with the flowers she brought for me at the center. I refill our glasses, and we eat. In silence at first. The food is phenomenal, and I can see that Nina loves it. I recall that night at Elias's house when she pushed the food around on her plate. This is nothing like that. She is nothing like she was that evening. This is a different Nina, with a big appetite; a Nina who talks and eats and seems very relaxed. A complete opposite to how she was that night at Elias's place.

It could also be that I won't talk about the things I know she hates. I won't bring up her past, or what happened to Elias, or any of that. I won't even talk about us, because I don't know if there will be an us. It's up to her.

I play it safe, so that she feels safe.

In fact, it's enough for me to watch her devour the food which she seems to be enjoying.

After dinner, we both go outside on the balcony. She walks around, surveying the terracotta pots and the plants and flowers inside them. "It's pretty."

"I haven't been out here," I confess, sheepishly.

Her jaw drops. "You have all this, and you haven't even been out. How long have you been here?"

"Long enough." It's shameful.

"This is wasted on you," she cries, touching the bright red petals of the flowers in a pot.

"Then it's a good thing you're here to appreciate all of this."

"I would kill to have something like this on my doorstep. I don't even have a yard. You're so lucky."

She's right. There are potted plants and flowers all around, and the lights have come on. I'm seeing them all for the first time. The whole of the balcony area looks so pretty, that even I am taken aback.

The air is cool, and it's quiet up here. I look down at the sea of lights spread out before us.

"Why have you never come out here?"

"I didn't have anyone to enjoy the view with." The words escape my lips before I get a chance to stop them.

"It's wasted on you." She deftly ignores it.

Coming out here to enjoy the view is nowhere on my list of important things to do, but watching Nina enjoy it gives me a sense of satisfaction. "I get in from filming, and there's nothing to do but shower, eat, and look over the next day's lines." I tell her.

"Or go to the diner in full makeup in order to deceive."

"Deceive?" I cry out in mock exaggeration. "I wasn't trying to deceive you, Nina. I told you I'd be coming in disguise. I just didn't say when."

"Maybe deceive is the wrong word. I'm pleased you did that."

"I'm pleased you came here."

She looks away, and I feel bad that I might have ruined the moment, changed the mood of the evening without meaning to. "I'm not looking for a girlfriend, Nina. I'm looking for a friend." I'm not entirely sure I mean that, but if it will make her continue talking to me, then that's what I have to say.

"That's a relief," she answers, "Because I'm not girlfriend material."

It shocks me how much this woman seems not to like herself. How she doesn't value who she is, or what she means to others. She's vulnerable, and soft, yet hard all at once. She is many things all wrapped up in different layers, like those little Russian dolls. "Why do you say that?"

She seems to be contemplating her answer, and her gaze lands somewhere in the distance. "Because I'm not."

"But the reason?" I press.

She rolls her eyes and looks away. It's obvious that she doesn't want to talk about it, and that this is her pushing me away again.

"You were telling me about Harper and your brother going to the mountains, before the food delivery came."

"He's going to Dwayne Bank's place where he went last year. Harper's going at the weekend and she asked me if I'd like to come."

"And are you?" From what I can tell, Nina only ever works, or goes to night school or does her assignments. Her friendship with Joni sounds flaky. It doesn't seem that she has much going on, or lets many people in. "It will be good for you."

"She also asked if you'd like to come along?"

"*Me?*" I'm so shocked by her suggestion that I almost turn to look around behind me. "Me?" I ask again.

"Harper suggested it. It wasn't my idea."

I frown, unsure if she's saying that because she feels a duty to pass on Harper's message or because she doesn't want me to come along. "It's not a date or anything," she adds.

"I didn't think of it as anything like that." But still, I'm shocked that she'd even ask me.

"Harper thinks you'd get to see more of what my brother does when he's working out, and ... and ... it would be a break for you, if you're looking to take a break."

She shrugs. "I could do with a break." She says this so quietly that I'm sure she didn't mean for me to hear it. But I did hear it.

"From what?" I ask quietly.

"What?"

"You said you needed to take a break."

"From the diner, and people." She goes quiet as she looks over the balcony.

"Dwayne Bank's place in the mountains," I say to myself. I'm considering it. It seems like it could be the perfect break for us both. "When?"

"Next weekend. I mean, I know it's short notice, but they did ask you last time, and Harper reminded me to ask you again."

"Next weekend?" My heart drops. Dottie reminded me yesterday about Alyssa's film premiere again.

She reads my reaction. "You can't make it?" Now she sounds disappointed. And I love that she does.

Maybe, just *maybe*, Nina sounds a little disappointed. "I have a film premiere I have to attend."

"Oh."

I wrap my hands over the balustrade of the balcony, and stare at the view of the city spread out before me like a jewel studded carpet. It's dark now, and the tiny twinkling city lights glow like a thousand fireflies over the city. It's breathtaking, and serene, and beautiful, and it's insane that I haven't been out here before. I'm also glad I'm out here for the first time to enjoy it with Nina. "I can't get out of it."

It's a secret. An industry secret. This fabricated

romance between me and my co-star Alyssa Watts. I need to tell Nina before she hears about it from someone else.

"That's a shame," she says, before I can say a word. "Harper was looking forward to it."

"Harper?" I stare into Nina's eyes. They're dark, and under the night sky, they sparkle like onyx. I can't decipher her expression though. I can't tell if she's disappointed, or relieved.

"She's a huge fan of yours."

"Why are we talking about Harper?" I ask. I want to talk about us. I want to know what Nina feels. I want to know *if* she feels anything for me. Or is this in my head? I never get it wrong, but I can't read her. I can't tell with her. "You could still go, though," I say. "If you want a break, and you need to get away."

"And feel like a gooseberry," she replies, looking out. The disappointment in her voice is hard to miss. My spirits start to soar, because it sounds like she kind of wanted me to come along with her.

I get it.

It would be safe, with Harper and Elias. It wouldn't be a getaway just for the two of us. I sense that would frighten her. And then I have an idea. It's crazy, and wild, and completely spontaneous, but I trust my instincts, and the worst that can happen is she could say 'no'.

But it would give me an inkling of how she feels.

"You could come with me to LA, to the film premiere."

She turns at me in surprise.

"I have to attend this event. It's with my co-star, Alyssa Watts, so it's not as if you're going to be linked with me, if that's what you're afraid of. But if you need a break, why don't you come along, anyway? Dottie will be there."

The fact that she doesn't say 'No' straightaway is a good

sign. She's thinking about it. I hazard a guess that mentioning my co-star, and Dottie being there are two pieces of information that might just sway her decision.

"What would people think?"

Good question. I have no idea what Dottie or Rudy might think, and I don't care. Dottie would ask questions worthy of the FBI, and Rudy won't be too happy. But the fact that Nina is asking me *that* question, instead of hitting me with a big fat 'No', is a good sign. Heck, it's a great sign. "Leave that to me."

Alyssa and I aren't real, but Nina and me, we could be, if she wants. "If it wasn't for the film premiere, I'd have gone to the mountains with you, but this is a contractual obligation I have to fulfil. I can't back out. If you want to come along, then come."

She's still mulling it over. I'm not used to women taking so long to consider their answer, not when it comes to something like this, a weekend away with me, but this time there will be no sexy interludes.

I'm okay with that. Nina isn't the type of woman to be interested in something like that.

"It would be a new experience," she says slowly. "And I've never been to a film premiere."

"I'll be with my co-star," I tell her quickly. "She'll be on my arm, and all that." It's on the tip of my tongue to tell her about the fake romance, but I need more signs from her that it would matter.

"That's okay," she murmurs, surprising me again. Most women I know would have asked me a whole heap of other questions. "You and Dottie could hang out during the premiere. I can get tickets, don't worry about that."

"It would be a weekend away," says Nina, as if she's slowly thinking about it. "And you'll be with your co-star."

I hate it when she says that. It's almost as if she's coming because she thinks I'm a safe bet. I won't do anything. I won't. I don't even know why I offered this.

"I've read some stuff in the papers, well, Joni did, and she showed me."

"What stuff?"

"About you and your co-star."

What am I supposed to say? I nod.

"I guess that must happen a lot, in show business?" she asks.

I scratch the back of my neck. "That's show business." How unreal is this conversation?

"Were you and Leanne Rose ever ... ?"

All of a sudden she wants to know about my love life. Well, this is weird. "No. Me and Leanne were just friends. Her mom got sick and passed away, and she was heartbroken. I was there for her."

We gaze at the glittering view, wrapped in a seal of silence.

"Just a weekend?" she asks, after a while.

"Just a weekend."

"Can I think about it?"

"Take all the time you need."

CHAPTER THIRTY-EIGHT

NINA

It's the most spontaneous thing I've done. Butterflies kiss the insides of my stomach each time I think about it. Going to LA with Callum Sandersby? Me? How did I ever allow myself to consider such a thing?

It's only when I get home after such a lovely evening, when I'm alone with my thoughts, that I start to have doubts.

It was all well and good, taking the leap, telling Callum I'd go with him, while I was standing on his beautiful hotel balcony, seeing the lights of Chicago spread out before us like a million stars in the galaxy.

But here, in the stark reality of my apartment, I'm scared that he'll think I want more.

What will it mean, me going with him?

He's not going with you.

He has a date. He's going with his co-star, I remind myself. It's part of the reason why I considered it. I have read the papers. I have looked him up online. I know there's gossip about him and his co-star. I'm not sure I believe it though. He didn't say much about it when I asked him.

Callum knows me, he knows me better than I give him credit for. This isn't a sleazy weekend away. This is us two being friends.

I pick up the phone and call the only person I can talk to about this.

"Are you alone?" It's late at night, and I know the answer already. Harper's probably with my brother.

"I am now." I hear a door shutting.

"I'm going to a film premiere in LA with Callum."

"Oh my god," her voice is breathless. "Tell me more."

"You can't tell Elias, he's so protective, and there's nothing going on."

"What do you mean there's nothing going on. You're going away with Callum Sandersby."

I put her straight, and tell her about our evening, and that I'd asked him to come to the mountains, but he couldn't, and how he invited me to go to the premiere instead. I tell her there is no romance, and that we're friends, and we're going in a group. "It's not what you think," I insist.

"Are you going to be on the red carpet?"

The idea stabs me like a knife to my chest. "No way. I'm hiding in the shadows. He'll be with his co-star, for the publicity—"

"You need a dress. You need shoes. You need accessories. And sexy lingerie."

"Harper! It's not like that." But her words set my heart racing. What am I letting myself in for?

"Come over, and we'll go shopping. You're going on a date with the biggest hunk in Hollywood."

"I'm not going with him, and this isn't a date," I insist. Trust her to see it like that when I don't see him like that at all. He's just a normal guy to me. Is it because of how we first met, in that alleyway, with him getting beaten up? I've never seen him as a superstar.

"I am going with his personal assistant." I set the record straight. "And he's going with his co-star."

"You need underwear. *Sexy* underwear. And heels. Sexy, fuck-me heels."

"This isn't that kind of weekend." But it doesn't matter, because she has selective hearing and she chooses not to hear me.

CALLUM

"The girl who's been bringing your lunch?" Dottie's mouth falls open. "You know you're supposed to be hopelessly in love with Alyssa?"

"Nina is a friend. She's Elias's sister. She invited me to the mountains, where Elias is training, but I can't go."

Whatever. I can't believe I'm having to justify Nina coming along with me to my personal assistant. "Just make sure her name is down on the list, so she can actually get into the theater."

"Does Rudy know?"

I exhale slowly, because he's going to be harder to break this to. I'm an A-list actor, and who I take along with me shouldn't be so goddamn hard, but this whole cloud of PR surrounds me wherever I go, whatever I do, and the studio has banked millions on my latest film. Even though we're not starting the whole crazy merry-go-round of post-film publicity until later, I still have to be mindful of who I'm seen out with.

"Don't worry about Rudy. I'll speak to him."

"And how is she getting there?"

I smile at Dottie sweetly. "With you. You're both spending the weekend together. You've seen her enough times at my trailer, delivering lunch."

Dottie sighs out loudly. "So you want me to get her flight and hotel tickets?"

"Book the hotel. Separate rooms. Don't worry about the flight. She'll probably want to do that herself."

Dottie raises both eyebrows as if I'm asking something big of her. "Okay, whatever you say."

I call Rudy next, and manage to get through his barrage of questions. He reminds me numerous times that Alyssa and I have a budding romance in the pipeline. I do my best to soothe his worries. "There's nothing going on with this girl."

"Then if there's nothing going on, why are you taking her?"

"She's a good friend. She's Elias Cardoza's sister. Think of the buzz this could create for the film."

"Are you fucking her?"

I grind down on my molars. I hate his pointed questions, but more than that, I hate the use of that word, especially when he's referring to Nina.

"No. She's just a friend."

"Since when have you been '*just* friends' with a woman you've met while filming? You don't have time for jack, so either you're lying, or you're desperate to get a ticket to the Cardoza fight."

"That's obviously it. It's impossible to get tickets." I hate having to explain myself to him and I hate having to label what Nina is. How is it that I'm this big Hollywood star and I still have to deal with these stupid little romance problems?

Rudy sounds pissed. His voice is tight. I can imagine those shrivelled little eyes of his getting even narrower as he imagines a publicity clusterfuck. "You have a contract, Callum."

"And I will honor it."

CHAPTER THIRTY-NINE

NINA

"This one," Dottie says, picking up Harper's short and sexy black number off the bed. "Actually, no. *This* one." She picks up another of Harper's dresses which I've laid out on my hotel bed. The one she likes is off-the-shoulder.

The only problem is that it's bright red, my least favorite color. Harper insisted I take it when I couldn't find the time to go shopping with her. Even now, I can guess that she's worried I don't have any sexy lingerie. I don't own sexy lingerie, and I will never make her understand that this trip is the last place I will need it.

"Isn't that too bright? Too noticeable? Aren't I supposed to be hidden in the shadows?"

"Don't worry, you won't outshine Alyssa. We're not going to be on the red carpet. We're entering through a side door, and we're going to be sitting at the back. We definitely won't be seen by the cameras."

"It's so bright," I lament.

"This might be the only time you get to go to something like this, make the most of it." Dottie and Harper are so similar, it's eerie.

Everything has happened so fast that this still feels like a dream to me. I'm grateful that Harper lent me a few of her dresses, and it's a good thing she made me take more dresses than I would have if I'd been left to my own devices. Most of them I would never even have considered, except that I'm wearing one of them now.

Callum's personal assistant has been super friendly and nice to me, which helps, because he told me to stick with her and I do.

Like chewing gum.

I don't know anyone here apart from him. I'm out of my depth. This is as far from the diner and my normal life as it can be.

It helps that I've met Dottie on a few occasions before. It helps that she's my age and she's likeable. I don't know her, but so far, she seems nice enough. Our hotel rooms are next door to one another, and apparently Callum is on the next floor up, in the fancier apartments.

I can't imagine him being anywhere else.

I end up wearing the bright red look-at-me dress. It's a little loose on me, but I don't mind that. In fact, I'm grateful for it. I would hate for it to be like a second skin, which is how it must fit Harper.

I follow Dottie around. We came on separate flights, and I've tried to pay her back for the hotel room, but she won't hear of it.

I haven't seen Callum since I arrived here this morning. He arrived here yesterday, and he called me before I flew out, to ask me if I was okay.

I am okay. Surprisingly, I'm better than okay. I'm not in my apartment, and there's no temptation of the blade, since I purposely left it behind.

Without trying too hard, I can put my normal life behind me and pretend to be a different me.

I can discard the old Nina.

I can pretend to be someone else.

I can pretend that this weekend is an adventure, because my life has been anything but that.

I can live a little.

"I'm going to get ready," says Dottie, walking away. "You should, too. I'll come by in an hour."

I do something which is alien to me, taking time to make myself look nice. I put on a face pack and paint my nails, then I take a shower. With my hair freshly washed, I take time blow drying it carefully, and then I apply my makeup slowly.

When I put on the dress and look in the mirror, I'm pleasantly surprised.

Okay, I lied.

I more than surprised.

I am astonished.

I twirl around, admiring my front, back and side views, and I pout and make silly faces at my reflection.

Who am I kidding?

I look fabulous.

Like a new woman.

My alter ego.

I take a selfie so that I can show Harper, but before I can send it, there's a knock on my door. It's not even been half an hour.

I open the door to find Callum standing there all dressed up in a tux. He is punch-to-the-gut gorgeousness.

His skin glows, his eyes glitter, and his smile—it seems to be speaking directly to my heart.

My mouth falls open.

A sigh might even have escaped my lips.

I forget to swallow.

And then I notice *his* reaction. He looks me up and down. It's the first time he's ever done that, and there's something in his gaze that I haven't seen before, amusement, or surprise, or something else, I can't work out what. His gaze burns through me. Goosebumps spring up along my bare arms. I fold my arms together, realizing that I've forgotten to put on my big chunky bracelet, and my watch. I couldn't cover up my scars, and Harper wouldn't let me take a dress with long sleeves, so, I had to cover up some other way.

Callum's lips part and it looks like he's about to say "Wow." But he doesn't. "I-uh...I uh... " He looks at the floor and ruffles his hair at the same time. "I uh... so you got here okay?"

I giggle. "Yes."

I open the door wider and tell him to come in. Callum being tongue-tied is something new to me. It suddenly feels as if I have power over him, that the way I'm dressed has rendered him speechless.

"Cool." He nods, and gives me another slow gaze that travels down the length of me. A burst of excitement crashes through me. Have his eyes always been so shiny? Have they always been such a dark green?

His tux is slick, rich black satin and crisp white shirt. Wide-shouldered, yet tapering in slightly at the waist. It's like he stepped out of a magazine and into my hotel room.

"This is a nice room," I say, biting my lip. This feels strange, me and him. Both of us dressed up like this. Maybe we can both pretend to be a different version of our usual selves?

"Dottie won't let me pay her back."

He scratches his nose, and glances at my feet. My sandals have thin, five-inch heels. I had to walk around in my hotel room to get used to them. There's a thin strap going around the ankles which makes them look extra strappy. Harper was going to lend me hers, but she's a bigger size than me and they didn't fit. I would have left it at that, but the minx went ahead and ordered me a pair. I was annoyed at first, but now I am so, so, so happy and thankful that she did. I love the effect they're having on Callum.

"Can I pay you?" I ask him, still talking about mundane things. That black tux looks so sexy on him. His crisp white shirt makes me wonder how well it fits. And his cologne. Can I smell it? Will I get close enough to?

"Huh, no. No way. Don't worry about stuff like that. The studio takes care of all that."

I stare at him and have forgotten what he's talking about. "The hotel room," he says, because I must have a dazed expression on my face. "We bill the studio."

"I'm not part of your entourage," I remind him.

"Don't worry about it." He steals another glance at my shoes. "You look ... different."

I was hoping for something more complimentary. "Different?" And then I realize that his eyes convey something that his words don't.

Interest.

Heated interest.

"I mean," his voice is low. "You look breathtaking."

A mega-watt smile lights up my face. If I didn't know any better, it's almost as if I'm mirroring his mega-watt smile.

"I'm not used to seeing you in anything like... those..." He throws another glance at my sandals. I'm always in pumps. Boring, black, safe-as-houses pumps. Feeling brave, I shuffle, pointing my feet as I make a pathetic attempt to show off the sandals. Note to self: get some tips from Harper on how to do this properly.

He coughs lightly. "You brush up really well, Nina Cardoza."

"And you always look good." The new Nina doesn't know how to hold back, how to gag her words, and the way I look at him, because of the way I'm allowing myself to see him, spills out. He can tell there's something different about me, because there is. I *feel* different.

"I could walk down the red carpet with you," he whispers.

"But you're going with your co-star," I remind him.

He looks at me for the longest time, his lips twisting as if he's about to say something, only, he doesn't.

This weekend in LA pushes back everything I know about my past. We smile at each other under this new spell of enchantment, but it is soon broken by the ringing of his cell phone.

"I'm on my way." Disappointment clouds his face. "My limo's here. I gotta go." He rakes another hand through his hair. I gaze at him, at his hands, and his face, slowly savoring every beautiful inch of his face. Every day he becomes so much more dangerously handsome in my eyes.

I see now why Harper was so goo-goo ga-ga over him.

Why Elias didn't like him at first.

Why Frankie told me to live a little.

Why Joni said someone like Callum would never be interested in someone like me.

"Come to the after party with me." Those sparkling

eyes are the ones I see when I'm balanced precariously between the edge of wakefulness and sleep.

"What?"

"Come to the after party with me."

"Me?"

He leans closer, and I forget to breathe then, when he looks straight into my eyes, his face only an inch or two away. "Do you see me asking anyone else?"

His voice is like honey. Sweet and seductive.

"What about Alyssa?" My breasts suddenly feel heavy, and shame creeps over me.

"She'll be there," he whispers into my ear. His scent— sea breeze and cool mint, lingers in the air. "No reason why you can't also come."

Our gazes lock, and I can't look away. Shame dissolves, heat replaces it. A tingle of desire creeps up my spine, coils between my legs. This man makes me think of things I have never let myself think of before. My heart bumps around in my ribcage. "The after party?"

I hate parties. I hate being in a place where I won't know anyone.

"Dottie's going. Stay close to her," he says, as if he can sense my reluctance.

"Okay," I hear myself say. "I'll come."

His lips curve up into the type of smile that does things to my insides, and when he lifts his hand and brings it close to my face, I almost miss a heartbeat. But he moves it away quickly, without it touching my skin, and I am already left feeling bereft.

"See you later," and he disappears, while I stand there, holding my own hand against my face and wishing it were his.

CHAPTER FORTY

CALLUM

Alyssa's talking, but my mind isn't on her. It's on Nina. Something weird happened back in her hotel room. She blew me away with that dress, and those heels, and the way she was.

I feel like there are so many facets to Nina, and she only reveals them when she is ready. The two of us have been dancing around one another for month. It's a tango of sorts, us getting to know one another. We've spent more time doing that, getting to where we are now, than the length of time most Hollywood marriages last.

She not only looks different, she *seems* different. Her hesitancy has gone. I no longer feel as if I'm taking one step forward and ten steps back. She's not pushing me away and I'm not left wondering what the hell I've done wrong.

This woman can be hard work, but now, she's leaning towards me, and I'm being careful not to lean towards her so fast. I can sense the change in her as easily as the perfume I could smell on her. I've never smelled it before. At the diner the aroma of coffee floats around, mingling with the sticky, slightly salty whiff of fried food. The scent she wore today was flowery and sweet. I noticed it straightaway. Her hair wasn't bunched up and away from her face the way it usually is. It was down, and soft, and flowing. She had on a touch of makeup. Dark eyes, luscious lips. The way I see them in my dreams.

But it was her dress that surprised me the most. It wasn't tight, and she wasn't spilling out of it, it looked to fit a little loosely, but she seemed even sexier for it, like she didn't even need to try. Like she doesn't know that other side to her, the side I see at the diner, and the side I've seen now. Her friends at the diner have hinted that Nina gets hit on. I know why. It's not just to do with Elias being her brother, even if that's what her jealous friend thinks. Nina is silently seductive. Ignorantly unaware of her allure.

"Hey." Alyssa taps my arm. "Did you even hear what I just said?"

I turn to her with what I'm sure is a blank expression. "Sorry, what?" Before she can speak, the limo comes to a halt, and we hear the raucous crowd outside Grauman's Chinese Theater.

"Are you ready, lover boy?" Alyssa asks in an over-the-top faux sexy voice as she moves her palm over my hand.

The games Hollywood plays, with us as the pawns. The acting doesn't stop when the director shouts 'Cut'.

I'm used to doing these publicity stunts, and the studio needs it, for me and Alyssa to look like we're at the start of our love story. My gut hardens at the thought of this new lie that I'm acting out.

We climb out of the limo, and instantly, we're showered

by the thousand flashes from the cameras. We hold hands, smile, and walk on the red carpet.

These photos of us will be in magazines and newspapers so fast.

I look around, wondering where Nina is and hoping that she can't see this. Alyssa gazes lovingly at me as we walk, like star-crossed lovers, flashing vacant smiles at the paparazzi.

Journalists call out her name, a few call out mine. Alyssa's smile becomes wider, and I follow her, still holding her hand, as she stops to answer questions about her film. She gives her smooth and practiced replies. Someone else asks a question about 'us', and she leans in closer to me as she answers.

It's not just what the fans see on the silver screen that's made up, but most of real life in Tinsel Town, too.

Hollywood owns us, and there is always a price to pay.

NINA

My mind is blown away. Grauman's Chinese Theater looks familiar. As we walk towards it I see two huge bright red columns holding up the roof, and the dragon carving at the entrance. I've seen it in magazines, only now I'm walking inside, but going in through the back entrance with Dottie.

I feel my old life slip away, and excitement fizzes in my belly. This is good, I tell myself, and I wonder if it is really that easy to shake off my past.

It's a good thing I'm not easily impressed by famous

people. But even so, I still find myself sitting in my plush seat, albeit right at the back, almost hidden from view, people-watching. Harper would have loved this.

The theater fills up fast. We got here about half an hour ago and we can now see celebrities as they file in and start to take their places.

Dottie tells me that there's a party afterwards at a club, and then someone else is having a party at his mansion. I tell her I'll be too tired, and I want to go straight home once this is over.

"Callum's expecting you to come to both."

Before I can protest, the screen before me fills up and I catch sight of Callum and Alyssa walking hand-in-hand on the red carpet.

"There they are," Dottie tells me. I hear her, but my eyes are already riveted on the screen. On his co-star. She's beautiful. Seeing Alyssa Watts up close on the huge screen, takes my breath away. Knowing that she is holding hands with Callum hits my gut hard. The blood in my veins turns icy. Everything from that moment in the hotel earlier with me and Callum has been a dream. But so fleeting, like the feel of a silk scarf as it slips through my hands. Flimsy, and gone.

Now, seeing him with Alyssa makes me want to stick a hot poker through her.

The force of my extreme emotions scares me. My feelings for Callum scare me.

I watch as they stop to talk to a reporter. I don't hear what they say, because there is no sound, just a visual of everything that's going on outside. There's noise inside the theater though; cacophony of sounds, the rumbling of chatter, the waterfall of laughter. This is the kind of place I never expected to find myself in, and I wonder what Joni and Frankie will make of it. I think of all the questions Harper will have for me when I get back.

"She's stunning," I whisper.

"They're Hollywood's next golden couple," Dottie answers.

Callum belongs in this world. I don't.

"They make a lovely couple," I reply evenly. I have no idea what Callum has told her about me coming here, but I feel as if Dottie is testing me. She knows I'm Elias's sister, because she asked me if there's any way she can get a ticket for her boyfriend to go and see the fight. I told her that I'd find out.

She doesn't know where to pigeonhole me. I'm guessing that someone like Callum doesn't have many women who are just friends. But me being Elias's sister has, I feel, helped our situation.

But what is our situation?

Who are we to one another?

The film starts and I sit back and watch, still not believing that I'm really here. Most of all, an uneasy sensation settles in my belly because I can't get those images of Callum with his co-star out of my head.

Hollywood's next golden couple.

CHAPTER FORTY-ONE

CALLUM

Alyssa and I walk into the film director's Bel Air mansion for the after party holding hands and looking very much together. I crane my neck and glance around trying to find Dottie and Nina. They're already here because Dottie called and told me.

I had to stick around with Alyssa because she wanted to change into another outfit, so we detoured a while. She spent two hours back at her hotel getting ready, while I waited at the bar.

In a few months' time we'll have our own film premiere for Legend. I picture walking up the red carpet with Nina, and all at once my mind tells me 'no'. But I imagine it anyway. This time next year our film could be up for an award. Even I could be. It's not impossible, and Rudy thinks I stand a good chance.

'Legend' is the closest I have come to making a film that is Oscar nomination worthy. It's a wild thought, as wild as thinking that Nina will be on my arm as we head for the Oscars.

I had no choice but to accompany Alyssa tonight, but I'm hoping to see Nina now. Alyssa won't mind. We're both playing the game, only, her boyfriend is here somewhere.

"Champagne," Alyssa announces. "I need champagne." She tugs at my hand, and I have no choice but to follow her as she heads for the bar. This isn't easy to do. The business of pretending to be in love with someone you have no affection for is tough. Not digging-for-coal tough, but mentally tough. All that posturing, and loving eye-gazing. The camera picks up everything.

The film director decided to throw the party at his place instead of at a venue and I can see why. His sprawling pad is stunning and it has everything you would expect. An infinity pool, a vineyard, pagoda and fire pit, and a mini golf course. There are plenty of other rich man's trinkets, Alyssa has told me because she's been here before. Still, I prefer my modest-in-comparison Hollywood Hills home.

"This is the bar I was telling you about," she says as we walk in.

"This is the bar?" It looks like something out of a top New York hotel. Chandeliers, mirrors, dark lights and velvet sofas.

I look around, but I don't expect to find Nina here. Alyssa hands me a glass of champagne from a passing server. I take it, even though I don't want a drink. I get out my phone and call Dottie, but her phone is dead. I call Nina next, and I hear her phone ringing but she doesn't answer and it goes to voicemail.

We work the room. People are congratulating her everywhere we turn. I smile perfectly, and put my arm around Alyssa's waist every now and then.

"There you are," Dottie exclaims, just as Alyssa starts talking to a group of people nearby.

I exhale in relief. "I called you."

"My battery died," Dottie explains.

"Where's Nina?"

"Over by the door." Dottie nods in that direction. Sure enough, Nina's standing there, holding onto her handbag for dear life. "She seems overwhelmed. You should go rescue her."

I don't answer, because I'm looking straight at Nina. Wesley is talking to her, and I don't like it. "What's he doing?"

"Talking to her," Dottie replies. She and Alyssa exchange pleasantries. They got to know one another well during filming. I clench my muscles, my gaze still pinned on Nina and that jerk. Wesley is a coke head. I need to rescue Nina. "Why did you leave her alone?" I say, interrupting their conversation.

"Leave who alone?" Alyssa asks.

"A friend," I say.

She looks in the same direction. "Ugh, Wesley." Her voice is full of disapproval. "He's cheating on his wife."

"The guy's an idiot." I knew Wesley from way back when. We both started out around the same time, but he went down the hedonistic lifestyle, drugs and drinking, and wild parties. I didn't. My parents grounded me, and losing Ben made me realize early on how fragile life is. I didn't want to fritter mine away.

"His wife doesn't know, and now he's found someone else to target," Alyssa says.

No way. "Excuse me." I march up to Nina and Wesley. Jealousy spikes and I put my arm around Nina's waist, not caring who sees. "There you are," I say to her, as if we are lovers.

Wesley looks at me, startled. "Is she with you?" He shakes my hand more firmly than I would like.

"She's a friend of a friend," I say quickly taking my arm off her waist, remembering that I'm supposed to be with Alyssa. "I'm keeping an eye on her."

"Alyssa will be looking for you." He winks at me. "I've got this one. She's in good hands with me."

No fucking way. "From what I hear, you've got your hands full," I toss back. He slips me a sly grin. "News spreads fast."

I glance at Nina. There's a grateful expression in her eyes, as if she's secretly happy that I came to her rescue.

"Nina was telling me she's a waitress," Wesley says.

"I am." Nina speaks up. I can tell by the tone of her voice that she doesn't like Wesley much, and that makes me happy.

Wesley laughs. "Everyone in this town is a waiter or waitress." He sizes her up, his gaze trailing all over her body. He's sizing her up, just like I've seen him do with most other pretty women. My fingers itch to hug her closer to me, but I can't.

"You're friends?" Wesley asks, cocking an eyebrow. "Aren't you and Alyssa meant to be ' friends'?" He airquotes the last words.

I toss his words back at him. "News spreads fast." I hold steady, refusing to give Nina up.

"Good luck with the new film," he says, obviously getting the hint. He winks at Nina, "if you get bored of hanging around with this guy, come and find me." I swear I feel her quiver.

"How did you end up talking to him?" I want to know, as Wesley snakes away.

"He came over, said he didn't recognize me, and wanted to know who I was. Why?"

"Why?" I lower my head and drop my voice to a whisper. "That guy is a player. He's the last person you should be hanging around with."

"Cal," Alyssa turns up with Dottie by her side. She looks from me to Nina, and then back at me again. "Hi, who is this?"

"Nina, meet Alyssa." They exchange careful looks, and forced smiles.

"And you are?" Alyssa is nice. She's been a good co-star, but the way she's checking Nina out makes me think she doesn't like the way I'm standing with her. This surprises me because she's obviously aware that our pretend romance is a farce. The studio can try to manipulate me, and make it seem that things are what they're not, but there's no way that Hollywood gets to tell me who I can and can't be with in my own private time. Or, in this case, who I can and can't be friends with.

"She's Elias Cardoza's sister," I say, snapping to my senses. I still have to be careful. News gets out. People talk, and I don't want to be hit with a lawsuit for breach of contract. I also don't want Nina to become the subject of a tabloid scandal.

"You are?" Alyssa shrieks. Excitement oozes from her eyes. I know it's not due to her appreciation for the sport of boxing.

Nina nods. "I am."

"You never told me!" Alyssa pokes me. "Have you met him?" she asks me, the tone of her voice indicating that she'd like to sink her claws into him at the first opportunity. I'm sure Harper would have something to say about that.

"I have. The guy's cool. Nice guy."

"Arrange a date," Alyssa orders me.

A what? I'm sure she told me she had a boyfriend.

Nina pipes up. "Elias is already spoken for."

Alyssa's enthusiasm deflates like a punctured balloon.

"He's so into Harper," Nina adds. "You should see them. They're cute together." I do a double take, because it's not like Nina to talk that much, especially to people she barely knows, and about Elias of all people.

"Just a meeting?" Alyssa suggests. "I saw the fight." She holds her hand to her chest, and for a moment I think she's going to fan herself. "He's ... he's ..."

"A great boxer. I know." Nina smiles again. This is definitely another side to her that I'm witnessing tonight.

"Shall we go mingle?" I suggest, seeing that Dottie has disappeared, and Alyssa won't stop going on about Elias. Wesley is still lurking around nearby, and I don't want him anywhere near Nina. Luckily, a guy I recognize, another famous actor, taps Alyssa on the shoulder, and they get talking, so it's easy for me and Nina to slip away.

I let go of my arm around her waist, as we step outside in the grounds of the mansion. An infinity pool glitters under the lights, and some partygoers are already in it. Others lounge around with drinks in their hands.

"I haven't seen you all day," I say, as soon as we're away from people. I haven't asked her if she wants to come out here, or if she wants to come out here *with me*, I assume she does. In any case, I'm more in need of her company. Nina will let me know pretty quickly what she does and doesn't want to do. But she says nothing. She's quiet. I continue walking, past people, and into the vast grounds. Alyssa said the film director had a Japanese garden, and I can hear water gurgling further down.

"You and your co-star," Nina comments, "You make a nice couple. You look good together, good and glamorous."

This pisses me off. Why can't she come out and say exactly what she's feeling? "Is that what you really think?"

"Yes."

"Sometimes, I wish you would be real with me, Nina."

"Be real?" she asks, astonished. "I am being real."

I got a vibe off her at the hotel, before I left. I tried to hold back, tried not to get caught up in her spell. Tried to resist, but I'm certain she felt it too. Now she's telling me this bullshit. Either she's as good an actress as me, or I've really messed up and got all her signals wrong.

There is more to her than meets the eye. Secrets. Things she wants to keep hidden. She puts up a façade, but the problem with that is, the cracks begin to show over time. It's not something you can keep up forever.

I contemplate my next move. We're away from everyone, out here on a beautiful night. Just me and her. No interruptions. No Joni, or Frankie. No Dottie or Rudy. Or Elias or Harper. I could lay out the whole line to her here.

Tell her how I feel.

Tell her that I like her.

Tell her the truth.

And then what?

With her I feel as if I'm on an eternal goose chase and it's a waste of my time because she is that elusive, rare thing; a beautiful woman who not only doesn't see herself as that, but who doesn't have any feelings for me. And that's a real kick in the balls for someone like me.

Maybe I'm wasting my time going after her. Doesn't matter, my time in Chicago will end soon and I can put this episode down to being nothing but a little experiment. It's taught me something. Made me realize that I am not God's gift to women. After years of being surrounded by women who would drop their panties at the slightest interest from me, it's been eye-opening for me to meet someone who is nothing like that.

"Hey!"

I turn around.

It's fucking Wesley again.

Under the light of the lamp it's plain to see that he's high on something. His eyes are red and there's a tell tale dusting of white powder under his nose.

"You never told me you were Elias Cardoza's sister." He ignores me completely and walks up close to Nina, completely encroaching on her personal space. She takes a step back.

"I didn't think anyone needed to know." Nina's voice sounds shaky.

"Back off, dude." He can be wild and unpredictable when he's high. I try to say it lightly, but I'm feeling pissed at Wesley's sudden interest in Nina, and it shows in my voice.

"Back off?" he echoes, clearly annoyed. "Are you together?" He points at both of us in turn. Neither I nor Nina respond. "Jesus. You sly dog, Sandersby. I thought you and Alyssa were a thing."

I grind down on my teeth. "We're friends, me and Nina."

Wesley's brow creases. "Then why are you trying to sneak her away from everyone? Here, alone, in the dark?"

My anger rises, not so much because Wesley's behaving like a douchebag, but because he's exposed a layer of wishful thinking, of stuff I've been mulling over in my head.

And he's made it sound as if I was making a cheap move, when the truth couldn't be more different. I wanted to get her away from the likes of Wesley so that we could talk, not to shove my tongue down her mouth. Most of the people here are phony and I was scared that she might leave early.

His accusation puts me on guard. "Don't make assumptions, dude. Cardoza's helped me out, and I was helping his sister out."

Wesley laughs. "I'm sure you were." He makes a lewd gesture with his hips, as if he's dry humping an invisible person.

"Fuck off," I tell him. He's being vulgar, and I know Nina hates talk like this. "Let's go," I say to Nina.

This is the last place either of us needs to be.

CHAPTER FORTY-TWO

NINA

The film premier was okay but I'm not sure about the after party. These people, they're from a whole new world. A place I don't want to ever be a part of.

Callum's holding my hand, and he pulls me away from his friend. Some drugged up actor who looks familiar. I follow him out, and see that he's making a call. Soon enough a stretch limo pulls up and we climb in.

"Sorry about that," he says. "That guy can be a jerk."

"I'm glad we left."

"I didn't mean to tell Alyssa that you were Elias's sister, but it kind of came out."

I wonder why he said that, but I let it go. I don't mind. I figure that he was only trying to save face in front of Dottie and his co-star. To them it must be strange that he invited me along at all. Explaining who I was, and my connection to Elias probably helped him.

This evening has been a welcome break from my

normal routine. It's been unlike anything I've ever encountered in my life and I'm not sure I want it to end. Watching Elias fight at Madison Square Garden, and then watching the press swarm all over him after the fight, is a little what this evening has been like, only being with Callum I feel as if I'm in the eye of the storm.

The limo pulls up outside the hotel, we get into the elevator. Callum presses the button to my floor, and then his, but when the elevator stops at my floor, I don't get out.

It seems relatively peaceful now, with just the two of us, but he's been relatively quiet, and I'm feeling a little daring. "Do you have a balcony?" I'm curious to know. I also don't feel like going back to my room right now and watching TV. It's late, and it's been a long day but I'm still buzzing from the events of the day.

Maybe I want to live a little, as Frankie would say.

"Yes, why?"

"I'm not ready to go to sleep. Can we sit outside and admire the view?"

The way his face lights up tell me he's pleased to hear this.

I walk in and see that he doesn't have a room. What he has is more like an apartment. It's similar to his suite back in Chicago, maybe a teensy bit smaller.

As soon as I see the doors to the balcony, I head straight for it.

He walks over and throws the doors wide open. "Here you go. Admire this all you want."

"Do you always have to have a balcony?" I walk over the railings and place my hands on it.

"I don't demand it, if that's what you mean. It just happens to come with some of the more expensive rooms."

"And those are the only kinds of rooms someone like you gets. You probably get everything you want."

He looks at me. "Almost anything."

An undercurrent of something hot and tingly zaps through the air. It's like an electric charge buzzing all around us. I force myself to stare out at the landscape before me, just so that I can pull myself out of this force field. My heart is beating so fast and my legs are suddenly unsteady. I've never suffered from vertigo, so it can't be that.

"This is pretty." Callum runs his finger lightly over my chunky bracelet. The four inch tall bracelet is the perfect thing to hide my scars. His fingers still on the cuff, and I wait for him to ask me if I'm okay, because he's not going to come out and ask me if I've cut myself recently. Yet he doesn't say a word.

"I'm glad I came here," I tell him.

He looks at me in silence.

"I didn't like it at the party, so much." I try to gauge his mood. He's been slightly off this evening, completely different to how he was when he knocked on my hotel room, when he saw me in my dress.

"Me neither. The whole thing was one big farce." He sounds annoyed.

"Did I get you in trouble?" I hazard a guess. He's mentioned about having an image, a façade to keep up. I know all about that.

"In trouble? With who?"

"With Dottie, and your friend Wesley, and Alyssa. About me being here."

"No."

It's seductive, being out here so high above the ground, closer to the night sky and its secrets. I feel as if I'm in a bubble. I'm with Callum Sandersby, in his hotel suite, on a beautiful night like this. This is a bizarre moment in my life and I am compelled to throw caution to the wind, to let down my guard, and to experience it fully. Leaving Chicago, and the diner and my dingy little apartment behind has made it easier for me to pretend to be a new me.

I understand now why people go off around the world in a bid to find themselves. I never understood that before, but I do now.

"Why am I here, Callum?"

"Because you wanted to be here."

"You asked me," I reply, biting the inside of my cheek, mulling things over. We've been friends for a while, and he's never tried anything, or come on strong. Maybe at the beginning he did, but I'm convinced now that it was part of who he is, and his bravado around women.

Along the way something changed.

He changed.

He changed enough for me to let him in.

"Because you asked if I wanted to go to the mountains with you."

"That was Harper asking."

"And you didn't want me to come?" he asks, softly.

"You came back with me," I state. "What happened to Alyssa?" My heart stops. I swear it stops beating because the look he gives me is so intense I feel as if my legs are going to buckle.

"Alyssa?" he asks, his voice throaty and hoarse. "Alyssa got busy, and why do you care."

"Shouldn't you be with her instead of me?"

CALLUM

. . .

"Shouldn't you be with her?" she asks, her doe-like brown eyes holding me captive. "Why is someone like you here with someone like me?"

"You really want to know?" I'm scared that telling the truth will push her away again. I feel as if we're finally being truthful with one another, stripped back from our facades, raw and vulnerable. But she seems willing to listen. Do I take a chance?

"I really want to know," she whispers.

I figure that there's a reason she wanted to come here instead of going back into her room. I can't gauge her mood, or what she's thinking but I have her to myself for now, and that's the best outcome I could have hoped for. "I like you, Nina, and I can't stop thinking about you." She blinks, her long eye lashes flutter. I'm fearful that this is too much.

"But you don't know anything about me at all," she says, softly, and even in that softness I hear an objection.

"Don't I?" I know more about her than she thinks. Fragments of stuff I've pieced together from those conversations with her brother and Harper. I've seen the cuts on her arm. I've read that there are many reasons why people cut. It's not so much a cry for help as it is a way of dealing with past trauma. "My problem is that unlike most women I meet, Nina, you have absolutely no interest in me."

She presses her lips together.

I continue. "I know that you're fragile, and brave, and kind." My voice drops as she turns to face me. "And you haven't yet told me to get lost."

She laughs. "I have, you just haven't heard me."

"If you had meant it, I would have."

She cocks her head as if she's thinking about my words.

"You were trying to figure me out, maybe, but you pushed me away for the longest time, because that's what you do, Nina."

Her lips part, almost as if she's surprised. "I find this hard; getting to know someone, and someone like you, so world famous, I wasn't sure. You've been patient with me, but ... "

There it is again. She stops just as she's starting to open up. "But?"

"Aren't you with Alyssa?" she asks.

"Do you really think I'm with her?"

She chews her lip.

"We are Tinsel Town's latest convenient romance story. She's with her boyfriend. They won't walk around so brazenly tonight, but she's going to spend the night with him. There's nothing real between us."

She blinks as if trying to make sense of my words. "I wasn't sure. I read what the papers said about you both, and I wasn't sure. I never believe what I read but seeing you both together this evening ... "

In the light of the moon, I swear her eyes have turned more glassy. I make my confession. "I got jealous when I saw Wesley talking to you."

"Jealous?"

I nod.

"The guy is a jerk," she says.

"The guys in your brother's gym, Jake and Santos, they aren't jerks, but I got jealous when you went outside with them at that last event."

"You did?" her voice is a whisper. "Jake and Santos are like my brothers."

I shrug. "How would I know that?"

"Why were you jealous?" she asks.

"Why do you think?" and when she doesn't answer, "I ask myself, how can I be jealous about someone who doesn't give a hoot about me?"

She touches her bracelet, and stares down at it. It's now or never, I tell myself. This is the only opportunity I'll have —not to get her into my bed—but to tell her how I feel.

"I got jealous seeing you with Alyssa," she says, beating me to it and knocking the air right out of my lungs.

"*You* got jealous?"

She nods.

Well, what do you know? Nina Cardoza has just hinted that she likes me. I rub my thumb over her hand and look up at the night sky because it seems like a magical moment. I've hooked up with girls I've only known for a few hours, and I've had fun sexy times in places that could probably get me arrested, but nothing is as unforgettable as this moment in which Nina confesses that she has feelings for me. Although, she hasn't actually said it out loud.

"Weird, right?" she asks.

"Weird." I smile.

We're not facing the city view anymore, we're facing one another. I stroke her face, move my thumb along her cheek and jaw, dare to move it to her lips. She gazes up at me as I run my thumb over her lower lip. It's taken me over a month to get this woman to notice me. And now it seems she has, and still I hesitate to kiss her.

I want to.

God knows I want to so badly.

And then she does something that surprises me again. She moves closer, and tilts her face up and touches her lips to mine. Electric darts shoot straight to my manhood, and I instinctively shift back a little so that she won't feel my hardness.

I exhale, because, again, I'm not sure how I should respond. I want to smack my lips over hers and kiss her for hours, and then I look into her eyes and I see the vulnerability that is always there.

But she kissed me first.

I lower my head and press my lips against hers. "Nina," I moan, against her lips.

We kiss again, arms wrapped around one another, and my fingers find goosebumps all along her arms. "Cold?" I ask her, then blanket her with my arms.

She nuzzles her face in my chest. "Better."

"Want to go inside?" I'm not holding my breath, but she surprises me again with a nod. Her dark eyes glistening as she looks up at me. We go inside.

"I should go."

There it is, her retreat just as sudden as the kiss she surprised me with. "Okay." I cup her neck, and stare into her eyes. I had a feeling she would back off once the magic spell of the stars and the night sky was broken.

"But I don't want to," she says.

"Okay." I'm not sure what she's asking, but I'll take it. I'll agree to whatever she wants.

"Kiss me again."

That's easy enough to do, so I comply.

CHAPTER FORTY-THREE

NINA

I lose myself in his kiss. It feels like I'm floating. Feels like my feet aren't on the balcony floor, but flying through the air.

Callum's arms are around me, and our bodies are pressed together, and then it comes, the tightness in my chest. "I can't," I say, wriggling out of his hug, I move away and put my arms around me, folding them, then holding onto them and making a barrier between him and me.

"That's okay. Hey," he lifts my chin up gently. "I'm not pushing anything." His voice is soft.

I move back, struggling to keep it together. I thought this time it might be different. With Callum, I thought I would forget. "I'm sorry. I can't." My voice is shaky and I'm suddenly embarrassed. What must he think? I turn my back on him and try to calm my breathing.

One moment I was in his arms, falling into his kiss, his

body, his scent, his warmth, and in the next I'm pulled right out of it. Images of the janitor bubble up, replacing the warmth and connection I just felt. I'm rummaging around in the stinky dark basement again, desperate to find those sweets.

I'm breathing hard and fast, rubbing my arms as I try to stop myself from shivering.

This is when I need my blade.

"It's okay, Nina. I'm not going to touch you." He doesn't come any closer, nor does he put his arms around me. I want him to, but he doesn't move. I'm giving off mixed signals again, so I should back off. I don't want to be labelled a tease, which is what my previous boyfriends said to me. "I'm sorry." It's not his fault, and I'd hate for him to think it is.

"Hey," he lifts his hand, and it hovers in mid-air as if he's unsure of what to do.

I want him to hold me. I almost ask him, but the words get stuck in my throat. His hand brushes my face, before resting against my cheek, a velvet touch that is soft and comforting. A beacon of something good in my life from someone who cares. I get that from Elias, but this is different. It feels different coming from this man who sets my heart racing, my blood pounding, and who ignites every inch of my body.

I wanted that feeling to last for more than a few moments. Maybe I can get it back. If I push away the old. "Hold me," I plead, and he does. His arms wrap around me, and I bury my face in his chest once more, breathing slowly, trying to put myself back together. We stand like that for a long time. I forget how long because time stops for me. I've found my soft rock, my place to anchor. I allow myself the gift of his solace.

I look up at him after a while wanting to see what he's thinking. His eyes glitter in the dim light. "It's okay. I've got you, Nina."

"You make me feel safe."

His lips curve up slightly, as if he understands. "I want you to feel safe. I'm not going to lay a finger on you unless you want me to."

He is different, and I never expected someone like him to understand. "Thank you," I muffle into his chest, and look away. He understands me. He doesn't know much about me, yet he understands me. This is priceless.

His hand smooths over my head. "What time are you leaving tomorrow?"

Home. Back to Chicago, and the diner, and my apartment and my blades. The same old, same old. Harper and Elias won't be back yet. "In the afternoon sometime."

His face registers disappointment. "You?" I ask.

"The day after. I figured it was the weekend, and I wanted to make the most of it. How about you extend your stay, if you want?" His voice is filled with hope.

I do want to extend my stay by another day. I have no desire to rush back. No desire to be rushed off my feet at work, or to sit at a home, tempted by the things I am trying hard to overcome. "What would we do?"

"Anything you want."

It's an appealing proposition. But if we spent the day out, he'd be mobbed by fans, unless he went in disguise.

"We don't even have to leave the room. We can stay here all day, order in, watch movies, play cards. We can do anything you want." It's as if he's read my mind.

Already that sounds like a better idea. "I'll see what I can do with the flight. I should really go now. It's so late."

He loosens his arms around me, and I already miss his hold. "Goodnight."

A part of me wants to stay but leaving is the right thing to do.

CHAPTER FORTY-FOUR

CALLUM

R udy calls me first thing in the morning. I've had about four hours sleep. He gushed about me and Alyssa looking like a proper couple. "Are you sure there's nothing going on?" he asks. I assure him there isn't.

I call Dottie afterwards to tell her that I don't need her to bring me anything today. No expensive coffees, or food, or dry cleaning to pick up or drop off. She can have the day off. I am supposed to have lunch with a few friends, but I've called and cancelled that too.

Nina texts me around noon to say that she's managed to move her flight to tomorrow evening. It instantly lifts my mood. The thought of spending all day here with her keeps the smile on my face.

Of course, I'm braced for more questions, from Dottie, and later Rudy, but I don't care.

Even though she already hinted, I text her to confirm. It

makes sense since my room is bigger, but it doesn't hurt to ask:

Are you sure you're okay to hang out here?

I wait for her to text back, but she doesn't, and then I hear the knock on the door, and her voice. "It's me."

I open the door to see her standing there, and my breath hitches in my throat.

We kissed. Me and Nina, we kissed.

Are we an item?

Is she my girlfriend?

Is this a one night stand without the thing that makes it a one night stand?

Are we still just friends who shared a moment?

As usual, when it comes to this woman, I have no idea.

There's no sexy red dress today. She's in a dress, though. I've only ever seen her in her waitress outfit, otherwise she's mostly in jeans. Today it's a summer dress. Dark green and simple, no frills or patterns. Nothing sexy, and yet she still looks different, and gorgeous. She walks in and kicks off her flip-flops.

I like that she's making herself at home here. I'm unsure what to do now that she is here. So much is up in the air. Going out would make things easier, but people would see us and hassle us, and she's right about wanting to stay inside. My problem is that I don't know how to be.

"Sleep well?" I ask.

"I fell asleep in my dress."

"Yeah?"

"I just crawled onto the bed, and I dozed off with my makeup still on." She makes a face. "I only woke up an hour ago."

"I couldn't sleep."

"No?"

"You were still probably buzzing from the events of the day."

More like from the events at the end of the day, on my balcony. "Had breakfast?" I ask her.

"No. I thought maybe I could make something for you." She wrings her hands together as if she's shy.

"*Make* something?" I laugh. "We're in a hotel. Ever heard of room service?"

I get out the menu, and we both study it. A short while later, room service arrives with a huge feast of fruit, and pancakes, croissants and orange juice.

The day runs smoothly from then on. Any reservations I had, any hesitation, has melted away. I was afraid that Nina would regret what we did last night, of how she was with me, letting me in a little. But she seems fine. Looking at her I see why she needed to get away. It wouldn't surprise me if she hadn't been away in many months. This is the welcome break she needed, and I needed. Out of the entire weekend, it's my time with her, with just the two of us, that makes this entire trip so worthwhile.

It's hot. Los Angeles weather is almost tropical compared to Chicago right now. Nina's at ease, and so am I, and I can't think of a nicer way to spend the day. We have breakfast out on the balcony and then stay out there for the rest of the day, lying on sun loungers that are side by side with a small gap between them. I notice that her toenails are painted a dark red. And that she has cute feet. Feet I'd like to hold and massage and kiss.

"Are you okay about hanging out here?" she asks, not realizing that I'm checking out her feet.

"There's no other place I would rather be."

We smile at one another. "Thanks for changing your flight."

"Thanks for suggesting it."

"I can't think of any person I'd rather spend it with."

She turns her head towards me. "Not even with Alyssa?"

I turn to her and raise an eyebrow. "What do you think?"

She smiles happily. "Truth is, I wasn't ready to go home. Elias and Harper aren't back for a few days."

"Do you spend a lot of time with them?"

"I see them at the diner, and I go around for dinner once a week. They're always at the end of the phone."

It sounds to me as if she's lonely. I get it. Living in a hotel room, even though I'm filming on a set, is not glamourous. It's a lonely existence. Nina never talks about friends much, and I know she doesn't have a boyfriend, so she probably spends more of her time alone. It's easy to see why she decided to spend another day here with me.

I reach over for her hand, and she puts it in mine. I squeeze it, and she squeezes it right back.

It's the best thing, lying here, with the sun shining down on me, and Nina holding my hand.

The best thing.

NINA

He's fallen asleep holding my hand. I stifle a giggle as I look over at him, then I turn on my side so that I can see him properly. I must be the luckiest girl in the world to be where I am right now.

Who would have thought?

Me, with Callum Sandersby, on a balcony, in LA. I let go of his hand and tiptoe back inside to get my cell phone. I take a picture of him sleeping so that I can show it to Harper later on, otherwise she'll never believe the type of weekend I've had.

I put my phone on the ground, and I push our sun loungers together, then curl up against him. I can do this, because we kissed. We shared a moment, or three together last night. I felt his heart beat against mine. I pressed my body against his. His lips claimed mine. I can do this. He's sound asleep, but he rouses as I snuggle up against him. When I place my arm across his chest, his arm goes over me and hems me right in.

***

"She awakens." I look up to find myself wrapped around Callum's chest. I pray that there is no drool sliding down my mouth. I lift my head to see his hooded eyes staring at me, causing a sizzle in my chest that is nothing to do with sun's rays beating down us.

I fell asleep just like he did.

He kisses the top of my head and I snuggle against him even more. That must have been one of the best naps I've ever had. "You fell asleep first," I point out, sniffing at the hint of his aftershave.

"That's because you are so huggable," he tells me. "And I trust you. I don't trust many people." This surprises me, because I am the same, but his lack of trust is due to his status and his wealth.

I smile at him, and we lie back, in our own little cosy bubble, in each other's arms. He thumbs my wrist, and because I'm not wearing the big bracelet, his fingers run over my scars. How is it that I can lie like this in his arms and I'm okay with him doing what he's doing? That I don't feel the shame of my cutting, or the desire to hide it.

There is a lightness, a relief, a lessening of the load, in having someone else shoulder my burden. After a while I look up at him and in the next moment we're kissing again.

I melt into his kiss, losing myself all over again. His touch is giddying and electric, and it zaps every nerve in my body. Being with him leaves me feeling light and warm, and clean, like the sun when it has dried the streets after heavy rain, and everything is bright and new again. Callum is the calm in the eye of my nightmares, the splendor in the dirt of my life.

I'm awkwardly angled, lying on my side, so I pull away from his wet lips and roll over him so that I'm straddling him. My dress rides up, and I place my arms on either side of his head before gazing down into his soulful eyes. Is this my alter ego, doing all of these things? She's showing me the way to what could be the life I can have, if I allowed myself to take a chance.

Letting Callum in is that chance.

I lower my head until our foreheads are touching and I press my mouth against his, falling into the sweet wetness. We're a bundle of heat and energy as his hands skate gently over my waist. Only, now I can feel his hardness against me. Desire rushes through me and heat coils between my thighs. I don't feel scared, or shy, but brave, and confident as I drop tiny, desperate kisses all over his neck. He likes it, I can tell, because his fingers dig gently into my waist. I slide my tongue further into his mouth and grind my hips against him because the heat below spirals out, flames fanning to every orifice. Shivers zigzag across my back when Callum's hands slowly slide under my dress. His touch is as soft as silk, as skittery as the flapping of a butterfly's wings. I moan in pleasure.

But the janitor's basement rears its ugly head.

I see the sweets in their shiny wrappers.

I see the janitor's rotting yellow teeth.

I freeze.

I bolt upright, my hands braced against Callum's chest, while his hands rest gingerly on my thighs.

Suddenly I'm not sure.

Callum looks at me in confusion.

My body is willing, but my mind isn't so sure. I'm scared again.

Scared, scared, scared.

"What's wrong?" he asks, pulling his hands away. He's had to put his brakes on which, judging by the huge package I'm feeling beneath me, can't be easy.

He must know, my heart whispers. He's not like the others.

"I want to, but I can't." I'm so broken that I will never be able to lead a normal life. I'll never be able to have the things that other women can have. I'll never be able to fall in love and stay that way.

"That's okay." He lifts up, propping himself on his elbows. "We don't have to do a thing, Nina."

I climb off him, and lie against him again, resting my arm across his chest. I can't look at him, but I want to tell him, because it might feel better if I do. He runs his hand up and down my arm, a comforting gesture which grounds me.

By not saying anything, by not judging me, he is giving me the freedom to speak. To confess.

I had therapy which helped me many years ago. It stopped me from cutting, but these last few months have been hard. I've crawled back to that dark place, hating the world and everything around me. Having Callum around, being here, for me, has been like a sliver of light coming in from the crack of my fragmented existence.

Elias said that talking to someone, especially to someone who cares, like this man in my arms, helps. I want to tell Callum why I'm like this. I want to move the boulder of shame which rests on my shoulders. I clear my throat, and his hand stills, and I dare not look at him. We lie still, in silence. I can tell from the sudden rise and fall of his chest that his breathing has sped up.

Callum's hand sweeps across my hair and he cups the side of my head, and still he says nothing. I open my mouth, not sure where to start, but trust that saying something will help him see why I am the way I am.

The way I am.

The way I am is not how he needs me to be. I am not Alyssa Watts, or Leanne Rose. I am not glamorous, or an extrovert. I am not used to the public stage. I can barely understand how Elias copes with the public scrutiny.

Am I ready for this? Life with Callum, even if all we have are a few weeks of fun?

What then?

He will return to LA, and I'll be back in my normal life.

Except he will know my dirtiest, darkest secret.

He will know the worst of me.

I'm no longer sure I can reveal my true self, because I don't know how long he will be around.

"Do you think about your brother a lot?" I ask, my survival mode kicking in as I find a deflection point. We all have things we don't want to talk about and I imagine this might be his. "Not every day, not in every moment, but he's with me. I feel he's always there, if that makes sense." His voice is somber, and now I wish I hadn't asked.

He strokes my back lightly, and I hear the gentle pitter-patter of his heartbeat. I could lie like this forever. "You must love your brother a lot," he says. He's good at deflecting, too.

This seals it for me. That's what he continues to think, that I have issues over my guilt for Elias. I mustn't ruin things by having him think anything else.

Especially not the truth.

CHAPTER FORTY-FIVE

CALLUM

We spent the rest of the day just lying down, talking about safe things. Nina's courses—she's always taking them, and learning new things. Elias and the fight, Harper and her new job. The goings on at the diner. I didn't bring it up, the way in which she froze, the way things become too much for her to handle. I'm aware that I have to be gentle with her.

I see her off to the airport the next morning, and I fly back later that same night.

Back in Chicago, our weekend in LA barely feels real. But it was real. Nina coming to the film premiere, Nina in my hotel suite, Nina lying with me on the sun lounger for most of the weekend—all of that was real.

When sex is out of the equation, things are so much simpler. All my past encounters with women have ended up in sex. Starting from the first kiss, it's always a foregone conclusion that me and the whoever are going to end up in bed together.

Not so with Nina.

I knew that going in.

I didn't expect anything. I was shocked when she said yes and agreed to come with me at all. How it all worked out was beyond anything I could have imagined and those precious days we shared are etched in my heart. I look upon them as our new beginning.

The film shoot will be over soon, but there's no way I will be ready to leave Chicago soon after.

Back on the set for the final week of shooting, Dottie makes a comment as she hands me my morning cup of coffee.

"Thanks." I wait for her to leave, as I look over my lines. She doesn't move. "That's all, thanks."

"You need to be more careful."

I shift in my seat. "About?"

"About you and Nina."

"What's your point, Dottie? Just say it."

"People saw you both together. You were with her more than you were with Alyssa. There were paps at the after party."

"We were talking."

"There are rumors going around."

Apart from Wesley trying to hit on Nina at the party, I can't think of how the rumors would start. We stayed in my hotel suite for most of the time. But I don't care. "I'll deal with them."

"I'm only letting you know, Callum. You should be careful."

"Thank you, Dottie. That will be all."

I call Nina and tell her that I can't come to the diner,

not even in disguise, and she tells me she misses me, and she doesn't care about missing night school, and then she asks when she can see me.

That's the best question I've been asked all day.

She comes over that evening, and for most evenings after that. We spend time in my suite. Just *being*. Ordering take out, talking, holding hands, kissing. I never know how far I can take it, so I let her set the pace because there is no rush.

NINA

Luckily, Harper didn't get back from the mountains until a few days ago, which means she hasn't been hounding me for an update on how my weekend went.

We have to catch up though. She wants me to come over for dinner before things turn hectic, and they will, in the run up to the fight. I showed her a few of the pictures I took of me and Callum, back at his hotel.

We look really cute together. It's the first time I've taken selfies and not cringed. He's staring at me adoringly in one shot. I never realized it at the time, but when I look at it when I'm alone, and pore over it, examining it in fine detail, I see it clearly. There's something in this frozen moment that I don't allow myself to see when he's with me. It's an unguarded snapshot, but if ever I needed proof that he likes me, this is it. I look at that picture every night before I go to sleep.

I don't know if this is love, or something similar, something warm, and mushy, and sweet, but I *feel* it. It warms me up inside. Lights me up like a lamp in a room on a cold, dark night.

Is this what people mean when they talk about the power of love? It gives me hope, that I can be more like the Nina I was in LA. That I can move on. Hope—that's what being with Callum gives me.

I didn't show this picture to Harper. I don't want her mouthing off to Elias, and I would rather tell her in person. But I couldn't help but show her the few selfies I took with Dottie, and some we took of ourselves outside the Chinese theater. I wanted to prove to Harper that I went with Callum's personal assistant, and that this wasn't a dirty weekend away for me and him. The fact that it turned into something else, something sensual and deep, is something she doesn't yet need to know. I also wanted to show her how I looked, all made up and wearing her dress, because, I really did look good. I *felt* good. I felt amazing. A different me, confident and happier.

And then I made the mistake of showing her the picture of Callum sleeping on the sun lounger on his hotel balcony. Harper's suspicious. She thinks that there's more I'm not telling her, and she's right. I don't know myself where this is going, so I tell her more about Alyssa and Callum being an item, even though it feels like I have a blade stuck in my throat when I talk about it.

Luckily, Harper's investigative skills aren't so sharp at the moment. Elias's fight is inching closer and soon he'll fly to New York. She's asked me a few times if I'll come, but so far, I've been avoiding it. I did consider asking her if Callum could come, but Dottie hinted back when we were in LA about Callum needing to make it look like he and Alyssa are an item, if only for the release of the film. As much as that grates on my nerves, I don't want to do anything to jeopardize his career or take any chances with his film. He's told me what this role means to him, how he finally got a chance to do something gritty, and real and I don't want to mess it up for him. Callum being seen sitting next to me at Elias's fight will set alarm bells ringing.

We don't even meet at the diner now. For the past week I've been sneaking into his hotel suite late at night. Most times I go back home late, but a couple of times I've ended up staying the night and have left first thing in the morning before Dottie comes over with his coffee. He was tempted to tell her to ditch the coffee, but he's worried she'll get suspicious.

It's not like we are up to anything.

Much.

Just a whole heap of kissing, and touching, and ... that's about it. I feel like we're teens sneaking behind our parents' backs and trying to spend time together.

Frankie looks at me with a knowing smile on her face. Twice she's commented on me missing night school. I missed it so that I could spend that time with Callum instead. I showed her the LA pictures as well. Joni didn't seem interested. She never even asked me about my trip, so I didn't bother telling her anything. She has a new guy now, he came into the diner a few days' ago. He seems okay but appearances can be deceiving, and they're still in the early stages.

I thought Rhys was nice until he opened his mouth, and I thought Callum was a big-headed actor guy, and he's not. He's the first man I've felt completely at ease with. When I'm with him, I don't see what everyone else sees. That might have been because of how we met, early on that first time in the alleyway. I see Callum for who he really is; a caring man who is helping me to become the woman I want to be. Though he doesn't know it, he's helping me to reclaim some of my power and being with him helps me erase the things I need to forget, the cruel memories that have wallpapered my past.

I'll tell him soon, when I'm ready. When I'm not worried that it will change things between us.

I go over late one evening, the day after he has finished shooting on the film. They had a big celebration on set yesterday. He didn't ask me to come along. I understand why he didn't. We can't be seen together. So tonight, it's our turn to celebrate. I go over with a bottle of champagne, and a selection of desserts from the diner.

"I didn't know what to get the man who has everything," I say, handing them to him. He tells me off, says he doesn't need anything from me, except my company. We kiss, and hug and my heart fills with something new and blooming, like the pretty pink cherry blossoms that herald spring and a new beginning.

"The only thing I want is you. Not *you*, not like *that*," he says, quickly, making me smile, reassuring me even though I'm finding it impossible not to think about intimacy when I'm pressed up against him, lost in his kiss.

He can light a fire inside me just through his touch. Each night, or morning, when I leave his apartment, I'm in the thick of my arousal. We reach that point, and then he'll stop. He doesn't want to push things, I sense that, but it's frustrating for me because sometimes, I want to go further and he always stops just when I could go on.

We never talk about it, and he's never brought it up again, about how I closed up back in LA.

I trust him, yet there is a tiny part of me that holds back. A warning bell in the back of my head that plants doubt and seeds the idea that this is fleeting. That he will leave soon, and I must prepare myself for fake romance stories of his love affair with Alyssa. I don't know if I will be able to see celebrity photos of him and her. I'd rather gut my heart out with a butcher's knife.

It unnerves me how quickly I seem to have fallen for him. My feelings run deep, feelings I thought I never had-- desire, lust, and jealousy. Love is complicated, and sometimes I'm not even sure that Callum will see me in the same way if he knows about my past.

I never knew what to label 'this' as and now I'm more confused than ever. I worry that my emotional scars and baggage will be too heavy for him to deal with.

Will he be a story I will tell my friends later on?

Or will he be a part of the story we tell our kids?

I don't know where we stand. I don't know if this is a fork in our road, or if this is where we make a stand. And tonight, I don't care. Sadness slides over me, and I go outside on his balcony, grip the railings and look out, remembering the first day I did this.

"Hey." He comes up behind me. "What's up?"

"You've finished your film."

His arms slide around me I hold onto his hands which rest against my belly. He drops a kiss on the back of my head. "So?"

"You'll be leaving soon."

"Soon. But this isn't goodbye."

"Isn't it?" Where does this go, when it hasn't even started? I treated him like I treated anyone who showed an interest, but Callum has a piece of my heart, and when he goes, he'll take a part of me with him. I won't even be able to tell anyone how it feels because I've never been like Joni, a loudmouth, spouting off to everyone.

"Hey." He nuzzles my earlobe, making me quake. I

push back against him, feeling the rock of his hardness against my back. His lips snake down my neck, and he kisses my skin, all along my neck and shoulder blade.

I turn around because I want him, and I'm sad that we have run out of time, so I kiss him back, and I take this moment as if it is my last. He, maybe sensing my urgency, kisses me back just as hard. We have made out for weeks, but there's a desperation as I cling to him now. I want him.

"Hey, Nina." He talks against my mouth, but I'm done with words for now. I suck his lower lip, taste his mouth and cling to his neck. He picks me up, and I wrap my legs around him.

I want him to take me to his bedroom, and lay me down, and do things to me. But somewhere deep in the back of my brain, I start to close off. I start to get scared. I breathe through it and focus instead on Callum instead. On his soft mouth, and his scent, and his strong hands around me. I squeeze my thighs together, and squeeze my legs, filling a void. Needing him. But instead of taking me to his bed, he puts me down gently on the couch, then stands up, looking down at me.

What now? Confusion and disbelief swirl around me. Why has he stopped before we've even started? "What are you doing?" I wonder if he's letting me down gently. "Is this where you tell me that this is goodbye?"

"This isn't goodbye," he insists, grinning. Sitting next to me he takes my hand. "This doesn't end here."

His words are like gold dust to my needy heart. I lean forward and kiss him, and I can tell that he seems surprised by my lustiness tonight.

"We don't have to do anything, okay?" he says gently.

"Don't you want to?" I ask.

He looks at me for what seems like the longest time. It's

as if he can see through me. My body responds in kind, my stomach turning light and feathery, my breasts longing for his touch. "I want to, but I'm not sure you know what you want, or need, from me. Sometimes I'm not even sure you completely trust me, Nina." His hand is light, yet for all that it's doing to my insides, it might as well be weighted.

"I do trust you. More than I have trusted anyone." His brow creases and I'm aware that he must have questions. His hand moves to my wrist. I shake my head. I don't want him to ask about that. I don't want to think about that. I move his hand away, back to my stomach. "You make me feel things I haven't allowed myself to feel before."

"I do?" he asks, unsure, this gorgeous creature who seems so unattainable and out of reach for many of his fans —and he's here, with me. I nod. I hold my breath, waiting for the question which I can almost hear on the tip of his tongue. "What do you want, Nina?" It's not the question I was expecting. "What would you like to happen?"

"Why?" I ask, disappointed.

My heart jumps, a surge of adrenalin, pure lust even, shoots through my veins. I don't know how to answer that. I was never asked that... then, and I don't know how to say in words what my body feels, or what I need, what I want from him. "What ... what would you like to happen?" I ask him.

"I want to kiss you all over. I want to lick you all over."

I groan in lustful anticipation.

"Would you want that?"

I bite my lip, hold my breath at the thought of that. Wondering how it would feel. "Yes." My voice is croaky. My panties are wet.

"I'll have to take your dress off."

Sweet baby Jesus. I'm too turned on to reply. "May I?" he asks, his voice turning husky as his hand presses against my stomach. I wonder what his touch will feel like on my naked skin.

"Yes."

"You just tell me to stop, and I will."

I let him undress me, so that I'm left in only my underwear. He's still in full clothes. "You're fully dressed," I protest.

"This isn't about me." But he fixes me with a searing gaze as he takes his T-shirt off but nothing else. The throbbing between my legs ratchets up a notch or five. I've seen him in many guises, his fat body-suit and tux and casual clothes. But not bare chested. This close and naked, his gorgeous physique is a vision to behold.

"You set the pace," he whispers, his voice dropping lower as he climbs back onto the bed and next to me again. His hand skims over my belly, his touch making my private parts tingle.

I want this. I want this so much.

But will I freeze up? Like I have before, with other less patient guys? Callum has shown me all the patience in the world. It's like he's being careful, empathetic, watching to see what I need. My hands slowly start to explore his bare torso, savoring the feel of his heat, admiring the hard outlines of his muscles.

He's in my arms now, with *me*.

At first he goes slow. Every nerve in my body tingles when he kisses my body, slowly, his lips lingering lazily over my heated skin. He worships me with his tongue and his lips, he sucks and kisses, while his fingers touch and tweak. He plays with me. When his hand slips inside my bra cap, and he tweaks my other nipple, he looks at me, as if waiting for my directions, but soon enough, his mouth sucks hungrily at my breast. I'm in heaven. He pushes the crotch of my panties to the side, claiming access, and his finger rubs my clit. The sensation rips through me. A livewire from my clit directly to my breasts. I writhe against him, clinging to him as if my life depends on it.

"Cal-lum," I cry out, rocking my hips towards him. He pulls down the cup of my bra and laves my breast with his tongue. Bliss such as I've never known before crashes over me like a tidal wave.

When he moves down my body, kissing my belly, my waist, my hips, then moves lower and kisses the tops of my thighs, I clench up. He stops and sits up. His lips are red, and wet. My gaze drops to his jeans, to the bulge that is hard to ignore. I moan, then bite my lower lip, desperate for all of him. He is all I need and want. I reach out, to touch his zipper, even though I don't know how to follow through.

"Don't go getting ideas, Nina," he says softly, taking my hand and kissing it as he bends over me. "Our first time, our first proper time together, we'll make it special."

"This *is* special," I protest, sounding like a two-year old. His finger glides over my clit again, teasing, tweaking, driving me to a frenzy. I lift my hips desperate for more, and he gives it to me. He strums my body even more intensely with his tongue and fingers, making me dance to his tune. Soft, strangled moans escape my mouth as I lie back and bask in the sheer loveliness of it all.

I want to do something for him, only I don't know how to, and I'm too embarrassed to even try.

CHAPTER FORTY-SIX

CALLUM

"Callum! I'm here. I've got your coffee."

Dottie's voice makes me bolt upright in bed, and the action wakes Nina. She stayed over last night; she fell asleep in my bed, and I didn't want to wake her and she had already told me that she was on the late shift at the diner today.

"Where are you?" Dottie cries, her voice getting dangerously closer to the bedroom. Something is off. Dottie would never do this.

And then I hear Rudy's voice. It's like shrapnel to my ears.

Shit.

What is *he* doing here?

I had a nice morning planned for us.

Had.

Nina gasps, then jumps out of bed and puts my T-shirt

over her head just as the door flies open. Rudy looks at us and his face crumples in disbelief.

"You're ... busy ... " Dottie appears behind Rudy looking sheepish. They stare at me with twisted faces. I'm sure Dottie would have tried to stop him but she's obviously failed.

Nina looks horrified as she rushes around trying to find her clothes. I'm naked from the waist up and I can guess what they're thinking. But this isn't what it looks like.

I climb out of bed, still with my boxers on. *That* didn't happen, but we got pretty close. Still, this is so new for both of us, and we're not ready to tell anyone about this when we're not so sure ourselves where this is heading.

Meanwhile Nina's hunting around for her clothes. "My dress?" she asks, frantically searching all over. "Where is it," she whispers under her breath.

"In the living room?" I guess. I can't remember exactly where we took it off. This isn't good. It's one thing Dottie knowing, it's something else Rudy finding out.

"Is this what you're looking for?" Rudy snarls, returning to the bedroom with Nina's dress.

"Lose the tone," I caution him, not liking that he's talking to Nina as if she's shit on his shoe. He can get angry at me, but not with Nina. I glance at her, and she's pale. I grab the dress and hand it over to her. She rushes away to the bathroom.

"What are you doing?" he says, quiet rage simmering under his outwardly controlled demeanor. He walks further into my bedroom as if he's my parent.

"Butt out," I warn. "What the hell are you doing here anyway?"

"I have a meeting later with the studio's marketing people. I came to see if you wanted to get breakfast. I see that breakfast is the last thing on your mind." He looks around.

"Watch what you say," I growl.

"Watch what you *do*. This isn't what the studio wants to see, Callum. Why can't you do as you're told, for once? You and Alyssa—*that's* the story they want to see. Not *this*." He looks around the room, at the disheveled bed, and draws his own wrong conclusions, I bet. "This better be a fucking one night stand."

Nina comes out at that moment, her face downcast.

I rush to her side. "Ignore him." She looks up at me with her big brown eyes. "I should go."

"Don't listen to him," I plead, but I'm not sure that she's heard me. I grab her hand, but she tugs it out of my clasp. There's a pleading look in her eyes, so I let her go.

Rudy glares at me, and I am so tempted to smack that stupid look off his face. Just as I'm contemplating on what to do with him, Nina slips past me with a breathless "'Bye." I'm tempted to run after her, but I can't, not with this jackass standing in the way.

"What the hell are you playing at Callum? Are the rumors true?"

"What rumors?"

He snorts. "Don't jerk me around."

I hold my breath and try to calm myself down.

"This better be history," he says, wagging a finger at me.

I bite down on my teeth.

"This is your one chance to be taken seriously. Don't mess things up. Don't piss off the big guns."

He disappears out of sight and I hear Dottie making small talk as their voices peter away.

CHAPTER FORTY-SEVEN

NINA

Dottie gave me an apologetic look as I slipped away. I couldn't get out fast enough. Waking up like that, half undressed and with people walking in on us.

I fell asleep in his bed, what was I thinking? I've never done that before. But things are different with Callum. Around him I feel safe; safe enough to fall asleep, safe enough that I *can* sleep and know that I will be okay. I've never done that before. What he did to me last night. I've never been pleasured before like that. Even thinking about it makes my cheeks turn red. I remember my hands sinking into his hair, and my legs over his shoulder.

I turn away, feeling the color creep into my cheeks. Frankie asks me if I'm okay, and I assure her that I am. I move away from her, scared that she'll know just by looking at me.

Callum calls me later that evening, to ask if I'm okay. I can hear the worry in his voice, but I'm more worried about him and his career, and the messed up ways his film people will do anything for publicity. I tell him not to worry, and that I'm okay, and that I was glad I fell asleep in his bed.

He's busy for the next few days, doing post-production stuff, so I make sure to stay well out of his way. He's becoming an addiction for me, and going to his hotel room in the evening was fast becoming my go-to. Maybe the enforced separation will be good for me.

I run my fingers over my scars, over the hard scabby raised skin—he touched this, and kissed it, and he didn't flinch. What I feel for him is hard to put into words. I'm scared that when he leaves, I'll fall back into my black abyss, so I push the thought to the back of my mind, I force myself to dwell on my present happiness instead.

I prepare myself for this being short-lived. Nothing lasts forever. Not the good, or the bad. I've braced myself for worse things before. When Callum returns to LA and back to his normal life forever, I will get over it because I'll have no other choice.

We must make the most of what we have now.

Staying away from Callum for a few days will give me the chance to catch up with Harper and Elias. I've been so preoccupied in my own life, for a change, that Elias's rematch hasn't been on my radar lately.

I go over later that evening when Elias is at the gym. My brother always kicks up his training to gruelling levels around this time, then takes a few days off just before the fight.

I'm glad that it will be just me and Harper because I am itching to tell her of my time with Callum. Unlike Joni, Harper will appreciate it. She has my back, and she deserves to be the first to know.

"How's Elias?" I ask her, as I make myself at home on her couch.

"Training super hard. You know what he's like. I keep out of his way." Harper offers me a glass of wine.

"I bet he's moody as hell?" I know from experience just how difficult Elias is to be around before a fight.

Harper rolls her eyes. "He's getting angry. The rumors are getting to him. People think he was a fluke. That he got lucky with the win over Garrison last time."

"He knows better than to let other people's opinions get to him."

Harper sits down, glass in hand. "This is different. He's at the top of his game now, being the world heavyweight champion. He dazzled them before when he was an unknown going straight to the top. It's harder now that he's at the top. He has to prove himself."

"But this is Elias. He's ready." My brother was born fighting.

Harper takes a sip of her wine. "Tell me about LA."

"You tell me about the mountains, first."

She makes a face. "There's no comparison. I'm sure your news is more exciting." But she goes on to tell me of how she read and made use of the sauna and the jacuzzi while Elias trained all day long. How they went to a lovely Italian restaurant that they went to last time. How it would have been nicer if I had come, and brought Callum along too. "Maybe next time?" she says, vampishly, raising an eyebrow. "There will be a next time, won't there?"

"I don't know where to start," I say out loud. Do I tell her about the film premiere, and the famous people I saw? About the way those glamorous women were dressed? Or do I talk about the after party, and tell her about that creep Wesley? Or do I move on to news about me and Callum?

Excitement charges through me like electricity as I remember that weekend.

"What are you holding back from me?" she asks slowly, reading my expression the way a clairvoyant reads tea leaves.

"So much has happened."

"Happened? With you? And Callum?" Harper sits forward, her eyes gleaming like dark emeralds. "I'm waiting."

"Should I start at the weekend in LA?"

"You mean there's more?"

"Well ... yes."

"You're seeing him, aren't you? You're with Callum Sandersby?" and when I don't say anything, she shrieks, "You slept with him?" She fans herself, and I thank goodness that my brother isn't here to witness this. She reaches forward and squeezes my hand. "That's the best news you've ever given me. You got laid! About time too."

I frown, shaking my head. "Not exactly."

"Not exactly?" she asks, confused. "Honey, you either did, or you didn't."

I tell her, starting from the weekend in LA, when I hung around with Dottie, to getting ready, and then having Callum come over to see if I was okay. Then I tell her the rest, being inside the Chinese Theater, and watching the film, seeing Callum and his co-star, and the after party. Then I tell her that we spent that night and the next day on his balcony, getting to know one another.

"Getting to know one another?" Harper asks, as if she's missed something. "You've had plenty of time to get to know him. You've been dropping off lunch to him every day. How much time do you need?"

"I'm not a fast mover," I say in my defense.

"Clearly. What were you doing on the balcony, admiring the stars?" I can see the million questions circling over her head.

"We kissed."

"You *kissed?*" She sounds unimpressed. "You mean you hadn't until them?"

"No!"

"All those trips to his set, and him taking you to night school, and you guys getting a cab back from Elias's place that night—all of that and you didn't even kiss him until you got to LA?"

I'm not trying to impress her, but she's obviously struggling to see how I can have Callum Sandersby to myself for an entire weekend and still not do much. I tell her that we've spent most of this week together, and that I've stayed at his suite a few nights. I tell her how I fell asleep last night in his bed. "Then his personal assistant and manager walked in on us. Well, not in on us in bed, but they see me hunting around the room for my dress."

"You have slept with him!"

"Not exactly. I had my underwear on?"

"Why didn't that come off?" she cries, surprised.

"It wasn't like that." I wonder if I was naïve in thinking I should confide in her.

"You've lost me somewhere," she says, gesticulating with her beautifully manicured nails. "Let me get this straight. You were naked, and in his bed, and you didn't sleep with him?"

"I didn't sleep with him."

Harper's long eyelashes flutter as she blinks rapidly. It's almost as if her synapses are having a hard time processing what I'm telling her versus the actions I carried out. She whistles. "Was *he* naked?"

"He was in his boxers."

"In his boxers." She fans herself again. "Well ... you're making progress, I'll give you that." She's still fanning herself, and then she stops and puts both her hands over mine and squeezes them, as if she's over-the-moon thrilled for me. "I'm so happy for you. I *knew* he had a thing for you."

"I wasn't sure if it was real. I wasn't sure I could trust him."

"You're a hard one to please. But I think this guy is real. He's nice. I like him."

"We know *you* like him. Elias knows you like him too," I counter with a smile. I underestimated how good it would feel to tell someone, and now I'm glad I did. Harper's reaction is all that I could have asked for. Joni would not have been as happy for me as Harper is. I'm happy for myself, that I've finally met the type of guy I never knew existed; one I could let my guard down enough to have him see the real me. All of me. He might not have seen my emotional scars, he might not know the whole story, but he's there for me, not rushing, not pushing, not goading, or coaxing. He lets me be.

"I don't understand what the problem is. Has he got a small dick?" she asks, giving me a look that suggests she is being serious. "Does it not work?"

I open my mouth. "Uh—" is the only thing I can mutter.

"You said you were naked and in his bed. So ... what went wrong?" She clears her throat. "Did it not get hard enough?"

I gasp at the shock of her words. I would force a laugh, except the real reason isn't funny.

"A man like that," Harper takes a sip of her wine. "I

would have thought Callum Sandersby knew exactly how to please a woman in bed."

"It's not him." The words leave my mouth before I have time to stop myself. "It's not him."

She looks at me, her mouth still open, and her lips forming into something like "You?" Only, she doesn't say it.

I look down at the stem of my glass. It feels as if I'm skating on ice. The longer I skate, the thinner the ice becomes. I can try to tiptoe across, pretending the cracks aren't there, even knowing that I'm in trouble and about to go under.

"Nina?"

"It wasn't just Elias who was abused at the care home."

"What?" Her expression signals her disbelief first. I watch as she wonders if she's heard right, and then it lands, the full impact of my confession. Like a car hitting a wall at two hundred miles an hour.

I can't bring myself to look at her. The shame of my past has burrowed deep in my bones, settled like grit in my pores so that I have always felt dirty. Yet during the last few weeks, I've felt the dirt and grime start to come loose, and the tar like stains of my childhood finally started to shift.

I hear the clink of glass on table as she sets her glass down. Harper shifts closer to me. "Nina?" Her hand is warm and soft over mine. "What do you mean it wasn't just Elias?"

I glance at her, and strangely, I have no tears. "The man Elias spoke of that day." I swallow because I still can't say his name. "He did that to me. He told me that he wouldn't touch Elias if I ... "

Harper squeezes my hand. I see the shock on her face. "Like he did Elias?"

I nod. "So I would let him. He would play a game with

me, and then he would take me to the basement and do things because I always lost the games he made me play."

"Oh, Nina." Her arms close around my shoulder.

"I'm okay," I insist. And I am. It doesn't feel as difficult as I thought it would, to say this out loud. "I'm .... I'm going to be more than okay."

"Yes, you are. Of course you are."

"That man is in my past."

She nods. "Yes he is."

"I ... I ...." And then the tears fall. "But I can't stop thinking of him doing to Elias what he did to me. That's what's killing me. He was only a young boy."

She lifts her hand and wipes away my tears. "You were only a child, too." She puts her arms around me again and we both hold one another for the longest time.

"Swain did that to you?"

I spring apart. Elias's voice ricochets through me like a bullet. He's standing at the door, his face is hard, his eyes feral. He walks in with his head cocked, as if he's spoiling for a fight. His huge body looking bigger, and scarier as he walks towards us. I recall my reaction to his news when I learned it for the first time.

He's like a walking grenade, getting ready to explode.

"When did you get back?" Harper asks, jumping up. But Elias's fists are clenched, the skin across his knuckles stretched so tight that I'm scared the bones are going to pop through.

My body feels like its shrinking. "How long have you been listening?" Telling Harper came easy, maybe I did it to practice for when I'd tell Callum. But telling Elias was never on the cards. I know the damage it can do. Finding out about him was the thing that drove me back to the blade.

He doesn't answer. It's like he's in a waking stance. His

expression dazed. He looks at me, but it's more like he's seeing right *through* me. "Swain did that to you?" he asks, again, shaking his head as if that will make it not be true.

"I'm okay, now." I force a smile as if that will help convince him. I know it won't. This will cut deep like an axe, severing all normal thought, and logic. It will inflict pain, and damage, turn normality to something dark and ugly. It will raise the ugly past, bringing it back into his present.

It will be the last thing he needs.

"Tell me, Nina."

I shake my head.

"Hey, Eli, let it go."

"Tell me," he insists.

"I don't want to talk about it." I can't.

"He did, didn't he? He put his hands on you too?"

I never wanted him to know. Never. Him talking about it pins it in front of my face. "Don't, Elias."

"I wish the fucker wasn't dead just so that I could be the one to finish him off now."

"Let it go, Elias. No more hurt. No more. Let it go," I beg, regret and shame twisting and crawling around me like creepers.

"I wish I had been the one to mutilate him. I wouldn't have spared him any mercy."

I shake him because I don't want him to spend any time in the past where I think he is right now. "Elias," I say gently, desperate to get my brother back. "Let it go."

For a second I think he's going to cry, but he doesn't. It's subtle, the way he straightens up, the way he puts himself back together again, even though I can tell he's shattered. He says nothing.

"You were supposed to be at the gym," Harper says, walking over to him, and putting her arms around him.

"I was. I walked in and heard you two talking."

I never wanted this. I know the damage this can do. "It's over now, Elias. Let it go. The past is in the past." I want him to see that I am okay but I recall all too clearly my reaction to the news when I found out about him. It is impossible to forget the impact of something so shocking that it puts a filter over the rest of your life. It changes you forever and you are never the person you could have been.

It was easier for me to deal with my own horrors than to accept that this had also happened to my brother. If I felt powerless in the basement against that man, it was nothing compared to how utterly and wretchedly useless I felt knowing that Elias had been abused, too.

After that, I looked back on our childhood with a different filter; something darker and bleaker. Nights were the worst when those memories flashed before me. I would try to remember my moments with Elias and look for clues so that I could figure out when the janitor got a hold of Elias without me knowing. Our story of decades' old abuse was impossible to bury, and when it reared its ugly head for the second time, I spiraled further into the abyss, feeling as helpless as I had as a young child.

That's when the lure of the blade called to me.

"Honey," Harper places her hand against Elias's face, her thumb skirts over his lips. "Nina's right. Let it go."

He shakes his face, then pushes her hand away. He looks broken. I know what it feels like to be that broken. I can guess every single thought that is going through his head and my staying here will only make things worse. "Our past can't touch us now, Elias," I whisper into his ear, as I attempt to hug him, but his body is hard, and he's still somewhere else.

I can't reach him, and maybe that's as well. He will need time to get over this, but he has a fight to focus on. A fight that I hope will distract him from all this, and then after, he will see me with Callum and see how happy I am, and he will forget that I ever said this. At least, that's the hope I console myself with.

"I should go," I say to Harper. She follows me to the door. "Look after him. He can't let this affect him. He *has* to get over it."

She looks at me with doleful eyes. "Are you okay?" Concern lines her face. "We didn't get to finish talking."

I force a smile. Try to make myself sound cheerful. "I'm okay. I never wanted Elias to know. I'm actually surprised at myself that I told you."

She squeezes my arm. "Thank you for trusting me enough to tell me."

I shrug. "It came out. I didn't mean to say it. It came out. Callum doesn't know. I never told him."

She nods, as if she understands. "So that's why you and he never … ?"

"Yeah."

"We can talk some more, if it helps you," she offers. "I'm worried about you."

"It's not me you need to be worried about."

She stares at me with concern. "Call me anytime."

"I'll be fine," I assure her.

"Will you, Nina? Or is that what you want us all to think? You're not alone."

"I'm on the mend," I tell her, and I'm not sure who I'm trying to convince more, me or her. "You know I am because I did something neither you nor I thought I would ever do."

I force a harder smile, clear my throat and pray that my voice doesn't falter. "Me and Callum Sandersby?" I say, fanning my hand across my chest, Harper-style. "Who would have thought?"

Her eyes don't turn all mischievous, and she can't force a smile, probably because she's never had to. She looks sad, and worse, she seems to feel sorry for me.

"Call me," she says.

"Take care of my brother."

CHAPTER FORTY-EIGHT

CALLUM

When I finish my workout and see eight missed calls on my phone I know something is wrong. Then when I return to my hotel suite, and see the papers which Dottie has thoughtfully left on my table, I understand the problem.

Love Cheat Callum Gets into Character

Love Rat Callum And His Mystery Woman

What Alyssa Doesn't Know

About three minutes after that, Rudy storms in. He has a habit of walking into my hotel suite when I am least prepared. "I thought we agreed this was a one night stand," he bellows.

Not that shit again.

"You might have said it. I never agreed." I wipe my hand across my face needing to take a shower.

"Elias Cardoza's sister? That was *her* the other day?"

I swallow. "Yes."

"You really did get into character," he snipes.

I glance at the headlines. Lies covering up more lies. I'm not a love cheat. Me and Alyssa never had a thing, and Alyssa doesn't need to know about stuff that is none of her business. "I'm going to sue these bastards."

"You won't have a career left after this."

"Drop the drama, Rudy. Leave that to me."

"You're not even taking this seriously. You and Alyssa are supposed to be in love."

"Well, we're not," I reply calmly.

"Your fans will see you as a cheat," he says, ignoring me. "And who loves a cheat? No one, that's who."

"As if I care," I toss back.

"You should. The studio is counting on you for this. You know how things work in this town."

"This town?" I smirk, knowing full well what he means. Skimming down the newspaper my heart comes to a skidding stop when I see Nina's name. "I'll sue the pants off them," I swear. They've picked on her probably because she's *someone*. She's Elias's sister, instead of a faceless waitress. The papers have been careful not to say anything bad about her, probably scared that Elias will come after them.

"Are you ... is this .... Are you together?" Rudy splutters to get his words out. I breathe out in annoyance. "That's none of your business, Rudy."

"It *is* my goddamn business. That's why you hired me. To take care of your publicity. You are always my business. Your love life is my business, now more than ever. You seem to forget that the studio owns you. You go where the studio tells you to go. You are seen with who they tell you to be seen with. You fall in love with who they tell you to fall in love—"

"No. I. Don't." I spit my words out slowly.

"You're supposed to be Hollywood's latest power couple."

I grit my teeth. Behind his back I see Dottie hovering around, looking at me worriedly. "The public will forget, Rudy. Calm down. They don't always fall for this shit. People aren't that stupid."

"The studio gave you a chance. Don't throw this away. Your new film releases in a month," Rudy cries. "This is the last thing we need."

I shrug. "The studio will get over it. The people will forget."

"I'm warning you, Callum. Don't get too big for your boots. Don't mess up this story just because you felt horny one night. Don't make that mistake."

I breath out slowly. I hate that he talks about Nina as if she's a mistake. I hired this jackass, and he's talking to me as if he's in sole charge of my career. Sure, he's the bridge between the studio and what needs to be done, but I'm not going to back down. I'm not going to forget Nina. I'm never going to forget her, as if it were that easy. "Is that a threat?"

"You already messed up on the set. You remember your little bust up when you went sightseeing late one night? You remember the delay in filming just because of that little detour that almost got you killed?"

"It did not almost get me killed."

"I beg to differ. You were stupid and incredibly lucky."

This man is pissing me off yet I somehow manage to hold my shit together and not explode. I could fire him. But then I'd have another asshole to deal with, and I'd rather not deal with the studio heads by myself. They piss me off more than Rudy does.

"This … waitress," he says, wiping his fat little hand over his jaw. "Even if she's the boxer's sister, she's still a waitress. That's not the story your fans want, not if you want this film to break records. Women need the *romance*. How many chicks do you think are going to sit through a *boxing* film?"

I can feel my nostrils flaring. "She's not just a waitress." Not to me.

Rudy waves his hand dismissively. "I've known you long enough, Callum. I know you have a hard time staying away from women, but I'm telling you now, for the next few months get your shit together and act like Alyssa Watts is the center of your entire fucking world."

"I can't do that. I *won't* do that."

His brow furrows as if he thinks I've suddenly gone insane. "You will do that. If you care about your career in this town, you will. You'll forget about the waitress the moment you leave this place."

Dottie looks at me, her expression one of worry. "You have a meeting at the studio," she tells Rudy. He turns to leave, but not before pointing a finger at me.

"I mean it, Callum. Don't fuck this up. Keep those headlines out of the papers. Take Alyssa to dinner."

"Kind of hard, given that she's in LA."

"Distance isn't a problem, your current sex life is. Think of this as damage limitation. Be seen doing something romantic with Alyssa, otherwise the studio will be forced to step in."

He slams the door behind him.

"What are you going to do?" Dottie asks. She knows me.

Gets me. Understands that Nina is so much more to me than all the other women I've met.

I point to the door Rudy left through. "I'm not going to do that." I'm not worried about what my fans will think, or the studio.

Screw them.

I'm worried about what Nina will think. She won't want her love life plastered all over the papers. She won't want her name or her photo out there. She's a private person, and she deserves her anonymity. I haven't worked it all out yet, how things would be, how she would handle it, if we get together. I'm sure we'll find a way.

I need to see her and warn her about the papers. She'll be embarrassed about these rumors. She'll hate them.

Worse, she might even hate me.

CHAPTER FORTY-NINE

NINA

Light. That's how I felt as I was opening up to Harper, but then Elias walked in and my heart sank.

I've called him a few times, but he's not picked up. I don't usually call him because we see one another either at the diner or at his place. But he's not returning my calls. Harper says his head's not in the right place, that he's been at the gym, training all day, and that I needn't worry. 'Give him time to work through it,' she said. She's worried, I can tell from her voice.

She asks me how I am, but of course I'm worried. Not for myself, but for Elias. He leaves for New York soon, and even though Harper wasn't going to go until the day of the fight, she's now going with Elias because she's so worried about him.

When she asks me if I'm going to come, I can sense the pleading in her voice. I've always told her I can't go. I *won't* go. I struggle to watch Elias fight, and I don't know how she does it, but maybe that's what being in love is about—making yourself do the things you don't want to do for the sake of the person you love. Being there on the night, by the ringside, I won't be able to look away. Yet I sense she needs me there, if only for her sake. Of course I have a duty to be there for Elias, now more so than ever.

Callum turns up on my doorstep, holding something in his hand. He looks worried.

"Did you see this?" He holds up a newspaper.

"Yes." I look away as I let him in. It was all that Joni and the other waitresses talked about the day that story broke. I close the door and walk into my living room. I know about the gossip in the papers. I know that Callum has been called many things. I know about Alyssa, and I nearly spat out my coffee when Frankie showed me a paragraph with my name in it.

She clenched her teeth before snorting with derision. "One night stand. You're not worried?" She sounded surprised. Any other day, I would have been. I'd have been a mess. I hate my business being out there for anyone to read. But I have other things which concern me at the moment, and these gossipy journalists with their click-baity headlines are the least of my worries.

This story isn't the one that's kept me awake at night. It's odd how something unexpected can blindside you to the point that the things which would have ordinarily made me hyperventilate don't even make me blink.

"I'm sorry. I didn't want this to come out, but those goddamn paparazzi, they're everywhere, like vampire dust mites." He sounds worried. "I should have been more careful. I should have—" He stops, and stares at me, when he realizes I'm quiet. He takes my hands, then turns them palm side up, running his fingers lightly over my wrists.

He's checking. "What is it?" he asks, seeing that I haven't inflicted any new damage to myself.

How do I tell him without giving up my story? "Elias isn't in a good place."

"He's got a big fight ahead of him," says Callum, scratching his jaw. I feel like he's got something to tell me. "*I'd* be worried sick if I was stepping into a ring for real, but your brother's going to be fine. Elias is a killer in the ring. He's trained for this. Perfectly natural for him to have nerves."

I'm not so sure. "He's not himself. Harper's worried."

"About what?"

About my secret. Something I never wanted Elias to know. Words which should never have reached his ears because he's not going to be able to unhear them. I'm worried about my brother who is about to step into the ring with "The Tank". That guy is even hungrier for a win, to prove that he is the true champ. I'm scared that Elias won't be at his best, and it's all my fault. I really need to see him before he goes, but I can't barge in on him at the gym or at his house. These days leading up to the fight are crucial, so I take my lead from Harper and stay away.

"Harper's worried about what, Nina?" Callum's hands slip to my shoulders and grounds me. The weight of them calm me down, and I don't even understand why, or how.

"About the fight." I can't stop thinking about Elias's reaction to my news. It was the look on his face, the fire in his eyes, the rage inside him. I can't get that vision out of my head. "He's nervous, I guess." I carefully sidestep what I know to be the real reason for Elias's mood.

"Should we arrange to meet him?" Callum suggests. "Do dinner, or drinks, or just see him before he leaves?"

I shake my head. "It's too close to the fight. He's irritable and moody." I look at Callum. "I'm going to go to the fight. Come with me."

"To the fight?" He seems caught off guard by my suggestion.

"I need to be there for him, and I would love you to be there for me. I struggle to watch him fight and I don't think I can do it alone."

"Sure. Yes. I'll be there for you."

"Will this get you in trouble? We can sit apart. You can go in disguise."

"Don't you worry about that."

But I do. I can't help worrying about him or Elias. There is the whole media circus going on around him and his co-star, and his douchebag manager guy seems to give him a hard time. I don't want to get him in trouble either, but I need him. "We can go for the night, watch the fight and come back the next day."

His hands pull me towards him, and I press against his chest. Suddenly, he has become my safe haven, the place I go to when in times of trouble. He holds me, his arms firm and possessive over my back. "We'll go. Can you get tickets?"

Of course I can get tickets. I'm Elias's sister.

CHAPTER FIFTY

CALLUM

"**B**ut Rudy said you can't see her!" Dottie scurries around the room as I pack my bag.

"I'm a grown man. I can see who I want. I can do what I want. I won't be dictated to by some big ass studio head."

She stares at me as if I've lost it. Maybe I have. All I ever wanted was a role like this, in a film like this. And now I have it. The shooting is over, and the best part begins; a round of interviews and publicity drives. Sucking up to the big guns, hoping to get noticed enough to be considered for an award. Elevate my career to the highest level.

But I'm not sure I want that so badly anymore. My life is pretty good. I have everything I could ever want. I don't need more money, or more fame. I don't need even more intrusion into my life.

I want Nina, and the chance to slow down, live life and appreciate each moment. I can't let her down. She's asked me to be there with her at Elias's match. Unfortunately,

Rudy's gone and set up a brunch meeting with the studio heads. I'll go to that, and I'll still be able to get my flight and make it to Madison Square Garden.

I'll wear my baseball cap and lie low.

"This is your career you're risking, Callum," Dottie says, doing her best to make me see sense. "Do you really want to do that?"

Every time I've started a new relationship, things have always gone well for me. They've been easy. People think I've led a charmed life. They have no idea what it is to lose your best friend and younger brother in the prime of his life. Most people only see what you show them, and they selectively always choose to see the good stuff. My friends have even said that everything is super easy for me. I get the women, I get the roles, I have the wealth. But I would give all of this up in a heartbeat if I could get him back. That's impossible, even I know that, so I try to make it the best life I have. It looks easy, the women, the wealth, the houses and cars. But this hasn't been easy—with Nina. Ever since we met, things have been decidedly different. *She* is the different I need and want.

"She's asked me to be there. She needs me. I can't let her down."

Dottie looks at me as if she doesn't understand. "I'll go and watch the fight, if it's support she needs. We get on, me and Nina."

"Nice try, but no." I've heard Dottie on the phone to her boyfriend who is desperate for a ticket. I think they might even have asked Nina to get one but Nina hasn't said anything about it..

"Rudy will go apeshit if he finds out where you are," Dottie reminds me.

"Who's going to tell him?" I heard Rudy loud and clear.

Heard the veiled threats. I'm aware of what studio heads do. The control that these invisible, rich men have over Hollywood and all the wanna-be's. We've all played along, and it has benefited me as much as it has them. But this time, on this one occasion, I won't bend to their bidding.

"This is the film you want to get the Oscar nomination for," Dottie reminds me. "Can you afford to mess it up?"

"Who says I'm going to mess anything up? Don't look so worried. I'm playing along. I'll go to this meeting with Rudy and the bigwigs now, and later I'll fly out. I'll be back before you realize."

Nina has never asked me for anything, and now that she has, I won't let her down. We're not leaving together. She's going with Harper and I'll meet her in the arena. I'll go in disguise, but I'll sit next to her. Nobody will know. We'll spend the night together and I'll come back before Rudy finds out.

I'm not worried.

This will work out.

Things always do.

CHAPTER FIFTY-ONE

NINA

There's not long to go before the fight now, another hour or so. Like last time, there is a packed undercard, boxing matches between two lesser known boxers before the main fight. I can't watch them, even though it would help mentally prepare me for Elias's fight. I am so not cut out for this stuff. I'm only here because I want to support my brother but I'm not being allowed. I want to go into his locker room to see Elias, but Harper warns me against it. Lou, his manager, and Jake and Santos, also tell me to keep away. Jake warns me that he's never seen Elias like this before.

I'm still jittery and nervous, but I tell myself that this is good. If he's angry, that's exactly how he needs to be.

Unlike last time, me and Harper aren't sharing a room together. Callum and I agreed to fly out separately and return to Chicago separately. He said he's coming in disguise, and if its anything like the stunt he pulled the last time, he could be walking towards me in a sea of faces and I wouldn't recognize him. I also managed to get him a pass to Elias's locker room after the fight.

I feel silly sitting here by myself. I feel left out. Everyone else is in there with Elias. I start to get paranoid and wonder if he is angry with me? Discovering his abuse broke my heart in a thousand places. I wanted to hold and hug him even though I fell apart at the time. I wanted to make sure that he was okay. I assumed he would have the same reaction, but Harper tells me that men handle things differently.

In a way I'm relieved that I didn't tell Callum about my past. Having him shun me would have been too much to bear. Talking of Callum, where is he? I need him here to support *me*. I look around in desperation for him, but he is nowhere to be seen. I scrutinize the faces of strangers in the misguided hope that one of them will be him in disguise. His plane would have landed hours ago. I've called a few times ever since I got here but it only goes through to his voicemail.

I feel left out. Alone and abandoned, sitting here by myself. Even Jake and Santos are in there with Elias. Harper will take her seat next to me only when Elias goes into the ring.

My stomach is knotty as I sit here in the raucous rambling noise of a braying crowd watching fights I have no interest in. Doubts, like vultures, begin to circle around my head, squawking before they swoop in and consume me.

There are empty seats on either side of me. Everyone I know and care about is in the locker room.

A vibration in my jacket pocket alerts me. I fish out my phone and see that Callum's calling. I look around in anticipation, trying to guess which direction he'll be coming from and what disguise he might be wearing this time.

"Hey."

"Where are you?" I ask, still looking around. The seats are filling up, and I wouldn't be able to single him out, unless he came carrying a huge banner.

"I'm still here. In Chicago. I'm sorry I couldn't—" His voice is barely audible, and I'm not sure I heard him right.

"Where are you?"

"Still in Chicago. I got held up in a meeting. I couldn't get away."

"You had a meeting?" On a Saturday? My heart sinks, dragging every ounce of hope with it. I can't hear him clearly, and I only catch words, something about Rudy, and a meeting, and the studio heads.

I thought he didn't care about those people? So, what changed?

"I'm sorry Nina. Rudy messed me around—"

A roar goes out around the auditorium and I crane my neck, looking towards the area where the boxers start their ring walk. "What?" I can't hear a word he's saying. Music starts up, and an announcement is being made. I look up, and the lights dim. Then lights begin to flash, and loud music blasts out. Garrison seems to have upped the razzmatazz for which he is known. Callum says something. "I can't hear you," I shout back.

There's nothing to do but hang up.

I hear booing, but it's quickly replaced by cheers from the audience as Garrison hops into the ring and dances around, mock boxing style. He is cocky, and playing to the audience. Up there alone in the ring, he struts around as if he owns it.

I'm eager to see Elias come in. I want to see his ring

walk. Harper has been telling me all about it. He had nothing last time, only a few of the guys walking up alongside him. He didn't even have music, or a light show, or a nickname. Come to think of it, I don't think he has a nickname even now, but he has music and light effects now. This should be epic.

The sound of the crowd lowers, then turns into a quiet buzz. And then the MC announces Elias's entrance, and everyone in the arena goes crazy. The air turns electric. I crane my neck, my ears straining for the music. And the lights. Where is the lightshow? Where is the music? Where is Elias?

He doesn't appear, but I know he's making the challenger wait, he's just building up the suspense.

But when moments pass, and there is no sign of Elias, I'm suddenly fearful. Then, just when everyone starts wondering what the heck is going on, Elias emerges from the tunnel.

I sit up taller, slip to the edge of my seat.

I can see Elias walking in, flanked by his entourage. He's wearing a white satin robe and his hood is up.

But still there is no music. There are no lights. Just one spotlight eerily showcasing Elias's walk to the ring.

What's going on?

My heart bangs against my ribcage.

I need to see his face. I need to gauge his mood. I haven't seen him since that day, and I won't rest until I do. His hood is up. His chin is high, but the rest of his face is shadowed.

And then it starts. I hear it behind me first, then the sound gets louder and louder, like angry waves crashing against rocks. The roar reaches a crescendo just as Elias jumps up and into the ring.

I don't know what happened to his entrance plans, but the crowd don't seem to know any different. Their support for him echoes in the jubilant cheers which shotgun all around me.

I push it away, that Callum isn't here. He must have good reason, I tell myself. He's not my priority right now. Elias is. My eyes are fixed on the ring, on Elias.

The crowd goes crazy when Elias's name is announced again, and the ensuing roar of admiration swells my heart. Harper takes a seat next to me. She looks happy. I have a good feeling about this. I smile at her. It must be tough for Harper to see the man she loves stepping into the ring, putting himself in harm's way. This is brutality, not entertainment. It's hard for me to watch, as Elias's sister, but it must be so much harder for Harper.

"Where's Callum?" She shouts in my ear.

"He couldn't make it."

Harper squeezes my hand.

She hates this as much as I do.

If Callum had been here, I would have squeezed his hand harder. Despite all his reassurances to the contrary, it seems that his career is more important to him.

It's not a big deal.

At least that's what I tell myself.

Callum's part is over. He'll be gone soon.

This is what matters, Elias, and this fight, and right now.

After he wins, we can go home.

And that's what I focus on.

I reach over and put my hand on Harper's. She squeezes it, and I squeeze it right back. We need each other, and as the fight begins we brace ourselves.

Elias starts off well, he looks fierce, and toned, and is lightning fast on his feet. In no time at all, Garrison walks straight into a jab. He looks as dazed as I feel watching that lightning fast move from Elias. The two of them move around, Garrison is slow, not as quick and sure footed as Elias, and they move around the ring warily, sounding one another out.

Before long the second round starts with Garrison lunging forward and throwing a punch to Elias's side. But Elias hits back, firing a jab and then landing a hook which catches Garrison unawares.

Garrison goes down.

In the second round! I sit up, struggling to contain my glee.

This looks easy.

The referee starts to count, but Garrison signals that he's okay, and gets up. As soon as he does, Elias lashes out slamming his fist into Garrison's jaw.

I breathe out, feeling happier.

This is brutal. It's not a 'sport' but Elias is winning. He's okay.

Tonight will be easy.

We'll be out of here in no time.

CHAPTER FIFTY-TWO

CALLUM

Screw Rudy.

He pulled a dirty one on me. It's not easy to walk out of a meeting with the studio head. The so-called 'brunch' meeting went on for hours. I'm pretty sure I didn't even need to be there for most of it. And then some wise ass suggested drinks. I have balls, but the studio head isn't the type of guy you say you've got other plans to. I went, because I was sure I'd get out of it and have time to get to the airport and catch my flight.

I had it all worked out. A simple yet effective disguise. A flight and then a car straight to The Garden.

Except that the 'drinks' went on for way longer than I expected, and Alyssa turned up. I smelled a rat. I'd been set up by Rudy. The bastard. This was *his* plan, the damage limitation exercise. Dinner followed later at a trendy restaurant even though by now no one was really hungry because all we'd been doing was hanging out and eating and drinking. Obviously the press had been tipped off to take shots of me and Alyssa leaving, holding hands as if we can't bear to be apart.

There will be plenty of gossip column inches and photos of this sham romance. I was too pissed off to even look at Alyssa, much less take part in the conversation. I was definitely in no mood to eat. I wanted dinner to be over and done with so that I could get back to my apartment and call Nina and tell her of the fuck-up I've been tricked into.

It was too late to get my flight. I couldn't even get the next one out. This is when having a private jet might have come in handy. I couldn't make it.

I called Nina as soon as I could to let her know, and to apologize, but I couldn't hear her properly, and I don't think she could hear me. I heard the roar of the crowd in the background.

She hung up on me. I'll have to catch up with her tomorrow, but I'm watching the fight sitting here in my hotel room alone and I can't believe what I'm seeing.

What the heck is up with Elias? I feel lousy anyway, and I'm drinking vodka because I'm in the mood for getting drunk, but I sober up fast when I see Elias taking the kind of punches he shouldn't be. He started to fall apart almost as soon as the fourth round started.

I sit up, and then I sit forward, then I put down my glass, my eyes riveted to the screen as I watch, shellshocked.

Elias is taking a beating.

What happened? It started off so well.

Garrison went down in the second and it all looked so promising, even when he managed to get up again.

Elias cut Garrison in the third round, and with blood

trickling from Garrison's left eye, the fight looked to be going the right way. Garrison getting beat, Elias showing the winning hand.

And then it all changed.

They continued fighting for another few rounds but it was hard to tell who was ahead.

Elias?

I don't know what happened. He looked so strong in the first two rounds. In the third round they seemed to be figuring one another out.

Now we're into the fourth round and I'm still waiting for a glimpse of the Elias magic that was there on the first fight.

Something is off.

Garrison is fast, he looks hungry. He looks like he wants to reclaim his titles and finish off Elias in the process.

Elias fights back, surging forward and landing a punch square on Garrison's jaw, but Garrison seems to have walked right through it. He lands a punch on Elias's jaw.

Elias goes down.

I sit forward.

Get up! Get up!

Elias is down and Garrison is battering him.

Hit back!

HIT BACK!

Elias manages to get up, but he's shaky. I sense a shift in the fight.

This isn't the Elias I know.

I sit on the edge of my seat, willing him to speed up, strengthen up, show us some of that Cardoza magic.

Then Garrison connects with a right that torpedoes Elias, knocking him down, and almost putting him through the ropes. Miraculously, he manages to upright himself and is saved by the bell.

What the hell is going on?

What happened?

Where is Cardoza? Because it doesn't look to me like he's in the fight.

My cell phone rings, and I grab it, my hopes sinking when I see that it's not Nina. It's a friend who's watching the fight. I was supposed to go and see it with a bunch of crew members. One of them is having a party and they're all watching it together. I was supposed to go, and I would have had Nina not asked me to go to the fight with her.

"Are you seeing this?" my friend says.

"I'm seeing it."

"What the fuck?"

"I know." I hang up. I feel bad for the Elias. He's not just some legend taking a beating in the ring, he's a guy I've come to know as a friend. This feels so much more personal. If I feel like shit watching Elias get beat this badly, I hate to think how Nina must feel. The only person I wanted to watch this with, the only person who needed me, I let down.

The fifth round starts and Garrison comes right at Elias from the opening bell. But this time, Elias fights back. A couple of his punches don't hit, it's like he's lost his aim. Seems to be Garrison who's doing all the chasing, and Elias is fighting a slow retreat. I shake my head watching Elias getting beat so bad. He gives back. I see he's trying to get back into the game, but this isn't the guy who the world watched take Garrison down so easily.

I sit on the edge of my seat, feeling utterly deflated.

Come on, Elias. I try to will him with every fiber of my being.

The sixth round starts and Elias is met with a hail of punches early on. He's being backed into a corner, and then he goes down again. He makes it to his feet but Garrison throws a barrage of hefty blows and Elias lies on the floor, doing nothing. Defenseless. Almost as if he's given up.

The referee stops the fight, and I bolt to my feet, hands on my face, in shock.

What?

The camera is on Elias sitting in the corner with blood trickling down his nose. I wince at the sight of so much blood pouring down Elias's face. He's been cut badly above the eye. He looks dazed, as if he literally doesn't know what hit him.

The camera catches Harper. She's holding her hands up to her mouth, fear swimming in her eyes. My heart skips a beat when I see Nina alongside her. I know that look. Of blame, and guilt.

I frown. This isn't her fault.

I call her, even though we couldn't hear one another last time. Her cell phone rings and rings and rings, but she never answers.

I watch in horror as a jubilant Garrison is being lifted on shoulders, showing off the many belts.

I don't even want to think what Elias is going through. Like they do, the journalists and the papers, they built him up soon after his first win against Garrison—hard not to when he had achieved such a phenomenal win. But in recent weeks I've seen the tabloid press throwing digs at him, doubting whether he was a champion at all and making him out to be a one hit wonder.

Now they will tear him to shreds.

Who we saw tonight, that wasn't the Elias we all know. The man I know is a beast. A fighting machine. A monster, full of rage, at least that's how I remember the guy in that first unforgettable fight with Garrison.

My thoughts are with the Nina and Elias, and I wish I hadn't let Rudy dick me over.

This is not where I wanted to be tonight. I should have been in The Garden. I should have been there for Nina.

CHAPTER FIFTY-THREE

NINA

"I need to see him." Harper and I wait outside Elias's locker room. He's been in there with the doctor for a good while now. Jake and Santos are outside with us. I hear them talking. They're saying out loud the things I've been thinking.

"What happened?"

"He fell apart out there."

"Never seen him lose it like that before."

"How did he lose so badly?"

"His head wasn't in the game."

I walk away, hanging my head in misery. *I* did this to him.

Me.

I know where his head was. I know why he couldn't get it together.

Because of me.

I feel an arm around my shoulder. "Don't blame

yourself." Harper hugs me. "Nina," she rests her head on my shoulder. "Don't beat yourself up about this. Not after everything you've been through."

"But it was because of me." I know. I fell apart when I found out about him. It took me days to get myself together and I was just a waitress, a woman going to different night classes trying to keep busy, trying to keep it together. Elias had to step into a ring with a man who wanted to finish him. He had the world's eyes on him. I had the luxury of breaking down in private. Elias didn't. He couldn't get it together. He got beat up instead because he couldn't fight back, and now the press will slaughter him.

They will think he's the one hit wonder.

I know where Elias's head was.

We deal with these things in our own ways. Elias dealt with it by fighting. He would always fight—street fights, underground fights—whatever it took to use up the anger inside him.

He was just starting to get his life together, and now they will break him. Except that Elias is unbreakable. He's stronger than me, but still, I worry what will happen to him. How he will deal with such a public failing. He took a real beating, and each time he watches that fight, he'll hate himself for it.

All because of me.

"You can go in," Santos comes over to tell us and Harper rushes off.

"How bad is he?" I ask him.

"The doc says he's gonna be fine. Nothing fatal."

That lifts my spirits. As we walk in, Harper has her arms around Elias's waist. She's holding him tenderly, as if she's afraid he might break.

I let them have their time and speak to Lou. He tells me

Elias has a suspected mild concussion and the usual cuts and bruises. Nothing too serious. "I don't know what happened out there." Lou looks as bewildered as I feel. "He trained harder, better and longer for this one. More than he did for the last fight. He was ready. The best I've ever seen him." He rakes a hand over his neck. "He lost it completely."

I know what happened. Guilt rolls over me like a deadly tsunami. I rest against a wall, glancing at Elias, unsure of whether he wants to see me or not. Wondering if the sight of me will bring back too many memories, and worse now —guilt.

For there is guilt. I let the janitor do what he wanted so that I could save Elias. I'm sure that monster would have said the same thing to him. Elias has gone through his whole life the way I did, putting himself in harm's way in the belief that it would save me. To discover the opposite is like drinking a poison slowly, rotting the flesh, constricting the airways, dealing a slow fatal blow.

"Go to him." Harper walks up to me. "He needs you."

Does he? I'm not so sure. I step towards him, my heart breaking into a million pieces. Elias is the picture of everything he wasn't supposed to be tonight. His eye is cut and it looks like he has butterfly stitches holding it together. His body is still bloody.

"Hey." I want to hug him and make everything be okay for him. I try to hold myself together, but it is hard to do that when Elias looks so broken. It's not the state of him that crushes me—the purple-ish bruises, and the battered body— it's the look of utter defeat in his eyes. "The doc says you're going to be okay," I say, feeling like a stranger grappling to find the right words of comfort.

"I'm going to be." His voice is low, husky. He sounds shattered. His heart and soul are crushed. For all his life he wanted to prove that he had what it takes. He wanted to show people who never so much as glanced his way. And he did with his first fight, and now he wanted to shore that up with a solid second win. He wanted to put the haters and doubters to rest, but now he will feel as if he's failed. Worse, he might even start to believe that he was only a one-hit wonder.

"This is ... " I swallow, but my mouth has turned dry. "This is all my fault." But Elias isn't even looking at me. His expression is vacant. I'm suddenly not sure that he's fine. He's gone. It's like he can't even hear me.

"Are you sure he's okay?" I ask Lou. "Shouldn't we take him to the hospital, get him properly checked out?"

"The doctor did." But Lou's assurances don't help assuage my worry. Elias's eyes are dark, and hard, like glistening flint.

"You need to rest, young man," Lou tells him.

"Nah." Elias wipes the back of his hand over his bloodied nose, and it starts to bleed again. Harper rushes towards him with a tissue and the white paper soon turns red. "I got this," I hear him say.

I get that he is mad, yet I want him to tell me that it's not my fault. I need some sort of reassurance from him, even though I know it was all because of me. I'm starting to feel lost again. Lost and rudderless. A failure and a waste of space.

"We should go," Santos tells me.

I walk away, desperate to leave. Each moment I stand here only reminds Elias of the things he would rather not remember.

"You sure you're going to be okay?" Harper asks,

lowering her voice as she touches my arm. "I'm worried about you."

"I'm fine."

"Is Callum not coming at all?"

"Something came up."

"Where are you staying?"

I mumble my hotel name at her.

"I'll come and see you tomorrow. You'll still be here tomorrow morning, won't you?"

I'm touched by her concern for me. "Don't worry about me. Take care of Elias. He's the one you need to worry about."

CHAPTER FIFTY-FOUR

CALLUM

"What the hell?"

I glower at the headlines of the paper on the newsstand. Pulling down my baseball cap, I survey the blatant lies.

Callum and Alyssa Back Together

Hollywood's Hottest Couple Share Cozy Dinner

Alyssa Forgives the One Night Stand

He Made A Mistake

There's some mention about 'the waitress' but the article focuses on me and Alyssa and our 'romance'. It goes on to say that we're flying off to the Bahamas now that filming has ended. There are rumors that I will pop the question.

What the hell?

We've gone from 'getting together' at the start of this film, to me proposing to her three months later.

Rudy.

Dinner with him and Alyssa and the others, two nights ago.

A huge mistake.

I was so pissed off about missing the flight to New York that I wasn't really present when we got to the restaurant.

I couldn't wait to leave.

But this? I smack the paper against the wall. This is a new low. Fairytale romances and glittering multi-million-dollar deals are forged here in Tinsel Town, a place which swims in lies and deceit. But this isn't fair to Nina. She's been dragged into this unknowingly. Because of me.

One-night stand?

He made a mistake?

No frigging way.

These are the types of headline that will make Nina see red, if she ever decides to talk to me again. She won't believe this, at least, I hope she won't, because she can see through the bullshit.

I walk off, wanting to be put my fist through Rudy's face.

I've left her numerous messages and texts since the fight, but she hasn't called back. Each time I call her, her phone goes to voicemail. I consider calling Harper, then as quickly I decide against it. Nina is annoyed at me, and it's better I speak to her first, besides, I won't be surprised if they're all still in New York.

I'm sick of Rudy and him telling me that the success of a film depends on rumors and giving the fans what they want.

'What they want is for you and your leading lady to fall in love.' He's always telling me I can't mess with the studio. I can't change the system.

Hollywood made you, Sandersby.

You'll never get a chance like this again.

NINA

I'm back. Elias and Harper are still in New York. Lou thinks it will be a good idea to go back to Dwayne Bank's place, and Harper agrees. She says it's peaceful over there. Elias is doing a few interviews today, but Harper tells me he's still not in a good place. Losing the fight has been the biggest setback for him.

Now that I'm here, I wish I hadn't rushed back. I wished I had braved Elias's wrath and stuck around. I would have owned up to my blame in this.

Callum has called me a number of times. He's left messages and texts, but I haven't returned them. I saw the newspaper headlines the day I landed. Alongside the huge gut-wrenching picture of a jubilant Garrison, and the bloodied and battered face of Elias on the front page, there's a small photo, also on the front page, showing Callum and Alyssa, and a small picture of me, looking a disheveled mess. It was probably taken as I left the diner one day. I didn't even notice anyone taking it. The headlines scream about how Callum has made up with Alyssa, and how I was the one-night stand. How he made a bad mistake.

Once upon a time, this would have killed me, seeing my photo and my story in a freaking local paper. But everything has been eclipsed by my worry over Elias and his state of mind.

Even Callum takes a backseat.

When I arrived at the diner this morning, Frankie told me to go home and take it easy. I couldn't. I can't go home. Not right now. There's nothing for me there. I'll be too close to temptation.

My saving grace is night school. I've missed a few classes over the past few weeks, but I need to get back to it. Night school gives me a much needed distraction, and I have a lot of assignments to catch up on.

I sit by the corner, catching up on my assignment when things are less busy. Joni comes over. We've been civil towards one another. I haven't been in a talkative mood ever since my return, so I've kept myself to myself. She asked me about the fight, and I told her what she wanted to know. She said she was back with Rhys, but I didn't have much to say about that. I was curious about the last guy she hooked up with, during her twenty four hour split from Rhys, but I didn't care enough to ask her.

She comes over again with a newspaper and spreads it out on the table. "*Did* you have a one-night stand with him?"

I ignore her and focus on my homework.

"You did," she gasps, taking my silence for an answer. I stop writing and feel the muscles on my face tighten. It's not a question I will answer. She's being who she normally is—a nosey bitch instead of a friend. I give her a hard stare.

"There's no need to get all moody with me. I'm only asking, Nina. 'Cause this isn't like you. You don't even *like* guys."

"Evidently I do."

"It says here he's back with Alyssa. Is it true?"

"If it's in the paper, it must be."

"Are you okay?" she asks, as if she gives a damn.

"I'm perfectly fine."

Joni folds the paper and moves it to one side. "We saw the fight. What happened to Elias? It's like he didn't even try."

I blink. What does she expect me to say to that?

"He must be upset?" she asks.

"He must be."

"You look upset. Do you want to come out with us tonight?"

Us?

"No, thanks."

"Scott won't be there."

Still no. I shake my head.

"Rhys says you could probably do with some cheering up."

I grit my teeth. "No thanks."

"Don't be like that, Nina."

"I've got assignments to catch up." I consider asking her why she's back with Rhys, but she might think I care, and I don't. She thinks it's love, what Rhys does to her, how he treats her. No amount of explaining on my part has ever made a difference in the past and I don't expect it will going forward. She'll only see what she chooses to see.

"We're going for something to eat. I know you don't exactly feel comfortable with him around, but it was his idea. He says you're likely feeling down and the papers haven't exactly been kind to you or Elias."

"I'm touched by his compassion." My sarcasm is layered on extra thick.

"Think about it. I'm going to the washroom to make myself look pretty. Let me know if you change your mind." She disappears.

I exhale slowly. I can't go home, but I don't want to go to night school either. I wish Harper were here. I can talk to her. I purposely didn't take up much of her time yesterday because she was with Elias the whole time, but I'm missing company. Good company with people who care about me.

"Hey, Nina. Seen Joni?"

His voice grates on my nerves more than Joni's voice does. I don't even look up at him. I can't stand Rhys, and surely, he must know that by now.

"She's getting changed," I say, picking up my pen and pretending to get busy. I won't look at Rhys even though he comes and hovers around my table.

"You must be feeling kinda down."

I sniff, then rub my finger under my nose. My eyes are still trained on my work, but then he puts his hand on my shoulder, and I flinch. "Back off." I snarl.

He grins. "Boyfriend troubles? I read the papers. What a day when both Cardoza's make it onto the front page. Only in Chicago, mind you. I doubt you're that important anywhere else."

I continue writing, but I'm not even sure that what I'm writing makes sense. I'm scribbling *something*, but my insides are all knotted up. I need rescuing.

Frankie. Where are you?

"Maybe Elias will come down a peg or two, instead of strutting around as if he's the king of this city."

I jolt my head up. "My brother never thought he was the king of anything."

"He's definitely not anything now. I didn't think he'd

last the whole distance, with Garrison this time around, but I didn't expect him to go down like he did so soon."

I pinch my lips together in a bid to stay calm. Rhys likes shooting off, and he's trying to rile me up.

"You don't look so happy, either. Can't be all to do with Elias getting beat."

This piece of filth wants me to react, but I won't. I refuse to give him the reaction he's trying to get. He puts his hand on my shoulder again, and this time his fingers dig into my flesh.

I'm dragged back into the janitor's basement. I am lost, hopeless and powerless to do anything. I try to open my mouth, but my muscles freeze up. "The papers called you a one night stand. I didn't think you put out for anyone. I guess you have different rules for famous guys." His fingers dig in. "Anytime you get lonely you —"

"Hey!" Someone sweeps in and gives Rhys an almighty shove. He goes flying backwards and hits the wall. "Get your fucking hands off her."

Callum.

My heart sinks.

Rhys is up and on his feet before charging towards Callum. The two of them grapple in the aisle, pushing and shoving like schoolboys.

"Stop it!" I yell, just as Callum pulls back on his arm, flexing his fist, his other grabbing Rhys's collar. Callum pauses to look at me, and that's when Rhys slams him in the face. Callum's fist flies and lands with a heavy thwack across Rhys's cheek.

"Hey!" Frankie bellows, as she marches over. "Break it up!" Her voice booms across the diner.

"Son of a bitch." Rhys holds the side of his face. It's red

and swollen. Callum shakes his hand which is just as red. He winces, and I can see that he's in great pain.

"What the—" Joni looks at the two men who are eyeballing one another. Frankie stands in the middle with her hands on her hips, daring either one of them to move.

"Get out," she tells Rhys. She waggles her finger at Joni. "If I ever catch him in here again, I will fire you."

"On what grounds?"

"On *my* grounds. Get out! The pair of you."

I close my eyes, wishing everything would disappear.

"I 'spose you need some ice?" she asks Callum.

"Ice would be great." He winces, and I can tell from looking at him that his hand is likely fractured, and he's going to be sporting another black eye. He sits down across from me. "Hey."

"I didn't need you to do that for me." It's been a while since we last met. Seems like so much has changed since then.

"I saw your face as soon as I walked in. I saw his hand on your shoulder. There was no way I was going to—"

"You're not my keeper, Callum. You don't need to play the hero."

"I wasn't playing the hero. I'm not going to let anyone do that to you."

I inhale deeply. "I don't need you to do that for me." I don't need heroes. I have managed just fine being my own hero. Even if I have occasional lapses.

"It's not true. About me and Alyssa. It's not true what they said about you, and the shit they made sound like I said about you."

"I know that's not true," I hiss back. It annoys me that he thinks he has to spell it out to me.

"That's not how I meant it. The media are bastards. You should know that by now."

"I do." Who's he trying to convince? I stare at my notes. Part of me wants him to go, and the other part wants him to stay. Callum makes things better, but someone like me doesn't need the headache that being a part of his life entails. It's a good thing I didn't make a mistake in telling him my story, that I never trusted him one hundred per cent. He's not a bad guy, but he's a big star, and I've seen at close hand how much of his life is lived under the microscope.

"I'm sorry I wasn't there for you. I was ready to come to the fight. I was ready to leave, but Rudy cornered me. They had it all set up. The meeting with the studio heads, the planned dinner with Alyssa."

"I don't need to know."

"I *want* you to know."

I tap my pen on my notepad. "But I don't need to. It doesn't matter."

"What's that supposed to mean?"

"That it doesn't matter. The fight is over with, it's done. It doesn't matter now."

"Don't push me away, Nina."

A quick glance around the diner tells me that people are staring. Some have their phones out and are filming. "You have an audience," I say, lowering my voice.

"Then let's go somewhere."

"No."

"No?" he asks, surprised. Why he is surprised comes as a shock. He let me down. Did he think he could waltz in here and kiss and makeup with me?

"No."

"You're doing it anyway. Pushing me away." He sounds weary, as if he was expecting this. "How's Elias?"

"How do you think?"

"You have every right to be angry with me. I wasn't there when you needed me, I get why you're angry, but let's talk it out. Don't shut down on me."

I lower my voice, "If you wanted to break up with me, with whatever it is that we have, you should at least have told me instead of giving me a feeble excuse why you couldn't come."

"Break up? What are you talking about?"

"I find it hard to believe that you—Callum Sandersby the famous actor—you couldn't be there for me when I most needed you." It's a long shot, and it's come down to him and the papers. I don't trust the papers, but now I'm starting to wonder if I should trust him.

He lowers his voice. "I told you. Rudy set me up."

"You expect me to believe that you're his puppet?"

He presses his finger and thumb against his brows, then looks at me. "You don't know how Hollywood works."

"This was important to me." I've never been one to rely on others because I could never trust anyone. Trusting Callum, relying on him, it was a risk for me.

"I know it was, and believe me, I feel bad. I feel *real* bad. You don't have to beat me up about it, Nina, because I'm already beating myself up about it. I'm sorry. I am so, so sorry." He reaches out as if he's going to take my wrist, then moves his hand away. "Are you ... are you okay?"

"You don't need to worry," I say, in case he thinks I'm going to start going back to my old ways.

"Let's go somewhere and talk this over. I know you feel bad for Elias. I know how close you two are. At least you have a brother."

I stare at him, wondering why he said that. Why he played that last card. "What?"

"It's my fault."

"What?"

It slipped out. He won't understand. "Nothing. I have to go." I rush to gather my work.

"You think it was your fault? For Christ's sake, Nina. Not everything is your fault. How can this be? Elias got into that ring to fight. You had no input in that."

I get this sounds crazy to him, but I also understand that I can't be a part of Callum's life. I like my privacy, my anonymity. I got lost for a few stolen moments being with him. I let my guard down and thought I could be normal; a normal woman with a normal life, with a normal guy. Maybe not so normal. He's not normal, and his lifestyle is not normal.

That, right there, tells me I picked the wrong guy.

Or the wrong guy picked me.

He pursued me.

For the wrong reason.

The logical side of my brain schools me on the truth, while the pitter patter of my heart tells me I should forgive him and forget. I've met Rudy, I've heard how he speaks. I knew Callum had contracts and obligations to stick to. I just didn't think asking him to be there for me was that big a deal. But it's not just that one night. I'm scared that I started to depend on him. I started to trust him, and in the end all I feel is let down.

That's what I'm scared of the most.

Despite who he is, I stayed away from Callum for the longest time, only letting him in because I thought he was different. He's not a predator, like the one I have known. He's not a slime bag, like Rhys. He's a nice guy, and he cares for me—it's not him, it's the getting used to someone and letting yourself feel vulnerable that scares me.

He stands up and grabs my arms, further up, so that he won't touch my scars. "We need to talk. You're upset, more than I realized. I messed up, but I couldn't get out of it."

"I have to go. I'll be late."

"There's something else, isn't there? Something you're not telling me? Something you've never told me?"

I stare at him, my mouth open, the breath stuck in my throat. How is it that he can see right through me?

"Let go of me," I say, feeling uncomfortable.

"I won't let you walk away, Nina, not until we talk things through."

I glance over his shoulder and see people filming us on their cell phones. "I can't be with someone who's life is on display for the public to consume."

CHAPTER FIFTY-FIVE

CALLUM

I expected her to be angry. I didn't expect her to stay angry once I had explained. There's more to it, I know. She blames herself for Elias losing, just the way she blames herself for most things.

I'm going to give her the space she needs, but I'm not going to give up. It's not the last of it when a few days later Dottie shows me the video of the altercation in the diner between me and that idiot who laid a hand on Nina. He's the boyfriend of her so-called waitress friend and he's lucky Frankie broke up the fight when she did.

I'm lucky Frankie stepped in. My temper got the better of me and it would have given me the wrong publicity if I'd landed a few more punches.

"This isn't great publicity," Dottie counters. "Are you pleased about this?"

"No." I'm not pleased but I saw the way that moron put

his paws on Nina. I saw the way she reacted. "It could have been worse."

"Nina's in the clip." Dottie shoves her cell phone closer in my face. Whichever idiot took this, got us talking afterwards. It's plain to see me and Nina sitting in one of the booths. I feel the color drain from my face and I can see the tawdry headlines already.

Dottie nods. "See, that's what I meant. Now you've dragged her into it."

"People film everything I do." I grit my teeth, hating the fact that I can't live my life without the whole world finding out what I'm up to.

"Maybe next time don't go and pick a fight in a public place."

"I didn't pick a fight. The guy was being a jerk."

"How's Nina going to feel about this?" Dottie puts away her phone. "What did she say, about you not making it to the fight?"

"She wasn't happy." I sigh out loudly. "She wasn't happy at all."

"It's a shame you couldn't go."

"It's not that I couldn't go. I had every intention. Deliberate obstacles were put in my path."

"I feel sorry for Nina. I like her. She's real, genuine. Nothing phony about her," says Dottie. There is nothing phony about her, and that's one more thing I cherish about her. "She left me a message apologizing about the tickets."

"The tickets?" I frown. "What tickets?"

"I'd asked her, rather cheekily, if there was a way I could get tickets to the fight. Sam's a boxing fanatic."

"That was a big thing to ask her. You barely know her."

"I got to know her in LA," retorts Dottie. "I would have

paid for the tickets, but she forgot. Says she had a lot on her mind and she's sorry."

I feel even more of a jerk now. If anyone should be sorry, it's me. I have to make it up to her.

"This has gone viral, Callum," Dottie taps her cell phone. "Rudy will be on the warpath."

I prepare myself for that eventuality.

NINA

The media is unforgiving. All morning, in between serving customers, I've been looking through the papers.

Cardoza stopped in the sixth by a fearless and better prepared Garrison

Elias got sloppy and paid the price

Cardoza stunned by relentless Trent Garrison in one of the biggest upsets in boxing history

"Boxing is an unforgiving sport at the best of times," Lou tells me when I pass by the gym. Lou only got back yesterday but Elias and Harper are still in New York. "But Elias will be back. He'll be fighting fit and better prepared."

"I hope so." Only Elias winning the belt back will make things better. I haven't been able to sleep. I haven't been able to do much. I'm pretty useless even at the diner.

"You're doubting him?" he asks, slowly lifting a wiry

white eyebrow. "He took a beating out there but there will be a rematch. No doubt about it. Six months max."

Lou's thinking of making Elias fight that soon? "Will he even be ready?"

"'Course he'll be ready." Ernesto, the gym handyman, walks into Lou's office with three cups of coffee on a tray. He offers mine up to me first. "Thanks, Ernesto."

"You doubting your brother?" he asks me, looking perplexed. "You've never doubted Elias before."

"She saw the same beating we all saw," says Lou, leaning back in his chair. "He wasn't complacent in there. He just didn't seem to know what hit him."

We all sound like a trio of doomsters as we pick through the remnants of Elias's fight. Ernesto heaves out a sigh. "But he *was* prepared. I seen him fight, I seen him spar with the guys. He was solid." He nods at Lou. "You said he worked till he dropped over at Banks's place."

Lou taps his pen on the desk. "He was fighting fit. He had it all under control. This should have been a win. It wasn't going to be an easy win, you saw Garrison, but it should have been Elias's win."

Ernesto takes a sip of his coffee. "Problem is, Garrison's been working out. Been in the best shape I've ever seen him. He was hungry to get those belts back."

"That he did, but Elias wanted to hold onto them just as much," Lou states. "Everything okay between him and Harper?" he asks me.

"Yeah. They're good. No problem there." It's not Harper who messed up Elias's head. It's me.

"Then what are you looking so worried for?" Ernesto asks me. "Elias got those belts and those world titles from Garrison once, when nobody but the three of us in this room believed he had it in him. He'll do it again, you wait and see. He'll get back what's rightfully his."

"He was beaten by a counter puncher with fast hands and fast footwork," muses Lou.

"Elias has fast hands, fast feet and fast instincts," Ernesto reminds us.

Lou looks weary. "So what the hell happened?" It's plain to see that he's taken this defeat as personally as Elias. Ernesto looks at me and Lou. "I'm standing here listening to the both of you and it sounds like you've both given up on him."

"I haven't given up on him," I reply quickly.

"This fight will go down in history as a huge upset," says Lou. Ernesto backs away from the wall and sets his coffee cup on the desk. "It wasn't so long ago that Elias did the impossible and wrested those titles from Garrison. I know it, and you both know it, and everyone with half a brain knows it. Elias was a nobody, just an underdog, and he did the impossible."

Lou and I sit there silently. I lap up the pep talk. "I don't know what happened this time. Sure, Garrison was fitter, thinner, faster and he seemed more prepared, but you've been training fighters for so long," he points at Lou, "and you said it yourself, you haven't seen anyone with Elias's hunger to win and the rage that burns inside him. He'll get it back, just you wait and see."

"They will rematch for the IBF, WBA and WBO world titles, and Elias has to win," declares Lou, as if saying it will make it happen. "I just need to figure out where he went wrong this time."

CHAPTER FIFTY-SIX

CALLUM

I venture back into the diner late in the evening. Late enough that there will be less people but early enough for Nina to still be here.

Luckily for me, she is.

I'm in my beanie hat and looking scruffy. Some people have noticed me, but I'm not attracting too big of a crowd to worry about. When Nina sees me, and our gazes meet across the room, she freezes. There's a menu in her hand and it looks like she's about to come over but because it's me she stops.

Another waitress, not her pain-in-the-ass friend, comes over instead and I order my usual milkshake.

I'm not going to approach her. That's not the reason I came. I'm still going to give her space, but I wanted to see how she was. I called Harper earlier, to see how Elias was doing. They had only just arrived back from New York. I told her I couldn't make it to the fight because film stuff got in the way. I was hoping Harper would offer up some news on Nina but I guess they're firm friends and she's not about to spill her friend's news to me.

Which is admirable, given the industry I'm from and what I'm used to.

We didn't get to talk for long because she was unpacking, and Elias had gone out for a run. She wanted to get everything done before he got back.

"We'll get together over dinner or something," she said, "When everything is settled."

That would be good, but I wonder when everything will be settled. Judging by the way Nina reacted to seeing me just now, it doesn't look like anything's going to be settled any time soon.

I have a meeting with Rudy, the director and the producer tomorrow. They want me to explain the news story, and why I've gone off script with the Alyssa romance.

I have no idea what I'm going to say.

Or what they'll say.

Rudy says the sequel for 'Legend' is on the fence, due to my 'not toeing the line'.

I'm not sure how I feel about that. I don't like being owned or being told how to live my private life. This wouldn't have been a problem ordinarily, but then Nina happened, and I don't intend to mess anything up just to fall in line with what the studio says.

"Here you go." Frankie delivers my milkshake and sits down. Now this is worth coming here for. She usually has a good old dose of Frankie common sense and wisdom and I'm hoping she'll enlighten me tonight.

"Cheers," I say, lifting the glass in the mid-air. "How about you have one, too?"

She snorts. "The smell of milkshake doesn't ever leave

me. I'm sick to death of it and all the other food smells that cling to my clothes and get stuck in my pores."

"Must be an occupational hazard, constantly smelling food everywhere?"

"I might have to consider giving this up soon."

"And do what?" I ask, smirking. Frankie's Kitchen is one of the most popular diners in Chicago. She has a good thing going here.

"That's just it. What would I do? What are you going to do?" she asks.

"When I leave? I could ask you to start a franchise and open a place in LA."

She opens her eyes with interest. "Keep talking. That sounds like a good idea to me."

We joke around, tossing ideas back and forth, as if our new LA diner would be a real thing. I'm not so sure that it can't exist, even though LA is full of diners, Frankie's has a certain something.

Maybe that certain something is Nina.

"You two fallen out?" Frankie asks, glancing at Nina who has been careful to stay away from where I'm sitting.

"I'm not sure."

"That was a mighty fine thing you did for her last week, standing up for her with that jerk. Has it cost you?"

I take a slurp of my milkshake, frowning. "Cost me? As in with the studio?"

She dismisses that notion with a wave of her hand. "I'm sure that stuff can be fixed. Maybe not the way you want it, but it can probably be fixed. Cost you with a certain Ms. Cardoza is what I mean."

Thinking about it like that, it cost me because Nina doesn't want anything to do with me. "She's not too pleased with me, as you can see."

"Oh, I can see alright," Frankie replies, smoothly. "Lemme guess, you're waiting for this situation to fix itself, by giving Nina more time."

I shrug.

"You can have all the time in the world but that little lady isn't going to come waltzing back to your door." She lowers her voice. "Just so you know, you got to her, and she's in full retreat mode."

This doesn't make sense. "I messed up. I did," I insist when Frankie rolls her eyes. "I was supposed to be at the fight, she asked me to, but I couldn't make it."

"I heard about that. The waitresses talk about everything you get up to, and who you get up to it with."

"None of that is true," I point out. "All that Alyssa stuff, it's made up."

"Oh, I don't believe that rubbish. I know most of it's not true. You probably did eat at a certain restaurant, but I doubt that you're about to swan off to the Bahamas and propose marriage to someone you barely know let alone care about."

I smile. "You're smarter than you think."

"How do you think Frankie's Kitchen became such a popular place?" She grins at me. "Now, how are you going to fix this? You know what I'm talking about."

"I figured I would wait it out," I tell her. I'm not going to put Nina under any pressure. She'll come to me when she's good and ready.

Frankie snorts with laughter. "You'll be shooting another film before she even thinks about it."

"I don't want to pressure her." She's too fragile. I won't push her.

"Then say goodbye," Frankie says.

I twist my lips, about to disagree.

"Say goodbye," Frankie repeats.

"You don't understand Nina."

"Oh, I understand her just fine," Frankie retorts. "You don't give her all the time in the world, you make her see sense. The thing she wants you to think she's angry about, is not the thing that's the problem."

I blink as I try to process what she just said.

"If you want her, you'll have to go up and claim her."

I don't see how this will work. I've worked Nina out. I think I have. There's no way I'll ever go up to her and impose my will, or demand to be heard.

As if she knows what I'm thinking, Frankie gives me a withering look as she slides out of the booth, "Okay then, suit yourself. Do it your way, because what you've been doing is working, huh?"

CHAPTER FIFTY-SEVEN

NINA

At least Ernesto believes in Elias more than Lou or I do. I believe in him, but I know what went wrong, and I want to help him fix it.

Harper calls me as soon as she and Elias return from Chicago. I want to go over and see Elias but she cautions me against it, and suggests that she comes over to my place, so that's what she's doing this evening. I've made dinner, in the hope that Harper will take some back for Elias. I've made his favorite chicken dish.

In all this, I've since discovered that the clip of the fight at the diner between Callum and Rhys has gone all over the internet.

Joni is still sour about Rhys getting banned from the diner, and there is more animosity between us than tolerance. Where and how did it go so wrong between us? I tried to help her, I tried to make her see, but there are some people who can't be helped; who don't *want* to be helped.

I can't help fix Joni, but I can help fix Elias. I can put him back together again.

I feel bad for Callum. Now that a few days have passed, I have calmed down and besides, so many things have happened that I feel less angry towards him. I know what I am doing, weaning myself off him. I got too close this time.

But I don't think about us. He said he wanted to talk and fix things between us, but there is no future for us. It's easier for me to discount these things—the good times in LA, getting to know him when we got back to Chicago, everything. The path to finding a new me. I thought I could become my alter ego and be the woman who could lead a normal life, untainted by past baggage. Now everything has reset back to my default.

While we eat, Harper tells me about all that happened in New York in the days after the fight. It sounds like they spent a lot of time just mulling around and sightseeing once the interviews were done and out of the way. Sightseeing isn't something Elias would have done willingly, not in his current frame of mind, but I am thankful that Harper insisted and dragged him around everywhere instead of him being stuck inside with nothing but bad memories and guilt eating away at him. I'm certain he's feeling guilty, because that's how I felt when I found out about his abuse. Guilt that it happened to him, even though I couldn't have done anything about it because I didn't know. Guilt, and hate, and utter wretchedness that the janitor tricked us both.

"He's hopeful," she says, when I ask her how he feels about a rematch. "He wants to get all his titles back."

"Did he say anything?" I fish for clues, trying to figure out where he's at.

"About?"

"About how he's feeling? What happened that night?" What was on his mind? What went wrong?

Harper scoffs. "I don't ask him about what happened that night. That's for Lou to work out. I keep his boxing life and *our* life separate."

"I want to see him."

"You should. He said he hadn't spoken to you properly, since that day ... he said he needed to. Give him a day to unwind, then go and see him."

"I've been trying to. None of you people would even let me near him before the fight." My anger bubbles up. "You kept me out. I sat in the arena by myself, wondering how he was doing. I know that what he heard about me messed with his brain."

"Then it was better I kept you away," Harper says softly. "Elias loves you. That bond the two of you have is like nothing I've ever seen. It's watertight. I love that you are both that close."

Watertight.

Seems like the seal broke and has stayed broken.

"Him losing wasn't your fault, you know that, right?" She's trying. I'll give her that. "He overheard and maybe it's a good thing he did."

She thinks Elias hearing about my abuse was a good thing? In which messed up universe would something like this be a good thing? "It's a *good* thing? How can it be when he lost the fight?"

"It's a good thing for both of you, otherwise you would never have told him."

"He never needed to know," I shoot back.

"But you didn't need to keep that all bottled up inside you."

I put down my fork. "I don't want to talk about it."

"Then let's talk about Callum." She sets down her fork. "What happened? Why couldn't he make it that night?"

"He had dinner with his co-star."

"I saw." She cocks her head. "I also saw the clip of him fighting some guy in the diner, and then the two of you sitting down talking."

I let out an I-don't-want-to-talk-about-it groan.

"No one believes the stuff about him and his co-star," she says. "It's so obviously contrived. But you ..." She sits forward and puts her elbows on the table. The mischievous glint is back in her eyes. "You and him, *that's* the real story. The actor and the waitress. That's the stuff of dreams. That's the fabric of fairytales."

I snort. "There is no story. There are no dreams, and there sure as hell aren't any fairytales."

"He doesn't know about what happened to you, does he?"

I shake my head.

"Why not?"

"He doesn't need to know." My past was responsible for my inability to trust anyone. I made an exception with him. I moved out of my comfort zone, put down my walls and I let Callum in. I almost told him, but I see what a huge mistake that would have been. Now I'm determined that he will never know. Soon, he will be gone, and none of my life will matter to him anymore. "We're not together, not that we ever really—"

"I call bullshit."

I blink because Harper is not one to swear. Elias is rubbing off on her.

"You were together. You were starting to be together. You can deny it all you want, Nina, but I've seen a change in you these last few weeks. You going to LA for a weekend with a *guy?* You've never so much as talked about a guy, let alone get up and gone away with him, and it being a mega movie star to boot. *You* changed. *He* changed you. Something about him made you get up and do the things that have scared you in the past—things like trusting, and believing and *being.* Letting go and having fun."

Harper is on a roll.

I open my mouth, but soon realize that I can't interrupt or reject anything she's saying, because what she's saying is the truth.

"Callum was the reason you did all those things." She huffs out a breath. "He didn't need to pursue you the way he did, for as long as he did, as relentlessly as he did, and probably, as gently as he did. He must have been patient with you because you're quick to ward people off. I've seen you do it at the diner. I've heard your witty one-liners when guys show an interest. So for Callum to have convinced you to step out of your normal routine and do the unthinkable, that must have taken something."

I swallow. It feels like I'm getting a dressing down. I can see why Elias went sight-seeing in New York when he didn't want to. If Harper can make a boxing champ see reason, she's going to make me see reason no matter how much I resist.

CHAPTER FIFTY-EIGHT

NINA

"Thanks for the chicken."

"I knew you'd like it."

I'm in Elias's living room. It's the first time I've seen him since the night of the fight. He looks a little gaunt, and I'm not sure if it's the fight or other stuff. I look away. Now that he knows about me, I find it hard to look him in the eye.

This is more awkward than I thought it would be.

"Do you want a drink or something?" he asks, leading me towards the kitchen. I'm relieved that we're heading into the kitchen, and not sitting on the sofas. I already feel panicky and fidgety.

"When's Harper back?" He told me she was having an overnight stay at a tech conference and I'm guessing that's why he invited me over tonight.

"Tomorrow."

Why does it feel so awkward? I've wanted to talk to him, ever since that day, but now that I have my chance, I'd much rather run away and hide. He opens up a bottle filled with dark green liquid. It looks gross. Like someone pureed spinach and added it to water.

"What is that?" I ask him, as I settle myself on a bar stool.

"A bottle of goodness."

"No, seriously, what is it?" He pulls open the refrigerator and pulls out a second bottle. "I made it for you." He hands it to me. "It's spinach, mango, pineapple, celery and kale. All good stuff. You should try it."

I wrinkle my nose when I open it and take a whiff.

"You should take more of the things that are good for you, Nina."

I look at him, unsure, then take a sip. It's actually not as bad as I thought it would be.

"It takes some time, getting used to it." He sits himself down next to me.

I take another sip. "It's not so bad. More like an acquired taste."

He smiles. The air is tense for a moment. I feel more awkward than ever.

"Harper says you feel responsible, that you think I lost the fight because of what you said about Grampton House and Sw—"

"Don't say his name. Please, don't say his name." I look away, but my insides are churning.

So quickly? I didn't expect him to move to the topic straightaway. Elias puts his hand around my shoulder, reassuring. "I didn't know he did that to you." His voice falters. It can't be easy for him either. Neither of us are looking at each other. I stare at the table, my head lowered because this is hard to hear. I can't talk. "I haven't been able to get it out of my head, Nina. I know

now why you reacted the way you did when you found out about me."

There is more awkward silence and I can't bring myself to say anything because the pain of revisiting the past is sharp and heavy.

Elias squeezes my shoulder gently, and the weight of his around me is a comfort I so badly need. "I don't want you to blame yourself for me losing. I should have been able to put that behind me. I should have been able to focus on the fight. Me losing is on me."

"But it's not," I protest, remembering how I couldn't function when I found out.

"The reason I can talk about what happened, the reason why I can say his name, is because I've been able to talk to people. I've got Harper, and I started seeing a therapist. I wonder if the thing that gave me my fighting edge was the anger bottled up inside me. I wonder if now that I can talk about my past, I have no rage. I've gone soft."

"You haven't gone all soft," I say. "You still have the anger to fuel you when it counts. Lou said you trained like a mad man."

"You spoke to Lou?"

"I was worried about you. You and I haven't spoken since that day. No one let me into the locker room on the night. And then I saw you fight, and then lose and I didn't know what to do, or how to reach you or tell you that I felt so bad."

"It's not your place to feel bad about a fight I lost, no matter what you say, or how you try to make it your responsibility and your fault for everything that goes wrong for me."

"If you hadn't heard. If I hadn't told Harper, you wouldn't have lost." I feel the energy leak out of me. What we're talking about drains me. Living in the past is an energy suck. Living in my past is deadly.

"You convinced yourself that it was only you who was to blame?" He hugs me to him. "You've always been more than a bigger sister to me. More than the mom we never had. You've looked out for me and protected me and you've always been there for me, Nina."

"We've always been there for each other," I correct.

"You've always done the right thing for me, but never the right thing for you," he whispers. "We can't let the past have any more power. I lost maybe because I got complacent, or I lost my edge, or talking to my therapist made me all soft. Maybe I lost because I walked in on a conversation I shouldn't have eavesdropped on. We'll never know. But I lost, and you had nothing to do with it. Got that?" He hugs me tighter. "Got that?" he says again, when I don't reply.

I don't reply because I don't agree.

"You overthink things, Nina. You live in the past. You don't talk. You wouldn't have ever told me, if I hadn't overhead, would you have?"

"Would you have?" I ask him. He didn't tell me either.

He takes a sip from his bottle. "So maybe it's not such a bad thing that I overheard. I needed to know. We both did. Because my story came out, I could deal with it, and part of that dealing with it is the thing that helps you to heal. We're broken people otherwise, Nina. *Broken*. I don't want to be broken anymore. Being complete is a whole lot better."

I frown, still not getting how the whole world knowing his business is a good thing.

"You don't get it, do you?" he says, his voice barely audible. "To heal and to move on, I want that for you more badly than I want it for myself." I look up at him again, more confused than enlightened. "You spend your life fixing things. Worrying about things, blaming yourself about things that you are blameless in. I don't want you to spend your life thinking and worrying about anyone else anymore. I want all the good things for you. I want you to be happy. Nina?" He studies my face. "Say something."

He wants me to take his advice and say I will be fine. He wants to hear it as badly as I want to fix things. "You want to talk about the future and I want to tell you I'm sorry about the past."

"The past is not your fault. Nothing is your fault. You were a girl. An eight year old girl." He loses it then, and the mask slips. He looks away.

It hurts. Knowing the truth of it hurts.

"What happened to us back then, doesn't define who we are today," he says, nodding his head as if he's talking himself off the ledge of pain. "We can't let Sw—" He stops, "We can't let that man have the power, because if we can't move on from this, he wins. It means that even in death, he still has a hold on us, and I don't want him to have a hold, do you, Nina?"

I shake my head. "I don't want any part of him. No memories, no nightmares, no nothing."

"And the best way to do that is to find the thing that makes you happy and run with it. And never let it go."

I lift my head.

"You have that thing, don't you?" he asks.

I roll my lips together, thinking.

"Maybe you need to take another look," he suggests.

I wonder what Harper has been telling him.

"I'm taking a couple of weeks off, me and Harper and Lou and his wife are heading back to Dwayne's place. Dwayne thinks it will be a good idea for me to go out there and clear my head. Why don't you and Callum come along?"

"Callum?" I don't want to get into an explanation about Callum. "I don't know. I'll see."

"You'll see?"

"Yeah."

"We good?" he asks, sounding like a seven year old Elias, wanting to make up with me.

"We're good."

We hug and hold onto each other for a long time.

CHAPTER FIFTY-NINE

NINA

I feel bad about that video clip going viral. At first I was angry because it invaded my privacy. It showed me and Callum talking after the fight, and that will only fuel the rumors about him and me.

The waitress and the actor.

Harper does love to come up with her taglines.

I can't imagine that this will work out well for him. People will forget who I am. They probably already did the second the video clip finished.

Soon the papers will stop mentioning me. The circus will leave town and he will be free to continue with whatever story he wants. In a way I feel sorry for him because he won't get his life back, he'll never have it belong only to him. His fans will always want a piece of him.

I did consider going over to him the other day when he came to the diner, when he and Frankie seemed to be talking for ages. She wouldn't tell me what it was about, though. Maybe I should have gone over to him but my pride —for the sake of my sanity—got the better of me.

I understand what Elias and Harper have said, about me needing to fix things, about moving on and talking more about what happened, about seeking help, but I'm not ready yet. I'll get there soon but I'm not there yet. I sense that they are keen for me to make things up with Callum. They think he was good for me.

Maybe he was, but I don't want to depend on anyone and I was starting to with him. I can't rely on anyone for my happiness because that's a slippery slope. I can't allow myself to be that vulnerable so I'll do what I do best, and that means staying away from him.

This is my way of handling things and its always worked well for me.

CALLUM

I'm not sure about the outcome, but I am sure about *this*, about me going to Nina's place. Frankie said Nina had left the diner a short while ago and was going home. I'll take my chances because Frankie's always been right before.

She looks surprised when she opens the door, but she composes herself quickly. "You're still here?" she asks. I smart at the coldness of her question and then I remind myself that she's a ninja at the art of not giving a fuck. That's not the question I would have expected from someone I can't stop thinking about, even someone as aloof as Nina. "I wasn't going to leave without saying goodbye."

She lifts her chin defiantly. Already I feel defeated. I

wasn't expecting her to be ecstatic, but I was expecting her to be friendlier than she is.

"Have you come to say goodbye?" she asks. I try to find some semblance of warmth in those dark eyes. It's only the tight press of her lips that gives me an inkling that all isn't as smooth under that exterior as she would like me to believe.

"Do you want me to say goodbye?" This is the type of question she hates—personal, slightly flirtatious, with double-meaning.

"I don't think it's a good idea for you and me to be seen together."

"I don't care about that."

"The clip went viral."

"It did." I wonder if we are destined to have this conversation on her doorstep. "Let me in?"

She hesitates.

"I'm not asking for a way into your heart, Nina. Just get me through the front door, please." I glance around for signs of any paps with their telephoto lenses.

She opens the door and grants me access.

"Was that really so hard?" I ask her as we stand in her living room." She's changed things around, rearranged where the sofa and TV went. This isn't going anywhere like how I expected it to. I was prepared for her being icy, and standoffish. I was prepared for her to not be willing to give me a chance. I wasn't prepared for this level of nothingness.

"How are your assignments going?" I opt for niceties.

"I ditched night school."

This is a shock. "What? Why?" Her night school kept her busy, just like the diner.

"I missed so many classes, and after the fight, I just lost interest. I'll probably start them up again when the course opens for registration again. The tutor said they'd give me a ten percent discount."

"Ten percent? Is that all? Frankie says you've gone through the A to Z of courses at that place."

"You and Frankie seem to know a lot about me."

"You don't talk to me much anymore, the only way I get to find out how you are is through Frankie or Harper."

She jerks her head to me. "You've been talking to Harper?"

"To ask about Elias. He must be feeling low after losing the fight."

She sits down, and suddenly she looks less guarded. Weary. As if she can't keep the cold facade up any more. I walk over and sit down beside her a few inches away, and not touching her, but close enough that I want to touch her face, and hold her hand and have to restrain myself.

"I'm sorry I wasn't there when you needed me."

"You don't have to keep apologizing for that."

"I feel like you're not hearing me," I tell her.

She stares at her hands. This is it. I have to have the courage of my convictions and I'm almost a hundred per cent certain. "I know what happened to you."

She doesn't turn her head towards me. Instead, she shifts her hands in her lap, picks at a seam on her dress.

"At the children's home," I say.

A tiny crease, the only telltale sign that I might be in the right track, forms in the middle of her brow. "I know it wasn't just Elias. There were other kids, and it happened to you."

"Did Elias tell you?" Her voice is unsteady.

"He never said a thing."

She pales. I literally see the color drain from her face. I've hit the truth. She seems to crumple before my eyes, her shoulders hunch, her head lowers. It's a fight to keep from putting my arms around her, from giving her the comfort and reassurance I so badly want to give her.

"Then how do you know?"

"Elias's biography. There were always rumors of abuse at that place. Never substantiated. Your scars. Small signs. These things added up."

"When did you know?"

"After LA, but I didn't know for sure ... until just now." It's the reason why I never took things further with her when we were making out even when she begged me to. I needed to know she was sure. I needed her to tell me, I needed her to trust me, and she never did, so I was willing to wait for when she would, just like I'm waiting for her to say something now.

Her lower lip quivers.

"It's okay, Nina. It's okay. You don't have to hide it anymore—"

"Okay?" she spits out. Venom in her voice, pure hate in her eyes. She changes in an instant. She's protecting herself. "How would you know? It's not okay. It never was."

"I didn't mean that. What happened to you was never okay. But you don't have to hide it from me. You don't have to close yourself off from me. I care about you." I've fallen for her, but I can't tell her. "Let me in, Nina."

"I don't want to let anyone in."

"You were starting to let me in before."

"I thought you were different."

What am I supposed to say to that? She still doesn't completely trust me. She still needs time.

"I've apologized about the fight, Nina. I don't know what else I can do to make you see that I'm sorry and that I want to get back to how we were before.

"And how were we before?" She glares at me, startling me with the acidity in her tone.

"We were getting to know one another. Tell me you didn't feel anything in LA? Tell me you didn't feel anything back here during those evenings you spent at my hotel? Tell me the night you stayed over was a mistake."

She can't.

I take her silence as a sign that all is not lost.

CHAPTER SIXTY

NINA

It was easier when he was trying to get me to deliver lunch. When his pursuit of me was based on some semblance of attraction, or whatever he claims it was that drew him to me.

I feel as if I'm going to hyperventilate. Or scream. And yet I have to sit here and pretend to be calm.

I can get through this.

Elias knows, and that was the worst thing. Callum is temporary. I can handle him knowing. I think I can trust him not to blab to the world. He's no Gerry.

But he knows, and I don't want to deal with him knowing.

Talking about it helps.

That's what Elias said.

He doesn't say anything. We sit in silence..

I was going to tell Callum before, but I hesitated. Do I tell him now? Do I do this?

It's going to take a leap of faith.

Maybe I can try to.

I clear my throat. "I was eight years old when it happened. He told me that he would leave Elias alone if I let him do things to me."

I can't face Callum, but I hear the subtlest of gasps.

"So I did. How could I let him do anything to my little brother?" I tell him about the game the janitor used to play with me, how he would get me feverishly looking for sweets, how he would count quickly, and how I would always lose.

"Nina," he whispers, his voice hoarse, not like the voice I am used to. He puts his hand on my arm, but it feels as if he's the one who needs to hold on.

"He didn't just take my innocence. He took my childhood. He chewed up the thing that made me human, and then he spat me out." There are days when I don't feel so good, but I put on my mask and I get out there.

"That monster didn't take away your humanness. He took away a part of you, but you're still whole, Nina."

"And all that time, he was telling Elias the same thing, that if he used Elias, then he would leave me alone. Neither of us knew, not until a few months ago. I only found out about Elias when his story broke, but he found out mine when I told Harper, just before the fight." I bite my lip, shivering at the moment Elias found out.

"Elias never knew?

"No one did."

"Then what made you tell Harper?"

You did. Something must have changed in me enough to make me open up to her. "I don't know."

"When?" he asks, softly.

"After we came back from LA." Something changed

inside me from the moment me and Callum started to get close.

He exhales a long breath. "So that's when Elias found out."

"He wasn't supposed to. I never wanted him to know. He walked in and heard us talking." I pick at the seams of my dress. "And that's why he lost the fight" My voice is all wobbly and weak. "I messed with his head."

"You didn't mess with his head," Callum is quick to say.

He doesn't know the damage that telling secrets can do. "That stuff, knowing that stuff, it messed him up."

"No way, Nina. No way."

"You're only saying that, like Elias did, because you don't want me to blame myself."

"You live your life blaming yourself, and you have no control over what Elias does, when he chooses to walk in and listen to a private conversation or not. That's on him, not you."

"But he heard, and he lost."

"He's a fighter. He's lived through moments as bad as hearing what happened to you. He gone into that ring plenty of times, with all of his past in his head, and he's won. This. Isn't. On. You."

I feel his arm around me and at the same time I inhale the merest hint of sea breeze and mint. For a second I'm back in LA, on the sun-lounger in the balcony, with the sun caressing me.

Callum hugs me closer to him. It's not what he says, it's what he *doesn't* say. It's what Callum does that tells me he gets me. That he cares. We sit like that without speaking. I don't have the energy to tell him all of it. I feel lighter for what I have told him, but right now, with his arm around me, with his chin just above my head, this feels like home.

After a while, because my body is slightly twisted, I move away from him and lift my head. To my shock, his eyes have welled up. I can't be sure, but it looks as if tears might spill over his lashes. "Why do you look so sad?"

"You ... " he says in a voice that doesn't sound like his. I chew the inside of my cheek, contemplating, because the sight of this world famous man—this larger than life movie action hero, who has been stripped right back so that he is as raw and as vulnerable as me—this is something I am unprepared for.

This is the real Callum, the one I have come to know. He cares about me, he feels for me, he understands all my fears and flaws.

"You're the bravest woman I know." Furrows crease his brow. "I can't imagine what you've been through. I look at you, and think of the times we've met and talked, and the things I didn't understand, I see them so clearly now. I had a feeling that you had experienced horrors, had lived through a childhood that must have been tough, but I never imagined this for you. Your wounds and scars, at first I thought they were because of Elias. I believed your guilt was because you couldn't be there for him, and then I started to think there was more." He gently trances over my wrists with his fingers. "Your wounds, your refusal to give me a chance, I knew there had to be another reason, and now I know. All I want to do is hold you forever and make things better again. I wish I could take away your pain. I wish I could make it all go away."

"You can't."

He touches my face, his fingers trembling, everything about him less sure and less confident. "I want to help you get over this, Nina. Don't push me away. I want to be by your side. I want to do whatever it takes. I want you to be happy."

"I am happy." I touch his lower lip. "You make me happy." I drop a light kiss on his lips, and he hesitates. I feel like he wants to kiss me back, but he's stopping himself.

He sees through me. Seems to understand me in a way no one has before. And he looks at me in wonder, wiping away the stains of my past. He waited, and was patient, and kind when he didn't have to be. He is the kind of man I can trust. The kind of man I want to be with.

"Come and lie down with me," he says, lying back on the sofa in a more comfortable position, his legs all spread out.

I lie on my side, against him, and we stay like that for the longest time. Hearts beating against one another, bodies pressed as if we were one, lying together in the stillness. I can feel and almost hear the beat of his heart against mine, with his arms wrapped around me. I don't want him to ever let go.

CALLUM

I once believed that Nina didn't trust herself with me. That was my fault, for thinking I was the big ass movie star who no one could resist. Turns out it wasn't that she couldn't trust herself with me, turns out she couldn't trust herself to open up.

Turns out her demons were bigger and darker than any I've had to deal with. I love her. It may be too soon to say it to her, but the way I feel about her, the way I would do anything, anything to protect her, to stop her from getting hurt, the things I feel, I've never felt them with such intensity for anyone before. If that isn't love, I don't know what is.

Losing that last picture of Ben was a huge loss, but I gained something so unexpected in return. Otherwise, how else would I have ever met Nina? Our paths might have crossed, I might have gotten fed up with Rudy and I might have walked into Elias's gym and met him and Harper. But I can't see how I would have pursued Nina without having experienced her indifference towards me from the start. That in itself was eye opening. She wouldn't have caught my eye.

I fervently believe that some things happen for a reason and going down that alleyway and getting mugged were a reason for me to meet Nina.

She has told me things that are hard to hear, but I listen, because she needs me to. She's healing herself by getting it out, and so I stay put. This won't be all of it. There will be more, and when she's ready she can tell me.

Now she's lying in my arms, lying on top of me. I never want to let her go. My heart aches for the girl she used to be and the woman she can be—the carefree and happy woman I saw in LA.

I want to punch this nameless faceless monster who did this to her. Not just her, but Elias too. My heart bleeds for both of them and I finally understand their bond, their closeness. She lies on top of me, light as a feather. I put my arms around her, needing to protect her and keep her safe.

I love her, and it's nothing to do with what she's told me but because I felt a connection to her right from the start. It's taken many different guises but this is what it is now.

Love.

Love that doesn't come from lust and desire because that's not how our attraction began. She was a stranger first, then a waitress, before she became a wary friend. Now she trusts me. She trusts me enough to tell me about the debris of her past.

We stayed like that for the longest time, and then we ordered food, and watched TV. I slept in her bed and I held her all through the night. It all makes such perfect sense, why she froze before. Why she pushed me away.

Sex is the last thing on my mind. She's hard to resist, especially when she puts on one of my big, baggy T-shirts and slips into bed with me. But she sleeps peacefully, even though I lie awake thinking of everything she's told me.

I will be there for her. I'll be the one to love her and help her to heal.

CHAPTER SIXTY-ONE

CALLUM

The studio was pissed off with me when I refused to stop seeing Nina and so defied their orders so brazenly in public, but then a funny thing happened as the weeks rolled by. The fans seemed to like the story about me falling for the waitress, and a waitress who just so happened to be Elias Cardoza's sister.

I'm leaving Chicago for a few weeks, doing some post-production stuff, and then taking a break. And Nina's coming with me.

No more night school, she says. It was her decision.

We sometimes meet at the diner, because Frankie has allocated us a table far in the corner, and she puts out those 'Cleaning in progress' boards which keep everyone away from us.

But we sometimes go out in disguise, Nina too now, since she's become known as my girlfriend, and not just as Elias's sister.

We've managed to do the Chicago Riverwalk and eat outside, and sometimes we'll hang out in my hotel suite, like we're doing tonight.

There's a knock on my door while I'm in the middle of making dinner. I smirk, because it's Nina and she will roll her eyes when she sees that I'm cooking. She once suggested making dinner for me here in my suite and I laughed at her.

The reason I'm doing this is because I want to pamper her. I want to make this evening be about her. She's so used to deflecting conversations and I don't want the interruptions or distractions that being outside offers.

I want Nina to myself, alone, so that she has the freedom and privacy to talk about whatever is on her mind.

I want for her to get that stuff out of her head. I want only good things for her.

So this is my way of creating a little safe haven for her, in my suite where I cook and she talks.

I open the door and she walks in, but there's a fire in her eyes.

Puzzled, I slide my arms around her and kiss her deeply.

"I've got something for you," she says, taking my hand and leading me towards the sofa.

I don't know what to think. Being a red-blooded man, it occurs to me that we might make out on the sofa for a while. But when she opens her bag and pulls something out, then holds it within an inch of my line of sight, I feel the air get sucked right out of my lungs. Ben's smiling face and his twinkling eyes make me gasp.

She has the photo I thought I had lost forever. I well up as I take hold of it.

"How?" is the only word I can manage to say.

I can't take my eyes of the picture. Of course, I have others of him, but this one, this is priceless.

She sits down next to me and clings to my arm, nestling her head on my shoulder so that we are both looking at a moment in time caught so many lifetimes ago; when I had a younger brother, and before Hollywood beckoned.

"Dottie got a call from the police station", Nina explains. It happened while she and Dottie were meeting for coffee one day.

She goes on to tell me how the police had managed to track down the guys who had mugged me, and they had raided the place where they were shacked up. Turns out they found a whole heap of stolen goods.

"They found this," she pulls out my wallet and hands that to me. "But there was nothing in it apart from this photo and a few scraps of paper. They're still in there. One had Dottie's number on it."

I don't even bother opening my wallet because the only thing of value in it is now in my hand.

I turn to her. "I never thought I'd see this again."

She kisses my shoulder. "I know what it meant to you. When Dottie said she was going to the police station, I went along. We looked through boxes of stuff before we found your wallet."

I leave a soft kiss on her lips. "Thank you."

"Don't thank me, thank Dottie."

I kiss her again, feeling thankful. It feels as if I've come full circle since the night I lost this. Now I have the things that neither money nor fame can buy. Important things like love and gratitude.

NINA

. . .

We didn't go to the mountains with Elias and Harper, even though Harper was keen for us to go. She seems to have her heart set on us being a foursome.

I told her we could hang out when they came back. Callum and I needed some time on our own, getting to know one another better.

When I get to his place, there are flowers in so many vases all around the living room and in the bedroom, as I find out later. He's lit candles all around the balcony.

And that's where we go, at first.

We talked about this before. About my first time. My first proper time.

Callum wanted for us to go away, somewhere hot and exotic. I didn't want to make such a big deal of it even though he has gone to great pains to want to put my bad experiences behind me.

Though we've made out a lot, and done a lot of intimate things, we haven't done *that*.

I'm the one who is impatient, but I also don't want or need any fancy things. Yet he has made tonight fancy for me, even here in his hotel suite. Flowers and candles grace the place. It's the thoughtfulness that touches me. The candles on the balcony, the scent of lavender and jasmine everywhere. Flames flickering in the dark of the night.

"Hey," he comes up behind me, and leaves a flurry of kisses along my neck. I tilt my head and sigh with pleasure.

His mouth grazes gently along my shoulder. I'm wearing a Bardot off the shoulder dress and my best underwear, and I'm feeling confident. I toss my hair to one side so that he can kiss me all over my neck and shoulders without anything getting in his way.

His tender lips put me at ease. My body loosens, and I lean back against him. My back to his chest. His hardness so evident as he presses against my hips. And so it begins, the excruciatingly slow build up in my belly, a flutter of excitement as arousal curls its way around my body. He sucks my earlobe, and his hand lowers to below my navel, and he's about to touch me there, when he spins me around. A sensual fog begins to cloud my brain. His fingers rub gently over my dress, over my panties, in the place where I hunger for him to touch me the most. I let out a mewl as he captures my mouth with his and his tongue slips deeper into my mouth. Real kissing, deep, sexy, slow, wet kissing—this is all I have survived on for weeks, that and his fingers exploring me. Mine exploring him.

Tonight I want it all. Tongues dueling, hearts crashing, his fingers snake through the buttons of my dress and find a way past my panties, I squeeze my legs and groan as his thumb slides over my clit. This is exquisite pleasure, that I have come to expect from him.

He breaks our kiss. "You let me know when you're ready."

"I'm ready."

"You sure you want to do this?"

He is so careful, so attentive, so not wanting to do anything wrong. So aware of what I have been through. He won't understand in words. With a newfound confidence, I take his hand and lead the way to his bedroom.

There are no candles here, but the room is awash with flowers and a few low light lamps. It's the perfect blend of sexiness and sensual. With a tap of my toe, I shut the door, then, not wanting to waste time, I reach down for the hem of my dress and pull it over my head, flinging it to the floor.

Callum looks at me as if I'm the only woman in the

world, and now that my boldness has brought me here into his bedroom, it vanishes.

I don't know what to do.

He takes a step closer, lowers his head then brushes his soft, velvet lips over my nose, my cheeks, my mouth. I tremble with anticipation, my breaths quickening, the nerves in my body zinging with his electric touch. "Is this okay?" he whispers, his hot breath caressing my skin. Every touch, every kiss, every breath of his electrifies me.

I reach for the zipper of his pants and lower it just as he unbuttons his shirt and throws it off. Climbing out of his jeans, it feels as if we've crossed some sort of milestone, we've been here before, but this is different. Concern in his eyes tells me he's still being cautious.

"I need you inside me," I whisper, letting my hands roam over his bare chest. I have come to know every bare inch of his muscles, the ridges and contours of his abs, but there are parts of him I've never seen before.

We kiss again, not kiss so much as melt into one another, his mouth claiming mine with a new intensity. I'm guessing that he's had to learn to hold back with me, but now given permission, his pent up frustration is finally on the way to release. We kiss, long and hard, and then my breasts are suddenly free. He tosses off my bra and I didn't even feel him unclasp it.

Pushing me onto the bed, his fingers hook into the sides of my panties. I school myself to breathe, because my breath hitches in my throat so much, each silky touch, each wet, sensual kiss, opens me up even more. When he pulls them down the length of my legs, I blush, but he probably doesn't realize in this light.

He's never seen me naked, not completely. Nor I him.

I husk out a breath because I feel his body heat, his

intention, his closeness. He stands up and takes off his boxers, and just as I gaze at this new unveiling, just as I start to lick my lips, needing him, he drops to his knees and pushes his tongue inside me. It's so fast it takes me by surprise. I arch off the bed.

I came so hard when he did this before, but this is too fast, too sudden. I'm going to come right now.

"Breathe," he says, kissing my folds, sliding his fingers over my clit. I suck in a breath feeling a million nerves dancing for joy in that one tiny bud he's stopped touching.

"Breathe," he coaches me.

I obey, because I want his lips back, I want his fingers back.

He rewards me, pumping his fingers inside me again as I struggle to contain myself. I cry out his name, and he stops.

This is beautiful torture.

"Please," I beg, and he obliges by brushing his lips over me before sucking my clit.

I'm going to come. Hard.

As I begin to pant heavily, he moves up on the bed. I was almost on the verge of coming when he stopped, now I'm lying spread-eagled as his dark eyes watch me intensely. He rolls a condom over himself, and I feel my heart miss a beat. Lowering himself on me, his bare skin caresses mine. We are hot and sweaty, and I have never been so ready, have never so badly wanted this as I do now.

"Nina." His voice is tender as he fixes me with a look that makes me melt. His gaze is so intense I think he could stare at me and lie naked on top of me and that would be enough.

"Do you want me?"

"I. Want. You." I pant because he is tempting mercilessly with his cock poised at my entrance, yet he doesn't move. My desperation drives me insane. I lift up, my pussy teasing him, needing him, *begging* him. He glides in slowly, then takes my hand in his, our fingers wrapping around as he pushes in deeper. With my eyes locked on his, I find myself falling deeper into him as he slides deeper into me.

This is beautiful. A soul connection, not just a physical one.

I moan as his mouth drops to my breast and he sucks hard. He gets into a slow rhythm with his thrusts, sliding in and out with a slow measured torturous pace. Each time he pushes in, I groan, drenched in pleasure, my arousal peaking higher and higher.

I claw his buttocks, then wrap my legs around him instinctively, as if I knew this would feel better.

And it does.

And when he pumps harder, and sucks my other breast harder, I squeeze my legs even tighter.

We're building together towards something momentous, and all consuming. Each thrust inflames, takes me closer to the edge, my heart pounds, my hips lift up, my muscles clench around him.

"I love you," he says, just as I scream, a long, contented, satisfied scream, convulsing and shuddering beneath him. Just as I finish, he thrusts, long and hard, and stays there, letting out a feral groan before pulling out and falling to my side, sighing as if he's just run a marathon.

He lifts his head and stares at me with a questioning look in his eyes. He's wondering how it was for me.

"I love you," I say, in answer, meaning it for the first time ever. I lift my head claiming his lips with my mouth before sliding my tongue over his. We kiss, softly at first, but the pace quickly intensifies. My breasts begin to tingle. Heat rushes south. I want him all over again.

"We might need a moment," he says, lying down beside me, taking my hand and kissing my fingers tenderly. "Just a moment, mind you."

"Promise?" I close my eyes and savor the touch of his velvet lips against my skin. This is what it's like to be with someone who cares, when it feels good, when it's not forced. This is what making love is all about.

I cling to him because I don't want to leave. I don't want us to part. I could lie like this forever.

NINA

"What do we do?" My heart is going crazy. The test is positive.

I'm pregnant.

Callum swoops me up in his arms easily and holds on to me, before dancing around the room, still carrying me.

"What do we do?" he cries, looking happier than I've ever seen him. "We're going shopping! We're refurbishing the nursery."

"We were being careful," I whisper.

"Except for that one time when you couldn't wait for me to put on a condom," he reminds me.

I remember that night. We hosted a party at his home in Vermont. Elias and Harper were there as were some of Callum's closest friends.

Vermont in the winter.

I'd never been to Vermont before.

I was overwhelmed.

The snow, the pretty town.

Callum's other home.

We threw a party, and I never knew that being a hostess could be so much fun.

When it ended, in the early hours of the morning, I was still flying high from the adrenaline.

I remember well that night without a condom.

I come back to the present. "Refurbishing the nursery?"

Where?

Where do we live?

I still work at the diner, I'm still clinging onto that normality, but it's only 'Cameo appearances' as Frankie keeps telling me.

I just need some normality. Something familiar and happy, and I think that's what I'm clinging onto even when I know I no longer need to work. It would be enough for me to have Frankie over for dinner every now and then, given that her warmth and wisdom are some of the things that reel me back there.

But I am so busy with other things.

I've been keeping an eye on Callum's books. My bookkeeping course came in handy. I don't do the books. Callum has too much money invested in too many places for me to feel confident to handle all that stuff. I keep an eye on his general expenses and, between that, and the diner, and no more night school, and having Callum in my life, I don't need anything else.

"You decide. Wherever you want. You'll have to give up your apartment now, you see that, don't you?"

I've been clinging onto that too.

When filming finished, he returned to LA, but travelled back and forth to Chicago.

Now we'll need a base.

A foundation.

Something permanent. No back and forth, because now we're going to have a child.

We're going to be a family.

He sets me down and disappears while I'm still giddy with happiness at this sudden change in my circumstances, and all the new things that this will bring.

I run my hand over my stomach.

A baby.

A new life.

And I will be the type of mother I always wished I had.

Elias. I can't wait to tell Elias and Harper.

Their wedding.

They're getting married in two months' time and I am Harper's maid of honor.

How much bigger will I be by then?

Harper has it all sorted out. She has copious notes of everything to do with the wedding, the cake, the flowers, the bridesmaids dresses. She gave up her tech magazine job just so she could concentrate on her perfect wedding.

My pregnancy will be a tiny blip in her plans.

A good blip. I smile at the thought of telling them both. I'm still smiling when I turn around, only, Callum is on his knee.

I gasp, and I think I'm going to cry.

Tears well up quickly because I see the ring.

"I wasn't going to do this right now," he says, clearing his throat and running his hand through his hair as if he's trying to tidy it. Not that he needs to do anything. I wake up beside this beautiful man each morning and consider myself to be the luckiest woman alive.

"I love you Nina Cardoza, and I want you to be my wife. Will you marry me?"

I stifle a cry, try to hold back the tears, but they come anyway.

I nod and splutter and a wave of pure heart bursting emotion crashes over me.

"Is that a yes?" he asks, getting up off the floor and holding the ring at the tip of my finger.

"Yes!" I cry, but it comes out as a smothered shriek. I compose myself. "Yes," I say calmly, "Yes, I will marry you."

He slides the rock—there is no other word for it—onto my finger. I haven't seen anything as big as this and it is going to take some getting used to; just like Callum took some getting used to.

He kisses me, as if to seal my acceptance, and our commitment.

I am no longer ashamed of my past. It was done to me. My scars are proof of my strength and resilience, rather than marks of regret. They remind me that even though I've been through so much darkness, I broke free.

My hand rests on my belly, the other around Callum's neck. He kisses me deeply this time, and it confirms that I have it all, a man who loves me deeply, and his child in my belly.

The things I thought I could never have—a normal life, someone to love me, happiness and a future that is bright— all the good things, are now mine to have and to hold forever.

Thank you for reading THE LIES OF PRIDE! I hope you enjoyed Nina and Callum's story, as well as catching up with Harper and Eli.

THE PRICE OF INERTIA is next. This is based on the

sin of sloth, and it's about a reclusive multi-millionaire author and the housekeeper who has to take care of him.

A reclusive writer, a desperate housekeeper …
Ward Maddox has a book to finish but he's only written six pages. His agent isn't happy.

Marianne Evers needs money and a break after a hellish week. Her boyfriend cheated on her, she got evicted and she lost her job - the one she needs to help pay for her mom's nursing home costs.

Serendipity strikes when she lands a last minute housekeeping contract.
The assignment is simple: to be a live-in housekeeper to a man she will barely see.

SIGN UP FOR MY NEWSLETTER to find out when new books release!
http://www.lilyzante.com/news

Read an excerpt from THE PRICE OF INERTIA below.

Happy reading!

Lily

EXCERPT: THE PRICE OF INERTIA

WARD

"Don't go dying on me," says Rob, my agent, and probably the only person whose opinion I value.

"I'm not going to die. I'm taking it easy. That's not going to kill me."

"You've been taking it *too* easy."

Easy isn't how I would describe the last few months. I throw him a resentful look. "I've had stuff to deal with."

"Do you have to work from bed? The same bed you sleep in?"

"I'm not in bed now."

"You're not at your desk, either." Rob exhales loudly. "I've given you the time you need, Ward, but you're not making any progress. You're in danger of missing the deadline. This book was supposed to release along with the film."

I grab a handful of potato chips and shovel them into my mouth.

"So, I've made the decision for you. You're going to Chicago. A change of setting will do you good."

I almost choke, and get up off the couch, dropping my bag of chips in shock. "I'm *not* going to Chicago." *Hell, no.*

"I've rented you a beautiful mansion. It might help."

"How?" How the hell will being in Chicago help me? My satin robe has fallen open. Rob looked at me oddly and made a sarcastic comment when he first saw me. I quite like this. It's comfortable. Far easier to sit and write in this all day than wearing sweatpants. I pull the sash tighter, but not before Rob gets a peek at my flabby torso. He winces and I turn away.

I've packed on a few pounds. My face might have rounded out a bit. I'm in a funk and have been like this for months.

"It's not permanent," Rob insists. "Three, four months. You need to finish the manuscript, Ward. You can't miss your deadline."

I sink back onto the couch. The words don't flow these days. They haven't for a while. For the second time in my life, I'm stuck with my writing. I used to be able to pull words out of thin air and piece together plots that would have my readers keep turning the pages.

I've lost that gift again.

"This is a seven figure deal and you need to honor it. What you don't want is to risk incurring a penalty. Think of the bad press. Think of the film that's coming out. Think of the book tour. The publicity. The talk shows. *Think.*"

I hang my head because all the things he's just mentioned weigh me down. Rob has done great things for me. He's been my agent for over a decade, my only agent. He's been more like a mentor, guiding me when I've had no real life role models. I hate publicity. I hate talk shows. I'm no good at them. I can't talk to people, much less laugh and joke with them, but because of this trilogy, this amazing book and film deal Rob negotiated for me, I have to do the whole publicity crap.

The first film in my *Morbid Trilogy* will release by the time the last book comes out but it's this last book that I've hit a wall on. I can't see me making the deadline. I haven't written much. I've tried and struggled, and I have failed.

"You're not doing yourself any favors slobbering in front of the TV all day," Rob complains.

I lift my legs onto the couch and lie back. "It's research."

He stares at the screen. "Grey's anatomy?"

"It's research," I repeat. "Wait till you see what happens to my main character during surgery."

"I'm looking forward to it. When will you get the manuscript to me?"

I say nothing, because I have no idea. Rob shoves his hands in his pockets and paces around my study. "This isn't good, Ward. You being stuck like this again."

My jaw tightens. "It's not like that," I throw back. I'm not in that same hell hole I was in all those years ago." This isn't like *that*. "Don't worry about the interviews and shit. I'll be okay by then."

"You need to write the book first!" He points at me. "When you clean up, when you take care of yourself, you come up looking good, when you look good, you feel good. It doesn't matter what you say in your interviews because most of those women readers of yours, they like that you brush up real good."

I groan.

"It's a damn shame that you look like a slob right now." He throws me a look that is soaked in disapproval. "When was the last time you shaved, or got a haircut? When was the last time you left the house?"

I lie. "Last week." It was two months ago, when I needed to get into my psychotically deranged murderer's head. I prowled around the streets of New Orleans in the early hours of the morning, trying to get into character.

"Last week?" Rob's tone indicates he doesn't believe me for one moment. "To do what?"

"Have a cup of coffee." Being a writer means that lies come easily. Making stuff up for a living is a skill that comes in handy in real life.

"You expect me to believe that you went outside and sat in a coffeeshop and had a cup of coffee, surrounded by people? You? Ward Maddox, the reclusive, hermit author?"

"Yeah, I had coffee. That's what I did." I rest my hand on my stomach and feel the soft, marshmallowy flesh. I have packed on a few pounds too many. "I re-plotted the ending, then I had to go back and change the middle, and then I hit a bar and restaurant in the evening." I lie again. He knows me too well and will see right through me.

If I could have things my way, I would never leave my writing cave. That's why I bought one of the most expensive and beautiful of houses here. A twelve bedroom home with chandeliers and fireplaces in each room, stained glass windows and elaborate architecture. This is my castle. A place where I reign, where I am at my happiest.

A place where I feel safe.

Good for nothing piece of shit. That's what my stepdad called me. The bastard would turn in his grave if he could see me now. I wish my mom had come here and seen my home and what I made of myself. She could have lived here, I even asked her to even though she didn't deserve an ounce of my kindness. She turned me down, and we barely saw one another over the years.

"Yeah, sure you did." Rob stares out of the window. "You also brought home a beautiful woman you picked up at said bar and spent the whole night showing her a good time."

Bastard.

Now he's messing with me. I can tell he's annoyed because it's not like him to bring up that stuff. He knows I'm cautious around women. Dating a basket case will do that to you. Sometimes I wonder if I am always drawn to insane people. Or maybe they are drawn to me because of what I write?

Rob stares at me as if he knows everything about me. And the problem is, he does. This guy who is supposed to be my agent, has become the only person I ever have any proper contact with.

"How many pages have you written?"

This is the question I've been dreading. "Six."

"Today?"

I laugh, because that is hilarious. "Today?" Hell, no. "Six in *total.*"

His brows squish together like angry caterpillars. "In total?" He massages his temple. "You can't afford to miss your deadline."

I never miss my deadline. Unless I'm in a funk. "I'll get it done." But I've been in this funk for months.

"That's what you said last time." Rob knows what it does to me. He's helped me through it before.

"I will get it done."

He strides towards me. "Damn straight you will. I've made arrangements."

I sit up slowly. He said something about Chicago. No

way am I leaving my house, especially to go *there* of all places. "I'll get it done," I insist. I don't want to hear what he has to say.

He nods. "You will. In Chicago."

"No."

"Yes."

"Hell, no."

Rob scratches his eyebrow. "James Garvey approached me. Wants me to represent him."

"And?" I clench my teeth and wonder why the guy needs a new agent. I can't stop another author wanting Rob to represent them. But James Garvey hates me too. Considers me to be an upstart. That's because he's in his sixties, and I've just turned forty-one. He and I often compete for the number one slot on the New York Times Bestseller list.

"I'm just letting you know. Say what you want about him, but the guy is prolific He's written three books this year, and he had a heart attack two years ago. He managed it somehow."

I clap my hands together mockingly. "Let's hear it for James Garvey."

Rob looks at me, and his eyes trail down me from top to toe. "If you're not careful, you're going to end up with a heart attack. Maybe even a stroke. Sitting down all day isn't good for you."

"I used to take care of myself." I used to be good. Good diet, I hardly touch drink, and I'd work out regularly. That was until my mom fell ill and summoned me to her deathbed. I went running, like a fool.

"Then what's gone and happened to you again?" He looks genuinely concerned.

I don't want to talk about it. "If you want to represent Garvey that's your call."

"I don't want to represent too many authors. Sally wants me to slow down and take it easy. We want to vacation more and spend more time with the grandchildren." He makes me feel as if I'm too much trouble. "I don't want you to die on me, Ward. Hearing about Garvey's health scare, and seeing you," he jerks his chin at me, immediately making me feel self-conscious. "it worries me. I've made a decision."

I lift an eyebrow and brace myself because it involves Chicago. He knows I hate that city. I'm surprised that he's suggested it.

"You need to get back on track, Ward. This writer's block you've been fighting has gone on too long. You look out of shape and you sound unmotivated. Freya says you wander around the house all day—"

"You grilled my housekeeper?"

"I can't rely on you to give me all the facts."

I manage to stare at him without blinking. It's frightening how well he knows me.

Freya has been with me for years. The stern but efficient housekeeper is the only person I see on a daily basis. She has the key to the house, and is there by the time I wake up, right through until the evening, when she has my evening meal ready.

Sometimes she brings her ten year old grandson along with her. I'm worried she's going to leave me. I don't want to think about replacing her. She's irreplaceable. She doesn't talk much, I barely notice when she's around because she hardly makes a sound. She makes my meals, takes care of my laundry, and cleans all the rooms slowly, one room at a time. I don't want a cleaning company. I don't want a live in cook, cleaner or housekeeper. I want my mansion to myself.

"You need to get your act together and finish the book on time, and you need to get into shape for the book tours and interviews, and don't forget the film premiere."

I groan loudly because that stuff makes me want to retch. The first two books in this trilogy sold millions of copies worldwide. Both are getting made into films. I should be ecstatic, but I'm not. The publicity, the idea of having to meet other people and pretend to like their company, makes me come out in hives.

"Are you stuck on the plot?"

I'm stuck, but it's not the book. It was facing my mother on her deathbed that did it. She pined for the monster she had married. The man I was supposed to call my dad, but I never did. The man who punished me for it. "You don't need to babysit me, Rob. I'll get over it. I just can't function the way I need to at the moment but I will. I promise you I will."

"Has your magic pen stopped working?" he asks.

"My magic pen is safe and sound." I write everything longhand with my MontBlanc. Notes, first thoughts, basic ideas, the first rough, rough, rough draft. It's all done on paper first.

"I can't lift you all the time, Ward. It's exhausting, so you're either going to do what I say, or ..."

"Or what?"

"There is no other alternative."

I swipe my hand over my face in exasperation. "You want me to go to Chicago to finish the book there?"

"You've always said your past defined you. Maybe go back and face your demons."

He doesn't know what he's talking about. What makes a child grow up and want to write horror. A stepfather who locked him up in the dark. That's what. But that didn't hurt as much as watching the mother I doted on, who doted on me, change into someone I barely recognized the moment she met him. "Chicago is the last place on earth I want to visit.'"

"I've rented you a house, nothing as beautiful as this, but I've tried to find you something to your standard. All paid for by you, of course."

"I'd expect nothing less."

"You have bad memories of your time there. You're stuck and, given what's happened, maybe you need to go back to the source of your pain."

"You think, huh?" I pick up the bag of crisps from the floor and stick my hand into it.

"And there will be no more of that." Rob nods at my chip packet, then picks up and shakes each of the four empty Coke cans that are lying on the coffee table. "I've got you a personal trainer and I'm still looking into getting you a—"

"A what?"

"A personal trainer, and I'm still looking into getting you a housekeeper."

I draw in a slow and steady breath. "I don't need people. I'm a fucking writer."

"Then write, for goodness sake, *write*."

"I'll take Freya," I throw back. The only problem is that she'd have to live with me, and I don't want anyone living with me. In fact, the best part of having Freya as my housekeeper is that she goes home every day.

"I've already asked her and she doesn't want to go. She doesn't want to leave New Orleans."

The wily little fox. Rob's been making plans behind my back. "I don't need a personal trainer."

"You've turned into a sloth. You're out of shape. Your face is puffy. When did you last shave?"

I raise a hand to my beard. It's thick and prickly but there is no need for me to shave. Or get a haircut.

"When was the last time you got a haircut?" I knew that would be his next question.

"A couple of months back."

"Try to look presentable. You don't want to scare the new people away."

"I don't think that's necessary. I can work out on my own."

Rob crushes the cans between his hands. "You look like you've been working real hard," he snorts. "You leave next week, and by that time, I'll have found you a housekeeper.

"A housekeeper? I don't need a housekeeper."

"I beg to differ." Rob looks around the room in disgust.

"What I need is a box of donuts," I tell him. I'm being serious, too.

Rob snorts. "You're going to end up looking like a donut if this continues."

"I'm processing things."

"It's been months, Ward. Months. Is this going to be like the last time?"

I close my eyes. The last time I went into freefall, I couldn't write a word for months. I open my eyes and glare at him.

"That's what I thought." He walks towards the door. "Chicago will jolt you into action."

He has no idea. Chicago is full of bad memories.

"Get a haircut. Try to look decent."

MARI

I've lost everything, in the space of a week.

Sitting on a park bench with Jamie, listening to the happy cries of children playing, I wish I could be as carefree and as happy as they are.

"It's a lifeline," I say, staring at the sheet of paper with the description of the only job I could find that needed someone urgently. I'm going for an interview tomorrow. "This is so beneath my current pay grade and position," I wail.

"It *was*," Jamie reminds me. "It's only temporary." He accompanied me to the recruitment agency which was my first stop this morning, after he'd helped me move stuff out of my apartment.

"Only temporary," I repeat, feeling the need to reassure myself. Being a housekeeper is not the career move I had in mind, but then, Jamie and I never expected to get laid off when we went to work a few days ago.

"Hey," Jamie nudges me gently. "Think of it like a new start, from everything."

"For you, too." I say, nudging him right back. I'm so grateful for a friend like Jamie. My life has gone to shit in the space of a week. We worked at a small family run hotel. I was the front desk manager, and Jamie worked behind the scenes, overseeing the hotel's amenities. We had no idea that our boss was taking part in shady money laundering activities. The hotel shut down immediately and all the staff had their contracts terminated.

And, not only did I lose my job, and a very well paid and satisfying job at that, but I found out that Dale, my boyfriend of two years, had been secretly seeing someone else and had gotten her pregnant. I made the mistake of stupidly forgiving him after I found him cheating on me the first time.

Jamie was lucky. He found a job almost the next day, working in the local gym. It's nothing like what he had at the hotel, but at least it's something.

"This will cheer you up." From his backpack, he pulls out a bar of my favorite chocolate. This guy knows all about the small things which make me happy, and right now, I'll grab any slip of happiness that comes my way.

Grinning, I take it from him and waste no time in peeling it open. "Thanks." I offer him some, but he refuses to take it, probably because he knows just how much I love my chocolate.

"I'm going to apply for other jobs in the meantime," I tell him, taking a bite of the chocolate bar.

"Me too. I can do better than where I'm at."

"We can both do better. At least you have a roof over your head."

"You can stay with me for as long as you want, Mari."

He's a good guy. A good friend. Someone I can depend on, unlike the douchebag who was my boyfriend. "You're too kind, but it's not ideal."

"Seriously, you can stay as long as you want."

I ditched Dale, of course. I don't need someone like him in my life, but I wish I'd learned my lesson the first time round. I deserve better. Jamie always says I'm too nice, too forgiving, that I always see the best in people, and that's my downfall. My mom always used to say that, too—back when she was my mom, before the dementia hit and slowly made her forget who I was.

A few days after that? My landlord told me to leave after I couldn't pay the rent for my apartment for the third month running. The well paid job? I'd used most of my savings to pay for my mom's hospital bills because in the last year she'd had a few falls, and there was always something wrong. We had lots of tests done over the course of the last year and then I had to pay for my mom's move into a nursing home.

She lived with me in my small apartment, but during the last year I noticed that she would get upset when she forgot something, because it started to happen a lot. I didn't think anything of it at first. Then one day she got lost when coming home from grocery shopping.

That's when I took notice. Over the next few months, she would become irrational, and get upset easily. She thought she was seeing people walking around in the house, or outside. I was starting to find it difficult.

Then she fell down and broke her arm and while in the hospital, she was diagnosed with stage four dementia. Maybe that's why I couldn't keep an eye on what Dale was up to. I'd stay at his place a lot, but the more ill my mom got, the less I saw him. There was no possibility of him coming to stay at my place. It was tiny as it was. With my mom being there it was hard.

Still, she was my priority and I nursed her back, but it wasn't easy, what with her new forgetfulness and mood swings. It was when she left the stove on all day, that I decided she would be better off in a nursing home.

So I tried to explain to her, and she understood it. She flits in and out of being 'my mom' and being a stranger. The trick, and the gift, the beauty, is to have her for as long as possible, being my mom. And this week, this week out of hell, I was told that she has stage five dementia.

It's good that she's in a nursing home, having someone keep an eye on her all the time, but I still worry. She's only been there a few months, and I've been paying to keep her there, thinking that the promotion I was going to get was going to come through. My boss had told me it was. And then the crook himself messed things up for us all.

I'd been paying a third of my rent for the past few months, needing to get my mom settled but my landlord got impatient and threw me out.

"Why so quiet?"

"My life is a shit show."

"It's not. This, right now, your life and everything that's happened, this is what's meant to happen. This is where you're meant to be. Hopefully you'll learn this time."

I narrow my eyes at him. "Learn what?" I scoff. "Being broke, discovering my mom's dementia is worse than I thought? Losing my job? Having a cheating boyfriend?"

"That you are too nice, too forgiving, too ..." He pauses, then presses his lips together, as if he doesn't want to say.

"Say it."

"You're too reckless, especially when it comes to guys. You can do better. Dale is a jerk. He was a jerk the first time he cheated on you, and now he's a ..." He shakes his head, and I can tell he wants to swear.

"I fell in love," I say, putting the chocolate wrapper in my pocket now that I've gobbled it all up greedily. I was in love. I am reckless, perhaps. I give my heart too easily, without thinking. I don't second guess when my insides go all mushy, or when someone kisses me and my toes curl. I'm not a hussy, but I can't *not* react at times like this. And Dale was so handsome and lovely in the beginning.

"Who's it with?" he asks. "The interview tomorrow? A family, with kids?"

"I think it's a guy. A businessman." That's what the recruitment consultant told me. She said it was a new job placement that came up and they didn't have many details about it yet. I look at him and widen my eyes, exaggerating my very-scared face. "A perv, you think?"

Now Jamie looks worried. "I'll come with you, if you want."

"To the interview? How stupid would that look?"

"The offers there if you want."

"I'll be okay. I'm a grown woman. It's just an interview. Oh, my goodness!" I squint at the paper with his address, as it hits me. "He lives in the Gold Coast area."

Jamie's eyes widen.

The famed Gold Coast is one of Chicago's most prestigious areas. Suddenly, my woes have evaporated and I feel suddenly uplifted. In the nightmare of my week, this new revelation is as shiny as a diamond. But Jamie stares at me as if there's an axe murderer standing behind me. "Maybe you shouldn't go alone."

"I'm going, and I'll call you before I go in, and as soon as I come out, okay?"

"Deal."

A red football bounces towards us. I look over to see a bunch of teens yell at us to kick it back so I get up and give the ball a hefty kick. Too bad it shoots off in the wrong direction, about five yards wide of where the guys are.

"And remember, you have a lot going on at the moment. Don't worry about finding a place to stay. You can stay with me for as long as you want."

"Awww." I squeeze his arm slightly. "You're very sweet."

"Just trying to help you out," he mumbles, before moving his arm and looking away.

Now I've upset him. This is a strange thing. Me and him being such good friends. He's not been lucky with women either, though as far as I know no one has cheated on him. We went out as a foursome once last year, and I met his girlfriend, but they split up a few months ago and he never really gave me a reason why.

Me sleeping on his couch might raise eyebrows with some of my friends, or even my mom, depending on what sort of mood she's in and if she remembers who I am, but it's the only way my life works right now.

"I worry about you," says Jamie, staring at me pensively.

"Awww, stop that. You have plenty of worries of your own without adding me to the list."

THE PRICE OF INERTIA is available at all major retailers.

BOOKLIST

**Buy Direct from Lily at
https://shop.lilyzante.com**

The Seven Sins:(New Series) A series of seven
standalone romances based on the seven sins. Steamy,
emotional, and angsty romances which are loosely
connected.

Underdog (prequel)
The Wrath of Eli
The Problem with Lust
The Lies of Pride
The Price of Inertia
The Other Side of Greed

The Billionaire's Love Story: This is a Cinderella
story with a touch of Jerry Maguire. What happens when
the billionaire with too much money meets the single mom
with too much heart?

The Promise
The Gift, Books 1-3
The Offer, Books 1-3
The Vow, Books 1-3

Indecent Intentions: This is a spin-off from The Billionaire's Love story. This two-book set consists of two standalone stories about the billionaire's playboy brother. The second story is about a wealthy nightclub owner who shuns relationships.

The Bet
The Hookup
Indecent Intentions 2-Book Set

Honeymoon Series: Take a roller-coaster journey of emotional highs and lows in this story of love and loss, family and relationships. When Ava is dumped six weeks before her Valentine's Day wedding, she has no idea of the life that awaits her in Italy.

Honeymoon for One
Honeymoon for Three
Honeymoon Blues
Honeymoon Bliss
Baby Steps

Italian Summer Series: This is a spin-off from the Honeymoon Series. These books tell the stories of the secondary characters who first appeared in the Honeymoon Series. Nico and Ava also appear in these books.

It Takes Two
All That Glitters
Fool's Gold
Roman Encounter
November Sun
New Beginnings

A Perfect Match Series: This is a seven book series in which the first four books feature the same couple. High-flying corporate executive Nadine has no time for romance but her life takes a turn for the better when she meets Ethan, a sexy and struggling metal sculptor five years younger. He works as an escort in order to make the rent. Books 4-6 are standalone romances based on characters from the earlier books. The main couple, Ethan and Nadine, appear in all books:

Lost in Solo (prequel)
The Proposal
Heart Sync
A Leap of Faith
Misplaced Love
Reclaiming Love
Embracing Love

Standalone Books:

Love Among the Ruins
Tomorrow Belongs to Us
Love Inc
An Unexpected Gift

ACKNOWLEDGMENTS

I owe a huge thanks to the wonderful ladies in my proofreading group for their patience and support, as well as their tolerance for my ever-changing deadlines. They check my manuscript for errors, typos, inconsistencies and the many strange words and phrases which often find their way into my stories.

They give me the confidence to release each book and I am eternally grateful for their help and support:

Marcia Chamberlain

April Lowe

Dena Pugh

Charlotte Rebelein

Carole Tunstall

I would also like to thank Tatiana Vila of Vila Design for creating the awesome cover.

ABOUT THE AUTHOR

Lily Zante lives with her husband and three children somewhere near London, UK.

Connect with Me

I love hearing from you – so please don't be shy! You can email me, message me on Facebook or connect with me on Twitter:

Website **|** Email | Newsletter sign-up